Global Shake

CW00505283

Series Editor
Alexa Alice Joubin, Department of English, George
Washington University, Washington, D.C., USA

The Global Shakespeares series, edited by Alexa Alice Joubin, explores the global afterlife of Shakespearean drama, poetry and motifs in their literary, performative and digital forms of expression in the twentieth and twenty-first centuries. Disseminating big ideas and cutting-edge research in e-book and print formats, this series captures global Shakespeares as they evolve.

More information about this series at
http://www.palgrave.com/gp/series/15016

Sarah Olive · Kohei Uchimaru · Adele Lee ·
Rosalind Fielding

Shakespeare in East Asian Education

With an Afterword by Chen Yilin

Sarah Olive
University of York
York, UK

Kohei Uchimaru
Osaka City University
Osaka, Japan

Adele Lee
Emerson College
Boston, MA, USA

Rosalind Fielding
University of Birmingham, UK

Global Shakespeares
ISBN 978-3-030-64798-8   ISBN 978-3-030-64796-4   (eBook)
https://doi.org/10.1007/978-3-030-64796-4

This Palgrave Pivot imprint is published by the registered company Springer Nature
Switzerland AG
The registered company address is: Gewerbestrasse 11, 6330 Cham, Switzerland

PREFACE

This book is the first monograph in English dedicated to the topic of Shakespeare in East Asian Education. The need to fill a gap in the literatures—both sustained, critical studies of Shakespeare in education generally and Shakespeare in East Asian education in particular—inspired us to write this book. We also wished to proliferate the literature that falls on the continuum between global (or world) Shakespeare and local (or national) Shakespeare: a literature that might be called regional Shakespeare, that is concerned with Shakespeare in multiple nations within a shared, larger area or construct, such as East Asia.

Regional Shakespeare, such as Asian Shakespeare, acknowledges the heterogeneity of Shakespeare 'done' in that area—translated, staged, filmed and (previously given less attention) taught and learnt—while exploring some of the intra-regional flows and similarities. This book builds on regional Shakespeare studies since it contains chapters on Shakespeare in education that take the reader on a journey through Hong Kong, China, Japan, and Taiwan. We also recognise that not all educational experiences with Shakespeare take place in a classroom—at school or university—but also in the theatre. So, there are chapters focused on each of these three sectors. We cover various aspects of education: policy, pedagogy and practice.

As authors, we approach Shakespeare in East Asian education from a variety of experiences and perspectives: as those who live and work in Asia on a daily basis and those who visit to research, teach and work in other sectors there; as citizens of countries as diverse as America, Australia, England, Japan and Northern Ireland and migrants between those countries; as native speakers of Asian languages and world Englishes, multilinguals, monolinguals, and language learners; those working in departments such as English literature, theatre studies, English (as an additional) language, and education. We are united by our interests in and scholarship of Shakespeare, education, theatre and East Asia.

York, UK · Sarah Olive
Osaka, Japan · Kohei Uchimaru
Boston, USA · Adele Lee
Birmingham, UK · Rosalind Fielding

The original version of the book was revised: The author name "Uchimaru Kohei" has been corrected. The correction to the book is available at https://doi.org/10.1007/978-3-030-64796-4_8

CONTENTS

About the Authors

Rosalind Fielding gained her Ph.D. from the Shakespeare Institute, University of Birmingham, in 2018. She is a researcher and theatre practitioner working in Japan and the UK, and an editor for *Re-imagining Shakespeare in Contemporary Japan: A Selection of Japanese Theatrical Adaptations of Shakespeare* (Arden, 2021).

Adele Lee is an Associate Professor in Early Modern Literature at Emerson College, USA. She is the author of *The English Renaissance and the Far East: Cross-Cultural Encounters* (Farleigh Dickinson, 2017) and has published articles in such journals as *Shakespeare Bulletin, Early Modern Literary Studies, Contemporary Women's Writing*, and *Borrowers and Lenders: The Journal of Shakespeare and Appropriation*. Current projects include an edited collection of essays on *Shakespeare and Accentism* (Routledge, 2021).

Sarah Olive is a Senior Lecturer in English in Education at the University of York, UK. She is the author of the book *Shakespeare in Education: Policy and Pedagogy, 1989–2009* (Intellect, 2015). She became the founding editor of the British Shakespeare Association's *Teaching Shakespeare* magazine in 2011. This free, online publication has a worldwide readership of educators across school, university, theatre and heritage sectors.

Kohei Uchimaru is an Associate Lecturer in the Faculty of Literature and Human Sciences at Osaka City University. Previously a Lecturer at the University of Tokyo, he completed the M.A. in 'Shakespeare and Education' at the Shakespeare Institute of the University of Birmingham after completing doctoral coursework at the University of Tokyo. His recent works include 'Teaching Shakespeare in Early Twentieth-Century Japan: A Study of *King Lear* in Locally Produced EFL School Readers' in *Shakespeare Studies* 56 (2018).

Chen Yilin is Professor of English, Director of the International Education Center, and Director of the Global Foreign Language Education Program at Providence University. She received a Ph.D. in Drama and Theatre from Royal Holloway, University of London. Her articles are published in journals including *Popular Entertainment Studies, Studies in Theatre and Performance, Fiction and Drama.* She is a contributor to *Doing English in Asia: Global Literature and Culture* (Lexington, 2016) and *Epoch Making in English Teaching and Learning: Evolution, Innovation, and Revolution* (Crane, 2016).

CHAPTER 1

Introduction

Sarah Olive, Adele Lee, Kohei Uchimaru, and Rosalind Fielding

Abstract 'Asian Shakespeare(s)' is an area of Shakespeare scholarship that has flourished in the twenty-first century. Monographs, edited collections and themed journal issues on Shakespeare in, and from, Asia written in (or translated into) English encompass translation, theatre, and film, but rarely education. Shakespeare in Asian education, written in English, is occasionally dealt with in individual articles and chapters as well as the British Shakespeare Association's *Teaching Shakespeare* magazine. This chapter introduces key works in these areas but also identifies their limitations and some ways in which this book redresses them.

S. Olive (✉)
University of York, York, UK
e-mail: sarah.olive@york.ac.uk

A. Lee
Emerson College, Boston, MA, USA

K. Uchimaru
Osaka City University, Osaka, Japan

R. Fielding
University of Birmingham, UK

S. Olive et al., *Shakespeare in East Asian Education*, Global Shakespeares, https://doi.org/10.1007/978-3-030-64796-4_1

1

The chapter evidences the way in which the authors of this volume approach Shakespeare in East Asian education from a variety of disciplinary expertises, experiences and perspectives. It does so using the notion that all researchers are positioned somewhere along a continuum of insider-outsider and flows of influence are bilateral east-west. Finally, this introduction offers an overview of each chapter.

Keywords Asia · Asian · Shakespeare · East Asia · Education

'Asian Shakespeare', sometimes written in the plural to reflect the heterogeneity of offerings and experiences, is an area of Shakespeare scholarship that has flourished in the twenty-first century. Of course, it has earlier origins.[1] Like Shakespeare studies generally, it is dominated by scholarship written in (or translated into) English. That said, many Asian countries have Shakespeare societies that publish research in their national language(s) or bilingually. Likewise, Shakespeare performances and events regularly use local languages alone or in combination with English. In this book, Kohei Uchimaru's and Rosalind Fielding's chapters draw on such Japanese language publications, performances and presentations. With regard to the East Asian region alone, scholarship in (or translated into) English on Shakespeare's theatre and film manifestations includes considerations of him as global[2]; national—often demarcated by the inclusion of a country's name in the title[3]; regional—usually signalled by the titular use of 'Asian'[4]; local[5]; or something negotiating, or flowing between, multiple sites or identities. Scholarship on this latter phenomenon is commonly signalled using terms such as 'intercultural', 'transcultural', 'global/local'[6] or its portmanteau, 'glocal'.[7]

Monographs, edited collections and themed journal issues on Shakespeare in, and from, Asia encompass translation, theatre and film, but rarely education—whether at school, university or in more informal settings. This reflects a more general status quo in Shakespeare studies internationally, whereby translation, theatre and film are valued as more prestigious areas in which to research Shakespeare than education. Andrew Hartley, in his edited collection *Shakespeare on the University Stage*, notes that productions happening in, or coming out of, universities have been relatively neglected in comparison with their professional and amateur equivalents.[8] Shakespeare in Asian education is occasionally dealt with in individual articles, book chapters and themed issues of *Teaching Shakespeare* (by way of disclosure, Olive is the founding editor of the magazine and Uchimaru the guest editor of issue 16).[9] Publishing on Shakespeare in East Asian education, and Shakespeare in education more generally, is impeded by the editorial policies of some academic journals and publishers in Shakespeare studies, which refuse to send for peer-review even critical articles on Shakespeare in education or silo even scholarly books on the topic away from 'mainstream' Shakespeare series.

There is a tendency, where Shakespeare in Asian education features in existing publications, for it to focus on *how* to teach Shakespeare, or to stop at recounting personal, anecdotal experience of teaching or learning Shakespeare, rather than offer sustained, critical analysis or theorisation— a situation which is broadly representative of work on Shakespeare in education.[10] Increasingly available are resources with which to teach, as well as research, Asian Shakespeare and Shakespeare for English as an Additional Language written or led by Asian academics.[11] This book identifies and analyses some of this existing material but also contributes fresh information and perspectives gathered from local teachers, students and institutions who are at the forefront of Shakespeare in education in their countries and sectors. Our preference would have been for more educators working in East Asia to contribute chapters to this book. We approached colleagues from China and Korea and sought to involve them as co-authors. These countries are, however, ultimately not well-represented in this volume, although Chapter 2 references Chinese education policy and practice, while Chapter 3 features the performances, experiences and words of mainland Chinese students. Their relative absence from this book is in spite of the fact that both countries have several monographs devoted to their national histories of Shakespeare an performance. Contributing a chapter to the book proved impossible for those colleagues due to the pressures on their time and the lack of support available from some institutions for academics to pursue research and publication activities. We note that, in this way, academics in East Asia are sometimes hampered in their desire to contribute to international research on Shakespeare in education. Moreover, this represents a relative inequality compared to colleagues working at research intensive universities in, for example, Europe and North America. This inequality— and others identified in a paper by Lee, stemming from assumptions about language, critical apparatus and distribution of roles[12]—must be addressed if international research on Shakespeare in East Asian education is to be written by those working in the region. The book in its present form—a blend of local and 'outsider' perspectives—was the feasible and next most effective way for us to represent the experiences and voices of Shakespeare educators in Hong Kong and Japan. We trace our individual expertises, and some limitations to them, as researchers in Shakespeare in East Asian education in the subsequent section.

The emphasis on Shakespeare in Asian education has historically been on India—we say 'India' rather than 'the subcontinent' advisedly, as neighbouring countries' experiences of Shakespeare in education are relatively absent. To some extent, this can be explained with reference to (1) the long tradition of Shakespeare studies in Indian academia; (2) the teaching and assessment of Indian people on Shakespeare in a variety of sectors—schools, universities and civil service entrance examinations; and (3) the use of English as an official language (and lingua franca) in India due to British colonialism and the plurality of languages spoken regionally.[13] This literature encompasses both examples of Shakespeare in education as a vehicle through which education, and other institutions, were westernised in British colonies as well as instances of Shakespeare being localised in teaching, particularly in the wake of countries' regaining their independence in the twentieth century. However, there are some similarities in these accounts from India with Hong Kong, Malaysia and Singapore, which makes their under-representation in literature in English on Shakespeare in education somewhat perplexing. Some authors who eschew this trend include Tam Kwok-kan et al. and Dorothy Wong.[14] Andrew Dickson's *Worlds Elsewhere: Journeys Around Shakespeare's Globe*, a trade book rather than an academic publication, samples and draws popular attention to some of the scholarship available on Shakespeare in the education systems of Hong Kong, as well as India and South Africa, and glimpses Shakespeare in some of these countries' classrooms.[15] Our book builds on existing writing on Shakespeare in colonial and postcolonial education by including countries with multiple colonial histories or non-British colonial pasts.[16]

This book is the first monograph in English dedicated to the topic of Shakespeare in East Asian Education. The need to fill a gap in the literatures—both sustained, critical studies of Shakespeare in education generally and Shakespeare in East Asian education in particular—inspired us to write this book. We recognise that not all educational experiences with Shakespeare take place in a classroom—at school or university— but also in the theatre. This might be a campus theatre with students performing (as in chapter 3) or a professional theatre with a series explicitly targeted at children (as in Chapter 6). So, there are chapters focused on each of these sectors or spaces: schools, higher education and theatres. We cover various aspects of education: policy, pedagogy and practice. Key questions that the book will explore are:

- What practices of, policies and resources for, teaching and learning Shakespeare, formal and informal, exist in East Asian educational institutions?
- How do they diverge (or not) within institutions, countries and across East Asia?
- How do educators and students in East Asia explain educational practices, policies and resources for teaching Shakespeare with reference to local (perhaps institutional), national, regional, western or global culture within and beyond education?

Apart from its relevance to those teaching, studying and researching Shakespeare in East Asia, this book offers some context to inform, stimulus to reflection and professional development for, educators who teach Shakespeare to East Asian students at schools and universities outside of the region. It is equally relevant to these educators regardless of whether their East Asian students are met as visitors on shorter, study abroad, exchange programmes and summer schools; international students taking a longer, degree programme; or through distance learning programmes. The book does not aim to be a comprehensive account of the history and practice of Shakespeare in education in Hong Kong, Japan or Taiwan. Rather, it presents six, related snapshots covering a range of Shakespeares in these countries' education systems: past and present; policy and pedagogy; school and university; student and professional performances aimed at young people. These snapshots are frequently interlinked by a concern with the same country, sector, concerns with performance pedagogies or English as an Additional Language. They are also interconnected by their overlapping research methods, including documentary analysis, secondary data analysis, and observation of Shakespeare events in the field. The chapters are a diverse set of jumping off points intended not just to inform, but also to inspire, future research topics and methods for Shakespeare in East Asian education. This book represents a start to sustained, critical analysis of Shakespeare in East Asian education in English, by no means the last word on it.

1.1   Authors' Contexts for Researching Shakespeare in East Asian Education

The authors in this volume approach Shakespeare in East Asian Education from a variety of experiences and perspectives: as those who live and work in Asia on a daily basis and those who visit to research, teach and work in other sectors there; as citizens of countries as diverse as America, Australia, England, Japan and Northern Ireland and migrants between those countries; as native speakers of Asian languages and world Englishes (which, where used, this book retains throughout rather than enforcing standard British English), multilinguals, monolinguals and language learners; those working in departments such as English literature, theatre studies, English (as an additional) language, and education. Sonya Corbin Dwyer and Jennifer Buckle argue that all researchers are positioned somewhere along a continuum of 'insider-outsider' and that the hyphen in that compound adjective is a dwelling place for researchers: we may be closer to the insider or outsider position, but our perspective is shaped by our researcher role as well as the developmental, dynamic nature of belonging to a community.[17] All contributors to this volume, including Chen Yilin as the author of our 'afterword', sit at different places along this continuum. We variously share, have at some point shared, and do not share, membership of some of the communities about which we write: Chinese, Hong Kongers, Japanese, Taiwanese, student, academic, theatre practitioner, theatre spectator, bilingual, multilingual, learner and teacher of English as an additional language. Some of these identities are themselves hotly contested: for example, Lau Chi-kuen and Michael Ingham both excellently problematise the notion of being 'authentic' Hong Kongers in the introductions to their respective books, *Hong Kong's Colonial Legacy* and *Hong Kong: a cultural history*.[18] Furthermore, Corbin Dwyer and Buckle offer the following caveat: 'Holding membership in a group does not denote complete sameness within that group. Likewise, not being a member...does not denote complete difference'.[19] Debates about the affordances and constraints of researchers belonging, or not belonging, to the group they are researching continue to rage and occasionally yield some surprising, even counter-intuitive, arguments. For example, Alison Phipps, specialising in Language and Intercultural Studies, has controversially critiqued what she identifies as the reification of linguistic competence, celebrated the extra-lingual aspects of multilingual research, and—albeit tongue-in-cheek—championed the benefits of researchers' 'linguistic incompetence'.[20] Some of her writing chimes with Corbin Dwyer and Buckle, who conclude that: 'The core ingredient [for successful research] is not insider or outsider status but an ability to be open, authentic, honest, deeply interested in the experience of one's research participants, and committed to accurately and adequately representing their experience'.[21] We certainly aimed for this. Pen portraits, such as those presented in the next few paragraphs, reject the over-simplistic binary of insider-outsider researcher, instead embracing Corbin Dwyer and Buckle's argument that all researchers are positioned somewhere along a continuum of 'insider-outsider'.[22]

Sarah Olive conceived the idea of a co-authored monograph dedicated to Shakespeare in East Asian education and set about approaching collaborators who could ensure that a range of countries and sectors would be covered. She began researching Shakespeare in UK education in 2004 and has carried that work on in both Education and English departments. Her PhD thesis first got her looking at policies and practices of teaching Shakespeare outside the UK, something she later fully embraced as founding editor of the British Shakespeare Association's *Teaching Shakespeare* magazine. In addition to East Asia, this publication has commissioned articles on Europe, the Middle East, Australasia and the Americas. Her research in East Asia began as a result of a single academic mobility funding opportunity but morphed into an ongoing research programme with multiple funders and countries involved, as well as frequent, even repeat, invitations from university departments in East Asia. She has visited universities in Tokyo and Takasaki, Seoul, Hong Kong, Hanoi and Ho Chi Minh City and continues to mentor colleagues from those institutions and others in China, particularly with regard to publishing research in English, in international titles or series, and applying for international funding opportunities (something made challenging in some East Asian countries by the widespread, relative paucity of institutional support for such activities). She is a co-director of the York Asia Research Network and, since 2017, she has organised its seminar series, which particularly aims to foster doctoral and early career researchers' dissemination with international students heavily involved. She also learns about East Asian education from her international students at the University of York: around two-thirds of the undergraduate students on her modules are from the region. Most of her international students are Chinese, with fewer coming from Hong

Kong, Japan, Malaysia, Singapore, Taiwan and Vietnam. Her teaching includes texts from Japan and Korea, written in or translated into English. The majority of her dissertation students (masters and undergraduate) are East Asian, completing empirical projects on education in their home countries, often with a focus on English language education, though she also supervises British students researching international schools in East Asia. She gained invaluable insight into English literature outside the classroom, in China, through her PhD student Zou Ying's research on Chinese parents' use of English picturebooks with their children. Examining doctorates on Shakespeare in Hong Kong theatre and Korean society historically has been a similarly instructive experience. These details are important because writers on Asian Shakespeare consistently stress the importance of knowledge and skills gained by researchers in East Asia. However, they more rarely recognise the influence on, and the contributions to, the work of academics in Anglophone countries that international students, and migration from East Asia more generally, make. This is in spite of Asian Shakespeare performance studies and area studies repeatedly problematising the assumption that influence flows unilaterally, west to east.[23]

Adele Lee's interest in Shakespeare in Hong Kong started while she was working on her PhD in English at the Queen's University, Belfast. Forming one chapter of her thesis, *The English Renaissance and the Far East: A Study in Cross-Cultural Encounters*, the subject of how this icon of Englishness ended up in the *Extrême-Orient* and in what ways the case of Shakespeare in Hong Kong challenges the 'colonial paradigm' also stemmed in large part from her mixed-race heritage.[24] It resulted in the publication in *Shakespeare Bulletin* of the first essay to examine Hong Kong film adaptations of the playwright's works.[25] Later, after taking up a position as Lecturer at the University of Greenwich, London, Lee was presented with, and eagerly seized, the opportunity to be a part of the British Council's 'Shakespeare: A Worldwide Classroom' project, a project that led to her gaining some invaluable experience teaching Shakespeare at selected schools in Hong Kong. Her involvement in 'Shakespeare: A Worldwide Classroom' then developed into a Research Excellence Framework (REF) impact case study designed to examine the role of Shakespeare in Hong Kong post-1997; whether Shakespeare's works are still relevant; and how it might be possible to reimagine Shakespeare in the territory. To address these questions, she conducted a medium-scale survey as well as interviewed actors and theatre directors, teachers and pupils, curriculum designers and academics. While the implicit, somewhat imperialistic goal of this University of Greenwich funded study was to influence decision-makers and demonstrate 'an effect on, or change or benefit to ... society, culture, public policy or services ... beyond academia' (according to the project's impact case study submitted for REF 2014), Lee ended up reaping as much wisdom and advice from her eastern counterparts about Shakespeare, and pedagogical approaches thereto, as she was able to impart. Indeed, some of the lessons she learned, and wishes to share, from her experience form the bulk of the subject of her chapter here. Her edited collection on *Shakespeare and Accentism*, on Shakespeare's own accentism and discrimination against various accents in contemporary Shakespeare industries, was published in 2020.[26]

'I began with the desire to speak with the dead', runs the famous quotation from Stephen Greenblatt.[27] For Kohei Uchimaru, the 'dead', however, include not only Shakespeare but also Japanese teachers of Shakespeare in the early twentieth century. His chapter is an attempt to re-create a conversation with them. Shakespeare is currently being marginalised in Japan, and in some other countries across the globe. However, this was not the case in late nineteenth- and early twentieth-century Japan. What was the teaching of Shakespeare like then? Why was the prominence attached to Shakespeare significant? These are his points of departure for investigating Shakespeare's reception in education. His primary concern, therefore, is Shakespeare in the English curriculum in Japanese higher education. The early Japanese encounter with Shakespeare took place when the book entitled *Self-Help* by Victorian moralist, Samuel Smiles was translated as *Tales of Successful Men in the West* by Masano Nakamura in 1870. This best-selling book offered readers numerous inspiring 'illustrations of CHARACTER AND CONDUCT', among which those concerning Shakespeare figured prominently. In Smiles' view, Shakespeare was 'a close student and a hard worker', and 'prospered in his business, and realized sufficient to enable him to retire upon a competency to his native town of Stratford-upon-Avon'. This portrait of Shakespeare as a self-made man resonated strongly with the young rising generation in modern Japan. As a result, Shakespeare's works came to be seen as suitable for educational purposes, particularly for intellectual and moral development. His works found their way into not only English reading textbooks produced locally for use in Japanese secondary schools but also into Japanese school readers. Additionally, Shakespeare's *sententiae* were flagged up in reference books produced for the university entrance examination in the English language. A majority of the Japanese people have encountered Shakespeare in the English-language classroom, and his works served as an integral component of cultural literacy for learners and teachers of the English language in Japan. The echoes of the past were still part of the English department when Uchimaru was a university student. An English-intensive reading course that he took as a compulsory subject was led by a distinguished Japanese Shakespearean scholar, Anzai Tetsuo (1933–2008), who was also a director of a Japanese theatre company, En. Professor Anzai used, as material for English teaching, a prose version of *Julius Caesar* (from Peter Milward's *Shakespeare's Tales Retold*), and then excerpts from the original play. However, as business- or career-oriented English language teaching began to gain power, the emphasis started to shift from an essential part of cultural literacy for learners of English towards a user of English deemed irrelevant to the needs of more utilitarian language learners. His historical research is, therefore, an attempt to hold a mirror up to the past, thereby re-considering Shakespeare as a possible educational resource. His chapter focuses on Okakura Yoshisaburō (1868–1936), the leading authority on English studies in early twentieth-century Japan, who viewed English language teaching as education. Okakura's staunch belief that Shakespeare should serve as an educational resource, rather than as a professional subject, in higher education institutions, continues to empower Uchimaru. His desire to re-create a conversation with him about Shakespeare encouraged him to write the chapter.

Rosalind Fielding studied Japanese at the University of Manchester as an undergraduate student, before writing a masters dissertation on Meiji era adaptations of Shakespeare and their contemporary influence on performance. She received her PhD from the Shakespeare Institute, University of Birmingham, in 2018, having written about the impact of social and political developments on the performance of Shakespeare in Japan since 2010. Her current research is on community theatre practices (particularly on older-age performance) and post-disaster theatre. She was a Visiting Research Fellow at Waseda University from 2017 to 2018. Having attended the 'Shakespeare for Children series: for children today' event hosted by the Tsubouchi Memorial Theatre Museum, she became interested in theatre for young audiences as another form of community and social theatre. She has worked for the Education departments at Shakespeare's Globe Theatre in London and the Royal Shakespeare

Company in Stratford-upon-Avon, besides various theatres and organisations in Japan including Saitama Arts Theater and the Japanese Centre
of the International Theatre Institute. She is an editor and translator of
*Re-Imagining Shakespeare in Contemporary Japan: A Selection of Japanese
Theatrical Adaptations of Shakespeare*, due to be published by Arden. In
spite of these wide-ranging, jumping-off points for creating this volume,
all three authors are united by their interests in and scholarship of
Shakespeare, education, theatre and East Asia.

The author of our afterword, Chen Yilin, is Professor of English,
Director of the International Education Center, and Director of the
Global Foreign Language Education Program at Providence Univer-
sity. She received a PhD in Drama and Theatre from Royal Holloway,
University of London. Her articles are published in diverse journals
including *Popular Entertainment Studies, Studies in Theatre and Perfor-
mance, Fiction and Drama*. She is a contributor to the book *Doing
English in Asia: Global Literature and Culture and Epoch Making in
English Teaching and Learning: Evolution, Innovation, and Revolution*.
Her research interests include Shakespearean translations, adaptations and
performances in Asia, digital and mobile learning for Shakespeare, and
graphic novels and *manga* adaptations of Shakespeare.

1.2   An Overview of the Chapters

In Chapter 2, Adele Lee reflects on the rise of China in Shakespeare and
performance, before pondering whether the nation could also be said to
be influencing or having a similarly 'remedial effect' on Shakespeare and
pedagogy. Drawing upon first-hand experience and scholarly research, and
focusing specifically on the case of Hong Kong—a special administrative
region of China that is under increasing national government control—
this chapter explores the extent to which Chinese educational systems
might help shape the future direction of how Shakespeare is taught in
the west. Taking into account recent reforms in China's education sector,
Lee argues that not only is Shakespeare playing a more prominent role
in Chinese classrooms, he is also serving as a catalyst for current adjustments to teaching strategies. She also argues that, as in Shakespeare on
stage, China could potentially hold the key to improvements in the west
and the Hong Kong classroom, where pedagogical approaches might be
deemed intercultural due to the territory's colonial past *and* the influence
of Confucian values and beliefs, in particular could serve as a model to the

west. This argument necessitates separating our opinions of the Chinese political system in our appraisal of its education, of course, and depends upon a willingness to diversify teaching methods with the same rigour and enthusiasm as we are willing to diversify curriculum content (so far, the 'intercultural turn' in Shakespeare Studies has not led to the adoption of intercultural teaching strategies). As Yong Zhao writes in *Who's Afraid of the Big Bad Dragon? Why China Has the Best (and Worst) Education System in the World* (2014), 'although it's unlikely that many western democratic nations will seriously borrow China's form of government any time soon, it's already the aspiration of many western nations to out-educate China, and to do it in the Chinese way'. More specifically, the examples of good practice Lee identifies in this chapter, and suggests are worth emulating globally, include successful group work, rewriting activities and even memorisation, all of which attest not just to the growing success of the Chinese system in the twenty-first century, but to the benefits of combining the best of both worlds, east and west, in how we teach Shakespeare.

In Chapter 3, Sarah Olive explores the Chinese Universities Shakespeare Festival as an extracurricular activity exemplifying prominent approaches to English as an Additional Language (EAL) learning. She opens with Amos Paran and Pauline Robinson's argument that there are three main approaches to literature and its use in the EAL classroom. Each of these is underpinned with a distinctive rationale and associated with distinctive teaching methods and activities, even different types of literary texts.[28] The three approaches are: literature (1) 'as a body of knowledge and content – for example, examining styles in literature, studying the history of English literature, dealing with the facts of authors' lives etc.'; (2) 'as language practice material', where the focus is 'on the language used in the literary text' and on activating learners' language skills; (3) 'as a stimulus for personal development', using 'activities which relate to students' personal experiences, thereby developing their imagination and emotions'.[29] In this chapter, she looks at the way in which the organisers' and participants' constructions of the Chinese Universities Shakespeare Festival (CUSF), which brought university students from greater China together to rehearse and perform twenty-minute Shakespeare scenes, align with these approaches (see the chapter itself for an explanation of the term 'greater China' and why Olive chose to use it in her writing). Knowledges featured in the festival included knowledge of Shakespeare's plays, their content and style, of his 'matchless' canonical status, his life and times, but also of literary theory and western theatre-going conventions and popular culture. English language skills ranged, if not evenly, across the domains of reading, writing, speaking and listening, with a particular emphasis on language in relation to dramatic performance (audibility, modulation, emphasis and so on). A particularly notable part of modelling English language skills was the emceeing by staff and graduate students—a mix of native speakers of English, multilinguals and EAL learners. There were also performances and workshops in English by professional theatre practitioners. This combination enabled participating and audience-member students to encounter a number of different varieties and registers of English. Personal development was constructed in terms of fostering literary and performing arts appreciation, creativity, empathetic associations students made with the plays, other affective experiences, teamwork and interpersonal communication—including between students from different regions of greater China who had previously been strangers to each other. The chapter offers the most extensive consideration of the festival's ten seasons available in English. It is written at a time when the festival's online presence, such as the Chinese University of Hong Kong's website for the event, is declining. The chapter concludes by considering whether CUSF provides a model for other higher education institution Shakespeare in countries where English is usually learnt as an additional language. In doing so, it suggests some improvements that might strengthen any successors.

In Chapter 4, Uchimaru considers the way in which Shakespeare is being marginalised in classrooms in Japan today, but this was not the case in late nineteenth and early twentieth centuries. English studies were enlisted in the national project of modernisation, at a time when the British Empire was encompassing the world. In seeking to improve the nation, the young rising generation in Japan learned English to imbibe knowledge and values from the west. This absorption and espousal were eagerly embraced, particularly in higher education institutions. Shakespeare was not exempted from this eagerness. The presence of Shakespeare in the English curriculum in institutions of higher learning can be best illustrated by reference to the likes of *Eigo seinen* (*The Rising Generation*), prestigious journals devoted to English studies in Japan, which featured lists of lectures on English studies and English textbooks between the 1910s and 1940s. They demonstrate that not only English-major students but also English learners in non-English departments were expected to read Shakespeare's plays, or Charles and Mary

Lambs' *Tales from Shakespeare*, as a platform for Shakespeare's original text. Since Shakespeare's plays were firmly placed within the English curriculum, knowledge of his work was naturally considered a prerequisite for English teachers engaging in higher education. They were not considered qualified teachers of English without profound knowledge of the plays. Shakespeare was thus esteemed as an integral component of cultural literacy for learners and teachers of English.

The first government-administered higher education institution in modern Japan that taught Shakespeare was a precursor of the Imperial University of Tokyo (now the University of Tokyo). The primary method for introducing Shakespeare to Japanese students during the formative years of higher education depended on the Anglo-American specialists hired by the Japanese government. The teaching of Shakespeare led by Anglophone professors can be seen as a unilaterally westernising force. Whilst their roles were taken over by Japanese scholars, Shakespeare was increasingly turning into an object of formal and professional study fit for experts. Japanese professors were also extreme in their contribution to Shakespeare teaching as a unilaterally westernising force in the sense that they strove to replicate Shakespeare studies on western model.

An attempt to teach Shakespeare as a professional subject was, however, problematised by the head of the English Department at Tokyo Higher Normal School, Okakura Yoshisaburō, who instead distilled the educational values of English as a means of learning about Anglophone 'thoughts and feelings' considered necessary to shape a 'great Japanese citizen'.[30] He staunchly believed that Shakespeare should serve as an educational resource for mental, cultural and national improvement. In this connection, his pedagogy was also peculiarly unique. In his reflections on educational psychology, knowledge acquisition took place when an unfamiliar idea is assimilated by the mass of ideas already in the mind. This led to his preference for the use of equivalence in the understanding of Shakespeare's plays. This was intimately related to what he perceived as education, which was best achieved by the discovery of the relative merits of different cultures or universal truth across them, rather than the study of Shakespeare for its own sake. In so doing, Okakura strove to read Shakespeare on his own terms. Okakura's ideological thrust, however, becomes more apparent when it is framed as his unwillingness to align himself with western criteria of literary greatness. For him, deference to Shakespeare, particularly to the words of Anglophone scholars, inevitably reduced the Japanese to passive imitators of an external model, which would establish a hierarchy of west-east relations. Instead, Okakura sought a way to use Shakespeare as a means of measuring Japan's greatness by finding Japanese equivalents to the plays. This coexistence of the desire to exploit Shakespeare as an educational resource with the urge to dissent from its unilaterally westernising force encouraged deviations from the model 'to secure the mobilization of those traditional characteristics and peculiarities that bolster the competitive edge of the developing country'.[31] In twenty-first century Japan, Shakespeare is no longer central to English studies in English departments nor are English departments a place to produce many academicians. By the same measure, the study of Shakespeare is no longer a unilaterally westernising force that reduces Asian people to passive imitators, as prominently exemplified in Asian-led 'Global Shakespeares' studies. Arguably, this makes Okakura's claim for Shakespeare's value in higher education all the more important. His comments on Shakespeare are perhaps most worth re-reading today for anyone interested not simply in the history of Shakespeare's reception in Japan, but also in the educational values of working with Shakespeare beyond the centre.

In Chapter 5, 'The west and the Resistance: perceptions of teaching Shakespeare for and against westernisation in Japanese higher education', Sarah Olive explores the question 'Is Shakespeare still perceived as one of the powerful global icons through which local education is westernised?' with regard to Japan. The question is adapted from one originally posed by Sonia Massai in her book *World-wide Shakespeares*: 'Has Shakespeare become one of the powerful global icons through which local cultural markets are progressively westernised?'.[32] Massai posits secondary and tertiary education as modes of cultural production alongside theatre, film and other media. Her collection is focused on analysing creative, rather than classroom, appropriations of Shakespeare. This chapter alters the wording of Massai's original question partly to focus on education rather than cultural markets and partly because this is not a longitudinal study. Its rewriting clearly foregrounds the perceptions of people studying and teaching Shakespeare in the region in the early twenty-first century. It demonstrates that some of these perceptions around Shakespeare in Japanese higher education are predicated on a binaric understanding of Shakespeare as the 'foreign'/'other'/west, distinct from the 'indigenous'/'our'/East Asian. His foreignness is perceived varyingly along a continuum from positive to malignant. However, other perceptions explicitly or implicitly trouble this supposed polarity, emphasising Shakespeare as local, regional and Asian. The question 'Is Shakespeare perceived as one of the powerful global icons through which local education is westernised?' is answered affirmatively in terms of the nature and purpose of subject English; the use of western productions in the classroom; and the delivery of a westernised 'world view' through Shakespeare. However, the chapter goes on to detail instances in which Shakespeare is not perceived to westernise Japanese education, or in which his teaching can be seen to resist or problematise westernisation. These include the negotiation of possible affronts to cultural sensibilities caused in Japan by Shakespeare's *shimo-neta*, or bawdy humour, as well as the demands of western pedagogies (i.e. pedagogies perceived to be western in origin by these educators and students); an emphasis on Japan being akin to Britain; and national pride in using local, cultural products to teach Shakespeare.

In Chapter 6, Rosalind Fielding examines the history, staging and reception of the Shakespeare for Children series, established in 1995 by actor and director Yamasaki Seisuke at the Tokyo Globe Theatre. The series, which creates specially adapted productions of Shakespeare for younger audiences, has staged over twenty shows and toured both nationally and internationally since its first production. Yamasaki's series is considered within the wider context of theatre for young audiences in Japan. Having outlived its original venue, the Tokyo Globe (which closed in 2002 and was reopened under new managed in 2004), Yamasaki's series has toured across Japan for the last two decades, bringing its unique take on Shakespeare to a wider audience. The series' productions run at around two hours, with cuts made to the text to help the young audience's understanding, although Yamasaki himself has stated that it is important not to 'underestimate children's capability' to understand Shakespeare since they can 'enjoy Shakespeare's plays just as adults do'.[33] A number of techniques are employed to create what the series terms its 'not difficult' take on Shakespeare which 'anyone can enjoy watching', including rearranging scenes to clarify the flow of the story, adding excerpts from other plays to provide background (e.g. adding scenes from the *Henry VI* plays to *Richard III*) and repetition, besides adding visual and verbal jokes such as references from daily life and popular culture.[34] The series is known for its theatricality, its use of simple sets, small casts and cross-casting, a Chorus that take on multiple roles during the performance, and its 'Shakespeare puppet' which helps to introduce the story in every production. These techniques help make the productions accessible for young audiences and reflect Yamasaki's desire that they get a feel for the story and the characters, and know that it is fine not to understand everything that they see and hear. The series is examined here in detail through case studies of *Cymbeline* and *A Midsummer Night's Dream*. Very little has been published on the Shakespeare for Children series in either Japanese or English, and so this chapter aims to re-examine this example of theatre for young audiences which has been, as Jan Wozniak writes, 'implicitly devalued in academic and pedagogical discourse and practice', taking its inspiration from the 'Shakespeare for Children series: for children today' event held at Waseda University, Tokyo, on May 29, 2017.[35]

The volume closes with an afterword by Chen Yilin who suggests that *Shakespeare in East Asian Education* is the first book exploring the ways in which Shakespeare has been incorporated into classrooms across the region, including both subjects of English and Theatre studies. She argues that the book is important for western readers not only to understand traditional approaches to teaching Shakespeare in this region, but also to reflect on new pedagogies in terms of making Shakespeare relevant to local cultures in the global context nowadays. Foregrounding the latter, Chen offers an insight into the rationale and pedagogies of the Global/Local Shakespeare Massive Open Online Course (MOOC), in the context of regional policy-makers' demands for graduates to have '21st century skills' including visual and Information and Communications Technology (ICT) literacy, as well as online teaching and learning becoming more mainstream, especially during the COVID-19 pandemic. She focuses in particular on the MOOC's incorporation into Taiwanese higher education using a flipped classroom and Bloom's Taxonomy of Educational Objectives to align objectives, teaching and assessment, from *manga* to mobile applications. Her closing argument is that the teaching of Shakespeare in East Asia must be more than English language and cultural competence teaching: it must raise students' awareness of the ways in which Shakespeare is interpreted and adapted in different social, political, and cultural contexts.

A note on our rendering of East Asian names: throughout, we have followed the regional custom of giving surnames before given names, except in cases where the individual is more commonly known by a different name order e.g. Uchimaru Kohei and Chen Yilin, rather than the westernised order Kohei Uchimaru and Yilin Chen.

NOTES

1. Zhang Xiaoyang, *Shakespeare in China* (Newark: Delaware University Press, 1996). Dennis Kennedy, *Foreign Shakespeare: Contemporary Performance* (Cambridge: Cambridge University Press, 1993).
2. Sonia Massai, *World-Wide Shakespeares: Local Appropriations in Film and Performance* (London: Routledge, 2006), 4. Mark Thornton Burnett, *Filming Shakespeare in the Global Marketplace* (Houndmills: Palgrave, 2007). Sharon Beehler and Holger Klein (ed), *Shakespeare and Higher Education: A Global Perspective* (Lewiston, New York: Edwin Mellen Press, 2001). Alexa Alice Joubin, 'Global Shakespeare 2.0 and the Task of the Performance Archive.' *Shakespeare Survey* 64 (2011): 38–51. Alexa Alice Joubin, 'Global Shakespeares as Methodology.' *Shakespeare* 9.3 (2013): 273–290. Paul Prescott and Erin Sullivan, *Shakespeare on the Global Stage: Performance and Festivity in the Olympic Year* (London: Bloomsbury, 2015).
3. Kishi Tetsuo and Graham Bradshaw, *Shakespeare in Japan* (London: Continuum, 2005). Alexa Alice Joubin, *Chinese Shakespeares: Two Centuries of Cultural Exchange* (New York: Columbia University Press, 2009). Murray Levith, *Shakespeare in China* (London: Continuum, 2004). Minami Ryuta, Ian Carruthers, and John Gillies (ed), *Performing Shakespeare in Japan* (Cambridge: Cambridge University Press, 2001). Takashi Sasayama, J.R. Mulryne and Margaret Shewring, *Shakespeare and the Japanese Stage* (Cambridge: CUP, 1998). Dominic Shellard (ed), 'Shakespeare in Japan.' Special Issue, *Shakespeare* 9.4 (2013).
4. Bi-qi Beatrice Lei, Judy Celine Ick and Poonam Trivedi (ed), *Shakespeare's Asian Journeys: Critical Encounters, Cultural Geographies, and the Politics of Travel* (London: Routledge, 2016). Joubin, *Chinese Shakespeares*. Poonam Trivedi and Minami Ryuta (ed), *Replaying Shakespeare in Asia* (London: Routledge, 2010). Alexa Alice Joubin and Charles S. Ross, *Shakespeare in Hollywood, Asia, and Cyberspace* (West Lafayette, IN: Purdue University Press, 2009). Alexa Alice Joubin, 'Asian Shakespeares in Europe: From the Unfamiliar to the Defamiliarised', *Shakespearean International Yearbook* 8 (2008): 51–70. John Russell Brown, *New Sites for Shakespeare: Theatre, the Audience, and Asia* (London: Routledge, 1999). Dennis Kennedy and Yong Li Lan, *Shakespeare in Asia* (Cambridge: CUP, 2010). Lingui Yang, Douglas Brooks, and Ashley Brinkman, *Shakespeare and Asia* (Lewiston: Edwin Mellen, 2010).
5. Martin Orkin, *Local Shakespeares: Proximations and Power* (London: Routledge, 2005).
6. Tam Kwok-kan, Andrew Parkin and Terry Siu-han Yip (ed), *Shakespeare Global/Local: The Hong Kong Imaginary in Transcultural Production* (New York: Peter Lang, 2002).

7. R.S. White, 'Introduction,' in *Shakespeare's Local Habitations*, edited by Krystyna Kujawińska-Courtney and R.S. White (Łódź: Łódź University Press, 2007). Lee Hyon-u, Shim Jung-soon, and Kim Dong-wook (ed), *Glocalizing Shakespeare in Korea and Beyond* (Seoul: Dongin, 2009).

8. The collection includes chapters on Shakespeare productions in Chinese and Malaysian universities that might interest our readers. Lee Chee Keng and Yong Li Lan, 'Ideology and Student Performances in China', in *Shakespeare on the University Stage*, edited by Andrew Hartley (Cambridge: Cambridge University Press, 2014), 90–109. Nurul Low bt Abdullah, 'The Politics and Economics of Malaysian Campus Productions of Shakespeare', in *Shakespeare on the University Stage*, edited by Andrew Hartley (Cambridge: Cambridge University Press, 2014), 168–184.

9. This list is intended to be illustrative, not exclusive. Sukanta Chaudhuri and Lim Chee Seng, *Shakespeare Without English: The Reception of Shakespeare in Non-Anglophone Countries* (Delhi: Pearson Longman, 2006). Kennedy and Yong, *Shakespeare in Asia*. Trivedi and Minami's *Re-playing Shakespeare in Asia*. Li Ruru, *Shashibiya* (Hong Kong: Hong Kong University Press, 2003). Li Jun, *Popular Shakespeare in China: 1993-2008* (Beijing: University of International Business and Economics, 2016). A.J Hartley (ed), *Shakespeare on the University Stage* (Cambridge: CUP, 2014), 211. Sharon Beehler and Holger Klein (ed), *Shakespeare and Higher Education: A Global Perspective* (Lewiston, New York: Edwin Mellen Press, 2001). Kate Flaherty, Penny Gay, and Liam Semler. *Teaching Shakespeare Beyond the Centre: Australasian Perspectives* (Basingstoke, Hampshire: Palgrave Macmillan, 2013). Joubin and Ross, *Shakespeare in Hollywood, Asia, and Cyberspace*. Yang, Brooks, and Brinkman, *Shakespeare and Asia*. There is no East Asian chapter in G.B. Shand's comparable volume (to our book) also focused on Shakespeare in higher education. *Teaching Shakespeare: Passing It on* (Chichester: Wiley, 2009).

10. Sarah Olive, *Shakespeare Valued: Education Policy and Pedagogy in England, 1989–2009* (Bristol: Intellect, 2015).

11. Asian Shakespeare Intercultural Archive (A|S|I|A) (website), accessed 28 November 2018, http://a-s-i-a-web.org/en/home.php. Lau Leung Che Miriam and Tso Wing Bo Anna, *Teaching Shakespeare to ESL Students* (Singapore: Springer, 2016).

12. Adele Lee, 'How Do You Solve a Problem Like China? "Global Shakespeare" and the Limitations of the "Cosmopolitan Model"', paper presented at the 'Rethinking the Global' Seminar of the Shakespeare Association of America Annual Meeting, Los Angeles, CA, April 2018. Key inspiration for Lee's paper came from Rey Chow's, 'Introduction: On Chineseness as a Theoretical Problem,' in *Modern Chinese Literary and Cultural Studies in the Age of Theory: Reimagining a Field*, edited by Rey Chow (Durham and London: Duke University Press, 2000), 3.

13. Kishi and Bradshaw, *Shakespeare in Japan*. Ania Loomba, *Colonialism/Postcolonialism* (London: Routledge, 1998). Sukanta Chaudhuri, 'Shakespeare in India', in *Shakespeare's Local Habitations*, edited by Krystyna Kujawínska Courtney and RS White. Łódź: Łódź University Press, 2007, 81–98. Supriya Chaudhuri, 'The Absence of Caliban: Shakespeare and Colonial Modernity', in *Shakespeare's World/World Shakespeare's*, edited by Richard Fotheringham, Crista Jansohn and R.S. White (Newark: University of Delaware Press, 2008), 223–236.

14. Dorothy Wong, '"Domination by Consent": A Study of Shakespeare in Hong Kong', in *Colonizer and Colonized*, edited by Theo D'haen and Patricia Krus (Amsterdam: Editions Rodopi, 2000), 43–56. Tam et al., *Shakespeare Global/Local*.

15. Andrew Dickson, *Worlds Elsewhere*.

16. Ania Loomba and Martin Orkin, *Post-colonial Shakespeares* (New York: Routledge, 2002).

17. Corbin Dwyer and Buckle, 'The Space Between', 60. Sarah Olive, 'To Research, or Not to Research? Some Dilemmas of Insider-Outsider Research on Shakespeare in South East/East Asian Higher Education,' *Researcher Stories Blog. British Sociological Association*, accessed May 5, 2017, https://bsapgforum.com/2017/05/05/dr-sarah-olive-to-research-or-not-to-research-some-dilemmas-of-insider-outsider-research-on-shakespeare-in-south-easteast-asian-higher-education/.

18. Lau Chi-kuen, *Hong Kong's Colonial Legacy* (Hong Kong: Chinese University Press, 1997). Michael Ingham, *Hong Kong: A Cultural History* (Oxford: OUP 2007), xviii.

19. Corbin Dwyer and Buckle, 'The Space Between', 60.

20. Alison Phipps, 'Giving an Account of Researching Multilingually', *International Journal of Applied Linguistics* 23 (2013): 329–341.

21. Corbin Dwyer and Buckle, 'The Space Between', 59. Kishore Mahbubani, *Has the West Lost It? A Provocation* (London: Allen Lane, 2018). Iwabuchi Koichi, Stephen Muecke and Mandy Thomas, *Rogue Flows: Trans-Asian Cultural Traffic* (Hong Kong: Hong Kong University Press, 2014).

22. Sonia Corbin Dwyer and Jennifer Buckle, 'The Space Between: On Being an Insider-Outsider in Qualitative Research', *International Journal of Qualitative Methods* 8.1 (2009): 60.

23. Adele Lee, *The English Renaissance and the Far East: A Study in Cross-Cultural Encounters* (Lanham, MD: Farleigh Dickson University Press, 2018).

24. Lee, *The English Renaissance and the Far East*.

25. Adele Lee, '"Chop-Socky Shakespeare"?! The Bard Onscreen in Hong Kong', *Shakespeare Bulletin* 28.4 (2010): 459–480.

26. Adele Lee, *Shakespeare and Accentism* (London: Routledge, forthcoming).

27. Stephen Greenblatt, *Shakespearean Negotiations: The Circulation of Social Energy in Renaissance England* (Berkley: University of California Press, 1988), 1.

28. Amos Paran and Pauline Robinson, *Literature* (Oxford: OUP, 2016.)

29. Paran and Robinson, *Literature*, 27.

30. Okakura Yoshisaburō, '*Eigo to eibungaku* (The English Language and English Literature)'. *Eigo seinen* (*The Rising Generation*) 53.12 (1925): 368.

31. Messay Kebede, *Radicalism and Cultural Dislocation in Ethiopia, 1960–1974* (New York: University of Rochester Press, 2008), 65.

32. Massai, *World-Wide Shakespeares*.

33. Yamasaki Seisuke quoted in Tanaka Nobuko, '*Hamlet* Marks Take #18 in Shakespeare for Children Series', *Japan Times*, 3 September 2014, https://www.japantimes.co.jp/culture/2014/09/03/stage/hamlet-marks-take-18-shakespeare-children-series.

34. '*Engeki*', *Canon Kikaku*, accessed 10 February 2019, http://www.canonkikaku.com/engeki.

35. Jan Wozniak, *The Politics of Performing Shakespeare for Young People: Standing up to Shakespeare* (London: Bloomsbury, Arden Shakespeare, 2016), 11.

References

Beehler, Sharon A. and Holger Klein, ed. *Shakespeare and Higher Education: A Global Perspective*. Lewiston and New York: Edwin Mellen Press, 2001.

Brown, J. Russell. *New Sites for Shakespeare: Theatre, the Audience, and Asia*. London: Routledge, 1999.

Canon Kikaku. '*Engeki*.' *Canon Kikaku*. Accessed February 10, 2019. http://www.canonkikaku.com/engeki.

Chaudhuri, Sukanta and Chee Seng Lim. *Shakespeare Without English: The Reception of Shakespeare in Non-Anglophone Countries*. Delhi: Pearson Longman, 2006.

Chaudhuri, Supriya. 'The Absence of Caliban: Shakespeare and Colonial Modernity'. In *Shakespeare's World/World Shakespeare's*, edited by Richard Fotherigham, Crista Jansohn and R.S. White. Newark: University of Delaware Press, 2008. 223–236.

Chow, Rey. 'Introduction: On Chineseness as a Theoretical Problem.' In *Modern Chinese Literary and Cultural Studies in the Age of Theory: Reimagining a Field*, edited by Rey Chow. Durham and London: Duke University Press, 2000.

Dwyer, Sonya Corbin and Jennifer Buckle. 'The Space Between: On Being an Insider-Outsider in Qualitative Research'. *International Journal of Qualitative Methods* 8.1 (2009): 54–63.

Dickson, Andrew. *Worlds Elsewhere: Journeys Around Shakespeare's Globe*. New York: Henry Holt, 2016.

Flaherty, Kate, Penny Gay, and Liam Semler, *Teaching Shakespeare Beyond the Centre: Australasian Perspectives*. Basingstoke, Hamps: Palgrave Macmillan, 2003.

Greenblatt, Stephen. *Shakespearean Negotiations: The Circulation of Social Energy in Renaissance England*. Berkley: University of California Press, 1988.

Hartley, A.J., ed. *Shakespeare on the University Stage*. Cambridge: CUP, 2014.

Ingham, Michael. *Hong Kong: A Cultural History*. Oxford: OUP, 2007.

Iwabuchi, Koichi, Stephen Muecke, and Mandy Thomas. *Rogue Flows: Trans-Asian Cultural Traffic*. Hong Kong: Hong Kong University Press, 2014.

Joubin, Alexa Alice. *Chinese Shakespeares: Two Centuries of Cultural Exchange*. New York: Columbia University Press, 2009.

Joubin, Alexa Alice and C.S. Ross, *Shakespeare in Hollywood, Asia, and Cyberspace*. West Lafayette, IN: Purdue University Press, 2009.

Kebede, Messay. *Radicalism and Cultural Dislocation in Ethiopia, 1960–1974*. New York: University of Rochester Press, 2008.

Kennedy, Dennis. *Foreign Shakespeare: Contemporary Performance*. Cambridge: Cambridge University Press, 1993.

Kennedy, Dennis and Yong Li Lan. *Shakespeare in Asia*. Cambridge: Cambridge University Press, 2010.

Kishi, Tetsuo and Graham Bradshaw. *Shakespeare in Japan*. London: Continuum, 2005.

Lau, Chi-kuen. *Hong Kong's Colonial Legacy*. Hong Kong: Chinese University Press, 1997.

Lau, Miriam Leung Che and Anna Wing Bo Tso. *Teaching Shakespeare to ESL Students*. Singapore: Springer, 2016.

Lee, Adele. *Shakespeare and Accentism*. London: Routledge, forthcoming.

Lee, Adele. '"Chop-Socky Shakespeare"?! The Bard Onscreen in Hong Kong'. *Shakespeare Bulletin* 28.4 (2010): 459–480.

Lee, Adele. *The English Renaissance and the Far East: A Study in Cross-Cultural Encounters*. Lanham, MD: Farleigh Dickson University Press, 2018.

Lee, Adele. 'How Do You Solve a Problem Like China? "Global Shakespeare" and the Limitations of the "Cosmopolitan Model"', paper presented at the 'Rethinking the Global' Seminar of the Shakespeare Association of America Annual Meeting, Los Angeles, CA, April 2018.

Lee, Chee Keng and Yong Li Lan. 'Ideology and Student Performances in China'. In *Shakespeare on the University Stage*, edited by Andrew Hartley. Cambridge: Cambridge University Press, 2014. 90–109.

Lee, Hyon-u, Shim Jung-soon, and Kim Dong-wook, ed. *Glocalizing Shakespeare in Korea and Beyond*. Seoul: Dongin, 2009.

Lei, Bi-qi Beatrice, Judy Celine Ick, and Poonam Trivedi, ed. *Shakespeare's Asian Journeys: Critical Encounters, Cultural Geographies, and the Politics of Travel*. London: Routledge, 2016.

Levith, Murray. *Shakespeare in China*. London: Continuum, 2004.

Li, Jun. *Popular Shakespeare in China: 1993–2008*. Beijing: University of International Business and Economics, 2016.

Li, Ruru. *Shashibiya*. Hong Kong: HKUP, 2003.

Loomba, Ania. *Colonialism/Postcolonialism*. London: Routledge, 1998.

Loomba, Ania and Martin Orkin. *Post-colonial Shakespeares*. New York: Routledge, 2002.

Low bt Abdullah, Nurul. 'The Politics and Economics of Malaysian Campus Productions of Shakespeare'. In *Shakespeare on the University Stage*, edited by Andrew Hartley. Cambridge: Cambridge University Press, 2014. 168–184.

Mahbubani, Kishore. *Has the West Lost It? A Provocation*. London: Allen Lane, 2018.

Massai, Sonia. *World-Wide Shakespeares: Local Appropriations in Film and Performance*. London: Routledge, 2006.

Minami, Ryuta, Ian Carruthers, and John Gillies, ed. *Performing Shakespeare in Japan*. Cambridge: Cambridge University Press, 2001.

Okakura, Yoshisaburō. '*Eigo to eibungaku* (The English Language and English Literature)'. *Eigo seinen* (*The Rising Generation*) 53.12 (1925): 368.

Olive, Sarah. *Shakespeare Valued: Education Policy and Pedagogy in England, 1989–2009*. Bristol: Intellect, 2015.

Olive, Sarah. 'To Research, or Not to Research? Some Dilemmas of Insider-Outsider Research on Shakespeare in South East/East Asian Higher Education.' In *Researcher Stories Blog: British Sociological Association*. Accessed May 5, 2017. https://bsapgforum.com/2017/05/05/dr-sarah-olive-to-research-or-not-to-research-some-dilemmas-of-insider-outsider-res earch-on-shakespeare-in-south-easteast-asian-higher-education/.

Orkin, Martin. *Local Shakespeares: Proximations and Power*. London: Routledge, 2005.

Paran, Amos and Pauline Robinson. *Literature*. Oxford: OUP, 2016.

Phipps, Alison. 'Giving an Account of Researching Multilingually'. *International Journal of Applied Linguistics* 23 (2013). 329–341.

Prescott, Paul and Erin Sullivan. *Shakespeare on the Global Stage: Performance and Festivity in the Olympic Year*. London: Bloomsbury, 2015.

Royal Shakespeare Company. *Wiki Shakespeare—Teaching Shakespeare Around the World*. Web. 26 February 2012.

Sasayama, Takashi, J.R. Mulryne, and Margaret Shewring. *Shakespeare and the Japanese Stage*. Cambridge: CUP, 1998.

Shand, G.B. *Teaching Shakespeare: Passing It on.* Chichester: Wiley, 2009.

Shellard, Dominic, ed. 'Shakespeare in Japan.' Special Issue, *Shakespeare* 9.4 (2013).

Tam, Kwok-kan, Andrew Parkin, and Terry Siu-han Yip, ed. *Shakespeare Global/Local: The Hong Kong Imaginary in Transcultural Production.* New York: Peter Lang, 2002.

Tanaka, Nobuko. '*Hamlet* Marks Take #18 in Shakespeare for Children Series.' *Japan Times,* 3 September 2014, https://www.japantimes.co.jp/culture/2014/09/03/stage/hamlet-marks-take-18-shakespeare-children-series.

Thornton Burnett, Mark. *Filming Shakespeare in the Global Marketplace.* Houndmills: Palgrave, 2007.

Trivedi, Poonam and Minami Ryuta, ed. *Replaying Shakespeare in Asia.* London: Routledge, 2010.

White, R.S. 'Introduction.' In *Shakespeare's Local Habitations,* edited by Krystyna Kujawińska-Courtney and R.S. White. Łódź: Łódź University Press, 2007.

Wong, Dorothy. '"Domination by Consent": A Study of Shakespeare in Hong Kong'. In *Colonizer and Colonized,* edited by Theo D'haen and Patricia Krus. Amsterdam: Editions Rodopi, 2000. 43–56.

Wozniak, Jan. *The Politics of Performing Shakespeare for Young People: Standing Up to Shakespeare.* London: Bloomsbury, Arden Shakespeare, 2016.

Yang, Lingui, Douglas Brooks, and Ashley Brinkman. *Shakespeare and Asia.* Lewiston: Edwin Mellen, 2010.

Zhang, Xiaoyang. *Shakespeare in China.* Newark: Delaware University Press, 1996.

CHAPTER 2

Shakespeare in the Hong Kong Chinese Classroom: Exploring an Intercultural Approach to Teaching

Adele Lee

Abstract This chapter reflects on the rise of China in Shakespeare and performance, before pondering whether the nation could also be said to be influencing or having a similarly 'remedial effect' on Shakespeare and pedagogy. Focusing specifically on the case of Hong Kong, it explores the extent to which Chinese educational systems might help shape the future direction of how Shakespeare is taught in the west. Lee argues that not only is Shakespeare playing a prominent role in Chinese classrooms, he is also serving as a catalyst for current adjustments to teaching strategies. More specifically, she argues that, as in Shakespeare on stage, China could potentially hold the key to modifications in the west with the Hong Kong classroom, where pedagogical approaches might be deemed intercultural due to the territory's colonial past and the influence of Confucian values and beliefs, serving as a potential model.

A. Lee (✉)
Emerson College, Boston, MA, USA
e-mail: adele_lee@emerson.edu

S. Olive et al., *Shakespeare in East Asian Education*, Global Shakespeares,
https://doi.org/10.1007/978-3-030-64796-4_2

Keywords Shakespeare · China · Hong Kong · Performance ·
Intercultural pedagogy · School

Reflecting on anxieties that western theatre has hit a creative impasse and
Shakespeare on stage in particular has become stilted, dated and inau-
thentic, Jang Tso Fang made the bold claim in 1986 that 'Shakespeare is
sick in the west, and much in need of traditional Chinese medicine'.[1] His
opinion was heartily embraced by scholars and directors on both sides of
the hemisphere, including Dennis Bartholomeusz, John Russell Brown,
Ariane Mnouchkine and Leonard C. Pronko, who argued in *Shakespeare
East and West* (1996) that:

> Using Asian techniques may seem exotic, but we need something radical
> to make us see that almost all the Shakespeare...productions of the past
> twenty or thirty years...have been filtered through more than a century of
> realism and naturalism, to the point that we have lost our ability even to
> see how realistic they are.[2]

As problematic as such sentiments are—they imply the spatial movement from west to east mirrors a temporal movement from modern-day
logos to pre-modern *mythos*—it is evident that in the last couple of
decades, Chinese dramaturgy has played a significant role in reinvigo-
rating Shakespeare performance, changing how we understand the plays,
as well as pioneering new, globalised artistic styles. Such a role attests
to the increasing 'soft power' of China and the extent to which cultural
capital typically accompanies economic development or, more accurately,
education and economics are inseparable. Indeed, some have gone so
far as to suggest that just as 'East Asia has become the most dynamic
center of Capitalist growth, the center of creativity in Shakespeare performance is shifting from Europe and the US to Asia'.[3] Certainly, some
of the most innovative and critically-acclaimed versions of Shakespeare
to emerge since the turn of the twenty-first century hail from China
and include *Richard III* (dir. Wang Xiao Ying, 2012–), *King Lear* (dir.
Wu Hsing-Kuo, 2001–) and *The Great General Kou Liulan* (dir. Lin
Zhaohua, 2007).

However, could China also be said to be influencing or having
a similarly 'remedial effect' on Shakespeare pedagogy, i.e. educational

policy, teaching methodologies or curriculum design? Drawing upon first-hand experience and scholarly research, including a range of qualitative and quantitative data (interviews, questionnaires and classroom observations), and focusing specifically on the case of Hong Kong—a 'Special Administrative Region' of China increasingly being absorbed into the 'Mainland'—this chapter explores the extent to which Chinese educational systems might help shape the future direction of how Shakespeare is taught in the west. In particular, taking into account recent reforms in China's education sector, which have led to the adoption of more heuristic and participatory teaching practices and a purported shift from rote learning to the cultivation of more critical thinking, I argue that not only is Shakespeare playing a more prominent role in Chinese classrooms, but he has the potential to act as a catalyst for current, ongoing adjustments to teaching strategies. As Yuan Yang recently noted, 'new, creative ways of teaching the plays in schools and performing them in theatres, coinciding with a surge of interest in Shakespeare, are stretching Chinese families' experience of art and education under an otherwise increasingly censorious regime'.[4] In this chapter, I also tentatively propose that, as in Shakespeare performance, China could potentially hold the key to improvements in the western academy which might benefit from the selective incorporation of elements from the Chinese education system, particularly in Hong Kong where teachers combine the best from the west and the best from the east and have developed 'a transformed pedagogy that [takes] into account student cognition and social infrastructure, integrating Chinese *and* western approaches in scaffolding student inquiry, collaboration and understanding'.[5]

Ultimately, an intercultural approach to teaching is not only appropriate given the '*inter*cultural turn' in Shakespeare studies (which has heightened awareness of the global dimensions of production and exchange), but might even be said to form a necessary but oft-neglected part of general, ongoing efforts to diversify and globalise the field. All-too-often efforts are made to revise curriculum content but not pedagogical practices and philosophies, even though the latter are as entrenched in Anglo-centric thinking as the canon of 'dead white men'. Put another way, it is ironic that while western higher education pundits advocate the development of an intercultural curriculum, they are much less open to the development of an intercultural pedagogy. This chapter therefore, and perhaps controversially, proposes that we scan other cultures, specifically Hong Kong, which, because of its Confucian heritage and British colonial legacy is 'an area that invites scholarly enquiry and ongoing critical reflection on successful practice'.[6] Such an enquiry necessitates setting aside the Sinophobic sentiments that are so prevalent in today's society and separating our opinions of the Chinese political system in our appraisal of its education system. After all, as Yong Zhao writes in *Who's Afraid of the Big Bad Dragon? Why China Has the Best (and Worst) Education System in the World* (2014), 'although it's unlikely that many western democratic nations will seriously borrow China's form of government any time soon, it's already the aspiration of many western nations to out-educate China, and to do it in the Chinese way'.

2.1   SHAKESPEARE AND CHINESE EDUCATIONAL REFORMS

Despite attaching great importance to education, as ancient proverbs such as 'to establish a nation state, education should come first' and 'a man [sic] without education cannot be a knowledgeable and moral man' indicate, China has not historically been lauded by the international community for its education system. Nor has its system, which originated in 1100 BC and was once called *pi-yong*, served as an obvious model for western institutions.[7] Instead, Chinese schools are frequently derided as gruelling, elitist and even 'medieval' due to strict discipline, a competitive and rigorous exam system, and impersonal, authoritarian teaching styles. They are also generally conceived as beset by a number of problems, for example, overcrowding, overspecialisation and excessive test taking. As one critic puts it:

> The authoritarian Chinese educational model ... emphasizes a narrow band of readily testable skills where the goal of students is to select the correct answer ... [it] was originally, and remains today, one of social control where students seek to please at the cost of achieving creativity.[8]

Yet, if this is the case, how do we explain the surge in Asian students attending Ivy League schools in the US and, more pointedly, the country's top liberal arts colleges where the emphasis is less on STEM-related subjects and more on the arts, humanities and social sciences? Furthermore, why is the East Asian educational model currently 'high on the minds of many international specialists who seek explanations for the declining ability of western-educated students to compete with the academic highflyers from Hong Kong, Singapore, Japan, China and elsewhere in the region'[9]? Clearly, clichés about China overlook the growing success of its overseas students, students who are succeeding in international tests such as PISA, TIMSS and PIRLS and who get accepted at institutions where the criteria for assessment is often quite different from those used in their own schooling; thus the skills they have acquired are transferable and translate across education systems.[10] Stereotypical notions, stemming in part from the western superiority complex, further overlook the steady climb of China's universities up global league tables[11]; the rise in the number of American students studying in China; and significant reforms, since the new millennium, to the country's academic structures and strategies. This is especially the case in Hong Kong, which has come under increasing, and sometimes violent, control lately by the national government and has proven something of a testing ground since the 1997 'handover' for various kinds of Mainland Chinese reforms: economic, social and political.

Less examination-driven (the existing Hong Kong Certificate of Education Examination and Hong Kong Advanced Level Examination have been replaced with a Diploma of Secondary Education) and more student-focused, Hong Kong education is gradually doing away with 'tough exams' and learning by memorisation and instead stressing the importance of 'whole person' development and critical thinking skills, which would perhaps explain why high numbers of under 29-year-olds have taken part in recent protests. In other words, attempts have been made to broaden the education of Hong Kong students along the lines of the liberal arts or general education model. As stated in *Learning for Life, Learning Through Life: Reform Proposals for the Education System in Hong Kong*, published by the Education Commission in 2000:

> Adaptability, creativity and abilities of communication, self-learning and co-operation are now pre-requisites for anyone to succeed, while a person's character, emotional qualities, horizons and learning are important factors [...] The mission in education is to enhance the knowledge, ability, quality, cultivation and international outlook of the people of Hong Kong.[12]

The emphasis on creativity, individuality and internationalisation reflects the general sea change in Chinese education in recent years, a change that has been *mis*read as an attempt by the People's Republic of China (henceforth PRC) to adopt a more international (specifically American)

approach. For, as Yin Hong-Biao and Li Zijian point out, although
'the national curriculum reform (NCR) in China [has] adopted many
seemingly "Anglo-American" ideas and policies, such as decentralization,
curriculum integration, constructivist teaching, inquiry-based learning,
formative assessment, cultivation of generic skills etc.', the reform process
is certainly *not* a 'copy and paste exercise'.[13] In fact, when comparing
educational trends in China and the USA, Preus (2007) found that what
is happening in China education is precisely the direct *opposite* to that
of recent reforms in the States, where education is becoming more and
more centralised, test-oriented and STEM-focused: 'U.S. institutions are
now embracing the sort of regimented, uniform, standards-based, test-
driven education that has weighed down China's system for centuries.
What we are witnessing … is nothing less than a reversal of ideals'.[14]
Similarly, in the UK, current trends indicate that instructors are under
increasing government control and forced to teach centrally prescribed
subject-derived curricular content.[15] Overcrowding, underfunding and
redundancies because of a funding crisis are also major problems, with
some head teachers warning that the school system is at risk of 'implod-
ing'. This runs contrary to expectations that there is a 'centre-periphery'
or 'dominance-subordination' relationship in international educational
frameworks, with China emulating the 'colonisers' academic models' or
conforming to a westernised global culture.

Indeed, as the BBC2 series, *Are Our Kids Tough Enough? Chinese
School* (2015), which investigated whether British teenagers could cope
with the rigours of the Chinese education system and whether pupils
taught by Chinese teachers could outperform the rest of their year group
in a series of exams (which they did), demonstrates the west could
potentially learn from Chinese philosophies of education. Even when it
comes to teaching Shakespeare, that icon of Englishness, Chinese models
of learning can prove highly useful since, as Edward Berry observes,
'[Chinese] students are for the most part … committed to the study of
literature with an intensity rare in North America … [thus] if this climate
continues, we will see not only more western but more Chinese Shakespeareans in China'.[16] Certainly, Chinese Shakespeare criticism, typically
focusing on class and social struggle, has made a positive contribution to
international Shakespeare scholarship in recent years as the proliferation
of new books and essays written by prominent Chinese researchers attests.

As stated, Chinese educational reforms are less indicative of the globalisation or westernisation of education and, instead, homespun solutions

to local issues. Indeed, it is evident in recent years that China has evolved from a copycat to an innovator in several sectors. In particular, prompted by dramatic cultural, social and economic changes, modifications in the education sector are a response to anxieties about the competition posed by more knowledge-based economies, i.e. economies powered by intellectual creativity, innovation and risk-taking. This is not to say the Chinese education system has completely lost its traditional values and techniques: 'the *keju*'s spirit lives on', according to Yong Zhao, referring to the (now notorious) Imperial Examination System. Nor have the controversial patriotism classes, another cause of dissent in Hong Kong, been abandoned as officials are concerned that encouraging creativity and independent thinking might clash with Confucian values of collectivity and obedience. Nevertheless, the system is undergoing a substantial shakeup with the aim, arguably, of creating an education system that retains its traditional characteristics while simultaneously adopting more constructivist approaches to learning as well as other 'modern' theories and practices.

The Hong Kong classroom, which has always been a step ahead of the Mainland and, due to its oft-commented upon cultural 'hybridity', in many ways exemplifies an intercultural educational experience was (at the start of the twenty-first century, at least) being transformed in progressive and imaginative ways and demonstrating a more receptive attitude towards the arts and literature (whereas before the emphasis was squarely on science and technology). Stated priorities in the newly fledged broad-based liberal arts curriculum included the training of critical and creative thinkers, gifted communicators, and, reflective of a humanist approach to education, ethical leaders (morals have always been regarded as a central learning outcome in China). For this reason, literature, drama and music have rarely been valued as highly in the former colony than at the turn of the century. Thus Shakespeare, regarded as a staple in a liberal arts curriculum, seemed set to play a more prominent role in Hong Kong schools; certainly, this was the goal of the HK Education Bureau when I spoke with representatives in 2014.

2.2   Why Study Shakespeare in Hong Kong

First, though, it is important to provide an historical context for the study of Shakespeare in Hong Kong which, inevitably, began soon after colonisation in 1842, when famous scenes and lines from Shakespeare first featured in high school texts. It was not until 1882, however, that the dramatist's works were studied in earnest and his plays became part of the curriculum at the Hong Kong Central School, the first centralised government school in the territory. The reason for this is due to views held by nineteenth-century colonial administrators like Frederick Stewart who (infamously) claimed, 'the Chinese have no *education* in the real sense of the word. No attempt is made at [the] development of mental powers'.[17] Stewart continued, 'only with a higher idea of British civilisation and institutions could the Chinese know the true essence of education'.[18] Shakespeare, as 'an advanced subject of Western knowledge', was an instrumental part of this endeavour, but his main purpose of course, as in other colonies, was to ensure the Hong Kong Chinese thought in line with and shared the same values and beliefs as the British. As Dorothy Wong puts it:

> The canonical status of Shakespeare in English education in Hong Kong evolving through socio-political conditions, through which the British hegemony strove to consolidate itself, was inscribed with all the colonial aggression of implanting a sense of superiority of the colonizer's culture in the local people.[19]

There is no doubt that, historically speaking, Shakespeare functioned as a tool of domination in Hong Kong, deployed by the colonial government as a means of promoting 'the master's ideology'. As in other British colonies, knowledge of Shakespeare even became a compulsory prerequisite for entry into university, the civil service and other professions, thus augmenting the bard's centrality in the curriculum and his association with social advancement, an association that continues into the twenty-first century.

Today, many Chinese educationists share with, or have inherited from, their western counterparts several ideas about Shakespeare; namely, that through familiarity with his work, students acquire 'values', 'taste', 'class', 'wisdom', 'morals' and a better understanding of the 'human spirit' (even though Shakespeare more accurately served as 'a code signifying the "universal values" of the British'[20]). Still hailed a 'genius', Shakespeare in Hong Kong enjoys a surprising degree of popularity, especially among the theatre-going middle class. Further, as the results of my 2014 survey (see Appendix 2.1 for the questionnaire I put together)—which involved the participation of 172 students from five different schools and colleges—reveal, most young people in Hong Kong have studied Shakespeare at some stage in their academic careers.[21]

It is more likely, however, that students who attend either Band 1 (the most academically prestigious schools[22]) or International schools (both of which are EMI [English as the Medium of Instruction]) will be exposed to Shakespeare, which proves that Shakespeare continues to be associated with the privileged elite and his reach has yet to extend to the wider population, i.e. to students at local, government-aided schools. Explanations for this include the reluctance of some ESL teachers to tackle material they consider 'difficult if not formidable [and] out-of-date if not stale',[23] and the continued prioritisation of subjects such as science and mathematics over the humanities, despite the aforementioned reforms. The decline in importance of the English language in Hong Kong since 1997 is also a contributing factor. Notably, though, students who choose Shakespeare as an elective at university often do so because they had formerly attended government-aided schools and felt they had missed out. Their decision thus suggests a genuine desire amongst ambitious young people in the region to acquire knowledge of Shakespeare or, at least, the opportunity for the cachet or symbolic power associated with him. It could also, of course, be the case that, in the context of Hong Kong, the playwright functions as a symbol of Britishness and thus as a means for Hong Kongers to distinguish themselves from Mainland China.[24] Indeed, the overwhelming majority of all those questioned—91%—were of the opinion that Shakespeare studies should be mandatory in Hong Kong, even though there were aspects of his plays they found challenging.

Although some students admitted to finding Shakespeare's plays 'boring', 'archaic' and/or 'difficult' (about 25% of those questioned)—one disgruntled kid claimed 'the original text is just too difficult for us Chinese', while another blurted 'he has [sic] dead!' and 'has no use for our future career'—most consider him worth studying, almost as if they regard him as bad-tasting medicine.[25] The reason for the perennialism that distinguishes the Chinese classroom from the UK's and the USA's, is the belief that the plays (and the movies and YouTube videos they have inspired) are, on the whole, perceived as 'interesting', 'valuable', 'fantastic', and as having 'survived the test of time'. Moreover, students tend to consider 'the themes and main ideas [as] universal and timeless, and therefore ... definitely worthy to be introduced to a wide audience'. 'The culture and history that could be studied from Shakespeare's works are extremely fascinating', according to quite a few students too, while the playwright's 'vast influence on present drama' makes him deserving of study according to others.

But by far the most common opinion is that Shakespeare can help Chinese students learn English: 'English is an international language and studying Shakespeare can widen our horizons in the language', claimed one secondary-school pupil, while another made the interesting argument that, 'Shakespeare can improve Hong Kong citizens' English and prevent 'Chinglish' This is despite the fact 'Shakespeare's dialogue, 400 years old and written in verse, is seen as impractical for [ESL] students to learn … [and] tracing the Shakespearean affinities of contemporary English is seen as an unnecessary chore in their programme of acquiring … everyday language'[26]. As one 19-year-old university student pointed out, 'Shakespeare teaches people in Hong Kong how to be more creative with the English language'. The consensus, then, is that students in Hong Kong regard the development of their English as the main reason for studying Shakespeare: a staggering 90% consider the acquisition of 'common words and phrases' important. Additionally, 74% felt studying Shakespeare had improved their English either a lot or quite a lot, highlighting the perceived usefulness of Shakespeare in English language acquisition. Ironically, though, the answers to question 5 of my questionnaire exposed that few could actually tell the difference between sayings from Shakespeare and everyday maxims in the English-speaking world. This highlighted the extent to which the playwright is perceived as synonymous with English-ness and the effectiveness of his use in EAL is perhaps more imaginary than real.

Another commonly held idea is that Shakespeare 'can help us to understand how European people think' and 'find out more about British culture' in particular. The desire to learn more about the western mindset (the main reason undergraduates opt to study Shakespeare) emphasises both the kind of 'outward thinking' the HK Education Bureau was encouraging, and the role of Shakespeare in bridging cultural division. Evidently, Chinese students want to share a 'common topic with foreigners'; they want, in other words, to be part of a global classroom in which ideas and beliefs are exchanged. In fact, some students disclosed to me that 'as an "international city" Hong Kong should actively embrace all types of culture', a desire that aligns with government policies, such as the *World Class 2.0 Project* and the *One Belt One Road* initiative.[27] The desire to conceive of Hong Kong as a 'world city' on the part of so-called Generation Z also, of course, suggests either a willful forgetting of, or a nostalgic longing among many for, the territory's former Anglophone colonial status and Shakespeare's deep-seated role therein.

Generally speaking, the association of Shakespeare with British (high) culture is still problematic in Hong Kong. Firstly, in the minds of many, the dramatist continues to be inextricably linked to Britishness and, by extension, social status: 'there's a particular "air" to it [Shakespeare]', professed one 21-year-old female, and 'people seems [sic] to be very impressed when one can say something about Shakespeare' (20-year-old male). The colonised, of course, inevitably start to fetishise Shakespeare when 'the master's language becomes an important component of the formidable ally of the economy and politics deciding the social status of the colonized'.[28] Moreover, even though Shakespeare is undoubtedly in the process of becoming less a symbol of Britishness and evolving more into a global figure, he still, as noted, tends to be studied more in either EMI Band 1 schools or International schools. What is more, the editions often used include *No Fear Shakespeare* and *Tales from Shakespeare* by the Victorian duo, Charles and Mary Lamb, rather than Chinese versions. However, given the appetite for more 'popularized [sic] and more accessible (i.e. Chinese versions)' of Shakespeare, this is slowly changing; in fact, one of the most striking and praiseworthy features of approaches to Shakespeare in contemporary Hong Kong is the growing tendency to connect and assimilate his *oeuvre* to the host culture. This is particularly the case concerning theatre practitioners, who (as usual) are more likely than secondary and collegiate educators to localise Shakespeare and make his plays stylistically and thematically context-specific.

2.3   How Shakespeare Is Approached in the Hong Kong Chinese Classroom

Tending to stick with classroom staples, i.e. those plays popular in the Anglo-American academy, such as *Romeo and Juliet*, *Macbeth* and *A Midsummer Night's Dream*, Hong Kong educationists are not always catering to the specific tastes, interests and concerns of their students, nor are they planting the playwright firmly in Chinese soil. For instance, the most important sources of information about Shakespeare, from the perspective of students in Hong Kong, are: their teachers; films in English; the World Wide Web; school textbooks; and, to a lesser extent, the theatre. This indicates that Shakespeare is not necessarily considered part of their lives outside of school nor does he constitute a part of the wider culture to which they belong. Instead, Shakespeare is usually linked to educational institutions and the specifically British entertainment industry. This is what sometimes makes it difficult for students in Hong Kong to 'relate to the text from experiences that lie outside the text', since 'the text and its world are [largely] alien to the student's private stocks of knowledge'.[29]

Students in Hong Kong do not perceive adults outside of school as knowing much about Shakespeare either nor is there much mention of the dramatist on local television (only 9% think there is anything about Shakespeare on Hong Kong TV and 0% regard Mainland TV as a source of information) or in other media, such as newspapers or magazines (only 13% find the former useful and 15% the latter, a critique of perceived quality of mainstream, mainland Chinese media echoed in the next chapter). Most remarkably, from the viewpoint of the majority of young people, 'Chinese Shakespeare' is an almost completely alien concept; in fact, not one of the 172 students I interviewed could name a film adaptation of Shakespeare produced in Hong Kong or Mainland China, which perhaps indicates the extent to which Hong Kong views itself as separate from the PRC.

What emerged as one of the most thought-provoking discoveries, though, was not just lack of knowledge of 'Chinese Shakespeares'—a topic that has attracted considerable attention in the western academy—but a seeming lack of interest in indigenous appropriation. It appears that students (and most teachers) in Hong Kong appear unaware of the paradox of claiming Shakespeare's plays possess universal human value, while, on the other hand, admitting to possessing little-to-no sense of what the study of Shakespeare can bring to light to them about their own society (87%). Students also attributed little significance to the performance history of Shakespeare in Hong Kong since 'how and why people in Hong Kong have performed Shakespeare' was deemed by 39.5% as only 'somewhat important'. Again, one can infer that this is either symptomatic of Hong Kong's denial of its colonial past due to the stigma attached thereto, or it is a manifestation of the oft-commented predilection to disavow their Chinese identity and heritage, a predilection that is one of the byproducts of colonialism.[30]

It is paradoxical—and hints at contradictory values and attitudes—that students in Hong Kong think learning about how Shakespeare's plays relate to their lives is important, yet they have limited knowledge of the reception and appropriation of Shakespeare in China or Hong

Kong. Only 13% felt Shakespeare had helped them understand how Hong Kong people think, whereas 52% thought his works had helped them understand how westerners think, thus discrediting notions of Shakespeare's universality and revealing that current pedagogical practices in Hong Kong have not always been attentive to the history, traditions or experiences of its inhabitants (something Olive also remarks on in the next chapter). Therefore, it would seem that Shakespeare in some ways continues to contribute, as he did during colonial times, to the erosion (rather than recuperation) of indigenous culture. However, this is not to say that Shakespeare has not found a second home in the Hong Kong classroom, and that students aren't actively and creatively engaging with the texts, but he must be altered and reinterpreted to suit the context. More importantly, his works are increasingly being opened out as a site for debate and intercultural dialogue, with students encouraged to interrogate the values embedded within them and made aware of the political, social and historical factors that shape responses to his plays.

Setting aside these criticisms, many of which could easily be levelled at educationists in the western hemisphere where lessons could also be less passive and more student-centred, there is evidence that many teachers in Hong Kong (and China more generally) are making a concerted effort to address the need for a more active approach to Shakespeare, an approach anchored in local culture, and an increased openness to 'oppositional reading'. They are devising lesson plans that propose a 'literature as content or culture model' and 'literature as personal growth model' approach to Shakespeare, thereby extending the language-based model that has tended to dominate in the past.[31] More specifically, they are encouraging students to:

1. **Perform** Shakespeare. Role playing enhances student 'self-confidence and a team spirit'[32] as well as communication skills;
2. **Translate** Shakespeare. Literary translation empowers students and provides them with 'the room to think, explore and create'[33];
3. **Watch** Shakespeare (both local and western adaptations). Analysing the plays in performance assists students in developing 'an international outlook' as well as a heightened sense of their own traditions;
4. **Compare** Shakespeare. Linking the plays with stories the students find in local news and television facilitates the integration of 'all-round learning activities' both inside and outside of the classroom[34];

5. **Accompany** Shakespeare. Complementing the plays with actions, sounds and illustrations fosters 'intellectual development, physical development, and aesthetic development'[35] (see Appendix 2.2 for specific examples).

All five activities are examples of good practice and effective at increasing the popularity of Shakespeare and enlivening the student experience through making his works more 'relatable': one of the aims of the aforementioned reforms is 'to strengthen the relevance of curricula to students' lives', after all.[36] (Ironically, of the 1,043 people in China surveyed by the British Council in 2015 and asked whether Shakespeare was still relevant, 61% in Hong Kong answered in the affirmative compared with just 57% in Britain).[37] Additionally, these activities make lessons more interesting and serve to reinforce the need for students to watch Shakespeare performed (onstage and onscreen) as well as to get involved in performing themselves. Rather than 'just sitting in the classroom', students require lessons that are 'more interesting and we can go to the theatre and dig deeper' (16-year-old female). (Four of these activities are evident in the Hong-Kong based Chinese Universities Shakespeare Festival, which is the subject of the next chapter, with the notable exception of translation.) There is, of course, already 'a major agreement [in the west] on the need for theatre visits, video and film',[38] an agreement reinforced in Ayanna Thompson and Laura Turchi's *Teaching Shakespeare with Purpose: A Student-Centered Approach* (2016). Nevertheless, it was refreshing to witness this theory actually put into action and to watch young people produce their own versions of Shakespeare and get physically, emotionally and intellectually involved, as I did at Heep Yunn College.

Polite, articulate and enthusiastic, the girls at Heep Yunn College, an Anglican school founded in 1936, in many ways lived up to 'the ideal of the Chinese learner', characterised as diligent and dedicated.[39] Having visited the Globe Theatre and Stratford-upon-Avon on a trip to the UK, they were co-writing their own, feminist spin-off of *Macbeth* thereby demonstrating not only impressive knowledge and understanding of Shakespeare's work, but a high level of creativity and cultural progressiveness. Under the expert tutelage of Ms. Mandy Mok, they boldly and imaginatively reconceived the play in ways that made it more in tune with their world. In their truncated rewriting of 'the Scottish play', the protagonist is a teenage girl called Beth; the three weird sisters are replaced by an oracle (or fortune-teller); and instead of having ambitions to the throne, the protagonist is in pursuit of a trendy, high-end gadget, which is apt given the extraordinary appetite for new technology in Hong Kong.

What the students did, then, was engage inventively with Shakespeare and on a personal level, and it was obvious that they found the project stimulating and enjoyable, thereby reaffirming that Shakespeare really does require both demystification and 'uprooting'. Notably, the students involved in the production were more talkative and less inhibited than students from the same school who spent their time studying Shakespeare in a more traditional manner, i.e. close reading the text, though this is not to say the former group had not developed a rigorous and in-depth understanding of the script. In fact, as observed elsewhere, Chinese students tend to reveal an almost 'obsessive analysis of script and character'[40] and might even be regarded as 'superior to their Western peers at recognizing the subtlety and peculiarity of the language and gaining more insight into how Shakespeare uses sound to create emotions, ideas and feelings'. This is the opinion of Joseph Graves who was struck by how Chinese student actors 'painstakingly study Shakespeare's use of language, examining each vowel and consonant'.[41] I too noted that the students' knowledge of the text went far beyond the surface level when I set them a quiz on *Othello* that tested not just their grip of the plot, but their understanding of the deeper meaning and symbolic significance of words, places and objects. The difference, however, is that unlike in the west, where the focus on individualism suggests that students learn best when they begin by exploring and then move to an understanding of concepts, educators in China believe that understanding of content must occur *before* creative exploration.[42]

Given that performing Shakespeare appears to be gaining almost equal weight as close reading the text, and more and more Chinese instructors now incorporate performance into teaching the playwright, it is not surprising that educational programs offered by director William Yip's company, Theatre Noir, and Shiona Carson's Shakespeare4All are proving increasingly important in Hong Kong. It is also not surprising that the territory plays host to an annual and highly impressive Chinese Universities Shakespeare Festival, first launched in 2005 and discussed in detail in the next chapter by Olive. Including the participation of students from the Mainland, Macau and Taiwan, this competition was originally intended to promote appreciation of English literature and although 'overtly educational in purpose' and enforcing 'strict regulations in terms of language', is a great example of the efforts being made to make Shakespeare conform to Chinese conventions and resonate with contemporary politics.[43] Similar to organisations like Theatre Noir, then, the festival is not only bringing theatre and academia into greater dialogue, but helping students meet the objectives of the Ministry of Education's aim to 'not allow Western readings to reign/ruin their own'.[44]

In addition to resisting western interpretations of the Shakespearean text, students at Heep Yunn College proved that the latest generation of Chinese students 'debunk the construction of Asian learners as passive, rote, uncreative memorizers'.[45] More importantly, for my purposes here, they made the prospect of Chinese education shaping the future of how Shakespeare is taught in the west not inconceivable; after all, there is no longer an unchallenged ascendant power to learn anything from in the current changing global order. The same conclusion could easily be drawn from my second case study at St. Paul's School (Lam Tin), an all-female Catholic secondary school where students likewise embraced the opportunity to relate Shakespeare's *The Merchant of Venice* to the context of contemporary Hong Kong. More specifically, through identifying current prejudices towards 'Mainlanders' in the territory with the anti-Semitic sentiments towards Shylock, whose presence in Venice is likewise tolerated for primarily pecuniary reasons, the pupils discovered the ways in which Shakespeare both is and is not their contemporary. In addition, the students rather ingeniously linked *The Merchant of Venice* to stories on television, in newspapers or trending online that address loopholes within the criminal justice system as well as the rights and status of the LGBTQ community in Hong Kong. The exercise actively encouraged them to see in Shakespeare's play themes and concerns close to their personal and social experiences, and it served as an excellent instance of how the playwright can serve as material for life-wide learning, i.e. learning that takes place in 'real' contexts, not just a school setting.

The girls at St. Paul's enthusiastically embraced the chance to engage in role-playing games (RPGs), too, reenacting the (in)famous courtroom scene in their own words. In particular, students took turns to play the judge, and thus don a wig, before reflecting with curiosity on how both their self-perception and treatment of others changed when given power and status. This was a fascinating, inspiring lesson to witness which reinforced the pedagogical effectiveness of 'hot seating' and RPGs which ease young people into Shakespeare without, as Justyna Deszcz-Tryhubczak and Agata Zarzycka have noted elsewhere, 'resorting to conventional theatrical renderings or ready-made interpretations that leave little room for individual engagement with the plays'. This lesson, similar to another one I observed at Lim Por Yen Secondary School, wherein students also replayed scenes from *The Merchant of Venice*, paid testimony to the effectiveness of the measures undertaken to enrich the educational experience of Chinese students. More specifically, it highlighted some of the most admirable aspects of Hong Kong's education system in the twenty-first century. For example, less scripted lesson plans and more spontaneity and improvisation; cooperative and respectful group work, which aligns with the Confucian emphasis on community and socialisation; and an openness and receptiveness to western institutions and educators like myself who was given a warm welcome and whose presence itself testifies to how high internationalisation really is on the agenda.

Indeed, the extent to which teachers in Hong Kong are comfortable with having others observe and participate in their classroom was something I was particularly stuck by in general. As Janette Ryan has remarked, 'teachers in China regularly open their classroom for observation and critique by other teachers, a feature that is rare in western systems'[46] where, in contrast, the implementation of an observation system has been met with resistance. This, of course, is again indicative of the individualism-collectivism split between east and west, for, as de Lima and Silva put it, 'the cultural norms of individual professional autonomy that regulate relations among colleagues [in the west] prevented ... heads from using information, gathered through classroom observation, to nourish in-depth professional discussions about concrete educational practices'.[47] In other words, the relative freedom and autonomy of instructors in the west, where there is an absence of the societal culture that promotes sharing and collaborating, is arguably hindering the rate and extent of educational change and reforms, an issue that is less likely to be a problem in a Hong Kong Chinese context.

2.4 Lesson Summary

Writing in 1988, Edward Berry expressed that it would be beneficial if 'Shakespeareans of all kinds might take some interest in the fortunes of their subject abroad'.[48] In light of recent reforms in Chinese education, the consistently high performance of East Asian students in transnational studies of achievement, and the marked expansion and influence of China in cultural matters (the list of 'paradigm shifts' goes on), Berry's call for increased attentiveness to what our Chinese counterparts are doing could not be more timely. After all, it is no coincidence that it is Asian teachers who emerge as authority figures on Shakespeare in contemporary movies such as *American Pie* (1999), *The Glass House* (2001), and *The Emperor's Club* (2002).[49] And although, as my 2014 survey underscores and numerous studies have shown, there are still areas for improvement when it comes to teaching Shakespeare in Hong Kong (in large part due to the fact the playwright has yet to be fully unshackled from his association with the British empire), there are many lessons to be learned from the Hong Kong Chinese classroom, which given its socio-political liminal status is already in many ways an intercultural teaching environment. The more active, student-focused activities being pioneered at admittedly elite schools such as St Paul's and Heep Yunn College, clearly constitute a methodology worth emulating. The attempts at anchoring Shakespeare in the home culture while simultaneously paying close attention to historical specificity—'Chinese professors teaching Shakespeare will focus on social and historical issues in a given play and the ideological in Shakespeare'[50]—is also evidence of good practice, as is, more controversially, the strategy of memorisation.

Derided as an unprogressive, lower-order form of learning, memorising (and reciting) lines from Shakespeare is rarely incorporated into lesson plans in the US or UK, even though it has been proven that 'the strategy of memorization [is] an important method to achieve a deep understanding in which subject matter is internalized and actively reflected upon'.[51] Put simply, Hong Kong Chinese students memorise in order to understand; thus, the western belief that rote learning (or 'drilling') achieves little more than surface learning is subject to debate. In fact, students in the Anglo-American system, many of whom are averse to textual analysis, could benefit from the Chinese practice (which is much less excessive than previously) of committing passages to memory as these exercises heighten appreciation for Shakespeare's language as well as students' grasp of its intricacies and complexities. Further, exercises in memorisation 'deliver unique cognitive benefits, benefits that are of special importance for [those] who come from homes where books are scarce and literacy levels low'[52] and Shakespeare himself, after all, 'was the product of a memorizing culture in which huge chunks of literature were learned by heart'.[53] In this sense, and others, Chinese students and teachers might actually be said to demonstrate a stronger understanding of Shakespeare and his culture since it is in several ways closer to their own given their patriotism, less-than-democratic political process, and strong sense of filial piety. The third, incidentally, often manifests itself in the classroom in the form of 'teacher honor', a concept that is almost alien in countries like the US and UK where educators habitually report feeling undervalued and held in low esteem. By contrast, teachers in Hong Kong, occupying the dual roles of instructor and facilitator and coming across as authoritative yet approachable, enjoy noticeably more respect from their students.

To conclude, while China still imports more education services than it exports and sends more students abroad than it receives, the Hong Kong classroom can help provide western practitioners with not just various examples of effective teaching strategies (please refer to Appendix 2.2 for more specific examples), but with an alternative, positive cultural model in thought and behaviour. A liberal education *can* exist within a politically illiberal system, after all, especially now that measures to de-centralise education have been taken in China. In addition, it can offer a different, fresher interpretative slant on Shakespeare, for instance through looking at the plays from a more socialist-oriented perspective (Chinese Shakespeare scholarship is often based on Marx's dialectical materialism). As Philip Brockbank summarises, 'new truths about Shakespeare's art [can be] discovered in China'.[54] More specifically, teachers in Hong Kong tend to present Shakespeare's plays in a manner we would label 'behaviorist', i.e. as reflecting the role of external forces—societal or familial—on the individual, and to adopt a decidedly ideological approach to the text. Most importantly, Chinese students, especially on the Mainland where the bard is free from association with imperial aggression, simply *like* Shakespeare, more so than their western counterparts, if the aforementioned British Council survey is to be trusted. This enthusiasm translates into engaging group discussions, detailed close reading, and fresh and thoughtful interpretations of the text, interpretations that often challenge or debunk western understandings of the playwright as a talisman of liberal, individualistic values. Combining the teaching styles and values associated with both China and the west, the Hong Kong classroom 'brings together the classical values of education, along with personal development, through culture and humanism'. It therefore, and contrary to Senator Tom Cotton's declaration that 'if Chinese students want to come [to the US] and study Shakespeare and the Federalist Papers, that's what they need to learn from America', can serve as a potential model for western educators who are keen to reignite interest in Shakespeare and refresh moribund, monocultural pedagogical practices. Ultimately, however, the ebb and flow of influence should be multidirectional and successful teaching hinges upon an exploration and incorporation of pedagogical practices and philosophies both east and west, especially in the context of increased internationalisation of both the syllabus and the student body.

Acknowledgements and Author's Note   This chapter originated as a University of Greenwich research project called Shakespeare in Hong Kong, of which I was principal investigator, before being revised for publication here. My sincere thanks to Andrew King, William Yip, Tang Shu-wing, Rosana Wai-Mun Chong Cheung, the British Council (HK), and students and teachers at St. Paul's School, Heep Yunn College, Victoria College, Lim Por Yen Secondary School, and the Chinese University of Hong Kong for all their help and support. Please note that many of the ideas and arguments expressed in this chapter were written prior to recent, radical changes in the political landscape of Hong Kong.

APPENDIX 2.1: QUESTIONNAIRE

Hello

Dr Adele Lee has come to Hong Kong from the University of Greenwich in London to try to find out what Shakespeare means in Hong Kong today.

As part of her project, she's asking you what you think.

She can't speak to you all individually. This is why she's asking you to fill in this questionnaire.

This is not a test. Just say what you honestly think. If you don't have an answer to a question, just leave a blank.

1. Have you studied Shakespeare before?   YES/ NO

a. If yes, how old were you? _____

b. If yes, where ? _____

2. What Shakespeare plays do you know?

Play	Please tick if you've studied it	Please tick if you know the name
Richard III		
Julius Caesar		
Twelfth Night		
Macbeth		
Hamlet		
Much Ado about Nothing		
King Lear		
Romeo and Juliet		
If you've studied or know other plays, which ones?		

3. How did you find out about Shakespeare? Circle all that apply.

Theatre	films on TV
Teachers	Friends
Theatre school	Films in English
You've heard adults talking about him outside school	Films in Chinese
You've talked to adults about him outside school	Films in other languages
School textbooks	Other books
Magazines	Newspapers
Illustrated magazines (*manga*)	Hong Kong TV
BBC World TV	Mainland China TV
American TV channels	Internet (e.g. Wikipedia, blogs)
Youtube	Facebook or other social media

4. Which of these do you think has been most important in forming your current ideas about Shakespeare? Put the number 1 against the most important, the number 2 against the next important and so on. NB If you haven't studied Shakespeare, this still applies to you.

Theatre	films on TV
Parents	Friends
Theatre school	Films in English
You've heard adults talking about him outside school	Films in Chinese
You've talked to adults about him outside school	Films in other languages
School textbooks	Other books
Magazines	Newspapers
Illustrated magazines (*manga*)	Hong Kong TV
BBC World TV	Mainland China TV
American TV channels	Internet (e.g. Wikipedia, blogs)
Youtube	Facebook or other social media

5. Which of the following phrases do you think come from Shakespeare?

- I must be cruel only to be kind.

- Knock, knock! Who's there?

- Sharper than a serpent's tooth

- Parting is such sweet sorrow

- I will wear my heart upon my sleeve

- The Be-All and the End-All

- All the world's a stage...

- We are such stuff as dreams are made on ...

- To be or not to be...

6. *Write down the first 5 things you think of when you think of Shakespeare! (this can be <u>anything</u> – words, phrases, feelings)*

_____

_____

_____

7. *What do you think you should learn about Shakespeare? (1= irrelevant; 5 = very important)*

- Shakespeare's life   1   2   3   4   5

- How his plays relate to you   1   2   3   4   5

- History of Kings and Queens in

   Shakespeare's time   1   2   3   4   5

- What the theatre was like in

   Shakespeare's time   1   2   3   4   5

- What Shakespeare can tell us about

   life in general   1   2   3   4   5

- Common words and phrases that

   come from Shakespeare   1   2   3   4   5

- gender and Shakespeare   1   2   3   4   5

- 'race' and Shakespeare   1   2   3   4   5

- Social class and Shakespeare   1   2   3   4   5

8. *What (if anything) can you learn about Britain through Shakespeare?*

_____

_____

_____

9. *What (if anything) can you learn about Hong Kong through Shakespeare?*

_____

_____

_____

10. *How has Shakespeare affected you? Please write a number in the box on the right where 1 = I agree very much, 2 = a bit, 3 = I don't agree very much, 4 = I don't agree at all*

Shakespeare has…

Helped with my knowledge of the English language

Helped me understand how European people think

Given me the confidence to express myself

Introduced me to going to the theatre

Helped me to understand how Hong Kong people think

Given me the chance to act

Given me the confidence to be who I am

Made me feel bad because I don't understand it

Made me want to write things that will last for hundreds of years

Shakespeare hasn't affected me at all.

If you think Shakespeare has affected you in any other way, please write it here.

11. *Do you think Shakespeare should be studied and performed in Hong Kong?* YES/ NO

Why/ Why
*not?*_____

_____

12. *Is there anything you'd like to tell us about Shakespeare in Hong Kong tht we haven't asked you?*

If so, please write it here.

_____

_____

ABOUT YOU

Age _____   Male/ Female (please circle as appropriate)

School/ University / College _____

Thanks for taking the time to complete this questionnaire!

Adele

APPENDIX 2.2: LESSON ACTIVITIES

The following activities are suitable for younger students, though creative and confident older students may find them helpful too.

Performing Shakespeare is obviously one of the most dynamic and effective ways for students to experience the playwright. This active teaching method involves young people working collaboratively and exploring the plays creatively. Through encouraging them to transpose scenes to the contemporary Hong Kong classroom/home/street, the plays can also be rooted in local culture.

- **Example 1**: Exchange between Egeus and his daughter, Hermia, in Act 1 Scene of *A Midsummer Night's Dream*. Modify and perform this scene so that it's appropriate to the context of a modern-day Chinese home. Why would a twenty-first-century dad disapprove of his daughter's choice in partner? How would you respond to parental disapproval?

- **Example 2**: Act 1, Scene 6 of *Macbeth*. In this scene—which is charged with irony—Macbeth and his wife welcome King Duncan to their castle. Perform this short scene by placing it mentally in your own homes. What would the equivalents of the characters be? Maybe your parents and their friends or maybe you and your friends? In both cases, think about the rules of etiquette and hospitality: What would the guests be offered? How would they be treated? Then afterwards think about the scale and nature of the Macbeths' crimes that will come later in the play.
- **Example 3**: Act 3, Scene 2 of *Othello*. Again, imagine this play is set in twenty-first-century Hong Kong. Instead of a 'Moor' the hero is perhaps Filipino, Pakistani or even Northern Chinese. How would a native-born Hong Kong Iago and 'gentlemen' behave around him? What would their body language and facial expressions be like? In what tone would they deliver their lines?

The following activities are suitable for a variety of age groups, depending on the amount of material to set and the level of discussion aimed at.

Comparing stories on TV or
in local magazines and
newspapers that share the
same concerns as
Shakespeare's plays to the
'originals' is a helpful way to
anchor Shakespeare in the
student's world and, at the
same time, serves to draw
attention to cultural and
historical differences and
similarities. After bringing to
class appropriate newspaper
clippings, websites or
YouTube videos, students
should list and explain the
ways in which the local,
contemporary stories they've
come across are similar to
Shakespeare's and the ways
in which they differ.

- **Example 1**: *Macbeth* is a play about rebellion and excessive ambition; it warns of the dangers of rivalry and of challenging and usurping those in positions of power. Can you find a story that tells a similar story? (e.g. in what ways—if any—do you think the killing of a Triad boss ('Mouse Shing') outside a hospital in April 2013 might resonate with *Macbeth*?).

- **Example 2:** Racism is a scourge in almost every society, not just Shakespeare's; take, for instance, the reports of abuse during Hong Kong's home 'friendly' against the Philippines in June 2013 or the recent *Time Out* reports about society in Hong Kong that were widely reported. How do stories like this relate to the treatment of Othello in Shakespeare's play? Are they at all comparable?

- **Example 3:** In the headlines in 2013, there was the story of a couple committing suicide by jumping into the Yangtze River in China, where suicide rates among young people are particularly high. The lovers, it seems, despaired of being together due to financial difficulties. Examining the story in detail, in what ways is it similar to *Romeo and Juliet*? In what ways does it differ? List and account for the similarities and differences.

The following activities are suitable for a variety of age groups 14 + , depending on the amount and nature of material set and whether it is set as a group or individual activity.

Translating Shakespeare is an effective way of encouraging students to engage both critically and creatively with the text. Asking students to rewrite speeches or short scenes in their own vernacular and then asking them to provide a reason for decisions fosters analytical skills, self-expression and confidence: students can master, or mold, the Shakespearean text in order that it speaks to and for them. The process also throws into sharp relief the aspects of the Shakespearean text students struggle with or find uninteresting. (The cuts or changes they make can be very interesting).

Alternatively, students could pick out a poem or short story that is not by Shakespeare and translate it so that sounds as if it is! This activity would, again, improve student familiarity with the archaic language and form of Shakespeare as well as challenge the concept of the Great Author who cannot be imitated.

- **Example 1**: Macbeth's soliloquies (for instance, in Act 1, Scene 7; Act 2, Scene 1; and Act 5, Scene 5). Rewrite these speeches in your own language and idiom. This will require considerable 'chopping and changing'. How does the protagonist appear now? In what ways has his character been altered? What do you think has been lost or gained in translation? Has the meaning or significance of the whole story been changed?

- **Example 2**: The rude mechanicals' preparations in Act 1, Scene 2 and Act 3, Scene 1 of *A Midsummer Night's Dream*. Rewrite these scenes in the language of schoolchildren. Imagine Bottom, Quince, Snout, Snug, etc. are just like you and your classmates trying to decide which roles to play and how characters should be performed. What's been changed and why? In what ways can you relate to the characters and the scenario they find themselves in? How would you describe the subplot in *A Midsummer Night's Dream* now?
- **Example 3**: Jennifer Wong is currently perhaps Hong Kong's most famous English-language poet. Find one of her poems on love and rework it so that it would fit into Shakespeare's *Romeo and Juliet*. How did you go about doing this? How has Wong's poem been altered? Describe the process of translation and its effects on your perception of both texts.

The following activities are suitable for students who have already some knowledge of the plays and are aged 17 + . The questions are general and conceptually challenging.

Watching film or stage adaptations of Shakespeare is pivotal. Not only do films make the writer's work more entertaining and understandable, but they allow students to compare different versions and gain insight into the various factors – historical, geographical, cultural and political – that determine how Shakespeare can be interpreted. Watching adaptations of Shakespeare's plays stimulates debate and prompts students to write their own reviews / critical responses.

It is particularly important that students in Hong Kong become familiar with Chinese versions of the plays. Again, this has to do with anchoring Shakespeare's work in local culture. There have been many Chinese versions of *Romeo and Juliet, Macbeth* and *A Midsummer Night's Dream*, some of which are available to download from sites such as www.a-s-i-a-web.org and http://web.mit.edu/shakespeare/asia /

- **Example 1**: Compare how three directors—Polanski, Sutton and Xu Xiaozhong—interpret Act 1, Scene 7 of *Macbeth*. How do the

characters differ in each production? In what ways is the relationship between the couple portrayed in each production. Account for
the differences in approach. Which version is more faithful to the
original? Which do you prefer?

- **Example 2**: *Crocodile River* (1978) is a loose adaptation of *Romeo
  and Juliet* directed by Hong Kong's Lo Wei. In what ways has the
  story been changed to fit the context of Hong Kong? What does this
  version suggest about Shakespeare's play? What does it reveal about
  the nature of Hong Kong?
- **Example 3**: Compare Deguchi Norio's three versions of *A
  Midsummer Night's Dream*: the school version, the mask version
  and the bar version (available at http://sia.stanford.edu/japan/
  INTRO/DEGNORIO.HTM). Weigh up the merits of each
  approach: which is your favourite? Which conveys the tone and
  meaning of the text best in your opinion?

The following activities are suitable for younger students, though creative
and confident older students may find them stimulating too.

> **Accompanying** words
> with actions, objects,
> sounds and illustrations
> enhances cognitive and
> emotional responses to
> Shakespeare in addition
> to improving
> understanding of what
> the words really mean.

- **Example 1**: Draw key moments in the plays. These illustrations can take the form of manga, digital photography or tableaux (silent, physical representations of events in a scene). Get others in class to guess what scene is being illustrated.

- **Example 2**: Experiment with different sounds to discover the role that sound can play in helping to create the mood and change the meaning of a scene? The sounds you produce could be made with musical instruments 'offstage' (like a film score) or made by actors themselves 'on stage'.

In particular, you might want to think about the difference the use of Asian percussion and string instruments makes to your understanding and response to scenes and characters.

- **Example 3**: Perform a scene in complete silence. Use your body, facial expressions and costumes to express what's happening and how you're feeling. You can adopt whatever kind of approach you feel is appropriate, including acrobatics, martial arts, Chinese operatic movement: how would the incorporation of these kinds of theatre conventions alter the mood and meaning of Shakespeare's work? Is the play radically changed when it is performed in a non-realist style? Think about how and why.
- **Example 4**: Try using different kinds of props, e.g. the 'little western flower... love in idleness' that wreaks such havoc in *A Midsummer Night's Dream* or the weapons in *Romeo and Juliet* and *Macbeth*. What effect do the changes have on the relevance and meaning of the plays?

NOTES

1. Cited in Philip Brockbank, 'Shakespeare Renaissance in China', *Shakespeare Quarterly* 39.2 (1988): 195.
2. Leonard Pronko, 'Approaching Shakespeare Through Kabuki', in *Shakespeare East and West*, edited by Fuijita Minoru and Leonard Pronko (Tokyo: Japan Library, 1996), 23–24.
3. See http://web.mit.edu/shakespeare/asia/about/, accessed May 13, 2019.
4. Yuan Yang, 'The Bard in Beijing: How Shakespeare Is Subverting China', *Financial Times*, October 5, 2018. https://www.ft.com/content/cd9 97246-c57b-11e8-bc21-54264d1c4647. Accessed August 7, 2020.
5. C.K.K. Chan, 'Classroom innovation for the Chinese Learner: Transcending Dichotomies and Transforming Pedagogy', in *Revisiting the*

Chinese Learner: Changing Contexts, Changing Education, edited by C.K.K. Chan and N. Rao (Hong Kong: Springer, 2010), 204.

6. John Chi-kin Lee, foreword to *Learning and Teaching in the Chinese Classroom: Responding to Individual Needs*, edited by Shane N. Phillipson and Lam Bick-har (Hong Kong: Hong Kong University Press, 2011), ix.
7. Philip Altback and Umakoshi Toru, *Asian Universities: Historical Perspectives and Contemporary Challenges* (London and Baltimore: The Johns Hopkins University Press, 2004), 13.
8. Yong Zhao quoted in *Chinese Education Models in a Global Age*, edited by Chuing Prudence Chou and Jonathan Spangler (Singapore: Springer Singapore, 2016), 223.
9. Gerard A. Postiglione, Preface to *Going to School in East Asia. The Global School Room*, edited by Gerard A. Postiglione and Jason Tan (Westport, CT and London: Greenwood Press, 2007), xii.
10. Indeed, as highlighted by the authors of *West Meets East: Best Practices from Expert Teachers in the U.S. and China* (Alexandria, Virginia: ASCD, 2014), 'students of Asian origin have been able to excel on international examinations' (6).
11. Check out the most recent (2019) world university rankings, according to *Times Higher Education* (THE), here: https://www.timeshighereducation.com/news/world-university-rankings-2019-results-announced, accessed May 13, 2019.
12. *Learning for Life, Learning Through Life: Reform Proposals for the Education System in Hong Kong*, published by the Education Commission (2000), 3.
13. Yin Hong-Biao and Li Zijian, *Curriculum Reform in China: Changes and Challenges* (New York: Nova Science Publishers, Inc., 2012), 6.
14. Teresa Brawner Bevis, *A History of Higher Education Exchange: China and America* (New York and London: Routledge, 2014), 165.
15. Ibid., 7.
16. Edward Berry, 'Teaching Shakespeare in China', *Shakespeare Quarterly* 39.2 (1988): 216.
17. *Hong Kong Blue Book* (1865), 138.
18. Ibid.
19. Dorothy Wong, '"Domination by Consent": A Study of Shakespeare in Hong Kong', in *Colonizer and Colonized*, edited by Theo D'haen and Patricia Krus (Amsterdam: Editions Rodopi, 2000), 45.
20. Ibid., 45.
21. Please note that research for this chapter was conducted prior to the major, rapid political changes in Hong Kong that we are currently witnessing and some statements might not necessarily still hold up in the context of 2021.

22. Secondary schools in Hong Kong are divided into three bands that are ranked in order of merit and prestige.

23. Wu Yongan, *Teaching Young Adult Literature to ESL Students: An Experiment* (BiblioBazaar, LLC: Charleston, S. Carolina: 2011), 5.

24. See also Lau Leung Che Miriam, *The Making of Hong Kong Shakespeare: Post-1997 Adaptations and Appropriations*. PhD diss. (Shakespeare Institute, University of Birmingham, 2018). Sarah Olive, 'Outside interference or Hong Kong embracing its unique identity? The Chinese Universities Shakespeare Festival', *Palgrave Communications*, 5 (2019).

25. It is worth pointing out that Richard Wilson traces the same attitude toward Shakespeare in the western school system: see his 'NATO's Pharmacy: Shakespeare by Prescription', in *Shakespeare and National Culture*, edited by John J. Joughin (Manchester: Manchester University Press, 1997), 58–81.

26. Han Younglim, 'Korean Shakespeare: The Anxiety of Being Invisible', in *Shakespeare without English: The Reception of Shakespeare in Non-Anglophone Countries*, edited by Sukanta Chaudhuri and Lim Chee Seng (New Delhi: Pearson Education, 2006), 53.

27. For more on the Chinese government's attempts to internationalize higher education, see *CIHE Perspectives No. 9, The Boston College Center for International Higher Education, Year in Review, 2017–2018*, edited by Hans de Wit, Laura E. Rumbley, and Dara Melnyk.

28. Wong, 'Domination by Consent', 47.

29. Kate Flaherty, Penny Gay and L.E. Semler (ed), *Teaching Shakespeare Beyond the Centre* (London: Palgrave Macmillan, 2013), 5.

30. For more detail on the complex, contradictory or, as Howard Y.F. Choy's puts it, 'schizophrenic' identity crisis in Hong Kong stemming from 156 years of colonial rule, see his 'Schizophrenic Hong Kong: Postcolonial Identity Crisis in the Infernal Affairs Trilogy', *Global Cities* 3 (2007): 52–66.

31. The 'content model' refers, in brief, to the concentration on social, political and historical factors as opposed to simply stylistic features, such as aesthetic properties and rhetorical devices. The 'literature as personal growth model', on the other hand, encourages students to draw on their own personal experiences and emotions in literary analysis.

32. *Learning for Life*, 5.

33. Ibid.

34. Ibid., 9.

35. Ibid. 15.

36. Yin and Li, *Curriculum Reform in China*, 2–3.

37. For more details about the 'All the World's' survey, see https://www.british council.org/research-policy-insight/insight-articles/shakespeare-all-worlds, accessed, August 2, 2020.

38. Rex Gibson, 'Teaching Shakespeare in Schools', in *Teaching English*, edited by Susan Brindley (London: Routledge, 1994), 126.
39. Refer to David A. Watkins and John B. Biggs, *The Chinese Learner: Cultural, Contextual and Psychological Influences* (Hong Kong/Melbourne: CERC/ACER, 1996).
40. Tsai Chin, 'Teaching and Directing in China: Chinese Theatre Revisited', *Asian Theatre Journal* 3.1 (1986): 120.
41. Joseph Graves interviewed by Yi Ziyi, 'Teaching Shakespeare to China's Youth', *News China*, September 15, 2017, http://newschinamag.com/newschina/articleDetail.do?article_id=739&section_id=31&magazine_id, accessed August 1, 2020.
42. Leslie Grant, James Stronge, Xu Xianxuan, Patricia Popp, and Yaling Sun, *West Meets East: Best Practices from Expert Teachers in the U.S. and China* (Alexandria, Virginia: ASCD, 2014), 7.
43. See Bi-qi Beatrice Lei, 'Betrayal, Derail, or a Thin Veil: The Myth of Origin', *Shakespeare Survey* 68 (2015): 168-82.
44. See Chin, *Teaching and Directing in China* (1986).
45. Alistair Pennycook, 'ELT and Colonialism', in *International Handbook of English Language Teaching*, edited by Jim Cummins and Chris Davison (New York: Springer, 2007), 20.
46. Janette Ryan, 'Changing Concepts and Practices of Curriculum in China', in *Curriculum Reform in China: Changes and Challenges*, edited by Yin Hong-Biao and Li Zijian (New York: Nova Science Publishers, Inc., 2012), 13.
47. Jorge Ávila de Lima and Maria João Tavares Silva, 'Resistance to Classroom Observation in the Context of Teacher Evaluation: Teachers' and Department Heads' Experiences and Perspectives', *Educational Assessment, Evaluation and Accountability* 30.1 (2018): 7.
48. Berry, 'Teaching Shakespeare in China', 212.
49. For a discussion of the significance of the casting choices in these films see Richard Burt, 'Shakespeare and Asia in Postdiasporic Cinemas: Spin-offs and Citations of the plays from Bollywood to Hollywood', in *Shakespeare, The Movie II: Popularizing the Plays on Film, TV, Video and DVD*, edited by Richard Burt, Lynda E. Boose (London: Routledge, 2004), 265–303.
50. Murray J. Levith, *Shakespeare in China* (London: Continuum, 2004), 133.
51. See Watkins and Biggs, *The Chinese Learner* (1996).
52. Quotation taken from Michael Knox Beran, 'In Defense of Memorization', *City Journal* (2004), https://www.city-journal.org/html/defense-memorization-12803.html.
53. Michael Wood cited in ibid.
54. Brockbank, 'Shakespeare Renaissance in China', 195.

References

Altbach, Philip and Umakoshi Toru, ed. *Asian Universities: Historical Perspectives and Contemporary Challenges*. London and Baltimore: The Johns Hopkins University Press, 2004.

Beran, Michael Knox. 'In Defense of Memorization'. *City Journal* (2004). https://www.city-journal.org/html/defense-memorization-12803.html. Accessed May 13, 2019.

Berry, Edward. 'Teaching Shakespeare in China'. *Shakespeare Quarterly* 39.2 (1988): 212–216.

Bevis, Teresa Brawner. *A History of Higher Education Exchange: China and America*. New York and London: Routledge, 2014.

Brockbank, Philip. 'Shakespeare Renaissance in China'. *Shakespeare Quarterly*. 39.2 (1988): 195–203.

Chan, C.K.K. 'Classroom Innovation for the Chinese Learner: Transcending Dichotomies and Transforming Pedagogy.' In *Revisiting the Chinese Learner: Changing Contexts, Changing Education*, edited by C.K.K. Chan and N. Rao. Hong Kong: Springer, 2010. 169–210.

Chin, Tsai. 'Teaching and Directing in China: Chinese Theatre Revisited'. *Asian Theatre Journal*. 3.1 (1986): 118–131.

De Lima, Jorge Ávila, and Maria João Tavares Silva. 'Resistance to Classroom Observation in the Context of Teacher Evaluation: Teachers' and Department Heads' Experiences and Perspectives'. *Educational Assessment, Evaluation and Accountability*. 30.1 (2018): 7–26.

Deszcz-Tryhubczak, Justyna and Agata Zarzycka. 'Giving "to Airy Nothing a Local Habitation and a Name": William Shakespeare's Worlds of Imagination as Accessed Through a Role-Playing Game'. *Borrowers and Lenders: The Journal of Shakespeare and Appropriation*. 21 (2006). http://www.borrowers.uga.edu/783081/show. Accessed April 29, 2019.

Flaherty, Kate, Penny Gay and L.E. Semler, ed. *Teaching Shakespeare Beyond the Centre*. London: Palgrave Macmillan, 2013.

Gibson, Rex. 'Teaching Shakespeare in Schools'. In *Teaching English*, edited by Susan Brindley. London: Routledge, 1994. 124–131.

Grant, Leslie, James Stronge, Xu Xianxuan, Patricia Popp, and Sun Yaling. *West Meets East: Best Practices from Expert Teachers in the U.S. and China*. Alexandria, Virginia: ASCD, 2014.

Han, Younglim. 'Korean Shakespeare: The Anxiety of Being Invisible'. In *Shakespeare without English: The Reception of Shakespeare in Non-Anglophone Countries*, edited by Sukanta Chaudhuri and Lim Chee Seng. New Delhi: Pearson Education, 2006. 46–66.

Hong Kong Blue Book. The command of the Colonial Secretary, W. T. Mercer, 1865.

64   A. LEE

Lau, Leung Che Miriam. *The Making of Hong Kong Shakespeare: Post-1997 Adaptations and Appropriations*. PhD dissertation. Shakespeare Institute, University of Birmingham, 2018.

Lei, Bi-qi Beatrice. 'Betrayal, Derail, or a Thin Veil: The Myth of Origin'. *Shakespeare Survey* 68 (2015): 168–182.

Lee, Adele. '*One Husband Too Many* and the Problem of Postcolonial Hong Kong'. In *Shakespeare in Hollywood, Asia, and Cyberspace*, edited by Alexa Alice Joubin and Charles S. Ross. West Lafayette: Purdue University Press, 2009. 195–204.

Lee, Ann. *What the United States Can Learn from China*. San Francisco: Berrett-Koehler, 2012.

Lee, John Chi-kin, Foreword to *Learning and Teaching in the Chinese Classroom: Responding to Individual Needs*, edited by Shane N. Phillipson and Lam Bick-har. Hong Kong: Hong Kong University Press, 2011.

Levith, Murray J. *Shakespeare in China*. London: Continuum, 2004.

Loomba, Ania. 'Teaching the Bard in India'. In *Subject to Change: Teaching Literature in the Nineties*, edited by Susie J. Tharu. New Delhi: Orient Longman Limited, 1998. 33–51.

Olive, Sarah. 'Outside Interference or Hong Kong Embracing Its Unique Identity? The Chinese Universities Shakespeare Festival'. *Palgrave Communications*. Accessed March 2, 2020. https://doi.org/10.1057/s41599-019-0327-5.

Pennycook, Alistair. 'ELT and Colonialism'. In *International Handbook of English Language Teaching*, edited by Jim Cummins and Chris Davison. New York: Springer, 2007. 13–24.

Postiglione, Gerard A. 'Preface' to *Going to School in East Asia. The Global School Room*, edited by Gerard A. Postiglione and Jason Tan. Westport, CT and London: Greenwood Press, 2007.

Preus, Betty. 'Educational Trends in China and the United States: Proverbial Pendulum or Potential for Balance?' *Phi Delta Kappan*. 89.2 (2007): 115–118.

Pronko, Leonard. 'Approaching Shakespeare Through Kabuki'. In *Shakespeare East and West*, edited by Fujita Minoru and Leonard Pronko. Tokyo: Japan Library, 1996. 23–40.

Ryan, Janette. 'Changing Concepts and Practices of Curriculum in China'. In *Curriculum Reform in China: Changes and Challenges*, edited by Yin Hong-Biao and Li Zijian. New York: Nova Science Publishers, Inc., 2012. 13–30.

Wong, Dorothy. '"Domination by Consent": A Study of Shakespeare in Hong Kong'. In *Colonizer and Colonized*, edited by Theo D'haen and Patricia Krus. Amsterdam: Editions Rodopi, 2000. 43–56.

Wu, Yongan. *Teaching Young Adult Literature to ESL Students: An Experiment*. BiblioBazaar, LLC: Charleston, S. Carolina, 2011.

Yang, Yuan. 'The Bard in Beijing: How Shakespeare Is Subverting China'. *Financial Times*, October 5, 2018. https://www.ft.com/content/cd997246-c57b-11e8-bc21-54264d1c4647. Accessed August 7, 2020.

Yin, Hong-Biao and Li Zijian, ed. *Curriculum Reform in China: Changes and Challenges*. New York: Nova Science Publishers, Inc., 2012.

Zhao, Yong. *Catching Up or Leading the Way: American Education in the Age of Globalisation*. Alexandria, VA.: ASCAD, 2009.

Zhao, Yong. 'Reforming Chinese Education: What China Is Trying to Learn from America', *Solutions*. 3.2 (2012): 38–43.

Zhao, Yong. *Who's Afraid of the Big Bad Dragon? Why China Has the Best (and Worst) Education System in the World*. Hoboken, NJ: Wiley, 2014.

CHAPTER 3

The Chinese Universities Shakespeare Festival as an Extracurricular Activity Exemplifying Prominent Approaches to English Language Learning

Sarah Olive

Abstract In this chapter, Olive explores the Chinese Universities Shakespeare Festival (CUSF), which brought university students from across greater China together in Hong Kong to rehearse and perform twenty-minute Shakespeare scenes. She considers the way in which the organisers' and participants' constructions of the CUSF align with Amos Paran and Pauline Robinson's taxonomy of approaches to literature and its use in the English as an Additional Language (EAL) classroom as a body of knowledge, language practice material and stimulus for personal development. The chapter also offers the most extensive consideration, available in English, of the festival's ten seasons at a time when the festival's online archives are disappearing as institutional websites are renewed. The chapter concludes by considering whether CUSF provides a model

S. Olive (✉)
University of York, York, UK
e-mail: sarah.olive@york.ac.uk

for other higher education institutions staging Shakespeare in countries where English is usually learnt as an additional language. In doing so, it articulates some improvements that might strengthen any successors.

Keywords Chinese University Shakespeare Festival · Hong Kong · China · Higher education · English as an additional language

Amos Paran and Pauline Robinson argue that there are three main 'approaches' to literature and its use in the English as a Foreign Language (EFL) classroom, each underpinned by a distinctive rationale, associated with distinctive teaching methods and even different types of literary texts.[1] The three approaches are: literature 1) 'as a body of knowledge and content—for example, examining styles in literature, studying the history of English literature, dealing with the facts of authors' lives', plot, characters and literary devices used[2]; 2) 'as language practice material', where the focus is 'on the language used in the literary text' and on activating learners' language skills; and 3) 'as a stimulus for personal development', using 'activities which relate to students' personal experiences, thereby developing their imagination and emotions'.[3] Paran and Robinson add that many English language teachers now make the latter approach 'a major element of their use of literature, believing that it is important for learners to experience literature in a pleasurable, engrossing way'.[4] Indeed, they argue that 'enjoyment and appreciation' of literature need to come first in the English language classroom.[5] In most language classrooms, the various approaches interact.[6] For example, the first approach (body of knowledge) is often important in enabling students to 'express their thoughts and feelings about a text', including their enjoyment of it (i.e. stimulus to personal development). However, there are also tensions between them not foregrounded by Paran and Robinson,[7] but strongly highlighted in another volume, *Shakespeare in the EFL classroom*. Edited by Maria Eisenmann and Christiane Lütge, the book responds to the perceived threat to Shakespeare in English as a Foreign Language (EFL) classrooms of allowing an emphasis on skills (or 'competence orientation') to dominate over a focus on a Shakespearean body of knowledge.[8] In this chapter, I look at the ways in which the organisers' and participants' constructions of the Chinese Universities Shakespeare Festival (CUSF) align with Paran and Robinson's three approaches to literature, albeit in the context of an extracurricular activity rather than a formal, classroom setting.[9] My suggestion is not that the festival organisers used Paran and Robinson as a manual for designing the event. Rather, I am interested in the way in which CUSF's organisers developed this focus organically, informed by their years of experience teaching (and, for some, studying) in English language classrooms. I will demonstrate that CUSF participants seem, by the end of its span, also to have internalised the festival's tripartite approaches to EFL learning through studying the criteria, judges' and emcees' feedback.

3.1 Overview of the Chinese Universities Shakespeare Festival

CUSF was held annually at the Chinese University of Hong Kong's (CUHK) campus in Hong Kong's New Territories.[10] Ninety different institutions participated in CUSF during its span: seventy-six from mainland China, the rest from Hong Kong, Macau and Taiwan.[11] Two inner Mongolian institutions participated but did not make the finals. Over the decade, CUSF grew from twenty to thirty participating universities annually and from ten to twelve finalist teams in later years. Almost half of all participating institutions (forty-four of around ninety) reached the finals at least once. Universities that wished to enter submitted a video-recording of a performance of a short scene, which was used by the organisers to shortlist finalists (though it was not always the scene performed in the final). Shakespeare's texts could be cut-down for this purpose, even re-arranged, but the script could not translate or modernise the early modern English or interpolate newly written lines.[12] Only undergraduates were allowed in participating teams: no postgraduates and no previously participating students, 'in order to maximize the number of students taking part'.[13] Each team was allowed only three actors— so some doubling was usual. The festival was open to students and staff from beyond English departments, to non-English majors studying EFL as part of another degree.[14] Finalists had twenty minutes to stage their productions. In practice, this ranged from fifteen to twenty-five minutes, although time-keeping was more firmly policed as the years advanced.[15] Only minimal sets were allowed for the finals, to keep set change times between performances to a minimum, but also presumably to ensure parity between local teams and those who would otherwise have had to transport sets across a vast country. In between performances, while sets were being changed, the team fresh off the stage (and perhaps their director too) would participate in English language discussion with the emcees about the experience of participating, performing, and key production decisions. In addition to Jason Gleckman, emcees included Melissa Lam, Michelle Cheung, Carly Chan and Joseph Lin. The criteria used to judge the festival were broken down thus: acting and directing were worth 30% each, English proficiency 20%, technical arts and stage craft 15%, and imaginative selection of scene 5%. English was not just the language of the festival performances but also the emceeing, the speeches given at the opening ceremony and the festival banquet, the display boards of the Shakespeare exhibition in the theatre foyer, the PowerPoint synopses of the plays, and the official Facebook page of the festival, though this is far from an exhaustive list of its uses in the festival.

There were three judges for each festival who, in addition to awarding marks and the most significant prizes, ensured that each participating university received feedback.[16] They are described on the festival website as 'professional experts in Shakespeare from both the academic and theatrical worlds'. Certainly the festival consistently managed to attract academics and practitioners from the highest echelons of their fields. Some judges made just one appearance, others were stalwarts of the festival. Almost all judges had strong ties with members of the organising committee—a practical necessity when identifying and inviting their possible contribution and common in other areas of academia, from appointing external examiners to organising conference plenaries. One effect of this pragmatic recruitment, however, is that the judges were predominantly white, Anglo-Saxon men. Exceptions, notably in the early seasons, include Timothy Bond, an associate artistic director of the Oregon Shakespeare Festival—the first artist of colour to serve that festival in an executive artistic position,[17] and Professor Richard M.W. Ho, an experienced actor, director and translator of Shakespeare into Cantonese.[18] My reaction to the judges' demographic, watching later seasons of the festival unfold through the videos echoes that described by Dickson: it felt 'peculiar after everything I'd learned about colonial history that the students were Chinese and the judges white'.[19] It also demonstrates, importantly for this chapter, a privileging of those who have English as their first language (elsewhere referred to as 'native speakers'): an assumption about 'authoritativeness' common, but contested, in research on Teaching English to Speakers of Other Languages (TESOL) and language education more generally. Professor Susan Wofford, former

President of the Shakespeare Association of America, was a rare female judge. The final festival brought more women into the judging roles with Dr Philippa Kelly, resident dramaturg, California Shakespeare Theatre, and Paige Newmark, artistic director, of Shakespeare WA (Western Australia) on the panel.

Other judges included Professor Geoffrey Borney, 'Head of Theatre at the Australian National University and a renowned teacher of theatre students', who served as a judge for seven out of the ten festivals.[20] Colin George, Royal Shakespeare Company actor; the founding Artistic Director of the Crucible Theatre, Sheffield, UK; the Artistic Director of 'several major theatres', including the State Theatre of South Australia; and Dean of the Hong Kong Academy of the Performing Arts for eleven years, who 'directed and acted in all types of performance media', had two geographic points of connection with Parker.[21] This is also true of Professor Simon Palfrey, 'a renowned scholar from Oxford University', who had been Parker's student at the Australian National University (ANU).[22] Professor Tony Turner, former Head of Drama at ANU and previously Head of Voice and Acting at London's Mountview Theatre School. Some points of connection to Parker were grounded in more immediate proximity. Judge Joseph Graves, described in his introduction to the festival's audience as an actor, director, scriptwriter of film scripts and television series, 'world traveller, his current project is setting up the World Institute for Film and Theatre in Beijing'.[23] He had also taught at the same institution as some of the participating students and made a vital contribution to the tuition students and directors received in the masterclasses. Professional interests in global and Asian Shakespeare additional to those of George and Graves also existed for Professor Peter Holbrook, University of Queensland and Chair of the International Shakespeare Association, as well as John Gillies, who had worked at several Australian universities (Macquarie, ANU—like Parker and Palfrey, and LaTrobe), authored books and curated multimedia packages on Shakespeare in Asia. While several of the judges (particularly those who returned for multiple festivals) had worked professionally in China for extended periods, others had more fleeting experiences there. These include Raymond Caldwell, founder and 'artistic director of a very interesting, exciting theatre called the Shakespeare Texas Festival: a few years ago this festival visited China with a production called The Miracle Worker' had more fleeting experiences there.[24] He, Bond, Kelly, and

Newmark were all judges whose established festival Shakespeare pedigrees were referenced in their introductions.

The festival was replete with practices of teaching and learning, overt and otherwise, around and beyond Shakespeare. For participating, university students this included a festive, competitive opportunity to plan, rehearse, and stage a scene from Shakespeare—acting, directing (and articulating decisions), backstage work, cutting and arranging texts (dramaturgy); watching productions from other teams and guest experts; participating in drama workshops led by guest experts; reflecting on and responding to emcees' comments in the post-performance discussion slots live on stage as well as feedback from the judges[25]; viewing a Shakespeare exhibition in the hall foyer; viewing and commenting on YouKu festival footage; travel and tourism for the finalists to Hong Kong and for the winners to the UK; cultural exchange at the 'open mic' part of the festival banquet; plus all the EFL work described in 3.4. For school students and their teachers, there was the experience of watching live performances of Shakespeare in English; participating in a multiple-choice quiz; reflecting on performances to vote for their favourite teams; school workshops; and continuing professional development (CDP) events for teachers. This included, in 2012, a free workshop called 'Shakespeare reimagined, reinterpreted' run by William Yip. Yip was introduced to participants as the Founder and Artistic Director of Theatre Noir, Hong Kong, a graduate and teacher at various Hong Kong performing arts academies, drama educator, advisor to the Hong Kong Education Bureau on curriculum, and collaborator with the British Council Hong Kong on a programme, 'Shakespeare: a worldwide classroom', to promote Shakespeare's works in local schools. The remainder of this chapter goes beyond observing the practices of teaching and learning involved in the festival to explore the constructions of three particular approaches to EFL education in greater China by those involved. First, however, I give a brief account of methods and resources for researching the festival.

3.2   RESEARCHING THE CHINESE
UNIVERSITIES SHAKESPEARE FESTIVAL

The majority of constructions of the festival analysed in this chapter come from a Hong Kong perspective: the words of the faculty, senior management, and some postgraduate students of the Chinese University of Hong Kong as well as the sponsors, educational charities based in Hong Kong. The verdicts and reflections of the international judges—overwhelmingly America, Australian and British—have also been analysed. In the main, their words were transcribed by me from the festival videos publicly available on YouKu or published on the CUSF website. From the videos, I transcribed the words of the participating teams from across greater China (with some international faculty and occasionally international students also participating), spoken during the post-performance discussions, prize-giving ceremony or elsewhere in the festival banquet. One resource for researching the festival which I omitted to look at was the CUSF Facebook page, partly because I questioned the extent to which this would be used by participants in 'mainland China' given the 'great firewall' that makes accessing Western social media difficult unless using special virtual private networks (VPNs).[26] While on a research mobility visit to the campus in 2016, I was fortunate to be able to discuss my analysis with a handful of CUHK faculty, doctoral students, and former participants (student actors and directors, faculty directors) acknowledged below: they were able to share their memories and understandings of the festival, ask me questions about and challenge my analysis, and otherwise add nuance to my analysis. Any errors or omissions are mine alone.

To delimit this chapter, I am not primarily interested in whether or not English language (with or without the use of English literature) should be a part of school or university education in greater China.[27] Instead, I acknowledge here that English language instruction is currently a fact of life for many young people in greater China, especially in Hong Kong where English was the official language under British colonial rule, later with Cantonese also recognised.[28] If English is part of daily life in Hong Kong, it is possibly experiencing some decline. Miriam Lau notes that 'There seems to be a constant worry among academic circles in Hong Kong that since the handover of the city to mainland China, English language is gradually losing its importance, resulting in an inevitable decline in the English standards of Hong Kong students. The objective of the festival is in part a response to this anxiety'.[29] Meanwhile, Michael Ingham flags up the 'growing importance of Mandarin' for younger generations'.[30] Contexts for the festival's consensus about the educational value of Shakespeare, English language, and literature that readers may wish to explore in the existing literature include historical education policy advocating 'Western learning for utility' in Hong Kong[31]; the legacy of the colonial domination[32]; 'Hong Kong's role in the global economy mean[ing] that the school curriculum [particularly with regard to English] was not radically reformed in an anticolonial backlash'[33]; protestors (mainly parents) demanding more English language teaching, more places in English language schools, resisting a perceived push towards Chinese language education[34]; the city's quest for its own identity in the twenty-first century, distinct from a 'mainland Chinese'/PRC identity and drawing on its colonial past[35]; active debates about the threat posed by the PRC's emphasis on *Putonghua* (sometimes referred to as Mandarin or Standard Chinese) to minority Chinese languages[36]; and international debates about Englishisation.[37] This chapter does not offer a history of the teaching of Shakespeare or English more broadly, or campus Shakespeare, in greater China, since these are available in the works of Yong and Lee, Li and Tam et al.[38] Nor does it engage in theatre criticism of the productions staged as part of the festival. Dickson undertakes some theatre criticism of CUSF in 2014, its final year, fleetingly in his book. Scholars from China who participated in it offer more detailed theatre criticism of productions.[39] Notwithstanding these publications, some recent attention to campus Shakespeare generally, and campus spaces and groups as pivotal to the development of modern theatre in Asia specifically, there is a paucity of literature (at least, in or translated into English) and media coverage of CUSF.[40] There is also a degree of temporal urgency to researching CUSF: as the CUHK website is renewed, material pertaining to the defunct festival published there is being taken down. Furthermore, few (if any) of the existing studies (written in or translated into English) tackle the festival in its entirety, considering all ten festivals on video and the CUHK website, with a particular emphasis on the paratexts to the performances—the opening ceremony, the festival banquet, the emceeing and the post-performance discussions. This is despite the fact that these moments are so rich in educators' and students' constructions of EFL education in greater China.

3.3   A BODY OF KNOWLEDGE AND CONTENT

In this section, I explore ways in which CUSF approaches EFL Shakespeare 'as a body of knowledge and content—for example, examining styles in literature, studying the history of English literature, dealing with the facts of authors' and 'the public knowledge which a reader takes away from a text', e.g. plot, characters and literary devices used.[41] This emphasis might be explained by the festival's growing out of an English department with a strong English literature focus. It is inscribed in one of the aims of CUSF: 'to promote the study of Shakespeare and Shake-spearean plays'.[42] Participants were instructed throughout each festival, from the call for entries to the judges' feedback, about Shakespeare's sociocultural literariness, standing as a 'genius', a 'keen observer of human nature, great dramatist, great poet', 'the finest writer in the language', and 'one of the most wonderful things in the world'.[43] Similar statements positioning Shakespeare as a 'core of centered cultural literacy', with 'out-standing significance for the development of English language, literature and drama', and as the foremost example of 'eloquence in English' can be found in other publications on campus Shakespeare and English language teaching.[44] A scholarly impulse to evidence Shakespeare's reputation for greatness can be seen in the recurrent discussion and explanation—in the festival guidance, feedback and videos of the event—of Shakespeare's 'peerless' facility with genres; abiding themes (trust, hate, love, desire, evil, ambition, obedience); character; language (double entendre, bawdy, metre); and structure (soliloquies versus dialogue). By later festivals, students were able to watch videos, and read judges' feedback, from previous seasons online. They echoed some of these knowledges about Shakespeare in their contributions to the post-performance discussion: 'everything is [there in the text] because Shakespeare put it there' (actor playing Hamlet, Hainan) and 'Shakespeare is a master of plays' (Director, Fudan).[45] Participants were also encouraged to demonstrate their knowl-edge of the full breadth of Shakespeare's work. An 'imaginative selection of scene' potentially earnt marks. Choosing an unpopular play or unusual scenes was praised in the qualitative feedback from judges and emcees' comments. There was some tendency to rest or retire prize-winning plays, or to choose a less staged scene, or present an unusual edit of the play. This emphasis on Shakespeare's corpus had the consequence that 31 out of 37 (or so) plays were staged in the finals—an enviable range of works that even professional Shakespeare theatres struggle to provide.[46]

Other areas of knowledge about Shakespeare's work disseminated in the festivals—from the exhibition boards in the theatre foyer to the patter of the emcees—ranged from the chronology of writing and publica-tion to the dramatic function of particular roles, e.g. the early modern clown as speaking truth to power. Participants were also given insight into, and exposed to the idiom of, wide-ranging literary concepts and critical theories. These included Shakespeare's 'greenworld', feminism, postcolonialism, ecocriticism, as well as humanist approaches stressing the universality of Shakespeare's themes and emotions.[47] Participants were instructed in a variety of prevalent approaches to studying and performing Shakespeare through the judges' feedback and emcees' comments, from close-reading of the play-text to a range of performance styles and techniques historically. Topics covered here include naturalism, symbolism, ensemble work and alienation effects. In the judges' overall comments, for instance, knowledge about changing theatre conventions and audience attitudes towards transitions between scenes was imparted to festival participants: 'in western theatre, particularly in Shakespeare, we no longer have blackouts. Now there's a very good reason for this: it's because it stops the action and it slows everything down' (Tony Turner[48]). The way in which early modern theatre conditions and conventions shaped Shakespeare's writing was also invoked when Holbrook explained that Shakespeare wrote 'poetic drama...more for the ear than for the eye'.[49] That participating teams engaged in acquiring and demonstrating knowledge of historical conventions of European theatre is evident in the post-performance discussion with a director of *Romeo and Juliet* from Fudan: '[There is] Too much information to be shown on the stage [in twenty minutes] therefore we have resorted to the telling mode and chorus and ancient theatrical technique dating back to ancient Greece'.[50] The material that teams prepared for their PowerPoint introductions in later seasons also demonstrated that they had undertaken research using literary and theatre criticism and related it to their own production decisions.

In terms of acquiring knowledge of Anglophone culture, Adele Lee has described in the previous chapter some Hong Kong school students' sense that studying Shakespeare enables them to understand, what they framed as, the western mindset and to demonstrate 'outward thinking'. Audience members, including up to a thousand school students each day of the festival, were encouraged to acquire the organisers' Anglo-cultural, theatre-going etiquette. This involved requests not to leave the hall during performances, only in the intervals; to 'shut off your cellphones'[51]; and, on the same matter, some banter emulating Shakespearean English between the emcees:

> Joseph: 'This man is Joseph, if you would know
> This beauteous lady, Carly, is certaine,
> Your phones with texts and fb will make noise,
> Noise, that vile, noise
> Which will our dramas disturb...'

Carly: 'Hi! My name is Carly. His name is Joseph. He means lose your phones. Put them away and pay attention'.[52]

Such requests are heard and heeded to varying extents in arts venues the world-over but they were framed here as being particularly important because of the almost universal and ubiquitous use of mobile phones in many public settings in Hong Kong. CUSF organisers also taught students about Anglophone cultural and theatrical superstitions: Gleckman repeatedly mock-scolded himself when emceeing for naming *Macbeth*—'Oops, I'm not supposed to ever say that name in the theatre and now I've brought an awful curse down on everyone in the auditorium. I'm awfully sorry'.[53] He then used the euphemistic phrases 'the Scottish play' or 'this un-nameable play' instead. Emcees invoked British literature and culture beyond Shakespeare, by comparing CUSF productions to *Harry Potter* and *Downton Abbey*. Anglophone folk music was included when David Parker led CUHK staff, judges, and anyone else who cared to join in singing a rendition of 'Waltzing Matilda' (Australian) and 'There was a lover and his lass' (English) at the festival banquet.[54] This was in the spirit of cultural exchange, rather than a unilateral flow of Anglophone cultural material, since mainland Chinese teams, for example, performed traditional songs and dances as well as regional pop hits in Chinese languages (being unable to identify these myself is an example of the limitations of the 'outsider' researcher, discussed in the introduction to this book).

Indeed, the festival's emphasis on 'the integration of Chinese and western cultures in greater China' was described by Professor Lawrence J Lau—then Vice-Chancellor of CUHK—at multiple opening ceremonies and on the 'history' section of the festival website: 'the Shakespeare Festival provides an exciting annual opportunity to integrate Chinese and Western cultures'.[55] The sense that this might be an unspoken criterion for success was reflected in the knowledges of Anglophone culture demonstrated by performing teams throughout the festival, with their peers and school audiences as the learners. Familiarity with Anglophone films of the plays was shown through teams' allusions to performances by renowned actors such as Laurence Olivier (though this could also be problematised as 'copying', something outlawed in the criteria[56]). Teams used music from the soundtrack of the Nino Rota score from Zeffirelli's *Romeo and Juliet* movie, as well as other genres associated with the west such as classical music and American jazz. Soochow presented a *Twelfth Night* that worked Hollywood teen Shakespeare tropes hard, including references to pop and grunge music, break dancing, US sports uniforms, and roller disco.[57] Other testimonies to knowledge of western history and culture came from teams who had Shylock wearing a star of David (Shenzen[58]), made attempts at regional British accents (Macau's *King Lear*[59]), and invoked US singer/songwriter Taylor Swift's lyrics by describing one actress' feelings towards her character's love life as 'this is exhausting. You know, we are never ever ever getting back together' (Northeast Normal's *Two Gentlemen of Verona*[60]).

Cultures beyond China and Britain also informed performances. Based on my recognition of visual markers in the productions alone, Cyprus, Greece, the Middle East and Moorish cultures were represented. Domestic and regional theatre traditions, music, architecture and costuming from across greater China (including Tibet) were also well represented and rationales for their incorporation discussed by teams and emcees in the post-performance segments. One of the knowledges that participants in the festival took away with them, and reinforced further in their own performances, was that 'art can be a bridge to a shared world'[61] and that 'Shakespeare belongs to the whole world'. The latter comment was made to me by Sun Yu, a postdoctoral researcher at Xiamen who founded the Shakespeare Troupe of Heilongjiang International University and led the students taking part in the last three festivals in 2011, 2012 and 2013 (private conversation). She took away this understanding from her experience, though her team were not finalists, juggling it with her keen awareness of debates around Shakespeare and western cultural imperialism. I have explored the way in which the festival embodies tensions between its reification of English language and, perhaps to a lesser extent, culture—which could be interpreted as neocolonialist or anglicising—with the opportunities it presented for intra-regional cooperation, competition and sharing diverse, greater Chinese cultures in greater detail in a previous publication.[62] Here, it is sufficient to highlight the way in which the knowledges displayed by the participants included of global, trans- and intercultural Shakespeares—especially in performance, jostling alongside constructions of his being 'English' or 'western'. The latter notions connect to and reinforce the approach of Shakespeare considered in the following section: Shakespeare as practice material for achieving fluency in English (narrowly conceived in a way that downplays world Englishes).

3.4 Practice Material for Activating English Language Skills

That English language skills can be enhanced by the use of English liter-ature as language practice material in the classroom has been widely argued in scholarship on English language teaching and learning beyond Paran and Robinson. Arguments include that the 'use of literature in EFL classes...improves reading skills', knowledge and use of complex vocab-ulary and sentence structures, as well as student and teacher motivation, turning 'learners into lifelong willing readers of English literary texts'.[63] Specifically, dramatic literature taught using performance methods with students has been described as benefitting English language skills because it is 'a holistic method that utilises different semiotic systems simultane-ously'.[64] These include linguistic, visual, gestural, audio, and spatial to think about 'how you could attract the viewers' attention'. Exponents of Shakespeare for developing EFL skills include Lau and Tso, Eisen-mann and Lütge, Christina Lima, Genevieve White (who acknowledges, but seeks to overcome, scepticism), and, specifically with reference to an extracurricular drama club, Kevin Bergman.[65] Such a conviction is explicit in the aims and criteria of CUSF. Lee's chapter in this book suggests that the Hong Kong school students in her research were committed to the idea of studying Shakespeare for improving their English, even though she felt that the resultant benefit was doubtful. So, the idea of Shakespeare as benefitting learners' English language skills is gener-ally prevalent but contested: in terms of CUSF, it is prevalent but not contested. In this section, I offer some examples of the organisers' and participants' constructions of the value of Shakespeare for EFL. Part of the CUHK's senior management, Professor Benjamin W. Wah's festival speech suggested the university's commitment to English as an additional language: 'We are the Chinese University and we're very proud of our name and our identity as a university with our historical roots in mainland china. But we are also strongly committed as part of our foundation to promoting the bilingual and bicultural aspects of education'.[66] This was reinforced by the judging criteria, with English proficiency worth 20% of the overall score.[67] It is not entirely clear to me what was included in judges' assessment of proficiency—solely the performance or also the level of English demonstrated in the post-performance discussion? Nonetheless, students were challenged to perform across various domains of producing and understanding English—reading, writing, listening, speaking and comprehension—even if they were not formally assessed on all of them in competing for the festival prize.

The first two domains were perhaps the least obviously required by the festival. However, with the exception of some areas of the website and some press releases offering Chinese language text, the written materials associated with the festival that I have found online were produced in English. Unless memorising their parts from oral transmission, participants would need to be able to read their English scripts. Cheung Man Yee, the first ethnically Chinese Director of Broadcasting in Hong Kong, speaking at the festival as Vice Chairman of the Shun Hing Education and Charity Fund, celebrated what she perceives as the spread of EFL skills in China, including reading: 'half a century ago, Chinese people read not English at all. And I am very happy that now in China so many of these students can learn English and read Shakespeare as first language'.[68] In addition to the university students, it was implicit that the Hong Kong school students attending would be able to read English, given that it was the language of the PowerPoint synopses of the plays used in later festivals: from the videos of the seventh festival onwards, projector screens are visible to the audience, with bullet-point text forming the basis for the emcees' introduction of each performance.[69] For example, before Hubei's performance of *Taming of the Shrew*, the slides explained the multiple meanings of the word 'shrew'. However, most of the material on the slide was also read out by the emcee, thereby including audience members who could understand spoken English but were not English literate. Additionally, this example demonstrates the treatment of Shakespeare as an opportunity to teach those present about unknown words, semantic change and the history of the English language.[70] Other instances show stakeholders engaging in expanding students' familiarity with English language vocabulary from the professional theatre. In his feedback on a production of *Pericles* by University of International Business and Economics, Borny explains that performers should avoid 'trucks', unnecessary pauses 'so long that you could have driven a truck through the space left between the two speeches'.[71] The YouKu videos give the impression that, in terms of writing, by the ninth festival (at least), teams had to submit a written document in English in which they detail their approach to the play, what elements of their performance they would like to highlight for the audience and judges' consideration in advance of the finals. It seems that this was then used as the basis for the emcees to introduce each performance. This offers some evidence of the way in which the festival evolved to require teams to produce modern English writing, as well as spoken early modern and modern English.

The aims of the festival foreground speaking English when they state that participation 'provide[s] an opportunity for students to display their acting skills in English'.[72] The organisers even provided each finalist team with 'a pronunciation CD to help them prepare for the final production'.[73] Given the emphasis on spoken English in the festival criteria and the preparatory stages, lack of proficiency in it during the performance could lose a team marks in spite of their achievement against other criteria. For example, Borny wrote of National Taiwan University's *Tempest*, in the eighth festival: 'The concentration on the physical and visual elements is sometimes at the cost of an adequate focus on language'.[74] His feedback to teams routinely emphasised the need for clarity of spoken English—in terms of audibility, accent, phrasing, pace, articulation and diction. Dickson too picks up on the latter quality being an aspect of performance that was emphasised by the festival. He praises teams that achieved in those areas. For instance, he describes Xiamen University of Technology's *Cymbeline* as 'by far the best performance' given in 'precise and believable English' and applauds CUHK's *Romeo and Juliet* for 'pronunciation [that] was pitch-perfect'.[75] Beyond using Shakespeare as language practice material, students were expected to improve their communicative (sometimes referred to as 'conversational' or 'transactional') English through participation in CUSF. Richard Liu, representing one of the festival's sponsors, is reported by the festival's organisers in one of the videos as having said that there is 'no doubt in my mind – in all areas, not just performance – [students'] level of English is sharper, clearer' year on year (prize-giving ceremony, sixth festival) and that English should be studied 'as a common language that we can communicate in among all the Chinese territories'.[76] Here, he seems to be picking up on aspects of the festival such as the post-performance discussions between the emcees and the actors and directors of the participating teams. The emcees asked questions about the teams' choices in terms of characterisation, themes, *mise en scene*, choreography, and rehearsal methods but also personal, moral, and philosophical questions (which I will return to in the next section on personal development). The participants listened and responded. These exchanges, between a mix of Hong Kong and expat emcees and (mainly) Chinese team members often seemed geared to test or impart conversational norms in English, particularly relating to informality and use of humour. So, they are concerned with cultural, not just linguistic, competence. An example of this comes when Gleckman asks one actor, after a discussion by his female team-mates of gender roles in *Taming of the Shrew*, 'What does Petruchio have to say?' Petruchio responds in character: 'Now I am tamed, so I have nothing to say', making a joke that cleverly allows him to control the direction of the conversation and gets him out of a further response (Hubei University[77]). Furthermore, they probe students' ability to partic-ipate in a kind of Socratic dialogue, often constructed as typically western in contrast to East Asian pedagogy as 'duck-stuffing' (a pejorative used by Adamson and Pang, where Lee discusses 'memorisation' in the previous chapter[78]). The discussions tally with Paran and Robinson's instruction to EFL teachers to 'Make sure that you elicit from students what they think, rather than telling them what acceptable answers are. In fact, discussion is likely to reveal that students have quite clear ideas. Accepting their points of view is likely to result in their experiencing a sense of freedom and creativity' as well as gaining 'useful fluency practice'.[79] At best, the discus-sions allowed teams to negotiate a range of registers, demonstrate their excellently idiomatic English, use of subject-specific vocabulary (such as 'green world' and 'naturalism'), and knowledge of etymology: one team explained their interpretation of Malvolio's character with reference to the origins of his name in the adjective 'malevolent'. At worst, they demon-strated that the ability to memorise and perform Shakespeare's lines does not always correspond to a holistic English language ability: there are occasions when a team member answers or translates for another who is unable to speak, or perhaps understand, English in these impromptu dialogues. However, it is worth noting that the excitement and stress of the performance immediately preceding these discussions might have negatively impacted on oral fluency for some.

Last, but by no means least, the festival required competency in English comprehension of Shakespeare's dramatic literature. The criteria explained that 'it is also very [important that] the actors perform-ing...have a good sense of the meaning of the dialogue. You will not act well if you do not understand what you're saying'. Participants needed to be able to understand plausible meanings of Shakespeare at the level of words, sentences, speeches, scenes and beyond; to demon-strate that understanding through their interpretations of the roles during the performance; and to present and defend the interpretation in the post-performance discussion (and, in later years, the production notes they submitted). This focus on comprehension of the Shakespearean texts can be seen from the judges' referencing of the criteria in their general remarks at the end of each festival and in their feedback for particular teams. A judge in multiple years, Holbrook wrote about the eighth festival:

> I also came away with the conviction that character, thought, and language are really at the heart of Shakespearean drama... I think that grasping the central role in Shakespearean drama of language and thought is the key to sound performance and production of his scripts. Shakespearean drama is not really much interested in spectacle for the sake of spectacle. But it is overwhelmingly interested in character and ideas, often complex characters and ideas, and these are conveyed only through words.[80]

Dickson wrote that his experience of the festival as an audience member was that it was 'as much a test of comprehension...as it was of acting'.[81] He uses this measure himself in critiquing Tsinghua University's *Twelfth Night* as an example of a production that was flawed in its lack of understanding of the play's bawdy humour, with the resultant effect that the 'vigour with which [Malvolio's] tights were deployed got more reaction than the word play'.[82] Comprehension was not only at stake for the participating university students. The organisers drew the teams' attention to the issue of English comprehension for the audience of bilingual/EAL Hong Kong high school students: 'You should also choose scenes that audiences will readily understand – scenes, for example, without too much wordplay, which are often difficult to follow for even native speakers of English'.[83] Participants were thus asked to take responsibility not only for their own comprehension of Shakespeare's English but, to an extent, for the comprehensibility of their performance for school audiences. When the organisers' felt that this had not been heeded, the emcee's offered advice to school audiences to ameliorate the potentially alienating effect of the language barrier: 'The language in *Hamlet* is also dense and sophisticated so don't worry about catching all the words, the actors' dynamics and gesture are also informative. Above all, enjoy'.[84] Not overwhelming pupils was important because the festival had been billed to school teachers as 'the perfect introduction for your students to Shakespeare and his mastery of the English-language'[85], i.e. Shakespeare as practice material for listening and comprehension; for students understanding if not yet, like Lee's students in chapter two, producing English.

The instances I have cited above give a small glimpse into the skills across a variety of domains and registers of English that CUSF demanded and with which the EFL participants and audiences engaged. Additionally, I have suggested that there is some variation between the perceptions of key stakeholders as to whether it was the Shakespearean English in the festival that was good for the students' language skills, or whether Shakespeare was more beneficial as the impetus to undertake mundane, English conversation. In this sense, the festival embodies some key debates around EFL teaching. However, there is a clear consensus in the available festival materials that English is a characteristic of a good education throughout China, at school and at university. There was no explicit evidence in the documents and videos I saw of concern over the potential Englishisation of language in greater China and its ramifications politically, socially or culturally. Rather, there was widespread embrace by the festival's organisers and sponsors of the positive ramifications for intra-regional communication, using English as the *lingua franca*, and for the greater Chinese economies.[86]

3.5   A STIMULUS FOR PERSONAL DEVELOPMENT

This final section considers the way in which organisers and participants construct CUSF as a stimulus for students' personal development. Paran and Robinson's rationales for literature in EFL learning define this as using literature in ways that connect it to students' 'personal experiences, thereby developing their imagination and emotions' including sympathy and empathy.[87] Similar arguments have been made specifically for the inclusion of Shakespeare.[88] This sense of students discovering 'unexpected connections' between the Shakespearean words they read and their own lives is praised by the Hong Kong author Xu Xi as outcomes of Ingham's trips with Lingnan students to London's Shakespeare sites.[89] Throughout CUSF, the belief in Shakespeare for personal growth was modelled for students in Gleckman's typically enthusiastic, self-deprecatory and humorous emceeing. In general terms, he declares 'combining education and entertainment…is a good goal for art – you can learn and you can have a good time as well'.[90] More specifically, he explains, 'Shakespeare is a wonderful thing, even better than Da Vinci, is Shakespeare. I won't say I think about Shakespeare every day, but I think about Shakespeare many days and sometimes when the clouds are out, when life is bad, I try to think of a quotation from Shakespeare to cheer me up...I'm still working on that'.[91] Along with linguistic and cognitive benefits, studying literature such as Shakespeare in these settings is described by Gleckman as educating the whole person, including their emotional development. Although there were no archives of school students' reactions to CUSF performances available to me (other than their applause on the video soundtrack and the award of audience choice awards each day), Hartley suggests that school students attending campus productions of Shakespeare can have an affective experience: 'these were young people who saw themselves – or something very much like themselves – in a text they had considered mouldering and alien, and that much of that association came very simply from the age of the principal players'.[92] So, not only is campus Shakespeare more affordable than commercial theatre (in this case, it was free), Hartley suggests that it can actually be more effective for pupils' empathic development. The benefit to Hong Kong's school students of seeing 'Chinese Shakespeare'—Shakespeare performed and directed by students and staff of universities in greater China—is further suggested by Lee's chapter in this book, which identifies a dearth of such opportunity in Hong Kong schools.

The benefit of the post-performance discussion sections of CUSF to students' speaking and listening English has been considered in the previous section, but the way in which they develop students' abilities in terms of 'explaining their likes and dislikes and discussing them, [learning] to articulate their feelings and opinions', as well as those of their characters, is also evident, even if tongue-in-cheek.[93] Emcee questions include: 'What do you think of your relationship with your mother? ... Good? Bad? Are you angry at her? Do you love her? (of Hamlet); 'What do you think about the idea of borrowing money from somebody?' (of a *Merchant of Venice* team); and 'Have you ever been in an experience of being torn between two women?' (of Lysander). Where the referent of 'you' is not clearly specified by the emcee, actors variously answer as themselves and in character, or as themselves but strongly identified with the character. For example, one Lady Macbeth responds to a question about how the team perceive their relationships with: 'After the performance he [the actor playing Macbeth] is still in love with me. You can see our connections. But he always treats me as a boy in real life' (Dalian Maritime University[94]). Her answer multitasks: it draws the judges' attention to the chemistry between the actors popularly held to be a key component of a good performance, perhaps factored into the points awarded for acting; expresses her desire for a personal, romantic relationship with her co-star;

indicates her confidence in her romantic allure—self-confidence and self-esteem have previously been identified as effects of active Shakespeare for EFL learners.[95] Earl Stevick has argued that 'for second language teaching "success depends less on materials, techniques and linguistic analyses, and more on what goes on inside and between the people in the classroom"'.[96] Certainly, the actor playing Lady Macbeth felt this to be the key to success in the competition and, romantically, beyond it.

Active encounters with Shakespeare for EFL, 'a Shakespeare that gets learners to talk and interact', are also thought to enhance personal development in 'fostering team spirit, co-operation, compromising and argument exchange'.[97] In this case, the festival aimed to nurture these interpersonal competences between 'students and drama coaches/directors from throughout China'.[98] This extended beyond their performance work in university teams to, for example, contributing to moments of joint performance and spectatorship involving all the finalists during the festival banquet.[99] These showcased a range of performing arts: music and dance were often chosen, including Chinese and western, classical and popular, traditional and modern. If predominantly through the medium of English, these additional performances and the social events they were part of contributed to 'the learners' understanding of cultures' not just in the Anglophone world but also within greater China.[100] The importance of an opportunity for these students to witness and exchange performing arts is further highlighted by Dillon's argument that, in China, the growth of new media and television has predominantly resulted in the production of material that is 'low quality', 'sensational', 'trivial' and 'ephemeral' as well as Li's and Lemos' findings that commercial theatre performances from Beijing to Chongqing are prohibitively expensive for students.[101] Furthermore, the residential nature of the finals—staying, eating and relaxing together on campus and at Hong Kong tourist attractions—offered a rare opportunity to bring into close physical proximity students from countries or regions often divided by their politics: mainland China, its Special Administrative Regions Hong Kong and Macau, and Taiwan (the Republic of China). This political division frequently impacts on cultural exchange within the region.[102] Furthermore, in Hong Kong, tensions between mainland Chinese and Hong Kong students (and occasionally between mainland Chinese students and expat lecturers) at Hong Kong universities have been well-publicised.[103] It is therefore not surprising that, while sponsors used to the cut-and-thrust of business tended to hype-up the competitive element of the festival, its organisers preferred to emphasise its value as a collaboration.[104]

Throughout the literature on EFL Shakespeare, emphasis is placed on the positive effect that engagement with literature and performance has on multiple forms of creativity: not just linguistic but also creative problem-solving, flexibility and other forms of creativity aligned with personal wellbeing and graduate employability.[105] CUSF argued for and enacted a continued role of the arts throughout formal education beyond the largely primary school confine that visual arts and music have held in greater China. Indeed, some participants in the festival, such as Joseph Bosco—who led a team from Beijing Foreign Studies University to victory performing *Othello* in the finals—used the festival as evidence to refute the stereotypes, 'myths, slanders actually, spoken so often by Westerners about Chinese university students, that they are not creative' in spite of the region's 'rich literary and artistic heritage'.[106] The website frames this event, involving the secondary and tertiary education sectors, as a form of achievement contributing to 'artistic life in China'.[107] That is to say, it makes a case for secondary and tertiary education as bolstering the arts in greater China. Gleckman's introduction to the performances in the second festival foregrounds the opportunity it affords students 'to demonstrate their creativity and imagination which is something that school life does not always give you opportunity to express'. Creative approaches to Shakespeare were sometimes cast by him as the antidote to perceptions of his works as challenging for a young audience. Introducing the performances, Gleckman highlights the contribution of creativity to audience appreciation of the plays: the 'words of Shakespeare...were written four hundred years ago...They may be a little dusty, at times, but we know that our young performers will make those words shine and live for us today'.[108] His emceeing seeks to give creativity further legitimacy in a Chinese educational context by claiming it as a form of hard work. That, beyond the organisers, CUSF participants also saw a lack of opportunity for personal development and creativity as a problematic aspect of their education is evidenced by a quotation in Li Jun's work from former student Li Yuzhuo, working for the multinational bank HSBC when this book was written, who describes the way in which University of International Business and Economics '(UIBE) students are often labelled with "shallow" and "utilitarian"' says that CUSF allowed students (who were not English literature majors) 'opportunity to shake off such labels by learning and performing Shakespeare'.[109] That the lack of creativity in education is seen as an issue across greater China is apparent in existing research: although Lee's previous chapter demonstrated that creativity is present in Hong Kong English classes, Lemos and Lau Chi-Kuen have suggested that 'pedagogy and teacher training could be reviewed to introduce a more inclusive approach with more varied levels and types of achievement for children of different abilities, rather than so strongly favouring narrow attainment in exams'.[110]

The potential for creativity in education to contribute to graduate employability is suggested by a CUSF video segment that shows participants visiting Hong Kong's Avenue of Stars (akin to Hollywood's Walk of Fame), seeing the statues, autographs and handprints that commemorate the likes of Bruce Lee and Jackie Chan.[111] Additionally, the festival's finals were held in the Sir Run Run Shaw Hall on the CUHK campus: the auditorium honours the founder of one of Hong Kong's most notable film studios and educational philanthropists (Shaw Brothers). By tapping into the rich lineage of the internationally celebrated, Hong Kong film industry, the CUSF videos suggest that its participants are stars in the making, the next generation of artists in greater China. Creativity's contribution to graduate employability is also demonstrated by Li Jun, who taught some of the CUSF-participating UIBE students. His book provides some evidence of the positive impact of CUSF on students' careers in the performing arts. For example, Zheng Guo, one of Li's students, was a non-English major who won the first festival's best actor award in 2005 and has now 'become a fairly well-known actor with many fans due to his impressive roles in … commercial performances'.[112] This CUSF participant's graduate success in the creative industries may owe some debt to the fact that the festival criteria took into account prowess in theatrical skills beyond acting such as dramaturgy, lighting, set design, costumes, music and direction.[113] Judges such as Peter Holbrook praising performances that were 'inventively choreographed' and the award of a prize for the 'most original production' are further evidence that the creativity demanded in the criteria was actively assessed.[114] In summary, one form of personal development championed by the festival included building participants' empathy and other interpersonal competences across political, geographical, cultural and linguistic boundaries. Another focused on creativity as a competence likely to enhance graduate employability. CUSF is not an outlier in constructing working with Shakespeare as able to foster these. Rather it, knowingly or otherwise, built on organisers' existing experiences of teaching, and scholarship from, EFL.

3.6 Model Shakespeare in an English Language Learning Context?

This chapter demonstrates that Paran and Robinson's rationales for literature in the EFL classroom can be applied extramurally, to explore whether, and how, a Shakespeare festival rooted in performance is constructed as benefitting English language learners. I have shown that the CUSF organisers developed a festival that tackled at least three key approaches to using literature in English language learning. These are identified by Paran and Robinson: 1) 'as a body of knowledge and content'; 2) 'as language practice material' activating learners' language skills; and 3) 'as a stimulus for personal development'.[115] Analysing the CUSF participants' words and performances demonstrates that they internalised these tripartite approaches to the use of Shakespeare in English language learning, through the 'feedback loop'—terms used by CUSF organisers when talking to me—created by the public accessibility of previous years' videos and judges' feedback. CUSF offers but one possible model for extra-curricular activities using Shakespeare in an EFL educational context. Some constraints in its set-up identified in this chapter could be addressed by its successors. For instance, if 'Shakespeare belongs to whole world' (as former participant Sun Yu said), the diversity of experts involved in these activities needs to better reflect that. Additionally, CUSF chose not to include literary translation activities, either from Shakespearean English to other languages or to modern vernaculars (including World Englishes) as a valuable form of language learning experience, unlike a comparable student festival in India.[116] Such stances have a demonstrable knock-on effect on the dramaturgy of young theatre practitioners, including those staging Shakespeare in China. Chinese theatre professionals generally, cited by Li, describe being almost fearful of altering Shakespeare's texts: treating it 'gingerly' and 'not daring' to adapt or change any of his 'original words'.[117] This does not sound like the best soil from which to grow lively Shakespearean productions that will attract local audiences in the twenty-first century. It also risks falling out of step with the growing popularity and critical acclamation of Shakespeares beyond English from East Asia, seen in the touring work of companies such as Ninagawa Yukio's from Saitama and Yohangza's from Seoul, on the Asian Shakespeare Intercultural Archive and MIT

Global Shakespeares websites, and in the sonnet translation competitions organised by the British Council as part of its 2016 Shakespeare Lives! programme. Furthermore, there is support for such activities in resources for EFL teachers as well as from practitioners and researchers in literary translation in education (see organisations such as Translators in Schools and Shadow Heroes in the UK).[118] Limited feedback from judges, sponsors and former students suggests that CUSF was effective in fostering students' knowledge of English literature and culture, language skills, and personal development. However, a future study by a multilinguist might undertake research with former participants to look at their perceptions of CUSF's longitudinal efficacy or might analyse university and newspaper webpages in English, Cantonese and Mandarin covering the festival. The next two chapters include consideration of historical and current ways in which Japanese school and university curricula and practices have embraced, rejected, and hierarchised these approaches to Shakespeare.

Acknowledgements This research would not have been possible without research mobility funding awarded to me in 2016 by CUHK. The English department at CUHK supported my application and were generous in hosting me. In particular, I would like to thank the following members of staff and students (some now graduates) there: Jason Gleckman, Julian Lamb, Simon Haines, Carly Chan, and Reto Winkler. Proof that the CUSF objective of collaboration with other English departments is still thriving is that they introduced me to Li Jun (UIBE), whose kind gift of his book on popular Shakespeare in China was a pleasure to read, and Mike Ingham (Lingnan), who generously spent time talking with me about the festival and showing me round his campus. Others who made me feel welcome in Hong Kong and discussed my project with me there include Athena Tang, Sarah Lee, Antony Huen, Chris Leung and Jingjing. Sun Yu, a postdoctoral researcher at Xiamen, shared experiences of CUSF with me by email. The English department at City University of Hong Kong hosted me to present my work, and I have had further opportunity to do so at the British Shakespeare Association, Asian Shakespeare Association, and Othering Shakespeare conferences in 2016 (special thanks to Eleine Ng for her invitation to the latter). In 2019, Hirohisa Igarashi organised for me to present this work as part of my research fellowship at Toyo University. In my own institution, Zou Ying assisted me with some queries regarding languages on YouKu, and several heads of department facilitated my presenting this research by allowing me to travel during term time. Our PhD student Katie Smith was funded by a departmental small grant to assist with the final presentation of the chapter and did so with her usual enthusiasm and attention to detail.

NOTES

1. Also referred to as 'English as a Second Language' (ESL) and 'English as an Additional Language' (EAL). Through this chapter, I will use EFL as it is the term preferred by the researchers whose writing offers the framework for this chapter: Amos Paran and Pauline Robinson, *Literature* (Oxford: OUP, 2016).

2. They demonstrate some overlap here with Louise Rosenblatt's 'efferent reading' approach, which 'focuses on the public knowledge which a reader takes away from a text'. *The reader, the text, the poem: The transactional theory of the literary work* (Carbonale, IL: Southern Illinois University Press, 1994).

3. Again, they observe some similarity with Louise Rosenblatt: this time, her notion of 'aesthetic reading'. This centres on 'the personal, private engagement of the reader with the literature: the immersion in a [text] which we find personally engaging; the feeling that the world outside has disappeared while we are watching a play; the sense of sympathy or empathy we feel when reading a particularly apt [text]'. Paran and Robinson, *Literature*, 27.

4. Paran and Robinson, *Literature*, 27.

5. Paran and Robinson, *Literature*, 28.

6. Paran and Robinson, *Literature*, 28.

7. Paran and Robinson, *Literature*.

8. Daniela Anton and Julia Hammer, 'To Shakespeare or Not to Shakespeare with Beginners? An Extensive Reading Project on *Romeo and Juliet*', in *Shakespeare in the EFL Classroom*, edited by Maria Eisenmann and Christiane Lütge (Heidelberg: Universitätsverlag, Winter 2014), 257–278.

9. Paran and Robinson, *Literature*.

10. 'New' is a bit of a misnomer, it describes one of three regions of modern-day Hong Kong—the others are Hong Kong Island and Kowloon Peninsula. Located on the mainland of China, it was leased to the UK for 99 years in 1898.

11. Participating universities listed include: Beijing Foreign Studies, Beijing Language and Culture, Beijing Normal, Beijing Sport, Beijing Technology, Bohai, Capital Normal, Central China Normal, Central Finance and Economics, Geosciences, CUHK, Dalian Maritime, Dalian Technology, Donghua, East China Normal, Fudan, Guangdong Foreign Studies, Guangxi, Guizhou, Hainan, Harbin Institute of Technology, Harbin Normal, Hebei, Hei Longjiang International, Huazhong Agricultural, Huazhong Science and Technology, Hubei, Hunan, Inner Mongolia Normal, Inner Mongolia, Jinan, Jishou, Lingnan, Ludong, Macau Inter-University Institute, Macau Polytechnic Institute, Mizu,

Nanchang, Nanjing, Nankai, National University of Defense Tech-
nology, National Taiwan, Ningbo Institute of Technology, Northeast
Agricultural, Northeast Normal, Northeastern, Pearl River College,
Peking, Providence, Qujing Normal, Renmin, Shandong Institute of
Business and Technology, Shandong, Shanghai International Studies,
Shaanxi Normal, Shantou, Shenzen, Sichuan International Studies,
Sichuan Normal, Sichuan, Soochow China, Soochow Taiwan, South-
east, South China Normal, South-Central Nationalities, Southwest,
Sun Yat-Sen, City University of Hong Kong, HK Institute of Educa-
tion, HK Polytechnic, University of HK, Macau, Tianjin Foreign
Studies, Tianjin Commerce, Tianjin Finance and Economics, Tongji,
Tsinghua, Tunghai, International Business and Economics, Wuhan,
Xiamen, Xiamen Technology, Xinjiang, Yuan Ze, Yunnan, Zhejiang,
Zhejiang Gongshang, Zhongnan Economics and Law. 'The Festival',
CUSF, accessed May 26, 2016. http://www.eng.cuhk.edu.hk/shakes
peare/aboutus4_festival02.php.

12. This rule contrasts with some popular practices in English language
teaching and artistic celebrations of Shakespeare which do alter the
text, including by translation, from the Royal Shakespeare Company
to productions on the Asian Shakespeare Intercultural Archive, not to
mention Hong Kong's long history of popular and critically acclaimed
bilingual productions. Lau, *The Making of Hong Kong Shakespeare*, 8
and 30. Lau and Tso, *Teaching Shakespeare*.

13. 'Competitions', *CUSF*, accessed May 25, 2016, http://www.eng.cuhk.
edu.hk/shakespeare/aboutus1_competitions.php.

14. This compares with Yu Jin Ko's experience that 'hard-core English
majors usually form only a small minority of the membership' of
extracurricular drama productions. 'Women Who Will Make a Difference: Shakespeare at Wellesley College', in *Shakespeare on the University
Stage*, edited by A. J. Hartley (Cambridge: CUP, 2014), 63.

15. Practicalities aside, pedagogic support for working on a limited amount
of the play is conveyed in Ahrens and Hammer's argument that in
English language settings 'the aimed target should not be to cover the
whole play'. '*Evil is at the bloody heart of Shakespeare's tragedies:* Teaching
William Shakespeare's *Othello* through an interactive reading project', in
Shakespeare in the EFL Classroom, edited by Maria Eisenmann and Christiane Lütge (Heidelberg: Universitätsverlag Winter, 2014), 201–218.
200.

16. Haines introduces the feedback to the seventh festival thus: 'these reports
are meant to be helpful, and survey about encouraging and honest. It
will help the directors and actors of the participating teams directly. But
they can also indirectly help or teens and all universities who may be

considering entering teens in the future'. 'News', *CUSF*, accessed May 25, 2016, http://www.eng.cuhk.edu.hk/shakespeare/apply.php.

17. 'Chinese Universities Shakespeare Festival', *YouKu*, videos for the first and third festivals.

18. 'Chinese Universities Shakespeare Festival', *YouKu*, video for the second festival.

19. Dickson, *Worlds Elsewhere*, 428.

20. 'Chinese Universities Shakespeare Festival', *YouKu*, video of the fourth festival.

21. Paul Allen. *Colin George obituary*, *Guardian*, accessed February 26, 2019, https://www.theguardian.com/stage/2016/oct/31/colin-george-obituary.

22. 'Chinese Universities Shakespeare Festival', *YouKu*, video of the fourth festival.

23. Li mentions that two students' of Graves at Peking University, Hu Xiao-qing and Zhang Zheng, the Assistant Director and lead actor of that university's prize-winning production of *Henry V* in the first festival (2005), went on to study directing at the Central Academy of Drama (Beijing), before a professional career as a director and playwright, and produce and act in Beijing theatre respectively—including and beyond Shakespeare's works. *Popular Shakespeare*, 183.

24. Li describes the way in which with 'invitation and support from Cald-well', two CUSF participants Zhang Suzhi and Gaoya Xiaozi from a Chongqing university of foreign languages took their production of *Hamlet* from the fourth festival to the Texas Shakespeare Festival he directed 'as the first Chinese troupe ever invited'. They formed the group Guangrong zhi xia (Summer of Glory) and took three further productions to Texas. Jun argues that CUSF 'provided a precious opportunity for these two talented young dramatists to set off on a fantastic journey'. *Popular Shakespeare*, 182. 'Chinese Universities Shakespeare Festival', *YouKu*, video of the fourth festival.

25. Haines introduces the feedback to the seventh festival thus: 'these reports are meant to be helpful, and survey about encouraging and honest. It will help the directors and actors of the participating teams directly. But they can also indirectly help or teens and all universities who may be considering entering teens in the future'. 'News', *CUSF*.

26. I could write 'People's Republic of China' instead, but 'mainland China' is the English language term I found most used in Hong Kong, perhaps because it differentiates Hong Kong as a Special Administrative Region from the rest of the country.

27. Excellent accounts of this include Zhang Y.F. and Hu G.W., 'Between intended and enacted curricula: Three teachers and a mandated curricular reform in mainland China', in *Negotiating Language Policies in Schools:*

94   S. OLIVE

Educators as Policymakers, edited by K. Menken and O. García (New York: Routledge, 2010), 123–142. Hu G. and S.L. McKay, 'English Language Education in East Asia: Some Recent Developments', Journal of Multilingual and Multicultural Development, 33.4 (2012): 345–362.

28. Michael Ingham, Hong Kong: A Cultural History (Oxford: OUP 2007), xviii.

29. Lau Leung Che Miriam, 'A Fusion of Small and Big Times: Chinese Shakespeares in the Universities Shakespeares Festival', Shakespeare Review, 12 (2014): 881–893. 881.

30. Ingham, Hong Kong, xviii.

31. Bob Adamson and Li Siu Pang Titus, 'Primary and Secondary Schooling'. In Education and Society in Hong Kong and Macau: Comparative Perspectives on Continuity and Change, edited by Mark Bray and Ramsey Koo (Second edition. Hong Kong: Kluwer, 2004), 39.

32. Andrew Dickson, Worlds Elsewhere: Journeys Around Shakespeare's Globe (New York: Henry Holt, 2016), 424.

33. Adamson and Pang, 'Primary and Secondary Schooling', 58.

34. Vaudine England, 'HK Marchers Demand More English', BBC News, accessed May 26, 2016. http://news.bbc.co.uk/1/hi/world/asia-pacific/6716095.stm.

35. Ingham, Hong Kong; Lau, The Making of Hong Kong Shakespeare; Adele Lee, 'One Husband Too Many and the Problem of Postcolonial Hong Kong', in Shakespeare in Hollywood, Asia and Cyberspace, edited by Alexa Alice Joubin and Charles Ross (Indiana: Purdue University Press, 2009), 159–204.

36. Dillon, Contemporary China (Abingdon: Routledge, 2009), 72, 204 and 212.

37. Tsuneyoshi Ryoko (ed). Globalization and Japanese "Exceptionalism" in Education: Insiders' Views into a Changing System (London: Routledge, 2018), 19. Maria Eisenmann and Christiane Lütge, eds., Shakespeare in the EFL Classroom (Heidelberg: Universitätsverlag Winter, 2014), 225 and 228. Philippe Van Parijs, Just Democracy: The Rawls-Machiavelli Programme (ECPR Essays Series, 2011). Andy Kirkpatrick, 'English as an Asian lingua franca and the multilingual model of ELT', Language Teaching 44.2 (2011): 212–224. David Graddol, 'The Future of Language', Science, 303.5662 (2004): 1329–1331. Lanvers, 'Language Learning Motivation', 1–25.

38. Yong Li Lan and Lee Chee Keng, 'Ideology in Student Performances in China', in Shakespeare on the University Stage, edited by A.J. Hartley (Cambridge: CUP, 2014), 101. Li Jun, Popular Shakespeare in China: 1993–2008 (Beijing: University of International Business and Economics, 2016), 38, 144–145 and 150–151. Tam Kwok-kan, Andrew Parkin and Terry Siu-han Yip, eds. Shakespeare Global/Local: The Hong

Kong Imaginary in Transcultural Production (New York: Peter Lang, 2002).
39. Dickson, *Worlds Elsewhere.* Lau Leung Che Miriam, 'A Fusion of Small and Big Times', 881–893. Jason Gleckman, 'Shakespeare Performance in Hong Kong: The Chinese Universities Shakespeare Festival', *Shakespeare Review* 46.4 (December 2010): 917–923. Danni Dai, 'To Achieve the Largest Effect Through Multi-Sympathies—My Personal Comments on Directing of *Hamlet* for the 4th Chinese Universities Shakespeare Festival', *Shakespeare Review* 46.2 (June 2010), 351–363. Li, *Popular Shakespeare in China.*
40. Andrew J. Hartley, *Shakespeare on the University Stage* (Cambridge: CUP, 2014), 7. Kevin Wetmore, Siyuan Liu and Erin Mee, *Modern Asian Theatre and Performance, 1900–2000* (London: Bloomsbury, 1999).
41. Paran and Robinson, *Literature*, 27.
42. Chinese Universities Shakespeare Festival', *YouKu*, video of the fourth festival.
43. Chinese Universities Shakespeare Festival', *YouKu*, video of the third festival. 'Mission,' *CUSF*, accessed May 25, 2016, http://www.eng.cuhk.edu.hk/shakespeare/aboutus2_mission.php.
44. Mark Pilkinton, 'Performance, Religion, and Shakespeare: Staging Ideology at Notre Dame', in *Shakespeare on the University Stage*, edited by A.J. Hartley (Cambridge: CUP, 2014), 42. Anton and Hammer, 'To Shakespeare or Not to Shakespeare with Beginners?', 210–211.
45. Chinese Universities Shakespeare Festival', *YouKu*, video of the eight festival.
46. The productions of the festival included, in order of most to least frequently performed, *Twelfth Night* (19); *Macbeth* (14); *Othello, Lear, Tempest, Romeo and Juliet* (8 each); *Shrew* (6); *A Midsummer Night's Dream, Hamlet* (5 each); *As You Like It, Measure for Measure* (4 each); *Henry V, Two Gentleman of Verona, Merchant of Venice* (3 each); *Winter's Tale, Richard III, Much Ado About Nothing, Merry Wives of Windsor* (3 each). The following were performed only once each: *Troilus and Cressida, Love's Labour's Lost, Julius Caesar, Henry VIII, Comedy of Errors, Henry IV, Henry VI part III, Anthony and Cleopatra, All's Well That Ends Well, Pericles, Coriolanus, Two Noble Kinsmen, Cymbeline.*
47. 'Remarks', *CUSF*, accessed May 25, 2016, http://www.eng.cuhk.edu.hk/shakespeare/public.php?festival=8. Resources for teaching these concepts and theories to EFL students using Shakespeare exist in Lau and Tso, *Teaching Shakespeare to ESL Students* (Singapore: Springer 2016); Eisenmann and Lütge, *Shakespeare in the EFL Classroom*, and the British Shakespeare Association's *Teaching Shakespeare* e.g. Smyth, 'Creative Monologues', *Teaching Shakespeare*, 1 (2012): 10–11. vi.

96   S. OLIVE

48. Chinese Universities Shakespeare Festival', *YouKu*, video of the tenth festival.
49. 'Remarks', *CUSF*.
50. Chinese Universities Shakespeare Festival', *YouKu*, video of the eighth festival.
51. Chinese Universities Shakespeare Festival', *YouKu*, video of the seventh festival.
52. Chinese Universities Shakespeare Festival', *YouKu*, video of the ninth festival.
53. Chinese Universities Shakespeare Festival', *YouKu*, video of the third and ninth festivals.
54. Chinese Universities Shakespeare Festival', *YouKu*, video of the ninth festival. Li, *Popular Shakespeare*, 154.
55. 'History', *CUSF*, accessed May 25, 2016, http://www.eng.cuhk.edu.hk/shakespeare/aboutus1_history.php.
56. 'The Festival', *CUSF*.
57. Chinese Universities Shakespeare Festival', *YouKu*, video of the ninth festival.
58. Chinese Universities Shakespeare Festival', *YouKu*, video of the sixth festival.
59. Chinese Universities Shakespeare Festival', *YouKu*, video of the first festival.
60. Chinese Universities Shakespeare Festival', *YouKu*, video of the tenth festival.
61. Chinese Universities Shakespeare Festival', *YouKu*, videos of the eighth and ninth festivals.
62. Sarah Olive, 'Outside interference or Hong Kong embracing its unique identity? The Chinese Universities Shakespeare Festival', *Palgrave Communications*, 5 (2019).
63. Anton and Hammer, 'To Shakespeare or not to Shakespeare with Beginners?', 259. Ahrens and Hammer, '*Evil Is at the Bloody Heart of Shakespeare's Tragedies*, 201 and 210. Richard Day and Julian Bamford, *Extensive Reading in the Second Language Classroom* (Cambridge: CUP, 1998), 28. Harmut Egert and Christine Gabe, *Literarische Sozialisation* (Stuttgart: Metzler, 2003), 1. Lütge, 'Determined to Prove a Villain?, in *Shakespeare in the EFL Classroom*, edited by Maria Eisenmann and Christiane Lütge (Heidelberg: Universitätsverlag Winter, 2014), 305. Göran Nieragden, 'People *WILL* Talk! *Much Ado About Nothing* in Grade Ten', in *Shakespeare in the EFL Classroom*, edited by Maria Eisenmann and Christiane Lütge (Heidelberg: Universitätsverlag Winter, 2014), 293. Laurenz Volkmann, 'Developing Symbolic Competence Through Shakespeare's *Sonnets*', in *Shakespeare in the EFL Classroom*, edited by

Maria Eisenmann and Christiane Lütge (Heidelberg: Universitätsverlag Winter, 2014), 15. Also Sun Yu, email to author, August 1, 2017.

64. Janice Bland, 'Slipping Back in Time: *King of Shadows* as Play Script', in *Shakespeare in the EFL Classroom*, edited by Maria Eisenmann and Christiane Lütge (Heidelberg: Universitätsverlag Winter, 2014), 332. Michèle Anstey and Geoff Bull, 'Developing New Literacies: Responding to Picturebooks in Multiliterate Ways', in *Talking Beyond the Page: Reading and Responding to Picturebooks*, edited by Janet Evans (London: Routledge, 2009), 28. Anike Bauer and Carola Surkamp, 'Shakespeare in Film, Filming Shakespeare', in *Shakespeare in the EFL Classroom*, edited by Maria Eisenmann and Christiane Lütge (Heidelberg: Universitätsverlag Winter, 2014), 109–128. 110. Eisenmann and Lütge, *Shakespeare in the EFL Classroom*, 226.

65. Lau and Tso, *Teaching Shakespeare*. Eisenmann and Lütge, *Shakespeare in the EFL Classroom*. Genevieve White, 'We Shouldn't Teach Shakespeare to Learners of English? False', accessed April 23, 2016, https://www.britishcouncil.org/voices-magazine/we-shouldnt-teach-shakespeare-to-english-learners-false. Christina Lima, 'Teaching Shakespeare to International Students', *Teaching Shakespeare*, 14 (2017): 5–7. Kevin Bergman, 'A Boys' Drama Club Performs *Romeo and Juliet*', *Teaching Shakespeare*, 6 (Autumn 2014): 14.

66. Chinese Universities Shakespeare Festival', *YouKu*, video of the seventh festival.

67. 'Competitions', *CUSF.*

68. Chinese Universities Shakespeare Festival', *YouKu*, video of the eighth festival.

69. For more on the use of plot summaries with EFL learners see Nieragden, 'People *WILL* Talk!', 287.

70. See also Lau and Tso, *Teaching Shakespeare*, and Ahrens and Hammer, '*Evil Is at the Bloody Heart of Shakespeare's Tragedies*', 210.

71. Chinese Universities Shakespeare Festival', *YouKu*, video of the eighth festival.

72. 'Mission', *CUSF*, accessed May 25, 2016. http://www.eng.cuhk.edu.hk/shakespeare/aboutus2_mission.php.

73. 'Competitions', *CUSF.*

74. 'Remarks', *CUSF.*

75. Dickson, *Worlds Elsewhere*, 429–430.

76. Chinese Universities Shakespeare Festival', *YouKu*, video of the fifth festival.

77. Chinese Universities Shakespeare Festival', *YouKu*, video of the seventh festival.

78. Adamson and Pang, 'Primary and Secondary Schooling', 59.

79. Paran and Robinson, *Literature*, 18 and 30.

80. 'Remarks', *CUSF*.
81. Dickson, *Worlds Elsewhere*, 428.
82. Dickson, *Worlds Elsewhere*, 429–430.
83. 'The Festival', *CUSF*.
84. Chinese Universities Shakespeare Festival', *YouKu*, video of the eighth festival.
85. 'News', *CUSF*.
86. See also Olive, 'Outside Interference?'
87. Paran and Robinson, *Literature*, 27.
88. Anton and Hammer, 'To Shakespeare or Not to Shakespeare with Beginners?', 259. Nieragden 'People *WILL* Talk!', 280. Bland, 'Slipping Back in Time', 331.
89. Ingham, *Hong Kong*, xx.
90. Chinese Universities Shakespeare Festival', *YouKu*, video of the fourth festival.
91. Chinese Universities Shakespeare Festival', *YouKu*, video of the second festival.
92. Hartley, *Shakespeare on the University Stage*, 5.
93. Paran and Robinson, *Literature*, 30.
94. Chinese Universities Shakespeare Festival', *YouKu*, video of the seventh festival.
95. Bland, 'Slipping Back in Time', 332.
96. Earl Stevick, *Teaching Language: A Way and Ways* (Rowley: Newbury House, 1980), 4.
97. Nieragden, 'People *WILL* Talk!', 293. Bland, 'Slipping back in time', 332.
98. 'Mission,' *CUSF*.
99. 'Mission', *CUSF*.
100. Anton and Hammer, 'To Shakespeare or Not to Shakespeare with Beginners?', 258.
101. Dillon, *Contemporary China*, 101. Li, *Popular Shakespeare*, 159. Gerard Lemos, *The End of the Chinese Dream: why Chinese people fear the future* (London: Yale UP, 2012) 265.
102. To take just one example from mainland China, 'Attempts are still made to restrict the sale of satellite dishes that are capable of receiving broadcasts from Hong Kong'. Dillon, *Contemporary China*, 100.
103. Su Xinqi, 'Why the Campus Feud Between Hong Kong and Mainland Chinese Students?', *South China Morning Post*, accessed April 10, 2019, https://www.scmp.com/news/hong-kong/education-community/article/2112609/why-campus-feud-between-hong-kong-and-mainland.
104. Olive, 'Outside Interference?'
105. Bland, 'Slipping Back in Time', 334.

106. Joseph Bosco, 'Creative Chinese Students Reveal Shakespeare's Depth', *Global Times*, 26 April 2009. Accessed 12 April 2019. http://www.globaltimes.cn/content/427989.shtml and Xu Xi introducing Ingham, *Hong Kong*, xviii.
107. Commentators have argued that in greater China, after primary education, there is a tendency for arts activities to be viewed as hobbies, popular extra-curricular activities, rather than academic or vocational subjects. Lau, *Hong Kong's Colonial Legacy*. Chinese Universities Shakespeare Festival', *YouKu*, video of the fourth festival. 'Mission', *CUSF*.
108. 'Chinese Universities Shakespeare Festival', *YouKu*, video of the sixth festival.
109. Li, *Popular Shakespeare in China*, 154–159.
110. Lemos, *The End of the Chinese Dream*, 212. Lau Chi-kuen, *Hong Kong's Colonial Legacy* (Hong Kong: Chinese University Press, 1997).
111. Chinese Universities Shakespeare Festival', *YouKu*, video of the first festival.
112. Li, *Popular Shakespeare in China*, 183.
113. 'Competitions', *CUSF*.
114. 'Remarks', *CUSF*.
115. Paran NS Robinson, *Literature*, 27.
116. Multani, 'Appropriating Shakespeare on campus: an Indian perspective' in *Shakespeare on the University Stage*, edited by A.J. Hartley (Cambridge: CUP, 2014), 75–89.
117. Li, *Popular Shakespeare*, 125 and 132.
118. Lau and Tso, *Teaching Shakespeare*. Edith Grossman, *Why Translation Matters* (New Haven and London: Yale University Press, 2010). Sam Holmes, 'Promoting Multilingual creativity: key principles from successful projects', *Working papers in urban language and literacies*, accessed April 11, 2019, https://kcl.academia.edu/WorkingPapersinUrbanLanguageLiteracies. Ulrike Nichols, 'Translators in Schools', *In Other Words*, 44 (2014), 18. Lawrence Venuti, *The Scandals of Translation: Towards an Ethics of Difference* (London: Routledge, 1998), 93.

References

Adamson, Bob and Li Siu Pang Titus, 'Primary and Secondary Schooling'. In *Education and Society in Hong Kong and Macau: Comparative Perspectives on Continuity and Change*, edited by Mark Bray and Ramsey Koo. Second edition. Hong Kong: Kluwer, 2004. 35–60.
Ahrens, Rüdiger and Julia Hammer. '*Evil Is at the Bloody Heart of Shakespeare's Tragedies:* Teaching William Shakespeare's *Othello* Through an Interactive

Reading Project'. In *Shakespeare in the EFL Classroom*, edited by Maria Eisenmann and Christiane Lütge. Heidelberg: Universitätsverlag Winter, 2014. 201–218.

Allen, Paul. 2016. 'Colin George Obituary.' *Guardian*. https://www.thegua rdian.com/stage/2016/oct/31/colin-george-obituary. Accessed February 26, 2019.

Anstey, Michèle and Geoff Bull. 'Developing New Literacies: Responding to Picturebooks in Multiliterate Ways'. In *Talking Beyond the Page: Reading and Responding to Picturebooks*, edited by Janet Evans. London: Routledge, 2009. 26–43

Anton, Daniela and Julia Hammer. 'To Shakespeare or Not to Shakespeare with Beginners? An Extensive Reading Project on *Romeo and Juliet*'. In *Shakespeare in the EFL Classroom*, edited by Maria Eisenmann and Christiane Lütge. Heidelberg: Universitätsverlag Winter, 2014. 257–278.

Asian Shakespeare Intercultural Archive (A|S|I|A). Accessed November 28, 2018. http://a-s-i-a-web.org/en/home.php.

Bauer, Anike and Carola Surkamp. 'Shakespeare in Film, Filming Shakespeare: Different versions of *Hamlet* in the EFL classroom'. In *Shakespeare in the EFL Classroom*, edited by Maria Eisenmann and Christiane Lütge. Heidelberg: Universitätsverlag Winter, 2014. 109–128.

Bergman, Kevin. 'A Boys' Drama Club Performs *Romeo and Juliet*.' *Teaching Shakespeare* 6 (Autumn 2014): 14.

Bland, Janice. 'Slipping Back in Time: *King of Shadows* as Play Script'. In *Shakespeare in the EFL Classroom*, edited by Maria Eisenmann and Christiane Lütge. Heidelberg: Universitätsverlag Winter, 2014. 331–346

Bosco, Joseph. 'Creative Chinese Students Rreveal Shakespeare's Depth'. *Global Times*. 26 April 2009. Accessed 12 April 2019. http://www.globaltimes.cn/content/427989.shtml.

'Competitions'. *CUSF*. Accessed May 25, 2016. http://www.eng.cuhk.edu.hk/shakespeare/aboutus1_competitions.php.

Dai, Danni. 'To Achieve the Largest Effect Through Multi-Sympathies—My Personal Comments on Directing of *Hamlet* for the 4th Chinese Universities Shakespeare Festival'. *Shakespeare Review* 46.2 (June 2010): 351–363.

Dickson, Andrew. *Worlds Elsewhere: Journeys Around Shakespeare's Globe*. New York: Henry Holt, 2016.

Dillon, Michael. *Contemporary China: An Introduction*. Abingdon: Routledge, 2009.

Eisenmann, Maria and Christiane Lütge, eds. *Shakespeare in the EFL Classroom*. Heidelberg: Universitätsverlag Winter, 2014.

Egert, Harmut and Christine Gabe. *Literarische Sozialisation*. Stuttgart: Metzler, 2003.

England, Vaudine. 'HK Marchers Demand More English'. *BBC News*. Accessed May 26, 2016. http://news.bbc.co.uk/1/hi/world/asia-pacific/6716095.stm.

'The Festival'. *CUSF*. Accessed May 26, 2016. http://www.eng.cuhk.edu.hk/shakespeare/aboutus4_festival02.php.

Gleckman, Jason. 'Shakespeare Performance in Hong Kong: The Chinese Universities Shakespeare Festival'. *Shakespeare Review* 46.4 (December 2010): 917–923.

Graddol, David. 'The Future of Language'. *Science* 303.5662 (2004): 1329–1331.

Grossman, Edith. *Why Translation Matters*. New Haven and London: Yale University Press, 2010.

Hartley, A.J. ed. *Shakespeare on the University Stage*. Cambridge: CUP, 2014.

'History'. *CUSF*. Accessed May 25, 2016. http://www.eng.cuhk.edu.hk/shakespeare/aboutus1_history.php.

Holmes, Sam. 'Promoting Multilingual Creativity: Key Principles from Successful Projects'. Working Papers in Urban Language and Literacies. Accessed April 11, 2019, https://kcl.academia.edu/WorkingPapersinUrbanLanguageLiteracies.

Hu, G. and S.L. McKay, 'English Language Education in East Asia: Some Recent Developments'. *Journal of Multilingual and Multicultural Development* 33.4 (2012): 345–362.

Ingham, Michael. *Hong Kong: A Cultural History*. Oxford: OUP, 2007.

Kirkpatrick, Andy. 'English as an Asian Lingua Franca and the Multilingual Model of ELT'. *Language Teaching* 44.2 (2011): 212–224.

Ko, Yu Jin. 'Women Who Will Make a Difference: Shakespeare at Wellesley College'. In *Shakespeare on the University Stage*, edited by A. J. Hartley. Cambridge: CUP, 2014. 60–74.

Lanvers, Ursula. 'Language Learning Motivation, Global English and Study Modes: a Comparative Study'. *Language Learning Journal* (October 2013): 1–25.

Lau, Chi-kuen. *Hong Kong's Colonial Legacy*. Hong Kong: Chinese University Press, 1997.

Lau, Leung Che Miriam. 'A Fusion of Small and Big Times: Chinese Shakespeares in the Universities Shakespeare Festival'. *Shakespeare Review* 12 (2014): 881–893.

Lau, Leung Che Miriam. *The Making of Hong Kong Shakespeare: Post-1997 Adaptations and Appropriations*. PhD dissertation. Shakespeare Institute, University of Birmingham. 2018.

Lau, Leung Che Miriam and Wing Bo Tso Anna, eds. *Teaching Shakespeare to ESL Students*. Singapore: Springer, 2016.

Lee, Adele. 'One Husband Too Many and the Problem of Postcolonial Hong Kong'. In *Shakespeare in Hollywood, Asia and Cyberspace*, edited by Alexa Alice Joubin and Charles Ross. Indiana: Purdue University Press, 2009. 159–204.

Lee, Adele. 'Shakespeare and the Educational Reforms in Hong Kong'. Accessed November 10, 2016. http://blogs.gre.ac.uk/shakespeareinhongkong/2013/02/26/shakespeare-and-the-educational-reforms-in-hong-kong.

Lee, Adele. 'Shakespeare in Hong Kong: About the Project'. Accessed November 10, 2016, http://blogs.gre.ac.uk/shakespeareinhongkong/.

Lee, Adele. 'How Do You Solve a Problem Like China?: "Global Shakespeare" and the Limitations of the "Cosmopolitan Model"'. Paper presented at the 'Rethinking the Global' Seminar of the Shakespeare Association of America Annual Meeting, Los Angeles, CA, April 2018.

Lemos, Gerard. *The End of the Chinese Dream: Why Chinese People Fear the Future*. London: Yale UP, 2012.

Li, Jun. *Popular Shakespeare in China: 1993–2008*. Beijing: University of International Business and Economics, 2016.

Lima, Christina. 'Teaching Shakespeare to International Students'. *Teaching Shakespeare* 14 (2017): 5–7.

Lütge, Christiana. 'Determined to Prove a Villain?—Approaches to Teaching Richard III'. In *Shakespeare in the EFL Classroom*, edited by Maria Eisenmann and Christiane Lütge. Heidelberg: Universitätsverlag Winter, 2014. 297–314.

'Mission'. *CUSF*. Accessed May 25, 2016. http://www.eng.cuhk.edu.hk/shakespeare/aboutus2_mission.php.

Multani, Angelie. 'Appropriating Shakespeare on Campus: An Indian Perspective'. In *Shakespeare on the University Stage*, A.J. Hartley. Cambridge: CUP, 2014. 75–89.

'News'. *CUSF*. Accessed May 25, 2016. http://www.eng.cuhk.edu.hk/shakespeare/apply.php.

Nichols, Ulrike. 'Translators in Schools'. *Other Words* 44 (2014): 16–18.

Nieragden, Göran. 'People WILL Talk! *Much Ado About Nothing* in Grade Ten'. In *Shakespeare in the EFL Classroom*, edited by Maria Eisenmann and Christiane Lütge. Heidelberg: Universitätsverlag Winter, 2014. 279–296.

Olive, Sarah. 'Outside Interference or Hong Kong Embracing Its Unique Identity? The Chinese Universities Shakespeare Festival'. *Palgrave Communications*. Accessed 2 March 2020. https://doi.org/10.1057/s41599-019-0327-5.

Paran, Amos and Pauline Robinson. *Literature*. Oxford: OUP, 2016.

Parijs, Philippe Van. *Just Democracy: The Rawls-Machiavelli Programme*. ECPR Essays Series, 2011.

Pilkinton, Mark. 'Performance, Religion, and Shakespeare: Staging Ideology at Notre Dame'. In *Shakespeare on the University Stage*, edited by A.J. Hartley. Cambridge: CUP, 2014. 27–42.

'Remarks'. CUSF. Accessed May 25, 2016. http://www.eng.cuhk.edu.hk/sha kespeare/public.php?festival=8

Rosenblatt, Louise. *The Reader, the Text, the Poem: The Transactional Theory of the Literary Work*. Carbonale, IL: Southern Illinois University Press, 1994.

Smyth, Stella. 'Creative Monologues'. *Teaching Shakespeare* 1 (2012): 10–11.

Stevick, Earl. *Teaching Language: A Way and Ways*. Rowley: Newbury House, 1980.

Tam, Kwok-kan Andrew Parkin and Terry Siu-han Yip, eds. *Shakespeare Global/Local: The Hong Kong Imaginary in Transcultural Production*. New York: Peter Lang, 2002.

Tsuneyoshi, Ryoko, ed. *Globalization and Japanese "Exceptionalism" in Education: Insiders' Views into a Changing System* (London: Routledge, 2018).

Venuti, Lawrence. *The Scandals of Translation: Towards an Ethics of Difference*. London: Routledge, 1998.

Volkmann, Laurenz. 'Developing Symbolic Competence Through Shakespeare's Sonnets'. In *Shakespeare in the EFL Classroom*, edited by Maria Eisenmann and Christiane Lütge. Heidelberg: Universitätsverlag Winter, 2014. 15–34.

Wetmore, Kevin, Siyuan Liu and Erin Mee. *Modern Asian Theatre and Performance, 1900–2000*. London: Bloomsbury, 1999.

White, Genevieve. 'We Shouldn't Teach Shakespeare to Learners of English? False'. Accessed April 23, 2016. https://www.britishcouncil.org/voices-mag azine/we-shouldnt-teach-shakespeare-to-english-learners-false.

Xinqi, Su. 'Why the Campus Feud Between Hong Kong and Mainland Chinese Students?' *South China Morning Post*. Accessed April 10, 2019. https://www.scmp.com/news/hong-kong/education-community/art icle/2112609/why-campus-feud-between-hong-kong-and-mainland.

Yong, Li Lan and Lee Chee Keng. 'Ideology in Student Performances in China'. In *Shakespeare on the University Stage*, edited by A.J. Hartley. Cambridge: CUP, 2014. 90–109.

Zhang, Y.F. and G.W. Hu, 'Between Intended and Enacted Curricula: Three Teachers and a Mandated Curricular Reform in Mainland China'. In *Negotiating Language Policies in Schools: Educators as Policymakers*, edited by K. Menken and O. García. New York: Routledge, 2010. 123–142.

CHAPTER 4

Teaching and Studying Shakespeare in Higher Education in Early Twentieth-Century Japan

Kohei Uchimaru

Abstract This chapter considers how teaching and studying Shakespeare evolved in higher education institutions in early twentieth century Japan. The first section demonstrates that Shakespeare was deeply incorporated and institutionalised within the English-language curriculum in order to reveal how powerful Shakespeare's presence was in early twenty-century classrooms in contrast to that in classrooms today. The next section examines how early professors of Shakespeare at the Imperial University of Tokyo, with their increasingly more specialist concerns, sought to make Shakespeare studies academic based on philological and literary-historical research. Their attempts to confine Shakespeare to a small corner of specialism, however, were questioned by the likes of Okakura Yohisaburô, who preferred equation pedagogy to explore the possibilities of literary studies as liberal education and to take local initiative in interpreting Shakespeare's plays.

K. Uchimaru (✉)
Osaka City University, Osaka, Japan

Keywords Shakespeare · Japan · Higher education · English · Okakura
Yoshisaburō · Curriculum

Shakespeare has been marginalised in Japanese higher education, largely
due to competition from career-oriented education. However, this was
not the case in the early twentieth century. Faced with Western pressure for trading ports, Japan reopened its doors to the world in 1868,
when the emperor decreed a restoration of imperial power to spear-
head modernisation and accepted the challenge to undertake monumental
reforms and adaptations in a struggle against perceived Western imperialism. English language acquisition was enlisted in the national project
of absorbing Western civilisation at a time when the British Empire was
encompassing the world. Amongst others, English literature was deemed
useful as material for the study of English because Stopford Augustus
Brooke's idea had taken hold in Japan that English literature was 'the
written thoughts and feelings of intelligent men and women'.[1]

In this climate, Shakespeare was vaulted to the forefront of Japanese
intellectual life, in the sense that the playwright was deeply ingrained
in English-speaking culture.[2] Regrettably, the way in which Shakespeare
was disseminated across the landscape of Japanese higher education in
the early twentieth century has not been fully documented. This chapter
seeks to remedy that oversight by exploring the under-researched early
formation of Shakespeare's curricular identity and by offering hitherto-
neglected instances of teaching and studying Shakespeare in higher
education between 1873 and 1945, the period when Shakespeare entered
Japanese higher education institutions and Japan surrendered to the Allies
in World War II.

The discussion is roughly divided into three parts. The first section
demonstrates how Shakespeare was institutionalised in higher education
during the time period. The next section gives a brief overview of the
germinal stage of teaching and studying Shakespeare by focusing on the
Imperial University of Tokyo, and then traces the ways in which scholars
sought to establish Shakespeare as a discipline. The merits of such an
academic specialisation, however, were questioned by the likes of Okakura
Yoshisaburō (1868–1936), the doyen of English language education in
early twentieth-century Japan. He served as head of the English department at Tokyo Higher Normal School, a principal teacher training, higher

education institution. The following section discusses how Okakura sought to square his beliefs and ideology with the teaching of Shakespeare by concentrating on his equation pedagogy. In so doing, this chapter attempts to unveil that teaching and studying Shakespeare in Japanese higher education was not conducted in an entirely straightforward or unilateral fashion.

4.1   INSTITUTIONALISING SHAKESPEARE

In order to precisely understand Shakespeare in Japanese higher education, it is imperative to offer a brief picture of the Japanese educational system in the late nineteenth and early twentieth centuries. In seeking to construct the Japanese educational system, the first National Plan for Education (*gakusei*), established in 1872, created a primary school, secondary school, and university system on a national basis.[3] Though school years more or less varied several times between 1872 and 1945, those who advanced to secondary schools from eighth-year (in 1881), and later sixth-year (since 1892), primary schools generally spent five years in middle schools (for boys), girls' high schools, normal schools (for prospective primary-school teachers), and (lower) technical schools. Those schools were attended by those aged approximately 12–17 years.

In the first three decades of the twentieth century, only 34% of middle-school students across the country advanced to higher education institutions: three-year higher schools or higher technical schools; four-year higher normal schools (for aspiring secondary-school teachers); and two- or three-year university preparatory courses attached to individual universities.[4] Those channels of post-secondary education, albeit not graced with the title of 'university', bore their fair share of the burden of higher education in early twentieth-century Japan. Most of those institutions were indeed transformed into universities in the 1920s, as exemplified by the promotion of Tokyo Higher Normal School to Tokyo University of Literature and Science in 1929.[5]

Prominently figuring amongst those institutions were higher schools that served to provide elite male students with a foundation to help them make the transition between secondary school and imperial university. Their graduates were automatically qualified to enter imperial universities, the zenith of Japanese higher education institutions. The curriculum primarily focused on the study of foreign languages not least because the school needed to prepare the students for admission to imperial universities in which they were expected to study through foreign books. The teaching of foreign languages was designed to 'precisely understand the features of the culture, life, and character of foreign countries, and then to cultivate wholesome thought, taste, and feeling, as well as to contribute to scholarship'.[6] The study of English in higher schools was thus intended not only to simply foster knowledge of the English language but also to serve as a cultural and literary subject considered necessary to foster the intellectual, cultural, and moral competencies expected of well-educated elites.

At the apex of Japanese higher education were imperial universities, which offered approximately three-year undergraduate courses along with two-year postgraduate courses, including the department of English Literature. Those imperial universities were attended by those aged approximately 19–22.[7] The faculty of English language and literature in those higher education institutions has been the local habitat of Shakespeare studies since the playwright's works entered the first Japanese university-level institution in the last quarter of the nineteenth century. Japan had no official bodies that prescribed a list of literary texts for the higher education curriculum and entrance examinations, but, as higher education institutions grew and became administratively standardised, there were occasions when educators indicated a set of literary textbooks, including Shakespeare's plays, for classroom use and teacher qualifying examinations. This contributed more or less to the institutionalisation of Shakespeare in higher education.

The works on which professors delivered lectures are succinctly indicated by an eminent Japanese magazine devoted to the study of English language and literature, *Eigo seinen* (*The Rising Generation*), which is probably the best contemporary source of information pertaining to English studies in Japan. This magazine listed lectures in the department of English literature at Japanese universities for 30 years from 1914 to 1944.[8] Those lists demonstrate that the most popular Shakespearean title amongst professors during the time period was *Macbeth* (27 lectures), which was followed by *Hamlet* (26), *The Tempest* (19), *Othello* (16), *King Lear* (15), *The Merchant of Venice* (15), *A Midsummer Night's Dream* (11), *Julius Caesar* (9), *Romeo and Juliet* (8), *Henry IV* (7), *Sonnets* (7), *Antony and Cleopatra* (6), *As You Like It* (6), *The Winter's Tale* (5), *Twelfth Night* (3), *King John* (2), *Cymbeline* (2), *Richard III* (1), *Coriolanus* (1), and *Timon of Athens* (1). The popularity of *Macbeth* makes sense given that the play is the shortest of all Shakespearean works, and is thus pedagogically most practicable for classroom use. The proportionally much larger numbers of *Macbeth*, *Hamlet*, *King Lear*, and *Othello* would reflect the influence of A.C. Bradley's 1904 highly regarded book, *Shakespearean Tragedy*, which often appeared as an assigned textbook until the 1930s.

English teaching at non-English major universities was another channel that helped to establish Shakespeare as a canon in higher education; extracts of the plays and the Lambs' prose versions were used as material for English teaching at schools, such as Kyoto College of Technology, Tokyo University of Commerce, and Shinto-oriented Jingu Kōgakkan. Research behind this study shows that *Eigo seinen* featured the lists of English textbooks used in approximately 60 universities, higher schools, higher normal schools, technical schools, and military academies (other departments of the same institutions are included) between 1920 and 1921, where teachers at 24 schools (32 classes) used Shakespeare's original plays or the Lambs' *Tales*.[9] The most widely circulated in those institutions was, with the exception of the Lambs' *Tales*, *Macbeth* (7 classes), followed by *Julius Caesar* (6), *Hamlet* (4), *The Tempest* (4), *Romeo and Juliet* (2), *As You Like It* (2), *The Merchant of Venice* (2), *King John* (1), and *Cymbeline* (1).

The prominence accorded to Shakespeare in the field of English language education can be evidenced by the fact that the plays were incorporated into the curriculum in the English departments of Tokyo and Hiroshima Higher Normal Schools, the principal teacher training institutions for secondary school. A look at the English curriculum in the humanities department of Hiroshima Higher Normal School indicates that Shakespeare's plays were regularly taught to prospective teachers of English.[10] Of further interest is that Okakura, head of the English department at Tokyo Higher Normal School, used *Macbeth* as material for English teaching, which reflects Shakespeare's canonical status in the educational sphere. The Bard was thus set in a hierarchy of literary texts to be appreciated by learners and prospective teachers of English.[11]

Students were carefully given a ladder towards Shakespeare's original texts in the English curriculum, as evidenced by the fact that several higher education institutions offered the Lambs' *Tales* to first-year (or preparatory) students and then Shakespeare's original texts to third- or fourth-year students. Something similar can be said about higher schools: seven higher schools, regardless of humanities or science courses, adopted the Lambs' *Tales* for first-year students as material for English teaching, and Shakespeare's original plays for third-year students.

These findings can be further reinforced by the 'List of Textbooks Used in 32 Higher Schools in Japan (1929–1930)' in the *Bulletin of the Institute for Research in English Teaching*.[12] This document evinces that the Lambs' *Tales* (in 6 classes) served as material to teach English for the first-year students, and then *Henry IV* (2), *The Merchant of Venice* (1) and *Othello* (1) were used for the third-year students. Other archival documents concerning higher-school curriculums followed a not dissimilar trajectory in using prose versions, *Tales from Shakespeare* and *Shakespeare in Short Stories*, to initiate first-year students into the world of Shakespeare, and then the original plays in the third-year classes.[13] Teaching Shakespeare in the prose form in the first year and the original texts in the third year was de facto higher-school curriculum in English.

4.2   STUDYING FOR EXAMINATIONS

This institutionalisation of Shakespeare can be taken to partly reflect practical requirements on the part of students preparing for (1) university entrance examinations and (2) the qualification examination for prospective higher-school teachers. Both of them required knowledge of English literature, including Shakespeare. A notable instance can be found in a 1936 entrance examination questions given by the English department in the Tokyo University of Literature and Science, which required students to answer the following questions in English:

> How many of Shakespeare's plays have you read? Which do you like best? Give the three groups (with one example from each) into which Shakespeare's plays are generally divided.[14]

Students had to study Shakespeare for examinations, and teachers needed to prepare them to take such examinations.

For prospective higher-school teachers, several of Shakespeare's original texts were also essential reading. For instance, *Eigo seinen* presents reading lists for the qualifying examination over time, and Shakespeare was an indispensable part. Excerpts of Shakespearean plays from its entire reading lists are set out in the adjacent table.

Works	Vol.	No.	Date	Page
The Merchant of Venice, A Midsummer Night's Dream, Julius Caesar, Macbeth	42	5	1919	158
Romeo and Juliet, The Merchant of Venice, As You Like It, Julius Caesar, Hamlet, Othello, King Lear, Macbeth, Antony and Cleopatra, The Tempest	52	10	1925	316
King Lear, Hamlet, The Tempest, A Midsummer Night's Dream	56	12	1927	428
King Lear, Hamlet, The Tempest, A Midsummer Night's Dream	61	1	1929	33
King Lear, Hamlet, The Tempest, A Midsummer Night's Dream	64	12	1931	430
King Lear, Hamlet, Macbeth, A Midsummer Night's Dream, The Merchant of Venice	73	8	1935	286
King Lear, Hamlet, Macbeth, A Midsummer Night's Dream, The Merchant of Venice, Julius Caesar	79	7	1938	222
Henry IV, As You Like It, Julius Caesar, Hamlet, Othello, Macbeth, King Lear, The Tempest	87	6	1942	188

It is fair to say, from this table, that a canonical status was given to particular Shakespeare plays. Also interesting is that those selected plays had some affinity with the aforementioned plays selected for classroom use. There was no official board for examination and text selection in higher education, like the College Entrance Examination founded in the United States around the turn of the twentieth century, but the selection of Shakespeare's plays for classroom use in higher education and the qualifying examination was likely to be mutually reinforcing.

Knowledge of Shakespeare was indeed tested in the qualifying examination for higher-school teachers, thereby furthering the orientation of Shakespeare as an integral component of cultural literacy for them. For instance, the 1929 and 1933 examination questions included a tough task of translating excerpts from *Macbeth* and *King Lear* in Japanese.[15] Following those translation tasks, the candidates were required to '[c]omment upon and explain any seven of the allusions contained in the italicised words and phrases':

a) A little month, or ere those shoes were old | With which she follow'd my poor father's body, | Like Niobe, all tears: — *Hamlet*.
b) Marry, our play is, | The most lamentable comedy, and most cruel death of *Pyramus and Thisbe*. — *A Midsummer Night's Dream*.[16]

In 1933, the candidates were required to answer the questions, 'When was *Hamlet* written?'; 'Which Shakespeare play did Miranda appear in?'; and 'Explain the double-time theory'.[17] They could neither have translated nor explained without being thoroughly acquainted with Shakespeare's works, including his use of Greco-Roman myths, his stories, historical fact, archaic language, and grammar. Consequently, the institutionalisation of Shakespeare was facilitated in higher education institutions. Once such tests had been created, teachers perforce prepared students to take them, leading in turn to the necessity of preparing teachers to offer such instruction in the classroom. This cycle resulted in constructing Shakespeare's plays as all but identical with higher education-level literacy in English.

Despite this ingrained belief in Shakespeare's canonical status, it is a fallacy to think that all the students were excited about reading Shakespeare in the English language classroom. For the majority of professors, translation and glossing were rather more central to teaching English. Since such teaching practices inevitably can be linked to disengagement due to its teacher-centred instruction, some students often fell asleep in English classes.[18] In addition, it is an overstatement to say that Shakespeare was more popular than other authors; rather, the playwright took his place alongside modern literary luminaries, such as Arthur Conan Doyle and Robert L. Stevenson. Indeed, the aforementioned *Bulletin* shows that Shakespeare was the fourth most popular as material amongst teachers.[19] It is more correct to say that English literature *per se* was most powerful in the English curriculum, in which Shakespeare similarly occupied an important place.

More significantly, English teaching in higher education was severely criticised in business circles as being irrelevant to the needs of more utilitarian language-learners, particularly in the aftermath of the Sino-Japanese War (1894–1895), and the Russo-Japanese War (1904–1905), when Japan embarked on a capitalist road.[20] Advocates of practical English voiced doubt about the English proficiency of university students in the department of English literature. A grenade was targeted at English literature in general, and Shakespeare in particular:

Not being versed in practical English is not worth a penny in instrumental terms. Bookkeeping, accounting, and practical English are essential weapons in business. Scholars of English are remarkable only in studying and criticising verses written by high-brow Shakespeare, Milton, Dryden,

Tennyson, Emerson, and Carlyle. Yet, they do not have a sufficient level of English proficiency to write a letter and to correctly understand a piece of newspaper, nor do they know how to write an invoice. All of them are upset if they are spoken to by foreign people.[21]

The view of Shakespeare as a representative user of non-utilitarian English was already existent in the first decade of the twentieth century. It is important to remember that the playwright was powerfully present in higher education but was simultaneously recognised as doubtful in instrumental terms. This survey begs one to ask: How was Shakespeare taught? The next section provides a fuller picture of an early history of teaching and studying Shakespeare at the Imperial University of Tokyo, now the University of Tokyo. The instruction will be inferred by focusing on the curriculum and examinations given by early professors.

4.3 THE TURN TO THE WEST

The first government-administered higher education institution in modern Japan to teach Shakespeare was Kaisei Gakko, which later developed into the nation's first university, Tokyo University, in 1877. This university was graced with the 'imperial' sobriquet in 1886 and was then reorganised into the Imperial University of Tokyo, when another imperial university, the Imperial University of Kyoto, was founded in 1897. The primary method for introducing Shakespeare during the formative years of higher education depended on foreign teachers recruited from Europe and the United States and employed by the Ministry of Education. The early university, therefore, functioned as the provider of Western knowledge, which students were expected to accept with deference.

Whilst the first foreign teacher to teach English at Tokyo Kaisei Gakko was an American ex-journalist, Edward Howard House, the evidence shows that the first professor to teach Shakespeare was James Summers, an Englishman appointed as professor of English literature and logic in 1873 and who gave lectures on *Hamlet* and *Henry VIII*.[22] How Summers taught the plays of Shakespeare can be inferred from the examination questions in 1875:

First Class: English Language and Literature.
Write out and paraphrase the first few lines of Wolsey's address: 'Farewell & c ...as I do.

Why is Shakespeare held in esteem? And why is Spencer less read than Shakespeare? Give the characteristics of these writers and those of Milton.
Write ten lines from Hamlet's address to his father's ghost and paraphrase a few lines'.

Explain the expressions: —
  'I find thee apt'.
  'Is by a forged process of my death Rankly abused'.
  'The serpent that did sting thy father's life, Now wears his crown'.
  'Taint not thy mind, nor let thy soul contrive
  Against thy mother aught'.
  'The glowworm shows the matin to be near,
  And 'gins to pale his ineffectual fire'.
  'Remember thee!
  Ay! thou poor ghost! while memory holds a seat
  In this distracted globe'.
  'I'll wipe away all trivial fond records,
  All saws of books'.

Second Class: English Language and Literature.
Write out and mark the quantities and accents in the passage from Shakespeare beginning, 'I could a tale unfold'.[23]

His examination questions consist of memorising passages ('Write out'), philological ('paraphrase' and 'explain the expressions') and literary-historical facts ('Give the characteristics of these writers'), with no attention paid to the content of Shakespeare.

Those examination questions were extremely similar to those of his contemporary Oxford and Cambridge Local Examinations, in which secondary English students were required to take examinations in literature, mainly Shakespeare. The 1904 Cambridge local examination included the following questions on *Richard II*:

Explain the following passages:
  (a) Thy word is current with him for my death,
  But dead, thy kingdom cannot buy my breath
  (b) My wretchedness unto a row of pins,
  They'll talk of state; for every one doth so
  Against a change.
  (c) Bound to himself! what doth he with a bond
  That he is bound to?

(d) Bearing their own misfortunes on the back
Of such as have before endured the like.[24]

This finding shows that Summers probably recycled the same format of examination questions as used in English schools and taught the plays in the way he had learned in his native country.

His Anglophone successors, such as William Haughton and James M. Dixon, also followed a not dissimilar trajectory in teaching Shakespeare. Amongst Dixon's students was Natsume Sōseki, who later became the first Japanese-born teacher of English at the Imperial University of Tokyo and then established himself as the greatest novelist in modern Japan. For him, Dixon was not the most inspiring lecturer. Sōseki expressed his frustration with Dixon's teaching of English literature and attacked it as fact-drilling:

> He would make us read poetry aloud, read prose passages to him, do composition; he would scold us for dropping articles, angrily explode when we mispronounce things. His exam questions are always of one kind: give Wordsworth's birth and death dates, give the number of Shakespeare's folios, list the works of Scott in chronological order.[25]

Such trends in literary studies extremely irritated Sōseki, who, therefore, problematised Dixon's pedagogy: 'Can *this* be English literature? Is this any way to instil an understanding of what literature is, English or otherwise?' He remarked in disgust that he 'did not know the answer to that after three years of furious study'.

Following his return from an official visit to Great Britain in 1900–1902, Sōseki became the first Japanese-born lecturer of Shakespeare in 1903 (until 1907) at the Imperial University. Another chapter would be required to discuss Sōseki's struggle with Shakespeare; suffice it to say now that in teaching Shakespeare, he apparently problematised a Japanese belief that re-enacting Anglo-European standards was a staple of progressive modernity, as recollected by one of his students:

> He neither had academic snobbery nor blindly accepted the judgement of Western scholars but tenaciously determined his own attitudes towards English literature, albeit not imposing them on his students.[26]

As Masao Miyoshi has observed, Sōseki's critical attitude presumably derived from his acute awareness that if the extent to which one could appreciate literature was decisively conditioned or determined by its underlying cultural traditions, then all that Japanese scholars of English literature could do was inevitably 'to either imitate what an English scholar had already said or make do with casual and arbitrary impressions, and thus he/she could not have the confidence of being a genuine scholar'.[27] To his mind, though, such studies left little room for local initiative but were no more than a slavish imitation.[28]

4.4   DISCIPLINING SHAKESPEARE

Regrettably, the critical space Sōseki had almost opened was closed by subsequent specialists who upheld the values, norms, and standards of Shakespeare studies as a discipline. In the words of David R. Shumway and Craig Dionne, disciplines are 'historically specific forms of knowledge production, having certain organisational characteristics, making use of certain practices, and existing in a particular institutional environment'.[29] Such a set of assumptions, methods, and practices serves as the source of their judgements resting on 'authority vested in an anonymous system of methods, of propositions considered to be true, of rules, definitions, techniques, and tools that may in principle be taken over by anyone who has been trained in them'.[30] Shakespeare in higher education entered the age of specialisation, increasingly becoming an object of scientific study.

The harbinger was Sōseki's successor, John Lawrence, a British philologist who taught English literature and philology from 1906 until 1916. Lawrence earned an MA from the University of Oxford in 1898 after his doctoral degree from the University of London. He brought to English studies, as a fact-grubbing philological subject, a more academic and professional refinement. As the quintessential philological scholar, Lawrence was much more concerned than his predecessors with teaching English literature as a scientific subject. His philologically-oriented literary studies covered not only Old and Middle English, but also the Indo-European languages, like Icelandic and Gothic. Within this rationale of research, the study of English literature, with philology as its principal method, was seen as the disinterested, and therefore, scientific, accumulation of objective knowledge.

It is certainly true that Lawrence's philological approach to Shakespeare's texts gained high acclaim amongst research-inclined students, but it seems to have dismayed those who were willing to study literature for aesthetic or uplifting purposes. Whilst cherishing the memory, several of his disciples admitted that 'although he was remarkable in his philological interpretations of poetry, literary criticism was out of his beat'.[31] For instance, a student's description of his *Macbeth* class gives an impression that it was so thoroughly trained in linguistic minutiae as to be insufferably boring. In struggling to interpret the plays, he seems to have borrowed opinions from English Shakespeare critics.[32] One of his students, Akutagawa Ryūnosuke, who later became a popular novelist, complained that Lawrence had given only a scene-by-scene outline of *Macbeth*: 'it has been widely acknowledged that his lecture was boring'.[33] A similar cynical view is shared in Nogami Yaeko's novel:

> The old professor's lectures were all historical investigations, quotations and philological commentaries [...] Deformed and weird Shakespeare stood before them [students]. He gave a lecture on *Macbeth*, entirely dependent on quotations from Sir Sidney Lee and Coleridge.
> [...]
> 'What, then, is his own opinion?'
> All the students were eager to listen to that in vain. He did not bring any opinions to Japan from London [...][34]

The evidence shows that Lawrence's concern focused exclusively on the philological study of Shakespeare's plays.

It is true that, as Martin Wallace and Gerald Graff have pointed out, it was necessary for English to be allied with philology, which had already been established as a discipline, in order to be accepted as an academic subject.[35] Yet Lawrence's lack of concern for literature *per se* would have been sufficient enough to provoke a question: Should the Japanese study English literature for investigation based on the accumulation of objective knowledge the majority of which derived from the opinions of Anglophone scholars?

In the aftermath of Lawrence, Shakespeare was left to a Japanese scholar, Ichikawa Sanki, who, as Lawrence's outstanding disciple, became the first Japanese to hold the chair of English with the title of full professor at the university. He started to teach at the university in 1916, immediately following his return from Great Britain and the United States (1912–1916), and delivered lectures on Shakespeare between at least 1920 and 1927. In seeking to establish English literature as an academic subject, Ichikawa carved out his rigorous, scientific identity as a specialised scholar through his academic works, including *Studies in*

English Grammar (1912) and his PhD thesis 'On the Language of the Poetry of Robert Browning' (1920). Ichikawa's philological interest in Shakespeare's plays was most apparent in his linguistically oriented annotated editions of Shakespeare's plays. Those editions offered exclusively a running paraphrase and his historical explanation of the language without any commentaries on the content of the play. His emphasis on philology can be seen in his 14 pages of the introduction to *Othello* in which only six pages are dedicated to its performance date, sources, and outline, whilst eight pages are devoted to 'Shakespeare's English'.[36]

Indeed, Ichikawa was counted as a trailblazer for promoting the scientific model of English studies, particularly the unification of literature and philology, as a scholar admired his achievements:

> Since Mr. Ichikawa, Ichikawa who left the old from Europe in 1916 and then started to deliver lectures at the Imperial University of Tokyo, promoted the scientific study of English everywhere, philological studies have become popular and contributed significantly to the study of English literature as well.[37]

His philological study of English literature was welcomed as providing a scientific foundation for literary studies to be accepted as an academic discipline. At issue is, however, that Ichikawa, the leading Anglicist as he was, may have exiled literature from the business of life, as acutely observed by Akutagawa:

> Students will be totally at a loss to study literature if they want to seriously. If they study English literature philologically as Mr. Ichikawa brilliantly does, I think it makes perfect sense. Yet, then, the works of Shakespeare or Milton cease to be plays and poetry, becoming simply a meaningless row of English words.[38]

Akutagawa confessed his weariness of the philological and historical study of English literature.

Ichikawa was discharged from teaching Shakespeare in 1927, and the task was then entrusted to Saito Takeshi, who wielded authority in teaching his plays as the first native professor of literature at the Imperial University of Tokyo. Saito worked on English studies under the guidance of Lawrence, but his concern focused on English literature rather than language. To his mind, though, the study of English literature should be based on literary-historical research, as Mukoyama Yoshihiko has summarised:

> [...] it was Dr. Ichikawa who left the old way of study of English literature which is commonly called the descriptive grammar and started scientific study of English language by observing the linguistic phenomenon as they actually are in their historical development, so it was Prof. Saito who left the then prevailing older way of study of English literature which is commonly called the impressionistic criticism and started factual study of the literature by observing the literary works as they actually are in the light of historical development of English literature.[39]

For Saito, literary-historical facts were necessary to present literary criticism under a scientific guise. His monumental engagement with the 'scientific study of English literature' was crystallised when he 'published "*A Historical Survey of English Literature with Special Reference to the Spirit of the Time* (1926)"', which scholars credited with heralding the advent of the academic study of English literature.[40] His rigorous scientific approach to the study of English literature can be also seen in his great emphasis on textual criticism, as he argued that Shakespeare's texts could not correctly be understood without comparing five to six editions of his complete works.[41] Saito gave primacy to 'textual criticism' and 'biographical discovery', but admitted in a self-depreciating manner that the subject realistically practicable for Japanese scholars to pursue was 'interpretation of the text or literary criticism'.[42] Thus, the advance guard of specialism in the field of English language and literature in Japan was the cadres of the Lawrence school, promoting the idea of the philological, biographical, and literary-historical study of English literature from the latter half of the 1920s.[43]

Such professionalising forces inevitably led scholars to preserve English literature in an English hermetically sealed box which could not be unlocked without knowing historical minutiae of biographical and cultural backgrounds against which literary works were incarnated. This is most apparent in Fukuhara Rintarô's perception of English literature as being confined to, not beyond, national boundaries, with reference to English critic, Herbert Read:

> [...] the soil, the physical climate and the actual landscape; the race, its upbringing, its reaction to material considerations, the resultant character of the people; the historical behaviours of such a people, the evolution of

their ideals, a formation of these ideals in institutions, in religion, art and literature; the various aspects of native genius.[44]

The late 1920s witnessed the Japanese reception of T.S. Eliot, who argued that what constituted a great English literary work and made it authentic were the values of Western European (within that English) culture.[45] Once the idea took hold that English literature should be only interpreted against the historical backdrop of English people, Japanese scholars dismissed the Sōsekian struggle and scrambled to conform to Anglophone standards of literary criticism. The way in which they evaluated literary texts was inevitably determined by Western hermeneutics and it eventually had to marginalise or override national identity.

In this academic climate, the doyen of English studies, albeit usually reticent about polemics, unusually voiced his concern about the study of English literature; the man was Okakura, the head of the English Department at Tokyo Higher Normal School. Regrettably, Okakura's approach to teaching Shakespeare has escaped significant scholarly attention, but it is worthy of study for the light that his propositions cast on issues concerning the study and teaching of Shakespeare as a discipline. Fortunately, his classes on English language and literature have been memorably taken down by dozens of students, the majority of whom remark that his pedagogy was peculiarly his own. By examining those recollections and his own writings on the teaching of Shakespeare, the following section attempts to reconstruct the pedagogical practice deployed by Okakura. An investigation into how he squared his belief with the teaching of Shakespeare provides a notable instance of a broad spectrum of pedagogical approaches to his plays in early twentieth-century Japan.

4.5   Okakura Yoshisaburō's Stand on Shakespeare

Okakura was not antagonistic with Ichikawa and Saito. Rather, he worked with them for the large-scale project of publishing the English Classics series from 1921 and highly regarded them as scholars. However, their approaches to Shakespeare were characterised by the stark contrast in their creeds and allegiances. Their opposing views stemmed from their different positions as scholars. Ichikawa and Saito took a purely academic path at the Imperial University of Tokyo, engaged in English studies for its own sake, and held a post at the same university. In other words, they aligned themselves with the values, norms, and standards the discipline upheld. By comparison, Okakura, who served as a professor at Tokyo Higher Normal School, was much more concerned than Ichikawa and Saito with English studies as education. More importantly, he was critical of a Japanese popular belief that replicating Anglo-American models was a staple of progressive modernity, as his elder brother who consistently resisted Western hegemony to re-validate Asian values, Okakura Tenshin, lighted the way to the critical acquisition of Western knowledge.

Okakura's misgivings about the specialised study of English literature were forcefully expressed in his essay entitled the 'Brown Study', which wrapped in purple prose his concern about scholarship oriented towards 'studying for the study's sake':

> It's a shame that the so-called scholars and artists tend to neglect their ultimate goal of raising themselves to another world. They are wasting precious time studying for the study's sake, despite the fact that scholarship *per se* is only a means, or tool, to an end. In so doing, they consider their work done. Due to this, current scholarship gives me no satisfaction.[46]

He was not explicit about what was meant by 'studying for the study's sake', but it is not hard to imagine that his impatience in the case of English studies emanated from academic research with no regard to its outward-looking relevance ('neglect their ultimate goal of raising themselves to another world'[47]). Indeed, Okakura argued that 'the scholars and artists of our country must seek to cultivate their minds so that they can follow the dictates of their hearts and row their way by the boats and paddles that they have crafted'. To his mind, the acquisition of such 'a spiritual force' was 'education (*kyôiku*)' and 'intellectual and moral development (*shûyo*)'.[48]

Shakespeare studies were also not exempted from his concern, as he expressed a deep sense of regret in the preamble to a locally-annotated edition of *Hamlet*:

> It is necessary for those inclined to read *Hamlet*, whether the Western or the Eastern, to ask themselves how *Hamlet* touches their hearts, why the play is a masterpiece, and then to seek those answers in themselves. Yet, large numbers of people, among whom even scholars are included, esteem literary masterpieces exclusively in terms of *kunko*, without any regard to the interactions between Shakespeare and themselves. Therefore, I feel the urge to say such a banal thing.[49]

The turn of the phrase, *kunko*, Okakura deployed is worthy of attention for the light that it casts on his stand on Shakespeare studies. The word *kunko* refers literally to the annotation of literary texts based on the accumulation of objective knowledge. However, at the same time, the *kunko*-inclined scholars and their practices were often a target of ridicule due to their lack of the curiosity to express their own hermeneutics, and to its corresponding escape from the business of life in favour of narrow pedantry. Given his dissent against 'studying for study's sake', Okakura's use of the word can be construed as his implicit critique of English literary scholars who tended to confine themselves to the accumulation of Western knowledge and annotation of Western literary texts and, by extension, to passively accommodate their opinions to Anglo-European opinions, with no priority given to their own engagements with texts *per se* and the wider applications. Okakura accused such a *kunko* study of *Hamlet* of its failure to contribute to developing cultured citizens.

Okakura was not alone in expressing his concern; several scholars also voiced dissent in favour of English studies to feed the mind. Indeed, the controversy amongst scholars loomed large in the *Eigo seinen* journal during the 1930s, and an advocate of Okakura's opinion complained that current scholars tended to rest contented to collect books about literary texts and to accommodate their views to Anglophone standards of literary scholarship:

> It is nice to read literature in terms of a grammatical study, to search for historical facts, and to find the sources of literary works. However, the study of the whole should come before that of the specific. We should be careful not to become too infatuated with sources or language to appreciate literary works as a whole. It is foolish that those who are unable to correctly understand literary texts indulge themselves in finding new facts and the peculiar anecdotes of authors and then determine their attitudes towards literary works only by reading British and American critical works.[50]

The accumulation of objective knowledge as an aid to literary evaluation ironically diminished the scholarly curiosity to engage with literary works on their own terms and eventually perpetuated a tenacious belief that reproducing Anglo-European standards was a staple of progressive scholarship.

Yano Kazumi was fiercer in his repudiation of the scientific study of literature as the accumulation of Western knowledge, using the same word *kunko* as Okakura did:

> The Japanese have not esteemed their advantages and instead have striven not only to swallow the opinions of Western scholars but also to imitate their arguments as an exemplar [...] In short, they have become unable to express any opinion without recourse to Western predecessors. They could not say anything even though they would. In essence, they have lost their selfhood to rely on.[51]

For him, Japanese scholars of English literature only re-enacted what Anglophone scholars had already done instead of appreciating texts on their own terms. As a result, English studies degenerated into 'the impotent repetition of Western discourse, and the banal replica'.[52] Yano arrived at the conclusion that this would be 'a common fault observable in Japanese academics in general, and university professors of English literature in particular'.[53] The antidote against it was sought in 'privileging self over others, rediscovering the lost self'.[54]

The target of Yano's assault was made more explicit in 1961:

> [...] philological and biographical approaches to English literature gave birth to the academic way of *kunko*, which led to a fallacy that it is literary studies. There is no denying that this trend has dominated academic circles for a long time [...] However, this phenomenon was not the case in Japan before Germany-based philology was introduced.[55]

Though he avoided naming them diplomatically, those who spearheaded 'philological and biographical approaches' to the study of English literature were the professional cadres of the Lawrence school.[56]

Fuelled by a counter-impulse towards outward-looking relevance in English studies, the opponents argued that most academic tasks, albeit extremely important for academic progress in Japan, were, nevertheless, not entirely relevant to the cultural and educational aims of the humanities considered necessary for the majority of students. What approach to English studies, then, was perceived to be desirable? One of the suggestions to those questions was given by Okakura, who demonstrated teaching practices that aligned with his educational ideals.

4.6   Okakura's Equation Pedagogy

As a professor at Tokyo Higher Normal School, Okakura first invested his energies in offering an instructional model as to how English language and literature could be made readily intelligible and manageable to the Japanese. This comes as little surprise given that the extent to which one can understand English has a high degree of control over the extent to which one can appreciate English texts. In a nod to the cognitive difficulty Japanese students would face in English studies due to its linguistic and cultural differences, what Okakura consistently advocated was the use of Japanese equivalents as an aid to comprehending English, which his disciple, Fukuhara, called an 'equation approach':

> In order to learn a language unfamiliar to our culture and customs and then to appreciate the language, it is necessary to have a grounding, or a kind of mirror, from which to infer the target meaning [...] in a way that we can infer oranges from Japanese mandarin oranges (*mikan*).[57]

In his view, knowledge acquisition takes place when an unfamiliar idea is assimilated by the mass of ideas already in the mind. New ideas should be gauged from and assimilated into the known.

Within this framework, students were first required to enlarge their own ideas when facing difficulties in understanding English literature:

> Some people say that the writings of Emerson or Carlyle are difficult [...] they should first seek to cultivate the habit of thinking and then enlarge their ideas by reading Chinese classics and Japanese books. It often happens that some idea, albeit easy to understand in Japanese, appears to be difficult in English. To remedy this, it is necessary to enlarge their ideas themselves first.[58]

Underlying this proposition was an assumption that the extent to which new ideas were assimilated in the minds of receptors was proportionate to what Okakura called 'empirical units', or the amount of pre-existing experience:

> [...] in much the same way that we cannot understand French and English cuisines without tasting Japanese fare [...] we cannot sufficiently understand what we have not experienced; on the other hand, we can fully

understand what we have already experienced. In this respect, our knowledge of the Japanese language is significantly related to the ability to interpret English texts.[59]

The learning of English language and literature was thus accommodated in a broad framework of finding affinities between English and Japanese thoughts and cultures.

Okakura promoted the application of this pedagogy to teaching Shakespeare at the Shakespeare Society of Japan, the first formal organisation on the study of Shakespeare in Japan, with an emphasis on the absorption of his plays in the Japanese equivalents as a catalyst to comprehend them:

> How can Shakespeare be made intelligible? An answer to the question is as follows: we had drama here in the age of Shakespeare. There are a number of similarities in the development of drama between there and here. What I find important is, therefore, to ask our drama of elder people who are familiar with it, to gather further materials from other people as well, and then to infer from our drama what their drama was like, based on research on the former. In other words, it is necessary to draw a parallel between the West and Japan and then to undertake comparative studies.[60]

In order to understand Shakespeare's plays, it was deemed desirable and effective to compare them with the Japanese equivalents. Okakura's students were indeed encouraged to listen to *kabuki* (classical Japanese drama) or *jōruri* (a chanted recitative accompanied by a string instrument, associated with *bunraku*, traditional Japanese puppetry, performance) recitation accompanied by the fuzz effect based on the sound of *shamisen* (a three-stringed Japanese musical instrument) as an aid to the understanding of Shakespeare's plays. In his words, 'you can't fully understand *Hamlet* without knowing *Tsubosaka*'.[61]

Okakura's juxtaposition of *Tsubosaka reigenki* (*The Miracle at Tsubosaka Temple*), particularly performed by a female reciter, Toyotake Roshô, with *Hamlet* was his favourite turn of phrase, and demonstrates his point. In the *jōruri* story, there is a blind man named Sawaichi, who lives with his beautiful wife, Osato, in Tubosaka Village. Osato is sincere of heart and helps her husband, but he suspects that when she quietly leaves the house each night, she is meeting clandestinely with a lover. However, it turns out that she has only been going to the Tsubosaka temple to pray to the goddess (Kwannon bodhisattva) to cure his eyes. He feels ashamed of his suspicions of Osato's honesty and chastity. After that, they visit the Tsubosaka temple together. With his wife back home, he says that he will complete three-day fasting alone; however, he decides to release Osato from her concern for him and throws himself off a cliff. Osato, sensing that something is wrong, hurriedly returns to the temple to find the body of her husband. Overwhelmed by grief, she also leaps into the valley, after which a miracle happens: the divine power of the goddess saves their lives and then cures his eyes. It is certainly true that the plot is totally different from that of *Hamlet*, but Sawaichi's suspicions of Osato's sincerity and his pangs of regret are sufficient to remember Hamlet's situation with Ophelia. Okakura brought the play close to a Japanese narrative tradition of a husband-and-wife (Sawaichi and Osato) love as a window into Hamlet and Ophelia.

The same note is struck in his annotated edition of Shakespeare's *Sonnets*, which frequently uses Japanese equivalents to obscure Shakespearean words. An eminent instance is his gloss of 'the frame' in Sonnet 24:

> Schmidt reads this as 'a case or structure to enclose and support a picture'. But that is roughly more similar to a miniature domestic Buddhist altar (*zushi*), in which to enshrine a Buddhist statue or picture.[62]

By appealing to the Japanese equivalent, Okakura made Schmidt's gloss more clearly recognisable to Japanese learners as being three-dimensional and sacred. His emphasis on the role of equivalents in teaching Shakespeare invited the students to appreciate the works by building upon their already existing competencies in their own cultural traditions.

The feasibility and usefulness of this equation approach for classroom use were also attested to by Fukuhara, who also employed equivalents in teaching Shakespeare's *Troilus and Cressida* in the classroom.[63] Fukuhara compared the massive Greek military attack on Troy to the thirteenth-century Mongol attempt to invade Japan, which brought an acute sense of national crisis home to the Japanese. The equation approach thus made the plays internally experienced by, rather than externally imposed on, Japanese students.

Notably, Okakura's approach aligned with pedagogy promoted by prominent educators of that time. For instance, Tanimoto Tomeri, the leading authority on general education, advocated the use of the ideas already in the minds of learners as an aid to teaching something new: 'when teaching something that students have never seen before, like a wolf and a tiger, teachers should begin with something that they have already known, like a dog and a cat'.[64] In the words of Higuchi Kanjiro, a teacher at Tokyo Higher Normal School, 'understanding happens when learners apperceive new ideas by evoking the known in their minds'.[65] Shimoda Jiro, professor at Tokyo Women's Higher Normal School, also asserted that 'it is necessary to base instruction on the past experience and knowledge to bind them with the new'.[66] In this educational psychology, new knowledge became best digestible when it was perceived in terms of a past experience. It should not be surprising that Okakura shared the pedagogy, given his position as head in the English department at Tokyo Higher Normal School and often asserted his conviction that English teachers 'should always refer to pedagogy or teaching methods'.[67]

It is certainly true that their statements were intended in large part as a contribution to primary and secondary general education, but their underlying concept can be subsumed under the broader concept of liberal education in higher education. For instance, an influential nineteenth-century Anglican minister who converted to Catholicism, Cardinal John Henry Newman, drew a line in university education between simply acquiring knowledge and expanding the mind, or, in his parlance, between 'the passive reception into the mind of a number of ideas hitherto unknown to it' and 'the mind's energetic and simultaneous action upon and towards and among those new ideas'.[68] Newman's emphasis was that the mind acted as a formative power that reduced to order and meaning one's acquisitions and made the objects of knowledge subjectively one's own. The enlargement of knowledge arose from a comparison of ideas one with another, and a systematising of them. The mind grew and expanded when one not only learned, but referred what one learned to what one knows already.[69] This dialectical process of the mind constituted liberal education in opposition to simply acquiring knowledge.

Okakura's preference was obviously for liberal education, as encapsulated in a statement that 'what the English call "liberal education" should be imparted in schools'.[70] His idealism shone through in the aforementioned 'Brown Study', in which he saw English studies as an attempt to 'show different elements born in the East and the West and then compare their respective advantages'.[71] The study of English literature, he argued, should be intended as a contribution to comparing the relative merits of different cultures and seeking universal truth across them. This constituted the educational value of English studies that could foster intellectual and moral development considered necessary for cultured citizens, or, in his favourite parlance, 'gentlemen' and 'ladies'. His ideals were indeed crystallised in his 1923 foundation of a literary association he presided over, *Yōyōjuku*, which was designed to 'reconcile between Eastern and Western cultures' through the study of literature.[72]

To that end, Okakura mobilised Japanese equivalents not only for simply understanding the works but also for analysing Shakespeare's plays from a Japanese point of view. For instance, he drew comparisons between *Romeo and Juliet* and Japanese traditional dramas in terms of *shinjū* (love-suicide, or death for love), in the form of fictional dialogues between Speaker A and Speaker B. Speaker A referred to Romeo's lamentation for the (supposed) death of Juliet, 'Eyes, look your last! | Arms, take your last embrace! and, lips, oh you | The doors of breath, seal with a righteous kiss | A dateless bargain to engrossing death!' (5.3.112–15), pointing out: 'it is certainly true that he shows love for her, but his motive to drink poison does not arise from his wish to come together with her in the afterlife'.[73] In his reflection on Juliet's speech to the dead body of Romeo ('I will kiss thy lips. | Haply some poison yet doth hang on them, | To make me die with a restorative' (5.3.164–66)), Speaker A doubted if 'this lamentation contains a sweet dream of reunion in the future'.[74] Subsequently, Speaker A argued that the quintessential idea of love-suicide in Japanese plays was: 'May we two come to rebirth together within the lotus—praise be to Amida Buddha'.[75] He continued: 'I cannot help feeling that the Japanese act of *shinjū* is the pick of the bunch'.[76] Eastern spirituality was made apparent by comparing the different representations of the afterlife in Western and Eastern literature.

Another instance can be found in his comparison of *King Lear* with the Japanese equivalent *noh* libretti (medieval drama familiar to Japanese intellectuals as part of cultural literacy), such as *Hibariyama* (*Hibari Mountain*), *Nakamitsu* (*The Loyalty of Nakamitsu*), and *Yoroboshi* (*Yoroboshi: The Blind Man*). *King Lear* and those *noh* libretti are similar in that children bear ill treatment at the hands of their fathers, but they are distinctly different in that the children of the latter are saved by loyal subjects similar to Kent, resulting in a happy ending. Those differences led Okakura to see *King Lear* as stunning and regard the venerable talents of Shakespeare as being 'beyond the scope of our mediocre minds'.[77] The play was considered exceptional because such a tragic story could not be found in the Eastern culture of filial piety. Similarities and differences between Shakespeare's plays and Japanese dramas were examined to gauge the local and the global.

However, Okakura's valorisation of English studies was not acceptable to specialised scholars who were not distracted by cultural differences or similarities but were willing to conceive the re-enactments of Western standards of English studies as the pinnacle of academic achievements. Rather, Okakura's ideas evoked negative reactions amongst them, as succinctly shown in a scholar's confession: 'I couldn't entirely agree with his attitude towards and approach to the study of English literature'.[78] Ichikawa also suggested that Okakura 'was aware that the so-called "specialists" or "scholars" were not beautiful, and, therefore, avoided defining himself that way'.[79] Even Fukuhara stated in his days of youth that 'it's only a cliché to say that English literature should be studied from a Japanese point of view, or should be evaluated as a Japanese. As English literature has its own organisation, the study of English literature should be undertaken against a backdrop of English culture'.[80]

4.7   The Re-turn to Japan: The Ideological Thrust of Equation Pedagogy

Fukuhara's words, however, irked Okakura: 'Well. The likes of Japanese artisans in the Edo period of the feudal age saw Western people and said, "how odd the red-bearded races are. How blue-eyed they are!" In that way, we should do'.[81] These are the words that sought to deflate or mock the West's racial hierarchies that the Japanese were trying to internalise. Indeed, Okakura's most ardent disgust was reserved for the exalted acceptance of English criticisms, and this was not exempted from those of Shakespeare:

> What irks me is to regurgitate panegyrics on Shakespeare by English critics, including the great poet Shelley, the masterly essayist Lamb, and, more recently, the doyen of literary criticism, Bradley.[82]

For him, the regurgitation of English opinions was most abominable due to its suppression of local initiatives, or Japanese points of view, in interpreting Shakespeare, thereby reducing the study of English literature to a task of passively accepting and introducing English opinions. This cast of mind, Okakura was afraid, would eventually perpetuate the West's cultural and racial hierarchies that the Japanese might internalise. Indeed, he lamented a Japanese mindset that tended to accept Westerners as 'a superior race that they can't contest', denouncing such 'servile obedience to things Western' as 'the downfall of the yellow race'.[83] In seeking to shy away from regurgitating Western opinions, Okakura invoked East Asian ideas as an aid to interpreting Western literary texts, as Fukuhara recalled:

> Professor Okakura abhorred assuming a pretentious air of Anglo-American people. He did not like to blindly admire them either. He was proud of being a Japanese [...] He placed greater emphasis on Japanese cultural literacy. Whilst teaching Western manners and customs, he consistently required us to look back on Japanese traditional culture. He always used East Asian ideas in interpreting Anglo-American ideas.[84]

His dissenting attitude resulted in the use of Japanese equivalents in interpreting Shakespeare.

Okakura's equation pedagogy, from this perspective, can be viewed not only as an educational means of teaching but also as an ideological process of realising already existing equivalent ideas and civilisation within, thereby raising Japan to a parity with Western powers, as attested by Fukuhara:

> Presumably, he [Okakura] was always thinking that the Japanese must be no less strong than the Western [...] If the Western have already stood on a six-feet higher footing, then we can no longer catch up and can't stand on the same footing as they do, no matter how hard we work on reading English books. However, if we study Japanese culture that parallels the Western one, then we can raise ourselves by the same six feet, and can eventually compete with the West. The relations between the Eastern and the Western are characterised by differences in the way of thinking and sensibilities. However hard we try to emulate the West, we must forever wear borrowed clothes without internal achievement.[85]

Since Western countries, in his view, developed naturally from within, Japan also needed to follow a trajectory similar to them. The discovery of affinities between the West and Japan was a testimony to Japan's internally motivated development. Therefore, they had to be unearthed to demonstrate its civilisational compatibility with the West. For Okakura, what was imposed from the outside—the West—was comparable to 'borrowed clothes' and did not congenially fit with the Japanese. It was necessary, therefore, to adapt it to their use, rather than externally imposing it on them.

In his view, Western thought that appeared to be new and unfamiliar had already been existant inside Japan, and it could be made clear through the acquisition with foreign knowledge. Such inference was more explicitly made in his English book entitled *The Life and Thought of Japan*:

> [Things mental and spiritual] will never take root where the soil is not propitious for their growth. If our mind can understand and appropriate what has originated and grown in your [Western] mind, is that not an evidence that ours has very much the same form and degree of developing as yours? No such nonsense as mere borrowing or imitation can at least be asserted of the learning of science and arts [...] there is no other means of approach to a higher and nobler state of mind but that of the tedious trudging along the wearisome road of natural evolution. If we have succeeded in adopting and assimilating rather quickly, some of the result of the Western civilization which had cost you many centuries of painful labour, it is because we had also been seriously, though silently, engaged in fostering the germs within the closed doors of political seclusion, for hundreds of years of equally painful investigation.[86]

Without the 'germs', Okakura argued, the Japanese would not succeed in appropriating Western civilisation. Since '[o]ur mental soil', in which the germs of such studies as 'literature' had already been fostered, had been 'well ploughed for the favourable reception of any intellectual seeds', the products of the Western mind could be readily assimilated through 'their parallels with those of ours'.[87]

Ideologically, Okakura's equation pedagogy was thus to trace how Japanese and English civilisations had evolved along similar trajectories. As Okakura argued by reference to a Victorian didactic preacher, Philip Gilbert Hamerton's notion of independence, the acquaintance with English literature was not designed to project or impose English values on the Japanese to annihilate Japanese innate self; instead, it should serve to make 'us more ourselves' than the Japanese should ever have possessed or known about 'ourselves' if their minds had not been opened by the acquaintance with foreign knowledge.[88] Okakura's equation pedagogy should be thus construed as his fierce willingness to study English literature for 'ourselves' and to adapt it to the use of the Japanese, rather than for imposing it on them.

4.8   CLASHING IDEOLOGIES AND VACILLATION

As Okakura expressed his concern, the study of English often has been perceived as an act of re-enacting Anglo-European academe and, therefore, inevitably entailed the anxiety of mental colonisation. This makes sense given that almost all South-East Asian countries (Burma, Malaysia, Indonesia, the Philippines, Cambodia, Laos, Vietnam, Macau, East Timor, and Hong Kong) had succumbed to Western powers by 1941. In demonstrating his deep concern for the Anglo-European colonial taming of Japanese intellect, a contributor to a newspaper quoted Okakura as saying that 'even Westerners cynically laugh at the spread of English words in Japanese advertisements, saying that Japan looks like a British colony'.[89] Okakura was far from alone in voicing concern about English. Sōseki was also adamant that English immersion in the classroom would be a sort of 'disgrace' to the Japanese, seeing such education as the same as that in colonial India.[90] Another scholar of English literature, Togawa Shūkotsu, embraced the same sentiment: 'The English language is a language used by *madorasu*, and by colonised peoples'.[91] Despite being a teacher of English, Togawa bitingly opposed the compulsory imposition of the English language in Japanese schools as a sort of 'colonial educational policies' that 'could disrupt Japan's independent spirit and then submit to servile obedience'.[92] They shared their concern about what can be perceived to be, in modern parlance, linguistic imperialism.

Yet, despite his association with Englishness, Shakespeare was not resisted as an image of what Guri Viswanathan calls the 'masks of conquest'. Instead, the Bard was curiously considered to deserve maintenance or seizure.[93] In 1941, when Japan decided to revolt against the United States and Great Britain, scholars of English began to vacillate between nation and profession. Whilst the majority of Japanese Anglicists observed dignified silence, some expressed their strong allegiance to the nation. The latter reached its zenith in Yamato Yasuo's jingoistic urge to seize Shakespeare as 'ours': 'Chastise the Fiendish America and Britain! They are our enemies. Seize Shakespeare! He is ours as well!'.[94] The willingness to opt for seizure over dismissal typically reflects clashing ideologies Japanese scholars of English faced: Westernisation, concern about it and re-validation of Japanese identity. Teaching Shakespeare in Japanese higher education thus has not been conducted in any straightforward way but revolved around clashing and competing ideologies.

Shakespeare used to occupy a firm position within the Japanese higher education curriculum. Students in higher education institutions, whether they liked it or not, were expected to encounter Shakespeare to advance to universities or to become a qualified teacher of English. Meanwhile, the perceptions about teaching and studying Shakespeare were different amongst professors; some scholars pursued the academic study of Shakespeare as a discipline, but such inward-looking specialisation came under doubt by a counter-impulse towards outward-looking relevance. This conflict was intensified by clashing urges to re-enact Western modernity and re-validate Japanese self. Such a conflict has not yet been resolved, as documented in the following chapter.

NOTES

1. Stopford Augustus Brooke, *English Literature* (London: Macmillan, 1876), 5. This book was widely read amongst Japanese students of English.
2. Dennis Kennedy, 'Shakespeare Worldwide', in *The Cambridge Companion to Shakespeare*, edited by Margreta de Grazia and Stanley Wells (Cambridge: Cambridge University Press, 2001), 251–264.
3. Benjamin Duke, *The History of Modern Japanese Education: Constructing the National School System, 1872–1890* (New Brunswick: Rutgers University Press, 2009), 11.
4. Ministry of Education, Middle and Elementary School Bureau, edited by *Zenkoku koritsu shiritsu chugakko nikansuru shochosa: Meiji 38 nen 2 gatsu* (*Investigations into Public and Private Secondary Schools Across the Country: February, 1905*) (Tokyo: Ministry of Education, Middle and Elementary School Bureau, 1905). Ministry of Education, Middle and Elementary School Bureau, edited by *Zenkoku koritsu shiritsu chugakko nikansuru shochosa: Meiji 44 nen 10 gatsu* (*Investigations into Public and Private Secondary Schools Across the Country: February, 1910*) (Tokyo: Ministry of Education, Middle and Elementary School Bureau, 1911). Ministry of Education, Middle and Elementary School Bureau, edited by *Zenkoku koritsu shiritsu chugakko nikansuru shochosa: Taisho 10 nen 10 gatsu* (*Investigations into Public and Private Secondary Schools Across the Country: October, 1921*) (Tokyo: Ministry of Education, Middle and Elementary School Bureau, 1921). Ministry of Education, Middle and Elementary School Bureau, edited by *Zenkoku koritsu shiritsu chugakko nikansuru shochosa: Showa 6 nen 10 gatsu* (*Investigations into Public and Private Secondary Schools Across the Country: October, 1931*) (Tokyo: Ministry of Education, Middle and Elementary School Bureau, 1931).

5. Kumiko Fujimura-Fanselow, 'Japan', in *Asian Higher Education: An International Handbook and Reference Guide*, edited by Gerard A. Postiglione and Grace C. L. Mak (Westport: Greenwood Press, 1997), 137–164.

6. Yamamoto Tsuyoshi, '*Kyuse koto gakko no seisin keiseishi kenkyu* (A Study of Mental Culture in Higher Schools)', *The Bulletin of the Graduate School of Education of Waseda University*, 20.1 (2012): 43.

7. This information is based on the educational system in 1919, when the University Ordinance (*daigakurei*) was implemented. No big changes were made to higher education system, including school years and student age, from 1919 to 1947.

8. Those lists were intermittently featured in *EigWo seinen* from vol. 30.2 in 1913 to vol. 91.3 in 1945.

9. Those lists were intermittently featured in *Eigo seinen* from vol. 43.5 in 1920 to vol. 46.6 in 1921.

10. Kobinata Sadajiro, *Eibungaku no shuyo to eigo kyoiku* (*English Literature and English Language Education*) (Tokyo: Kenkyusha, 1936), 34.

11. '*Tokyo hiroshima ryokoshi no eigo kyokasho* (English Textbooks for Use in Tokyo and Hiroshima Higher Normal Schools)'. *Eigo seinen* 43.5 (1920): 157.

12. 'List of Textbooks Used in 32 Higher Schools in Japan (1929–1930)', *The Bulletin of the Institute for Research in English Teaching* 62 (1930): n.p.

13. '*Kyusei koto gakko shiryo hozonkai*', *Kyusei koto gakko zensho* (*A Collection of Research Material on Higher Schools*) (Tokyo: Showa Shuppan, 1981), 3: 421–528.

14. Morimura Yutaka, *Zenkoku kanritsu daigaku nyushi eigo mondai seikai* (*Answers to National and Public University Entrance Examination Questions in English Across the Country*) (Tokyo: Kenkyusha, 1937): 186.

15. '*Koto gakko eigo kyoin kentei shiken*', *Eigo seinen* (*The Rising Generation*) 61.8 (1929): 292. '*Koto kyoin eigo kentei shiken*', *Eigo seinen* (*The Rising Generation*) 73.8 (1933): 284.

16. '*Koto gakko eigo kyoin kentei shiken*', *Eigo seinen* (*The Rising Generation*) 53.7 (1925): 217.

17. '*Koto kyoin eigo kentei shiken*', 284.

18. Ozawa Junsaku, '*Omoide* (Memoir)', *The Study and Teaching of English* 10.2 (1941): 20–21. 21.

19. Erikawa Haruo, *Nihonjin ha eigo wo do manande kitaka* (*A Socio-Cultural Study of English Language Education in Japan*) (Tokyo: Kenkyusha, 2008), 76.

20. Mark E. Linicome, *Imperial Subjects as Global Citizens: Nationalism, Internationalism, and Education in Japan* (Lanham: Lexington Books, 2009).

21. Ashikawa. '*Shoka jitsumu toshiteno eigo katsuyo ho* (How to Use English as a Business Person)'. *Jitsugyo no nihon* (*Business in Japan*) 8.14 (1905): 17–18.
22. Toyoda Minoru, *Shakespeare in Japan* (Tokyo: Iwanami-Shoten, 1940), 23–27.
23. Tokio Kaisei-Gakko, *The Calendar of the Tokio Kaisei-Gakko, or Imperial University of Tokio. For the Year 1875* (Tokyo: Tokyo Kaisei Gakko, 1875), 105.
24. John D. Jones, 'Shakespeare in English Schools', *Jahrbuch der Deutschen Shakespeare-Gesellschaft* 42 (1906): 111–126. 121.
25. Natsume Sōseki, 'My Individualism', in *Theory of Literature and Other Critical Writings*, edited by Michael Bourdaghs, Ueda Atsuko, and Joseph Murphy (New York: Columbia University Press, 2010), 248.
26. Nogami Toyoichiro, '*Daigaku koshi jidai no natsume sensei* (Professor Natsume at Imperial University)'. In the Supplementary Volume of *Sōseki zenshu* (*The Complete Works of Natsume Sōseki*) (Tokyo: Iwanami Shoten, (1918) 1995): 170–174. 173.
27. Miyoshi Masao, 'The Invention of English Literature in Japan', in *Japan in the World*, edited by Miyoshi Masao and H.D. Harootunian (Durham: Duke University Press, 1993), 271–287. 281–282.
28. Todd Andrew Borlik, 'Reading Hamlet Upside Down: The Shakespeare Criticism of Natsume Sōseki', *Shakespeare* 9.4 (2013): 383–403. 390.
29. David R. Shumway and Craig Dionne, ed. *Disciplining English: Alternative Histories, Critical Perspectives* (New York: State University of New York Press, 2002).
30. Shumway and Dionne, *Disciplining*, 3.
31. Saito Takeshi, '*Eibungaku 55 nen* (55 Years of English Studies)', *Eigo seinen* 109.5 (1963): 262.
32. E.N., '*Ko lawrence kyoju no macbeth kogi* (A Lecture on *Macbeth* Given by the Late Lawrence)'. *Eigo seinen* 35.9 (1916): 273.
33. Akutagawa Ryūnosuke, '*Anokoro no jibun no koto* (My Life in Those Days)', in *Akutagawa Ryūnosuke zenshu* (*The Complete Works of Akutagawa Ryūnosuke*), vol. 2, edited by Yoshida Seiichi, Nakamura Shinichiro, and Akutagawa Hiroshi (Tokyo: Iwanami Shoten (1919) 1977), 434–456. 436.
34. Nogami, Yaeko. '*Jokyoju b no kofuku* (The Happiness of Associate Professor B)', *Chuo koron* 33.10 (1918): 29–54. 34–35.
35. Martin Wallace, 'Criticism and the Academy', in *Modernism and the New Criticism*, edited by Walton Litz, Louis Menand, and Lawrence Rainey, *The Cambridge History of Literary Criticism*, vol. 7 (Cambridge: Cambridge University Press, 2000), 269–321. Gerald Graff, *Professing Literature: An Institutional History* (Chicago: The University of Chicago Press, 2007).

36. Ichikawa Sanki, ed. *Othello* (Tokyo: Kenkyusha, 1925).
37. Funyu Heizo, '*Taisho nenkan ni okeru eibungaku no kenkyu* (The Study of English Literature Between 1912 and 1926)', *Eibungaku kenkyu* (*English Literary Studies*), 7 (1927): 153–154.
38. Akutagawa, 227 [check – doesn't seem to be vol. 2].
39. Mukoyama Yoshihiko, *Browning Study in Japan: A Historical Survey, with a Comprehensive Bibliography* (Tokyo: Maeno Publishing Company, 1977).
40. Okada Akiko, *Keats and English Romanticism in Japan* (Bern: Peter Lang, 2006), 126.
41. Saito Takeshi, *Zousho kandan* (*An Idle Talk on Books*) (Tokyo: Kenkyusha, 1983), 23.
42. Saito Takeshi, 'English Studies in Japan', *Japan Quarterly* 2.4 (1955): 501–05.504–05.
43. A growing interest in the 'factual study' of English literature crystallized in the 103 volumes of *British and American Men of Letters* by Japanese scholars of English studies, which was an imitation of *English Men of Letters* published in Great Britain during the 1890s.
44. Fukuhara Rintaro, *Eibungaku kenkyuho* (*How to Study English Literature*), vol. 4, *Eigo eibungaku koza* (*Lectures on English Studies*) (Tokyo: Eigo Eibungaku Kanko Kai, 1934), 10.
45. Robert Eaglestone, *Doing English: A Guide for Literature Student* (London: Routledge, 2000).
46. Okakura Yoshisaburō, 'Brown Study', *Eigo seinen* 50.8 (1924): 248–249.
47. Okakura, 'Brown', 248–249.
48. Okakura, 'Brown', 248.
49. Okakura Yoshisaburō, '*Jo* (Introduction)', in *Suchu hamuretto* (*A Variorum Edition of* Hamlet), edited by Tsuzuki Tosaku (Tokyo: Kenkyusha, 1932), n.p.
50. Mori Masatoshi, '*Kenkyu to kansho* (Scholarship and Appreciation)', *Eigo seinen* 77.6 (1937): 209.
51. Yano Kazumi, '*Kenkyu ka hensan ka* (Scholarship or Annotation)', *Eibungaku kenkyu* (*Studies in English Literature*), 17.2 (1937): 304–308.
52. Yano, 'Kenkyu', 304–308.
53. Yano, 'Kenkyu', 304–308.
54. Yano, 'Kenkyu', 304–308.
55. Yano Hojin, *Nihon eibungaku no gakuto* (*The Orthodoxy of English Studies in Japan*) (Tokyo: Kenkyusha, 1961), iii.
56. Yano, *Nihon*, iii.
57. Shibuya Shinpei, '*Eigo taika rekihoroku: Okakura Yoshisaburo* (A Visit to Distinguished Experts in the Field of the English Language: Okakura Yoshisaburō)', *Eigo no nippon* [*The Nippon*] 9 (1916): 115. Fukuhara Rintaro, '*Kuregashi sensei no kyoshitsu* (Professor Okakura's Classroom)', *Eigo seinen* 76.8 (1937): 266.

58. Uei Isokichi, 'Okakura kyoju no eibun kaishaku ho (Okakura's Method of Teaching English Reading)', Eigo seinen 34.6 (1915): 178.
59. Uei Isokichi, 'Okakura kyoju no eibun kaishaku ho (Okakura's Method of Teaching English Reading)', Eigo seinen 34.5 (1915): 146.
60. Okakura Yoshisaburō, 'Achira no kanso (About a Country in Antipode)', Nihon sheikusupia kyokai kaiho (Newsletter: The Shakespeare Society of Japan) 3 (1933): 47–48.
61. Fukuhara Rintaro, 'Wakaki mono no tegami (A Letter from a Young Person)', Eigo seinen 43.4 (1920): 116.
62. Okakura Yoshisaburō, 'Notes', in The Rape of Lucrece and Sonnets, edited by Okakura Yoshisaburō (Tokyo: Kenkyusha, 1928), 305.
63. Fukuhara Rintaro, Fukuhara rintaro chosaku shu (The Collected Works of Fukahara Rintaro) (Tokyo: Kenkyusha, 1968), 5: 208.
64. Tanimoto Tomeri, Jitsuyo kyoikugaku and kyojuho (Practical Education and Pedagogy) (Tokyo: Rokumeikan, 1894), 77–78.
65. Higuchi Kanjiro, Togoshugi shin kyojuho (A Holistic Teaching Method) (Tokyo: Dobunkan, 1900), 48–49.
66. Shimoda Jiro, Joshi kyoiku (Women's Education), (Tokyo: Kinkodo, 1904), 365.
67. Uei Isokichi, 'Mombusho kaki koshukai', Eigo seinen, 33.10 (1915): 316.
68. John Henry Newman, The Idea of a University: New Edition (London: Longman (1852) 1891).
69. Newman, The Idea, 134.
70. Uei Isokichi, 'Okakura kyoju no eibun kaishaku ho (Okakura's Method of Teaching English Reading)', Eigo seinen, 33.12 (1915): 374–375. 375.
71. Okakura, 'Brown', 248.
72. 'Yōyōjuku umaru (The Birth of Yōyōjuku)', Eigo seinen, 76.8 (1923): 266.
73. Okakura Yoshisaburō, 'Chu to shinju (Loyalty and Love Suicide)', Eigo seinen, 48.7 (1923): 212. All references to his plays follow the act and line numbering of William Shakespeare, The Oxford Shakespeare: The Complete Works, 2nd ed., edited by John Jowett, William Montgomery, Gary Taylor, and Stanley Wells (Oxford: Clarendon Press, 2005).
74. Okakura, 'Chu', 212.
75. Okakura, 'Chu', 212.
76. Okakura, 'Chu', 212.
77. Okakura Yoshisaburō, 'Riao no daigomi (The Real Taste of King Lear)', Sao fukko (Shakespeare Renaissance), 13 (1934): 12–17. 13.
78. Sugiki Takashi, 'Rikkyo ni okeru okakura sensei (Professor Okakura at Rikkyo University)', Eigo seinen 76.8 (1937): 264.
79. Ichikawa Sanki, 'Okakura sensei wo tsuibo shite (In Memory of Professor Okakura)', Eigo seinen 76.8 (1937): 260.

80. Fukuhara Rintaro, *Atarasii i.e.* (*New Home*) (Tokyo: Kenkyusha, 1942), 304.
81. Fukuhara, *Atarasii*, 204.
82. Okakura, '*Riao*', 12.
83. Okakura Yoshisaburō, *Kone zappitsu* (*Collected Papers*) (Tokyo: Yōyōjuku, 1926), 45–49.
84. Okakura Yoshisaburō, '*Okakura yoshisaburō sensei* (Professor Okakura Yoshisaburō)', *Kamu kamu kurabu* (*Come Come Club*), 1.10 (1942): 24.
85. Fukuhara, '*Kuregashi*', 266.
86. Okakura Yoshisaburō, *The Life and Thought of Japan* (London: Dent, 1913), 45–46.
87. Okakura, *The Life*, 45–46.
88. Okakura, *The Life*, 38.
89. Takita, '*Shokuminchi ishiki* (Colonised Mind)', *Asahi Shinbun*, 22 September 1940. 1.
90. Natsume Sōseki, '*Gogaku yoseki ho* (How to Improve the Teaching of a Foreign Language)', in *Sōseki zenshu* (*The Complete Works of Natsume Sōseki*) (Tokyo: Iwanami-shoten, 1996), 392.
91. Togawa Shukotsu, '*Kanban no eigo to chugaku no eigo* (English on Signbords and in Secondary Schools)', *Tokyo Asahi Shinbun*, 6 July 1924.
92. Togawa, '*Kanban*', 9.
93. Guri Viswanathan, *Masks of Conquest: Literary Study and British Rule in India*, 25th ed. (New York: Columbia University Press, 2015).
94. Yamato Yasuo, *Eibungaku no hanashi* (*Tales of English Literature*), (Tokyo: Kembunsha, 1942).

REFERENCES

Akutagawa, Ryūnosuke. '*Anokoro no jibun no koto* (My Life in Those Days)'. In *Akutagawa Ryūnosuke zenshu* (*The Complete Works of Akutagawa Ryūnosuke*), vol. 2, edited by Yoshida Seiichi, Nakamura Shinichiro, and Akutagawa Hiroshi. Tokyo: Iwanami Shoten, (1919) 1977. 434–456.
Ashikawa. '*Shoka jitsumu toshiteno eigo katsuyo ho* (How to Use English as a Business Person)'. *Jitsugyo no nihon* (*Business in Japan*) 1.8 (1905): 17–19.
Atherton, Marth. 'Henry Sweet's Psychology of Language Learning'. In *Theorie unde Rekonstruktion*, edited by Klaus D. Dutz and Hans-J. Niederehe. Münster: Nodus. Publikationen, 1996. 149–168.
Borlik, Todd Andrew. 'Reading Hamlet Upside Down: The Shakespeare Criticism of Natsume Sōseki'. *Shakespeare*, 4.9 (2013): 383–403.
Brooke, Stopford Augustus. *English Literature*. London: Macmillan, 1876.

Duke, Benjamin. *The History of Modern Japanese Education: Constructing the National School System, 1872–1890*. New Brunswick: Rutgers University Press, 2009.

Eaglestone, Robert. *Doing English: A Guide for Literature Student*. London: Routledge, 2000.

'*Eigoka koto kyoin shiken kamoku oyobi sankosho* (Subjects and Reference Books for the Qualifying Examination for Prospective English Teachers of Higher School)'. *Eigo seinen*, 8.73 (1931): 222.

'*Eigoka koto kyoin shiken kamoku oyobi sankosho* (Subjects and Reference Books for the Qualifying Examination for Prospective English Teachers of Higher School)'. *Eigo seinen*, 12.64 (1931): 430.

'*Eigoka koto kyoin shiken sankosho* (Reference Books for the Qualifying Examination for Prospective English Teachers of Higher School)'. *Eigo seinen*, 11.73 (1935): 286.

E.N. '*Ko lawrence kyoju no macbeth kogi* (A Lecture on *Macbeth* Given by the Late Lawrence)'. *Eigo seinen*, 9.35 (1916): 273.

Erikawa, Haruo. *Nihonjin ha eigo wo do manande kitaka* (*A Socio-Cultural Study of English Language Education in Japan*). Tokyo: Kenkyusha, 2008.

Fujimura-Fanselow, Kumiko. 'Japan'. In *Asian Higher Education: An International Handbook and Reference Guide*, edited by Gerard A. Postiglione and Grace C. L. Mak. Westport: Greenwood Press, 1997: 137–164.

Fukuhara, Rintaro. '*Wakaki mono no tegami* (A Letter from a Young Person)'. *Eigo seinen*, 4.43 (1920): 116.

Fukuhara, Rintaro. *Eibungaku kenkyuho* (*How to Study English Literature*). Vol. 4, *Eigo eibungaku koza* (*Lectures on English Studies*). Tokyo: Eigo Eibungaku Kankō Kai, 1934.

Fukuhara, Rintaro. '*Kuregashi sensei no kyoshitsu* (Professor Okakura's Classroom)'. *Eigo seinen*, 8.76 (1937): 266.

Fukuhara, Rintaro. *Atarasii ie* (*New Home*). Tokyo: Kenkyusha, 1942.

Fukuhara, Rintaro. '*Okakura Yoshisaburō sensei* (Professor Okakura Yoshisaburō)'. *Kamu kamu kurabu* (*Come Come Club*), 10.1 (1948): 24.

Fukuhara, Rintaro. '*Watashi to shaikusupia* (Me and Shakespeare)'. In *Sheikusupia* (*Shakespeare*), *Fukuhara Rintaro chosakushu* (*The Selected Works of Fukuhara Rintaro*) Vol. 1. Tokyo: Kenkyusha, 1968. 124–130.

Funyu, Heizo. '*Taisho nenkan ni okeru eibungaku no kenkyu* (The Study of English Literature between 1912 and 1926)'. *Eibungaku kenkyu* (*English Literary Studies*) no. 7 (1927): 153–154.

Graff, Gerald. *Professing Literature: An Institutional History*. Chicago: The University of Chicago Press, 2007.

Higuchi, Kanjiro. *Togoshugi shin kyojuho* (*A Holistic Teaching Method*). Tokyo: Dobunkan, 1900.

Ichikawa, Sanki, ed. *Othello*. Tokyo: Kenkyusha, 1925.

Ichikawa, Sanki. '*Okakura sensei wo tsuibo shite* (In Memory of Professor Okakura)'. *Eigo seinen*, 8.76 (1937): 260.

Jones, John D. 'Shakespeare in English Schools'. *Jahrbuch der Deutschen Shakespeare-Gesellschaft*, no. 42 (1906): 111–126.

Kennedy, Dennis. 'Shakespeare Worldwide'. In *The Cambridge Companion to Shakespeare*, edited by Margreta de Grazia and Stanley Wells. Cambridge: Cambridge University Press, 2001. 251–264.

Kobinata, Sadajiro. *Eibungaku no shuyo to eigo kyoiku (English Literature and English Language Education)*. Tokyo: Kenkyusha, 1936.

'*Koto gakko eigo kyoin kentei shiken*'. *Eigo seinen*, 61.8 (1929): 292.

'*Koto gakko eigoka kyoin kentei shiken sankoshomoku* (Reference Books for the Qualifying Examination for Prospective English Teachers of Higher School)'. *Eigo seinen*, 12.56 (1927): 428.

'*Koto gakko kyoin juken chui* (Instructions for the Examination for Prospective Higher-School Teachers of English)'. *Eigo seinen*, 5.42 (1919): 158.

'*Koto gakko kyoin kentei shiken mondai* (Examinations Questions for Prospective Higher-School Teachers)'. *Eigo seinen*, 7.53 (1925): 217–219.

'*Koto kyoin eigo kentei shiken* (Qualifying Examinations for Prospective Higher-School Teachers)'. *Eigo seinen*, 73.8 (1933): 284.

'*Koto kyoin kentei shiken sankosho* (Reference Books for the Qualifying Examination for Prospective Higher-School Teachers of English)'. *Eigo seinen*, 10.52 (1925): 316.

'*Koto kyoin kentei shiken sankosho* (Reference Books for the Qualifying Examination for Prospective Higher-School Teachers of English)'. *Eigo seinen*, 87.6 (1938): 188.

'*Koto kyoin shiken sankosho* (Reference Books for the Qualifying Examination for Prospective English Teachers of Higher School)'. *Eigo seinen*, 61.2 (1929): 33.

Kyusei Koto Gakko Shiryo Hozonkai, ed. *Kyusei koto gakko zensho (A Collection of Research Material on Higher Schools)*. Tokyo: Showa Shuppan, 1981.

Linicome, Mark E. *Imperial Subjects as Global Citizens: Nationalism, Internationalism, and Education in Japan*. Lanham: Lexington Books, 2009.

'List of Textbooks Used in 32 Higher Schools in Japan (1929–1930)'. 1930. *The Bulletin of the Institute for Research in English Teaching*. 62: n.p.

Ministry of Education, Middle and Elementary School Bureau, ed. *Zenkoku koritsu shiritsu chugakko nikansuru shochosa: Meiji 38 nen 2 gatsu (Investigations into Public and Private Secondary Schools Across the Country: February, 1905)*. Tokyo: Ministry of Education, Middle and Elementary School Bureau, 1905.

Ministry of Education, Middle and Elementary School Bureau, ed. *Zenkoku koritsu shiritsu chugakko nikansuru shochosa: Meiji 44 nen 10 gatsu (Investigations into Public and Private Secondary Schools Across the Country: February,*

1910). Tokyo: Ministry of Education, Middle and Elementary School Bureau, 1911.

Ministry of Education, Middle and Elementary School Bureau, ed. *Zenkoku koritsu shiritsu chugakko nikansuru shochosa: Taisho 10 nen 10 gatsu (Investigations into Public and Private Secondary Schools Across the Country: October, 1921*). Tokyo: Ministry of Education, Middle and Elementary School Bureau, 1921.

Ministry of Education, Middle and Elementary School Bureau, ed. *Zenkoku koritsu shiritsu chugakko nikansuru shochosa: Showa 6 nen 10 gatsu (Investigations into Public and Private Secondary Schools Across the Country: October, 1931*). Tokyo: Ministry of Education, Middle and Elementary School Bureau, 1931.

Miyoshi, Masao. 'The Invention of English Literature in Japan'. In *Japan in the World*, edited by Miyoshi Masao and H.D. Harootunian. Durham: Duke University Press, 1993. 271–287.

Mori, Masatoshi. '*Kenkyu to kansho* (Scholarship and Appreciation)'. *Eigo seinen*, 6.77 (1937): 209.

Morimura, Yutaka. *Zenkoku kanritsu daigaku nyushi eigo mondai seikai (Answers to National and Public University Entrance Examination Questions in English Across the Country)*. Tokyo: Kenkyusha, 1937.

Mukoyama, Yoshihiko. *Browning Study in Japan: A Historical Survey, with a Comprehensive Bibliography*. Tokyo: Maeno Publishing Company, 1977.

Natsume, Sōseki. '*Gogaku yoseiho* (How to Improve the Teaching of a Foreign Language)'. In *Sōseki zenshu (The Complete Works of Natsume Sōseki)*, vol. 25. Tokyo: Iwanami-shoten, (1911) 1996. 391–400.

Natsume, Sōseki. 'My Individualism'. In *Theory of Literature and Other Critical Writings*, translated by Michael Bourdaghs, Ueda Atsuko, and Joseph Murphy. New York: Columbia University Press, (1912) 2010. 242–264.

Newman, John Henry. *The Idea of a University: New Edition*. London: Longman, (1852) 1891.

Nogami, Toyoichiro. '*Daigaku koshi jidai no natsume sensei* (Professor Natsume at Imperial University)'. In the Supplementary Volume of *Sōseki zenshu (The Complete Works of Natsume Sōseki)*. Tokyo: Iwanami Shoten, (1918) 1995. 170–174.

Nogami, Yaeko. '*Jokyoju b no kofuku* (The Happiness of Associate Professor B)'. *Chuo koron*. 10.33 (1918): 29–54.

Okada, Akiko. *Keats and English Romanticism in Japan*. Bern: Peter Lang, 2006.

Okakura, Yoshisaburō. *The Life and Thought of Japan*. London: Dent, 1913.

kakura, Yoshisaburō. '*Chu to Shinju* (Loyalty and Love Suicide)'. *Eigo seinen*, 48.7 (1923): 212.

Okakura, Yoshisaburō. 'Brown Study'. *Eigo seinen*, 8.50 (1924): 248–249.

Okakura, Yoshisaburō. *Kone zappitsu (Collected Essays)*. Tokyo: Yōyōjuku, 1926.

Okakura, Yoshisaburō, ed. *The Rape of Lucrece* and *Sonnets*. Tokyo: Kenkyusha, 1928.

Okakura, Yoshisaburō. '*Jo* (Introduction)'. In *Suchu hamuretto* (*A Variorum Edition of Hamlet*), edited by Tsuzuki Tosaku. Tokyo: Kenkyusha, 1932.

Okakura, Yoshisaburō. '*Achira no kanso* (About a Country in Antipode)'. *Nihon sheikusupia kyokai kaiho* (*Newsletter: The Shakespeare Society of Japan*), 3 (1933): 47–48.

Okakura, Yoshisaburō. '*Riao no daigomi* (The Real Taste of *King Lear*)'. *Sao fukko* (*Shakespeare Renaissance*), no. 13 (1934): 12–17.

Ozawa, Junsaku. '*Omoide* (Memoir)'. *The Study and Teaching of English*, 2.10 (1941): 20–21.

Saito, Takeshi. 'English Studies in Japan'. *Japan Quarterly*, 4.2 (1955): 501–505.

Saito, Takeshi. '*Eibungaku 55 nen* (55 Years of English Studies)'. *Eigo seinen* 109.5 (1963): 262.

Saito, Takeshi. *Zousho kandan* (*An Idle Talk on Books*). Tokyo: Kenkyusha, 1983.

Shakespeare, William. *The Oxford Shakespeare: The Complete Works*, 2nd edn, edited by John Jowett, William Montgomery, Gary Taylor, and Stanley Wells. Oxford: Clarendon Press, 2005.

Shibuya, Shinpei. '*Eigo taika rekihoroku: Okakura Yoshisaburō* (A Visit to Distinguished Experts in the Field of the English Language: Okakura Yoshisaburō)'. *Eigo no nippon* (*The Nippon*), no. 9 (1916): 114–116.

Shimoda, Jiro. *Joshi kyoiku* (*Women's Education*). Tokyo: Kinkodo, 1904.

Shumway, David R., and Craig Dionne, ed. *Disciplining English: Alternative Histories, Critical Perspectives*. New York: State University of New York Press, 2002.

Sugiki, Takashi. '*Rikkyo ni okeru okakura sensei* (Professor Okakura at Rikkyo University)'. *Eigo seinen*, 8.76 (1937): 264.

Takita. '*Shokuminchi ishiki* (Colonised Mind)'. *Tokyo Asahi Shinbun*, September 22, 1940.

Tanimoto, Tomeri. *Jitsuyo kyoikugaku and kyojuho* (*Practical Education and Pedagogy*). Tokyo: Rokumeikan, 1894.

Togawa, Shukotsu. '*Kanban no eigo to chugaku no eigo* (English on signboards and in secondary schools)'. *Tokyo Asahi Shinbun*, July 6, 1924.

Tokio Kaisei-Gakko. *The Calendar of the Tokio Kaisei-Gakko, or Imperial University of Tokio. For the Year 1875*. Tokyo: Tokyo Kaisei Gakko, 1875.

'*Tokyo hiroshima ryokoshi no eigo kyokasho* (English Textbooks for Use in Tokyo and Hiroshima Higher Normal Schools)'. *Ego seinen*, 43.5 (1920): 157.

Toyoda, Minoru. *Shakespeare in Japan*. Tokyo: Iwanami-Shoten, 1940.

Uchimaru, Kohei. 'Education Through the Study of English: Yoshisaburō Okakura as a Conservative Reformer'. *Language & History*, 2.62 (2019): 159–176.

Uei, Isokichi. '*Mombusho kaki koshukai*'. *Eigo seinen*, 33.10 (1915): 316.

Uei, Isokichi. '*Okakura kyoju no eibun kaishaku ho* (Okakura's Method of Teaching English Reading)'. *Eigo seinen*, 12.33 (1915): 374–375.

Uei, Isokichi. '*Okakura kyoju no eibun kaishaku ho* (Okakura's Method of Teaching English Reading)'. *Eigo seinen*, 34.5 (1915): 146.

Uei, Isokichi. '*Okakura kyoju no eibun kaishaku ho* (Okakura's Method of Teaching English Reading)'. *Eigo seinen*, 6.34 (1915): 177–178.

Viswanathan, Guri. *Masks of Conquest: Literary Study and British Rule in India*, 25th edn. New York: Columbia University Press, 2015.

Wallace, Martin. 'Criticism and the Academy'. In *Modernism and the New Criticism*, edited by Walton Litz, Louis Menand, and Lawrence Rainey. *The Cambridge History of Literary Criticism*. Vol 7. Cambridge: Cambridge University Press, 2000. 269–321.

Yamamoto, Tsuyoshi. '*Kyuse koto gakko no seisin keiseishi kenkyu* (A Study of Mental Culture in Higher Schools)'. *The Bulletin of the Graduate School of Education of Waseda University*, 20.1 (2012): 37–47.

Yamato, Yasuo. *Eibungaku no hanashi* (*Tales of English Literature*). Tokyo: Kembunsha, 1942.

Yano, Hojin. *Nihon eibungaku no gakuto* (*The Orthodoxy of English Studies in Japan*). Tokyo: Kenkyusha, 1961.

Yano, Kazumi. '*Kenkyu ka hensan ka* (Scholarship or Annotation)'. *Eibungaku kenkyu* (*Studies in English Literature*), 2.17 (1937): 304–308.

'*Yōyōjuku umaru* (The Birth of Yōyōjuku)'. *Eigo seinen*, 8.76 (1923).

CHAPTER 5

The West and the Resistance: Stakeholders' Perceptions of Teaching Shakespeare for and against Westernisation in Japanese Higher Education

Sarah Olive

Abstract This chapter explores the question 'Is Shakespeare perceived as one of the powerful global icons through which local education is westernised?' in Japan. It foregrounds the perceptions of people studying and teaching Shakespeare in Japan in the early twenty-first century. The chapter demonstrates that some of these perceptions around Shakespeare in Japanese higher education are predicated on a binaric understanding of Shakespeare as the 'foreign'/'other'/west, distinct from the 'indigenous'/'our'/East Asian. His foreignness is perceived varyingly from positive to malignant, with reference to the nature and purpose of subject English; the use of western productions in the classroom; and the delivery of a westernized 'world view' through Shakespeare. However, other

S. Olive (✉)
University of York, York, UK
e-mail: sarah.olive@york.ac.uk

© The Author(s), under exclusive license to Springer Nature   145
Switzerland AG 2021, corrected publication 2021
S. Olive et al., *Shakespeare in East Asian Education*, Global Shakespeares,
https://doi.org/10.1007/978-3-030-64796-4_5

perceptions explicitly or implicitly trouble this supposed polarity, emphasising Shakespeare as (adapted to be) local, regional and Asian, in terms
of perceptions of his bawdy humour, affinity with Japanese history and
culture, and use of locally-made or -inflected resources.

Keywords Shakespeare · Japan · Higher education · West ·
Westernisation · Local · Asian

This chapter explores the question 'Is Shakespeare perceived as one of the
powerful global icons through which local higher education is westernised?' with regard to Japan. A 'global icon' can be defined as someone
whose name needs no gloss to be instantly recognisable to households
internationally.[1] The westernisation of education invokes a process in
which provision becomes 'western in character', adopts, is brought or
comes 'under the influence of the culture, economy, or political systems
of Europe and North America' or 'the Anglophone model'.[2] It is particularly interesting to explore whether or not Shakespeare is perceived as
one of the powerful global icons through which local higher education
is westernised in Japan given prominent accounts of its fluctuating relations with the rest of the world. Recently, there is the claim that 'It is the
most resistant Asian country to English, maintaining a national language
system; it tends to do things differently in many spheres to the Anglophone model' with considerable success. Hence, 'it is one of the countries
which seems to challenge, albeit perhaps not consciously, the popular
assumption that perhaps the Anglophone way is the most efficient'.[3]
Historically, there are its periods of isolationism and nationalism; 'opening
up' and being forcibly opened up to western influences; military occu-
pation, continued military presence, and direct intervention in shaping
Japan's school system and curriculum design after World War II. Many of
these heavily involving the United States as well as Britain, through the
Anglo-Japanese Treaty of 1902.[4] These are highly relevant contexts, even
explanations, for Shakespeare's place in Japan. Existing research has established the role Shakespeare was made to play, for example, in westernising
and modernising traditional Japanese theatre as part of the wider 'Meiji
Restoration's sycophantic adoration of Western literature and mores' in
its 'dramatic drive for innovation and development' and to compete with

the global dominance of the British Empire.[5] There is less research avail- able, in English, on the effect of the Meiji Restoration on Shakespeare in education. Although it is still overshadowed by attention to Shakespeare in education in Britain's former colonies, publications on Shakespeare in Japanese classrooms are flourishing at the start of the twenty-first century: see issues six, seven, thirteen and sixteen of the British Shakespeare Asso- ciation's *Teaching Shakespeare* for examples of, what Bi-qi Beatrice Lei has called, the 'showcasing' of Shakespeare in Japan, where individuals present their experiences of and guidance for teaching or studying him.[6] There is a dominant focus in such work on what Shakespeare is done, when and how, i.e. what pedagogies are used—students' perceptions of and visions for Shakespeare. Publications that go beyond such show- casing include Daniel Gallimore's and Kohei Uchimaru's critically- and historically-engaged work on Shakespeare in Japanese classrooms and educational publishing.[7]

The previous chapter in this book, by Uchimaru, suggests that the attractiveness of Britain in, and somewhat beyond, Meiji Japan was pred- icated on—and went hand in hand with—a deficit view of Japan as an inferior nation in desperate need of modernisation. Such views were expressed in critiques written by its own sons (with some dissent from intellectuals and authors such as Natsume Sōseki and Fukuhara Rintaro).[8] Facility in English was held to be important less for communicating with English speakers than for gaining knowledge about 'manners and customs', 'thoughts and feelings', morals, values and culture from Anglo- phone countries with which to 'improve' Japanese citizens.[9] It is hard to imagine this scenario persisting today given either, depending on who you read, an apparent role reversal—Britain's seeming pursuit of isolationism (exemplified through its withdrawal from the European Union) and Japan's overall growth in cultural and economic power, notwithstanding its economic stall in the 1990s—or Japan's determined *galapagosuzation* or exceptionalism.[10] One of the concerns of this chapter is the extent to which western—no longer purely, or primarily, British—models and prod- ucts are constructed as desirable in Japanese higher education. Uchimaru explains that, as the twentieth-century progressed, Shakespeare's place in Japanese higher education was articulated more critically, even as he continued to be a mainstay of studies of English literature and language. He argues that currently 'Shakespeare is being marginalised in Japanese higher education, largely due to competition from career-oriented educa- tion' faced by the liberal arts and humanities.[11] So, this chapter's key question might be restated as, in twenty-first century Japan, 'Is Shakespeare *still* perceived as one of the powerful global icons through which local higher education is westernised?'

In the following section, I critically relate the methods used in researching this chapter from 2014 to the present. Subsequent sections answer the question 'Is Shakespeare still perceived as one of the powerful global icons through which local higher education is westernised?' affirmatively. They do so by analysing university educators' and students' constructions of the nature and purpose of subject English; the use of western productions in the classroom; and the delivery of a westernised 'world view' through Shakespeare. I then demonstrate contrary instances in which Shakespeare is *not* perceived to westernise Japanese education, or in which his teaching can be seen to resist or problematise westernisation. These include the negotiation of possible affronts to cultural sensibilities caused in Japan by Shakespeare's *shimo-neta* or bawdy humour as well as the demands of western pedagogies (i.e. pedagogies perceived to be western in origin); an emphasis on Japan's affinity with Britain; and the use of local cultural products to teach Shakespeare.

5.1   RESEARCHING SHAKESPEARE
IN JAPANESE HIGHER EDUCATION

The question explored in this chapter is adapted from one originally posed by Sonia Massai in her book *World-wide Shakespeares*: 'Has Shakespeare become one of the powerful global icons through which local cultural markets are progressively westernised?'.[12] Massai posits secondary and tertiary education as modes of cultural production alongside theatre, film and other media.[13] I have altered the wording of Massai's original question, not only to focus on higher education rather than strictly cultural markets, but also to remove any suggestion that this is a longitudinal study ('progressively' has been deleted) or that it will measure a cause-and-effect relationship between Shakespeare in higher education and westernisation. The chapter will demonstrate that some perceptions of Shakespeare by stakeholders in Japanese higher education are predicated on a binaric understanding of Shakespeare as the 'foreign'/'other'/west (with foreignness perceived varyingly from positive to malignant) distinct from the 'indigenous'/'our'/East Asian. Other perceptions trouble this supposed binary, explicitly or implicitly, drawing on concepts such as nationalising, localising, regionalising and Asianising Shakespeare.[14] They reject, as Thea Buckley terms it, 'a simplistic east-west binaric axis' in favour of recognising 'multidirectional complexity' and 'glocal inter- and intraculturalism between multiple local and global centres'.[15] So this chapter contributes to rewriting a dominant and overly-simplistic narrative of west-east influence on Shakespeare pedagogy.

It draws extensively on articles, written and published in English, by contributors from Japan. They were received in response to my calls for papers for the British Shakespeare Association's *Teaching Shakespeare*. This is an international, cross-sector publication for Shakespeare educators (teachers, lecturers, theatre and heritage workers mainly) freely available online and read in over sixty countries. I founded it in 2011 and continue to edit issues two or three times a year: this year saw the publication of its twentieth issue. The articles analysed here that appear in issue 6 were received in response to a call shared through multiple international, regional and local Shakespeare associations. Those in issue 13 of the magazine were volunteered by the organisers of a symposium, Shakespeare Film East West, co-organised by Waseda University and the University of Birmingham. Issue 16 similarly came out of a symposium on the teaching of Shakespeare in Japan held at Toyo University in January 2018. A couple of the articles drawn on in this chapter were commissioned by me for general issues. I gave little guidance, beyond house style, to these authors or the guest editors of the themed issues. Each contributor was asked to write between five hundred and two thousand words on their experience of Shakespeare as an educator and/or student from/in Japan. To offer some insight into the demographics of the contributors, the majority were Japanese nationals, the rest UK or US foreign nationals working in Japan, mostly on a permanent basis. Some were postgraduate students as well as educators in higher education.[16] Both public and private universities are represented.[17] Although Shakespeare is rarely a compulsory subject at university, contributors come from a variety of departments and programmes: mostly English departments (language and literature), but also law, global studies, life design, liberal arts and lifelong learning offered by institutions affiliated with universities (but not awarding degrees).[18] Many academics who might identify their home discipline as English Literature teach both English majors (e.g. British Literature, British Drama) and non-English majors (e.g. law and life science students studying English as an Additional Language or EAL). The educators represented in this chapter are working at undergraduate, postgraduate and non-award level. Their voices are crucial to this research given the absence of educators working inside 'the Japanese system' from much existing literature on Shakespeare in education.[19]

That the articles needed to be written in English for publication in *Teaching Shakespeare* means that the research was self-selecting of educators with strong written English skills. However, there is a long-held expectation in Japan that those delivering Shakespeare in higher education are familiar with and skilled in the English language, making it a reasonable proposition. Although this research exceeds the sample size of previous studies (such as the aforementioned publications showcasing Shakespeare in Japanese classrooms), an obvious limitation of this chapter is that these educators and students constitute a small sample of the total population currently studying and teaching Shakespeare in Japan. Additionally, the sample's representativeness—or lack thereof—must be taken into account. For example, the contributing educators consider themselves, in some respect, experts in and innovators with regard to Shakespeare and/or pedagogy. They are also sufficiently self-motivated to write about their experiences. Apart from these contributions to *Teaching Shakespeare* articles, this chapter is also informed by my attendance at and participation in a range of Shakespeare-related activities in Japan since 2014: teaching classes as a guest lecturer; informally mentoring small groups of undergraduate and postgraduate students; auditing and presenting at academic symposia; participating in student rehearsals; watching productions; auditing and presenting at public events for educators, students and Shakespeare enthusiasts. A limitation of my interactions is that they were all conducted in English (or that, occasionally where Japanese was spoken, I was dependent on translation into English by multilingual colleagues or students) so there is the possibility of mistranslation, missed nuances of speech, or that some English as an Additional Language speakers may not have felt as free or secure in their articulation as when working in their first language.[20] I have written on the challenges, benefits and pleasures of such outsider research more widely in the introduction to this book as well as in a dedicated blog post published by the British Sociological Association.[21]

To a lesser extent, this chapter draws on vox pops that I undertook with students at several higher education institutions for *Teaching Shakespeare*. They were drawn from universities in Tokyo and Kyoto as well as (relatively) smaller places like Gifu, Nishinomiya, Sendai and Takasaki. Additionally, many of the articles quote students' anonymous course feedback or surveys (again, anonymised) undertaken with students by the article authors. To help understand these students' perspectives, I offer here a brief sketch characterising Japanese students' experience with Shakespeare—although it cannot capture the full range of experiences. Although popularly extracted in EAL readers until the mid-twentieth-century, the plays are not generally now taught at high school.[22] However, school students may learn about Shakespeare as a historical figure from their world history textbooks.[23] Additionally, Igarashi Hiro-hisa and Anthony Martin argue that '"Shakespeare" is not entirely foreign to' higher education students in Japan but may instead be something to which they have had 'significant exposure', if serendipitously and unwit-tingly instead of through formal educational policy.[24] An example they give is that students may have unknowingly encountered him in the EAL classroom: 'English learning materials used in Japan are dotted with quotations from "Shakespeare"', although they are not always identified as such.[25] For instance, '"All that glitters is not gold" is often quoted in English grammar books to illustrate the proper use of "that" as a rela-tive pronoun. "To be, or not to be" is quoted to demonstrate the use of the to-infinitive'.[26] Moreover, young adults in Japan are familiar with the figure of Shakespeare and snatches of his work through their incorpora-tion into domestic popular culture. As Uchimaru explains, 'Shakespeare's plays are employed as material resources to exploit for Japanese youth culture, including *anime* and *manga*'.[27] Igarashi adds songs, television dramas and commercials—as well as reminding us of the long history of translations, stage and film productions of Shakespeare in Japan— to this list of local cultural appropriations of 'stories, moments and famous speeches'.[28] Furthermore, he cites various twenty-first-century examples of British theatre and BBC Shakespeare productions that circu-lated reasonably popularly in Japan in cinemas and on DVD. Rarer yet than these experiences of Shakespeare, but still a source of contact, are touring theatre groups, student and, occasionally, school productions.[29] However, reading Shakespeare's works in early modern English editions or extracts is repeatedly identified by educators as being too hard for both school and university students in Japan: some perceive this to be exac-erbated by the lack of attention given to reading sizeable literary texts, in any language, at school.[30] Shakespeare is not necessarily a compulsory subject at university, even for English/modern language majors. This may be more common where a choice is offered between studying English and American literature.[31] To summarise, Japanese higher education students are likely to have encountered a phenomenon called 'Shakespeare' by the time they reach English classes at university, but not to have studied his works.

5.2   Shakespeare for Global *Jinzai* and English as an Additional Language

That learning English problematically involves westernisation has already been made evident in this book.[32] With the particular example of Shakespeare, chapters two and three testify that studying language frequently involves encountering literature written in that language as well as cultural mores, predominantly from the west rather than the wider, English-speaking world. Uchimaru established in Chapter 4 that the study of English in Japan since the late 1800s onwards has been no different. This westernising effect of learning English—entailing coming under the influence of (among other things) the culture of Europe and North America—is actively sought in certain contexts and by certain stakeholders in education.[33] This is true of Japan, from Uchimaru's description of the Meiji period's equation of westernisation with modernisation and imperial power to something I focus on in this section: the idea that learning English (on the assumption that it is the global *lingua franca*) is a key aspect of 'global *jinzai*' or '*globaru jinzai*'. Otherwise known as global talent, global personnel and global human resources, the notion of 'global *jinzai*' has been foregrounded in Japanese higher education, especially since the 'burst of Japan's bubble economy in 1991'.[34] These global personnel should graduate with the potential to study and work abroad, be interested in and understanding of different cultures, and able to use foreign languages for professional communication. Under this banner, a particular target has been improving Japanese graduates' speaking and listening skills in English, which have for a long time been regarded as a weak point of EAL in Japan (with Japanese students' EAL generally held to be weaker than in neighbouring countries).[35] Gallimore notes that at the time of his arrival in Japan in 1987—roughly three decades prior to the report Motoyama Tetsuhito cites—'there was a perception that while educated Japanese people could read English, they lacked the skills and confidence to communicate in English with native speakers'.[36] Indeed, Uchimaru's previous chapter suggests an identical concern was expressed at the very turn of the twentieth century. This view is often explained by citing the context that 'spoken English is not necessary in daily life, and Japan still retains a strong national language system', the lesser place of English in schools (especially primary schools) in Japan than in neighbouring countries, and the pressure on graduates to 'have the qualities and skills to cope in the international arena [plus]...a stable Japanese identity' ahead of being a global citizen.[37]

This focus on particular aspects of, or approaches to, EAL has been enshrined in Japan's education policy. Evidence of this in higher education institutions, and its consequences for Shakespeare, includes an article by Motoyama, who teaches Shakespeare as part of EAL education in Waseda University's law school. He cites as an influence on his course design the final report of the Japanese Ministry of Education, Culture, Sports, Science and Technology (MEXT)'s Committee to Form a Grand Design for Education and Research for the twenty-first century's call for 'education that makes discussion in English possible'.[38] Motoyama explains the effect of this report on the work and curricula of Waseda Law School. Its 'non-area-major faculty members', including Shakespeareans, have offered 'language and general education courses' informed by their own humanities and social sciences disciplines, including 'a tutorial-style class in Shakespeare' since 2006.[39] The idea of such content- and task-based classes is to 'make students functional enough in English to be able to study law in English when necessary' and to take part in 'academic discussion' in English.[40] Additionally, students in the law school commented that studying Shakespeare enhanced their understanding of the culture and attitudes that have shaped English law.[41] Umemiya Yu's article in the same issue of *Teaching Shakespeare* cites a survey of school-leavers undertaken by MEXT to highlight that students have internalised their national government's concern and to explain their enthusiasm for studying English, including courses on Shakespeare.[42] He has recently developed an online teaching activity with students reading aloud, then submitting audio recordings of, and receiving feedback on monologues from Shakespeare to develop their spoken English. There is a particular emphasis on accent, pronunciation, stress, fluency and speed.[43] Where Shakespeare is included in English classes in twenty-first-century Japanese higher education, especially for those not majoring in Literature, it is because lecturers, such as Motoyama and Umemiya, have made a convincing argument for Shakespeare's being 'inextricably tethered to English-language' speaking and listening ability, including its benefits to vocabulary.[44] On the flipside, the policy emphasis on English for global *jinzai*—sometimes framed as a focus on English as skills over content; 'English language' rather than 'English literature'; or 'communicative competence' rather than English as a 'cultural and literary subject'—means that Shakespeare, as a literary giant, can be seen as getting in the way of learning English for professional communication.[45] Some lecturers report being asked not to cover Shakespeare, or have the time they spend on it, in their English language classes, limited.[46] The 'stampede towards English as a global language', specifically English for global *jinzai*, has split attitudes towards and behaviours around teaching and learning Shakespeare in Japan, perhaps along the lines of institutional ethos: liberal versus utilitarian education, embracing versus shunning.[47] Thus, it sometimes transpires in twenty-first-century Japanese higher education that Shakespeare is perceived as not westernising enough or, rather, not *functionally* westernising enough.

5.3   Western Productions
for Teaching Shakespeare

Given the emphasis shown above on Shakespeare for EAL and the Anglo-centric nature of much English language teaching, it is not surprising that western, Anglophone productions and adaptations of the plays dominated these educators' and students' experiences of Shakespeare in the classroom. Given the further value accorded to learners interacting with native speakers in many Japanese educational institutions—demonstrated by the use of native English-speaking teaching assistants in schools and lecturers in universities—it is perhaps also predictable that the majority of productions were not just Anglophone but western. Any attempt to explain the favouring of western Shakespeare productions with reference to a lack of availability of non-western, English language Shakespeare productions would be questionable in the digital age where online resources such as the Asian Shakespeare Intercultural Archive and MIT Global Shakespeares websites are freely available. Rather, watching British and American Shakespeare productions or adaptations on screen is portrayed by several educators in Japan as satisfying students' need to listen to native speakers in order to improve their communicative ability in English.[48] That is to say, the perceived westernising influence of these productions is strategically courted by some educators. For others, however, the films' geographic origins seem incidental: what matters is the sense that students engage better with films of Shakespeare than with reading tasks, especially as an introduction to or overview of the plot—something not unique to EAL Shakespeare classes. Productions mentioned include *Henry IV, part*

1 from Shakespeare's Globe, directed by Dominic Dromgoole (2010); the BBC's *Hollow Crown* (2012); the BBC's *Two Gentlemen of Verona* (1983) in a version with both English and Japanese subtitles; Baz Luhrmann's *Romeo + Juliet* (1996); and Michael Radford's *The Merchant of Venice*.[49] Koizumi Yuto, writing about teaching at Waseda University Writing Centre and Komazawa Women's University, describes teaching Shakespeare, specifically *A Midsummer Night's Dream* and *The Merchant of Venice*, using two 'modern films featuring Shakespearean lines, characters' and plot moments: *Dead Poets Society* (1989) and *The Man Without A Face* (1993).[50] Similarly, Morinaga Koji shows Anglophone films that quote Shakespeare as part of a focus on 'The Poetry of Film' such as *Sense and Sensibility* and *Mrs Dalloway*. Marie Honda taught *The Taming of the Shrew* drawing on American screen adaptations of the play such as the Zeffirelli film, *Kiss Me Kate*, *10 Things I Hate About You*, and the TV drama *Gossip Girl*, as well as Japanese spin-offs detailed below. These films range through the genres of literary adaptation, drama, romance, romantic comedy, crime and Shakespop, glossed by Christy Desmet as 'Hollywood teen Shakespeare'.[51] Desmet's article usefully puts into perspective for readers that Shakespeare and western productions of his work, encountered as part of curricula and assessments, are a minute part of the cross-cultural traffic these students partake of and participate in.[52] Shakespeare is not the prime westernising force in their lives: they are independently, avid consumers of western film and this enthusiasm is used by educators to engage them with Shakespeare, a less familiar western text.[53]

Another way in which Japanese higher education students may encounter western productions of Shakespeare is through touring Shakespeare companies. The two occasions on which Machi Saeko recounts hosting a British Shakespeare touring company, TNT, at Japan Women's University not only introduced students to the experience of hearing Shakespeare's English spoken by native speakers, but also to western theatre productions and conventions, including purportedly western values around gender, sexuality and equality.[54] This is in line with rationales articulated for subject English as extending students' realms of experience, making them 'open-minded' and 'flexible', understanding 'themselves and the world around them' no longer dominated by the local or national but international or global,[55] producing 'more cultured, critical and sympathetic world citizens', 'challeng[ing their] existing social consciousness' and addressing 'issues of importance'.[56] Machi observes that the touring production did not overtly introduce the audience to movements promoting and legislation around contemporary LGBTQ+ rights movements in the west.[57] However, she suggests that the students may have made connections between this western play's LGBTQ + resonances, heightened by its gender-blind casting of Maria, and international current affairs, such as the LGBTQ+ community's fears about backsliding on their rights under Donald Trump's leadership of America. Furthermore, she suggests they may have linked the production to institutional discussions about the inclusion of transgender students at Japan Women's University and national legislation on gender reassignment in the 2017 Family Register Law. Machi articulates support for what she perceives as progressive, western thinking about sexual equalities in Japanese policy and society in her statement that:

> ...the world has entered a new phase in terms of the concepts of gender, sex, masculinity, and femininity; their definitions are becoming more varied and flexible than they used to be. Unfortunately, LGBT rights and understanding of transgender issues in Japan are relatively behind compared to the US and some countries in Europe.[58]

Supposedly, western-style approaches to gender and sexuality are cast by this educator as desirable in Japanese education and society, and Shakespeare is welcomed as one possible stimulus to reconsidering local (Japan Women's University) and national (Japanese) constructions of them: 'I hope that the opportunity to watch *Twelfth Night* has not only inspired the students to learn more about the English language, culture, and plays, but has also given them the chance to question our notions of gender, humanity, and love'.[59] There are resonances here with the historical aims for Shakespeare in Japanese higher education expressed by Uchimaru, even if the outlook that studying Shakespeare is supposed to instil has shifted. In addition to exposure to western Shakespeare productions, on film or stage, as part of studying Shakespeare in Japanese higher education, Honda helps students to visualise early modern England by showing them photos of Shakespeare's Globe alongside *Shakespeare in Love*. Furthermore, she looks at eighteenth-century Shakespeare adaptation by teaching students about *The Tempest* by William Davenant and John Dryden and *King Lear* by Nahum Tate.[60] Tink developed students' awareness of the plays' historical context, asking them to explore extracts from Elizabethan sources, such as *An Homily against Disobedience*, as well as western literary criticism as diverse as E.M.W. Tillyard and Phyllis Rackin.[61] Kenneth Chan used multiple, English, short stories of the set play with his classes, by the Lambs and E. Nesbit.[62] Thus, teaching the global icon Shakespeare sometimes entails the use—even the multiplication—of other western texts in the classroom.

5.4   JAPANESE RESOURCES FOR TEACHING SHAKESPEARE

However, there is also evidence of the use of Japanese-originating teaching resources in the Shakespeare classroom in Japanese higher education. Their use troubles notions of Shakespeare as a powerful global icon through which local education is straightforwardly westernised. These resources are one way in which domestic or Asianised texts are brought into the English classroom in Japanese higher education that counterbalances with the western productions and additional texts cited above. Obvious examples are the textbooks for teaching EAL produced by Japanese publishers, including those with a literary focus.[63] Others include *haiku* in Japanese being brought into the classroom to read alongside Shakespearean verse and Japanese translations of Shakespeare. A benefit of the latter was described by one of Honda's students thus: 'Japanese lines move my heart more directly'.[64] For this student, experiencing Shakespeare in Japanese had a greater affective impact and was thus more engaging. Beyond strictly literary examples, Honda describes using Japanese *manga* such as *Hanayori dango*, translated as *Boys over Flowers*, in her session on *The Taming of the Shrew* (more details on this below). Matsuyama Kyoko similarly used Japanese-language *manga* and *anime* in her classes at Komazawa Women's University: not 'study manga', which offer a beginner's edition, but popular titles in their own rights which incorporate Shakespearean quotation or adapt his plotlines.[65] These include *Seven Shakespeares* and *Seven Shakespeares Non Sanz Droict* by Harold Sakuishi, *Black Butler* by Toboso Yano, *Blast of Tempest* by Shirodaira Kyo, Sano Arihide and Saizaki Ren, and *Requiem of the Rose King* by Kanno Aya. Matsuyama perceives them as highlighting key themes in the plays and conveying to students details about British history and culture, despite their Japanese origins—or because of them: perhaps, as Japanese cultural products, they assume less knowledge of the plays, British history and culture on the part of their readers than western equivalents. She also notes that these Japanese texts sometimes talk back to the Shakespearean originals. For example, they criticise Shakespeare and his western audiences' fondness for tragic 'bad-end' plays, rewriting them to fit with Japanese sensibilities concerning appropriate endings.[66] That is, they actively resist western genre conventions used by authors such as Shakespeare.[67] Gallimore uses Anglophone *manga* Shakespeare editions from a series by the British publisher Self Made Hero (perhaps inspired by the earlier, Japanese phenomenon of study *manga*). These combine cut-down playtexts from modern-spelling editions of his works with specially-commissioned work by international *manga* artists. Some are identifiably Japanese and create Japanese settings for the plays; others are not, do not, and their work is Japanese-inflected only in the sense of following *manga* conventions which originated with the creation and popularisation of the genre in Japan. In his guest editorial for *Teaching Shakespeare*, Martin argues that the contributors' use of Japanese or Asianised texts related to Shakespeare means that their students 'can gain a knowledge of the various Shakespearean worlds' and 'enjoy a process of understanding Shakespeare as part of their own world'; of Shakespeare de-centred from western literature and culture as well as the English language, part of the larger phenomenon of globalising or Asianising Shakespeare.[68] In return, the publicising of Japanese titles in an inter-national, Anglophone magazine contributes somewhat to the reach of Asian Shakespeare in education beyond that continent.[69] These scenarios offer some sense of Shakespeare, not so much as a global icon through which Japanese higher education can be westernised, but as a global icon receptive to localisation and Asianisation—with the results being shared internationally, not just for domestic readers and audiences.

The home-grown resources used to teach Shakespeare are not limited to popular visual and audio-visual media: they include bespoke pedagogic resources.[70] Umemiya describes, in his online lessons using Shakespearean verse to teach English stress pattern to students in Japanese higher educa-tion, requesting students to avoid watching and mimicking western film or audio recordings of their set speeches lest they pick up idiosyncrasies. Instead, students are given a recording of the speech by an expert, Japanese, EAL speaker. These examples of educators using domestic-made or domestic-inflected resources redress the situation of over-reliance on west-east flows that, decades previously, Sōseki and Fukuhara critiqued.[71] In fact, some of the students went further than their teachers (who were, after all, Shakespeare exponents) in suggesting local canonical authors who offer alternatives to the study of Shakespeare, such as Sōseki and

Akutagawa Ryūnosuke. 'We can learn much from Japanese classics', said one student who suggested that Shakespeare be saved for 15-16 year olds and upwards in Japan (an age by which they deemed students would have acquired sufficient EAL knowledge and skills). They also argued for equivalence in artistic merit, and the socio-cultural recognition deserved, between Shakespeare's plays and key works in popular Japanese genres such as *manga* and *anime*, like Studio Ghibli's *Spirited Away*.[72] Their words reprise the antidote to bardolatry in Japan suggested by older, Japanese, literary criticism in the previous chapter.

5.5 SHAKESPEAREAN BAWDY IN THE JAPANESE CLASSROOM

There is another way in which Japanese culture is perceived to locally influence teaching Shakespeare, offering some resistance to dominant twenty-first-century western norms[73]: the practice of censoring Shakespeare's bawdy in editions and performances, avoiding or not explaining passages with sexual or scatological humour.[74] In Chapter 4 of this book, Uchimaru suggested that this practice was introduced to Japan in the 1880s by the American William Houghton. The following section, however, shows that such treatments of the text still exist in Japanese universities, though not uncontested, particularly by lecturers who have studied Shakespeare in the west. Tip-toeing around Shakespearean bawdy produces a full range of responses from students. Ayami Oki-Siekierczak describes early twenty-first-century Japanese translators', editors', her own lecturers' and her students' struggles with Shakespeare's bawdy humour. She suggests that in Japan 'it is still an option for lecturers to skip parts of plays that would be considered inappropriate, such as when Mercutio and the Nurse indulge in questionable sexual eloquence in *Romeo and Juliet*' but argues that 'without these components, the play loses its appeal'.[75] From personal experience, she recalls that:

In 2005, in Japan, I was taught by a male...lecturer, who seemed extremely uncomfortable discussing Shakespeare's bawdy side with one male and six female students...When examining [our notes in] the textbook [that] this eminent scholar had given us, it was remarkable to note that certain passages were not covered...Our notes had the same untouched part: bawdy. In the Shakespeare course I attended in 2007, in the UK, the emphasis on the play was extremely different. In front of three male and nine female students, a male professor encouraged us to discuss innu-endo in Mercutio's jokes. Regardless of gender, we pursued the sexual undertones of the play.

One of the reasons Oki-Siekierczak gives for such bowdlerisation of Shakespeare in Japanese texts and classrooms is its treatment by some editors and academics in Japan as a form of *shimo-neta*, a somewhat illicit humour, more appropriate to bars than public places or classrooms. Such humour, they argue, has the potential to impact negatively on students' esteem for Shakespeare, to 'damage [their] image of the genius of Shakespeare'.[76] However, Oki-Siekierczak questions the sustainability of the divorce between Shakespeare and his bawdy humour in Japanese education given westerners' presence in and apparent willingness to talk Shakespeare, sex and scatology in Japanese classrooms—not to mention the privileging of native English speakers as Shakespearean experts and authorities. Oki-Siekierczak also problematises what she perceives as a double-standard around sex and scatology in Japan, given the widespread availability of and lack of controversy around such material in Japanese popular culture, even if such content is strongly bounded in terms of place (particular sections of cities such as Kabukicho in Tokyo) and time (night-time). She writes:

Why...is the sexual innuendo of the Elizabethan playwright too contro-versial to be taught in Japanese classrooms? Japan is a peculiar country in regards to its treatment of sexuality, which is different on the surface and in its depth. Exploring the shadows of its cities, it is possible to encounter sexual interests, from shooting photos of local idols and the sale of sexually explicit manga and anime, to visiting 'soapland', a sensual bathing service.

In trying to implode what she articulates as a national double-standard through her own teaching of Shakespeare, Oki-Siekierczak found that her students continued to take a conservative stance to Shakespearean *shimo-neta*. Eventually, both parties came to acknowledge different perspectives on the topic:

In 2014, when I brought an abridged version of *Romeo and Juliet*, without risqué expressions, to a class on [English literature]... my students felt content with their first Shakespearean experience. The romanticism of this version fulfilled their expectations. Later on, it was explained that all the problematic jokes were excluded from the text. Discussion of how students

felt about this omission deepened their understanding of language in Elizabethan plays and culture, as well as my own understanding of their feelings
towards the language of sexual humour. The students were unanimous in
their belief that romantic love should have been separated from sexual
matters by the author, and it was difficult for them to understand the idea
that sensual jokes could be so openly accepted.

These students spoke back to Shakespeare, troubling his creative choices
using criteria—particularly for adherence to generic conventions—from
Japanese literature, much like the *manga* and *anime* creators cited
previously by Matsuyama.

This reluctance to consider Shakespeare's *shimo-neta*, or view that it
debases his love stories so that they cannot belong within the romance
genre, might depend on the students' gender, institution or discipline, as
well as their level of study and rapport with the lecturer. Oki-Siekierczak
taught at mixed (Meiji University) and single-sex, women-only institutions (Sacred Heart University). At Japan Women's University, also
single-sex, Machi's students wrote comments on viewing a British touring
company's production of *Romeo and Juliet* that echo Oki-Siekierczak's
students' attitudes: 'many students claimed that they were shocked by
Shakespeare's bawdiness; as one student commented, "Some scenes were
much more rude than I had imagined!"'—although it is not clear here
whether the student was pleased or disappointed at this revelation.[77]
Additionally, 'many students shyly admitted that they blushed when they
saw Romeo and Juliet kiss, since kissing in public is taboo in Japan'.[78]
These comments were made on an already muted version of the production: Machi reports that the actors had been asked, by whom it is unclear,
'to tone down the overt sexuality of Shakespeare's bawdiness for the
Japanese audience, even though they were often able to connect with
the audience and break the ice by the very fact that they were being
rude on stage'.[79] Machi here weighs the pros and cons of staging bawdy
humour for Japanese student audiences. It challenges expectations of
what canonical literature and theatre should be, as well as what sort
of humour is acceptable in education settings, but it can also engage
student audiences as a novel educational and cultural experience. Furthermore, even the apparent drawback of performing traditionally taboo stage
business can be embraced with an appeal to global *jinzai*: 'seeing how
people danced, kissed and partied exposed the students to a different
set of cultural norms'.[80] Global *jinzai*, if not demanding that Japan's

citizens become westernised, at least demands that they be conversant with western cultural norms and able to use them for communication and commerce.

To further problematise a binaric understanding of western/Japanese responses to bawdy, by demonstrating the heterogeneity of these populations, Motoyama's students, at an elite mixed-sex institution rather than the women's universities above, are not held to experience Shakespeare's *shimo-neta* as problematic. Rather, he perceived them to be inspired by it to readily participate in discussion and, beyond that, to include consideration of the issue in their coursework: 'Some of the topics the students chose to discuss concerned the function of [Shakespeare's] sexual puns...Many of them wrote about the humour and wit in the plays'.[81] Motoyama's students articulated positively the 'challenge [Shakespeare's bawdy] made to the world-view they had developed "by living in Japanese society"'[82]—the challenge Shakespeare's western treatment of bawdy made to its treatment in Japanese culture. His article echoes Yang Lingyui, albeit writing on Shakespeare in Asian theatre rather than education, who discusses Shakespeare's 'use as a new force to challenge some traditional values that his localizers attempt to renovate or dispel'.[83] Motoyama perceives his students to be embracing Shakespeare as one of the powerful global icons through which Japanese cultural norms can be questioned and alternative stances explored. Perhaps the necessity of performing well in terms of global *jinzai* is strongest at elite institutions, given the employment prospects they project for their graduates.[84] Alongside the material in 5.2 concerning which institutions embrace a literary and liberal—versus a communicative and utilitarian—model of EAL, these differences in the treatment of bawdy by institution type are suggestive of some of the differences within Japanese higher education as well as those rooted in gender in Japanese society.[85] In summary, textual and pedagogical treatments of Shakespearean bawdy had a polarising effect. They tended to demonstrate *either* a resistance to modern, western norms around its inclusion and explication in texts and classes by some students and staff, *or* a welcoming of the opportunity such content presents to challenge Japanese cultural norms around sexual and scatological content.

5.6 Western- and Japanese-Style Pedagogies for Teaching Shakespeare

This section attends to the way in which pedagogies for Shakespeare are constructed by educators as being western and/or having a westernising potential but also as encountering local opposition and requiring local modification. One of the most noticeable ways in which Shakespeare is perceived to westernise Japanese higher education is through the classroom use of drama methods.[86] Kevin Bergman points out that, unlike many anglophone, western school and higher education systems, Shakespeare is not encountered in Drama.[87] Drama barely exists as an academic subject in Japan. Nonetheless, it does exist as a reasonably popular extra-curricular activity, if somewhat secondary to sports.[88] Furthermore, Kodama Keita describes the way in which drama methods for Shakespeare are used in his classroom with students spending one class 'acting out the ghost's visit' to Hamlet, while in later classes they acted out further scenes with encouragement 'to add their own lines to whichever scene they were doing at that time' to develop their dramatic creativity. They also use hot-seating (e.g. interviewing potential suspects in the death of Polonius)—an exercise taken directly from the Black Cat abridged text of the play, part of a series of graded readers designed for EAL students.[89] In this way, Kodama's article is a reminder of the way in which the use of western pedagogical resources in the classroom can be an impetus for introducing western pedagogical trends.

Umemiya's experience teaching a course titled 'Theatre, city and communication' at Yokohama National University offers another exception to the *status quo* around drama methods in Japanese higher education. His article offers a first-hand exploration of the difference between his teaching methods and those used to teach the 'previous generation', including himself.[90] As an outcome of the course, Umemiya wanted to convey to students the importance of the relationship between space, performers and audiences. His teaching contrasted Shakespeare's plays as 'inherently contain[ing] the possibility of audience participation' with the familiar theatre set-up in Japan 'of a proscenium arch stage, with a definite detachment between the performer and the audience'.[91] In such an environment, he explains: 'It is rather rare for the audience to laugh during the performance and they are reluctant to participate in interactions with the actors...Constructing the so-called fourth wall' has become one of the hallmarks of Japanese theatrical production in such spaces.[92] In order to explore the effect of different uses of space on audiences for Shakespeare, Umemiya had groups of students perform the balcony scene in the lecture theatre with the instruction to practice 'creating a firm connection between the stage and their observers'.[93] They were given free choice regarding what area of the space they used, taking turns to watch and be watched. Students also gave a presentation on their design for one of the plays where students embraced Japanese aesthetics and materials. For example, one

> group adapted *Othello* into the culture of Japanese Edo era (1603–1868). They ... created design images for the costumes and the settings...they pointed out the advantage of using the style of *buke* house (a place lived in by the people with authority at the time), which has a garden, multiple buildings for masters and servants. They also claimed that the Japanese classic *shoji* windows, the ones lined with sheer *washi* paper rather than glass, created an effect of projected shadows that works effectively for the eavesdropping scenes.[94]

If Shakespeare here is one of the powerful global icons through which local performers and students are made aware of current western trends in staging Shakespeare, it is also true that Japanese theatre design, including on campus, is one of the means through which Shakespeare is Asianised and some resistance to Shakespeare as a westernising force demonstrated.[95]

Several educators mentioned the use of small or whole group discussion in class as part of their pedagogy, stimulating students 'to ask questions' and display 'a spirit of inquiry'.[96] Discussion was popularly associated by some of the educators with western classicism in British higher education (e.g. Socrates) and contrasted with Confucian methods. Koizumi would ask a question to kick-start discussion about the relationship between the play and the film that quoted it.[97] Motoyama's 'students were assigned scenes and prepared questions about the plot and difficult expressions as well as discussion topics. The students asked [their] classmates the questions they prepared, and facilitated the discussion; [so] this became an opportunity for them not only to engage in but also instigate discussions in English themselves'.[98] Motoyama writes that 'Heated discussions followed questions as to whether Romeo or Paris would make a better husband, whether one's family name can or cannot be easily discarded, and whether parents should or should not have the kind of authority Capulet holds over Juliet'.[99] He portrays discussion as flowing easily—refuting stereotypes and contrasting with other accounts of teaching Shakespeare to Japanese students. Factors explaining this might be his substantial teaching experience, the intended profession of many of his students (law) and the status/entry requirements of Waseda (a nationally-prestigious, private university). At its best, educators like Suzuki Shinichi felt that perceivedly western-style discussion enabled students to realise and enjoy the plurality of possible interpretations of Shakespeare, by readers and film directors, rather than to seek a single and definitive one.[100]

In a contrasting vein, Honda wrote about her experience lecturing at Toyo, Waseda and Meiji universities as a doctoral student, including to lifelong learning students—often retirees who missed out on tertiary education due to the Second World War. Such returnees to education were studying on non-degree programmes. Unlike Motoyama's experience with classroom discussion, she highlights the perceived pervasiveness of local face-saving behaviours practised by students in her classes, and explains the way that she adapts her activities to these. She describes the dearth of student questions during sessions and the relative scarceness (or novelty) of interactive small group teaching in Japanese institutions as particularly problematic for and typical of Japanese pedagogy. She also mentions her own decision to 'never address questions to a specific student', suggesting that the challenge of fostering a collective, dialogic spirit of inquiry exists for staff as well as students in Japanese higher education.[101] After introducing the plays to be studied on the module, Honda says:

I assigned the remaining weeks' classes to group presentations of six or seven people. While one group gave a paper, the other students wrote questions and comments on worksheets. Then the representative of each group asked the questions or gave comments. However, this discussion did not work very well because Japanese students are not taught how to debate and express their opinions in schools: even though the students may have good ideas or criticisms, they do not want to voice them in public because they care about what other people think of their opinions very much. Therefore, at the end of the class, I collected some interesting questions or comments from the worksheets, put them together in a handout, and distributed them in the following class. The students whose ideas were chosen were glad to see the handout, and it motivated the other students too.[102]

In this instance, Honda elaborates a way of finding, what is for her, a workable compromise between western-style expectations for critical thinking about western literature with activities that respect, what she describes as, Japanese cultural preferences in terms of communication, particularly communicating dissent and criticism: having students hand in or complete online an 'exit ticket'—some comments on their experience of the class, what they learned, what they liked and any questions they have—is a widespread feature of the Japanese English classrooms that I have visited. She finds a way to meet educational objectives associated with subject English, specifically Shakespeare, internationally with locally-adapted activities in the vein of glocalisation.[103] Another example of a pedagogy which arguably Asianises students' experience of Shakespeare is the use of communal singing by Chan with his Shakespeare class, redolent of Hong Kong's tradition of singalong parlours and Japan's hi-tech take on them, *karaoke*: 'We ... learned and sang some of the songs in the play to liven up the atmosphere and improve the experience. [The class] were especially moved by the unfaithful Proteus' serenade to Silvia, that is, moved with a compassion for Julia'.[104] Such performance activities, bonded the class through a shared, local, cultural activity—a more familiar, perhaps comfortable, icebreaker to active methods than the story whoosh or tableaux favoured in western active methods approaches to and teacher handbooks for Shakespeare. In terms of multilateral traffic, the activity also shows one way in which Shakespeare offers an aegis for renovating traditional, local forms by drawing on western 'folk' songs which had not previously featured among *karaoke*'s repertoire.[105]

5.7   Affinities Between Japan and England

The use of affinities—or 'equation approach'—is traditional in Japanese reception of western phenomena, as Uchimaru demonstrated in the previous chapter, particularly in relation to Okakura's attempts to help students overcome cultural and linguistic differences in his teaching of English studies (*eigaku*).[106] The idea of likeness troubles that of an east/west binary. Both Japanese and English citizens have historically claimed a 'natural' affinity between the countries: for example, Dominic Shellard and David Warren—introducing a Japan-themed issue of the journal *Shakespeare*—assert that 'the United Kingdom and Japan enjoy a series of strong political, economic and cultural links, be it the number of times the two countries have voted together at the United Nations (the strongest compatibility or any states), the palpable love of British designers on the streets of Tokyo, a shared reverence for their respective monarchies, or a mutual attachment to the works of Shakespeare'.[107] We have already seen, in this chapter, the way in which Japan's island nature is used to explain students' struggle to master foreign languages: a similar explanation is commonly given in relation to British students. In the classroom, James Tink describes the way in which 'a discussion of Falstaff's question "What is honour?" allowed the class to explore ideas of conduct', particularly 'how both European chivalry and Japanese *bushido* [also known as the samurai code] are popularly understood' and analogies drawn between the two through discussion of Falstaff's incarnation as *The Braggart Samurai* in traditional-style Japanese drama by Takahashi Yasunari.[108] Tink found that, when studying the history plays, his students readily drew parallels between medieval England and medieval Japan.[109] Specifically, his students drew a comparison between Shakespeare's Duke of York and the sixteenth-century warlord Date Masamune, affiliated with Sendai where the campus is located. Like York, he switched his allegiance to the emerging power (in this case the Tokugawa Shogunate) in order to preserve his domain.[110] Tink's students proposed further analogies between Shakespeare's history plays and Japanese literature: 'the canonical 13th century poem *Heike monogatari* describes a civil war and the ruin of the Taira Clan, who are presented as corrupt but nevertheless courtly and refined'. For Tink's students, 'it provided a way of thinking about the allure and tragedy of King Richard [II, 14th century], and the pathos that can be attached to ideas of a defeated, distant past' in both countries' nationalisms.[111] Thus, his students effectively refute understandings of Shakespeare as a westernising force on Japan in favour of asserting an existing cultural similarity or 'special relationship', finding similarities between two supposed oppositions or poles, the 'foreign'/'other' (UK and/or Europe) and the 'indigenous'/'our' (Japan).[112]

Marie Honda's reflection on teaching *The Taming of the Shrew* has a rather different flavour to Tink's, although it is also rooted in notions of affinity. In this case, Honda lit on the idea of exploring an affinity between the play's concern with (traditional or conservative) gender and sexual relations, masculinity and femininity, and a sustained moral panic around deviations from these norms in modern-day Japan. Honda focused on concern about the purportedly increasing 'number of the so-called herbivore or grass-eating boys [who are] not interested in having girlfriends' as well as the criticism young Japanese women have faced for their 'lack of interest' in having boyfriends.[113] These (apparently) emergent identities are causally connected in reactionary media with the economic and social implications of Japan's long-declining birth-rate. Her article is a rare but valuable insight into an instance where teaching does not go as planned, where teaching activities do not achieve the intended learning outcomes with unqualified success. While Honda had hoped that teaching the play would raise discussion of this topical Japanese issue and encourage students to challenge—what she identifies as—outdated gender roles and gender politics in the play and Japan, it instead resulted in a significant number of her students retreating further into their echo-chamber. They continued to prefer readings of the play that gelled with their own, conservative views on gender and sexual norms. One female student wrote: 'Petruchio is always so cool and calm so Kate came to respect him. I reflected on my behaviour and decided to become such an elegant lady like Kate'.[114] Another suggested: 'A man generally wants his girlfriend or wife to obey him more or less like Petruchio...[He] is too much, but some women may prefer such a selfish but manly, strong men guarding women [sic]'.[115] Honda suggests that finding an affinity between issues in Shakespearean drama and modern Japanese society did not ultimately result in the criticality and progressivism that she had envisaged, but can instead have unpredictable—even retrograde—effects. Her experience in this educational setting chimes with Warren's experience that, in Japan, 'Britain is often seen as a centre of traditional values, sometimes enshrined in a very traditional reading of English literature'.[116] The students here ground affinity between Japan and Britain in cultural conservatism, against the expectations of their teacher (and evidence from Machi above) that Shakespeare, as experienced through modern productions from the west, can spark socially-progressive discussion.

5.8   De-Centring Shakespeare in Japanese Higher Education

Readers of both this and Chapter 4 may have noticed several continuities between teaching Shakespeare in Japanese higher education in the nineteenth and twentieth centuries and the early twenty-first century beyond the affinity or 'equation approach'. They include the emphasis on Shakespeare for English language acquisition, a blend of western and Japanese texts being used, and some bowdlerisation. Meanwhile, the palpable sense of a deficit model of Japan, so prevalent among the Meiji- and Taisho-period policymakers that Uchimaru cites is only occasionally still visible. For example, it is sparingly invoked by some of the educators in this chapter to critique social conservatism in Japan.[117] Perhaps the starkest difference between this chapter and the account Uchimaru gives is the greater weight placed latterly on perceivedly western pedagogies of drama and discussion for teaching Shakespeare, pedagogies whose ubiquity in the west is rather recent and, perhaps, somewhat over-stated.[118] In answer to the question, 'Is Shakespeare still perceived as one of the powerful global icons through which Japanese higher education is westernised?', on occasion, yes. Sometimes this effect appears to be positively received, even sought, in a way that echoes Yang's 'Shakespearization of Asia'—'the idealization of him as a modern cultural icon in a universalizing cele-bration of his authority in many sectors of modern Asian cultures'.[119] For example, his authority as the pre-eminent figure in shaping, and supremely skilled user of, the English language is harnessed by some EAL educators here in a way that strongly resembles a key approach of the CUSF organisers in chapter three. Study of Shakespeare's play-texts, or extracts thereof, often entailed the use of western productions as well as additional anglophone, western texts being brought into the classroom. This does not reflect well the phenomenon of English as a world language, spoken in western and non-western countries alike, and the quantity of Shakespeare from beyond 'the centre' available (often free-of-charge, online for educational use). However, these productions were sometimes actively preferred for their westernising effects in terms of influencing students' understanding of perceived western social, cultural, moral and romantic norms, as well as to fire-up 'western-style' discussion and literary criticality.

Nonetheless, any suggestion that teaching Shakespeare contributes to a straightforward, unilateral westernisation of Japanese higher education is also resisted, problematised or nuanced by stakeholders throughout. Educators described using Japanese resources, somewhat balancing out the presence of western texts in the classroom—although the aegis for their inclusion remains Shakespeare, routinely constructed as a western, literary luminary. In terms of pedagogies for teaching Shakespeare in Japanese higher education, the incorporation of dramatic and discus-sion activities in the classroom was explained with reference to their perceived status as western methods well-suited to meeting objectives for English, as a subject and a language. While the impetus for using some of these pedagogies may have come from the west, particularly through the international study experiences of Japanese educators, drama activities sometimes produced Asianised or localised creative choices for productions.[120] Additionally, where western norms for classroom discussion were perceived to be too uncomfortable for Japanese students, they were explicitly adapted to suit local conventions, localising or Asianising pedagogies for Shakespeare in Japanese higher education settings. Some students advocated for a greater focus on Japanese works, though presumably not as part of an English language or literature course. Responses to Shakespeare's bawdy were diverse, seemingly dependent on institution type and students' gender. They suggested either active cultivation or rejection of western norms and the inability of his texts to single-handedly steamroll over Japanese cultural norms, at least in the immediate aftermath of lessons. Finally, the finding of affinities, between Japan and Britain in particular, troubles the supposed polarity of Japanese and western higher education and culture implicit in the research question. That said, this chapter demonstrates that 'great convergence' that Mahbubani describes as an outcome of globalisation has not yet arrived in terms of the teaching of Shakespeare.

Critics of the term 'globalisation' argue that it effectively equates to homogenisation along western lines, repackaged as something more multilateral and culturally enriching.[121] Yet, Shakespeare in Japanese higher education demonstrates facets that are distinctly national, regional, local and glocal as well as western or cosmopolitan—that is, reflecting a homogeneity of experience between elites the world over, between top universities teaching Shakespeare in Japan and the west.[122] It remains true in the twenty-first century, as it was for James Brandon writing from Japan in the 1990s, that 'life [and education] for tens of millions of people in Asia's cities is an inescapable mixture of modern and traditional, Asian and western'.[123] However, this chapter, using the case of Shakespeare, educational research and Asian studies more generally, draws attention to the way in which this mix may not be passively experienced but actively and strategically sought: 'it is possible that we are seeing the emergence of a unique Asian model of higher education that selectively borrows from the West, yet freely draws upon its own solid academic traditions'.[124] For Mahbubani and other commentators, this is tied up with the rapid progress of Asian higher education institutions in international rankings and the cross-sector advent of the 'Asian century'.[125] The way in which Shakespeare educators' and students' experience in western higher education is becoming a mixture of 'Asian and western'—as, for example, Japanese Shakespeare follows Japanese popular culture into western consciousness and practices—is an avenue for future research.

Acknowledgements I wish to thank the British Academy, the British Council, the GB Sasakawa Foundation, York Research Champions Culture and Communications strand, the University of Hiroshima, and Toyo University for funding my research visits to Japan. Thanks also to the Education Department, University of York, for one term's research leave, which enabled one of my visits to Japan, the flexibilities that enabled a couple more, and its students (also those of the Shakespeare Institute, University of Birmingham) who indulged me in conversations about this research. I was fortunate to have multiple opportunities to discuss this work at conferences and seminars. I am hugely grateful to those who invited me, especially Kohei Uchimaru for a seminar at Toyo University, with students planning to teach English in Japan; Umemiya Yu for 'Shakespeare Day' at Waseda University; as well as Susan Bennett and Sonia Massai at their seminar 'Rethinking the "Global" in Global Shakespeare' at the Shakespeare Association of America congress in 2018. Uchimaru-sensei also read this chapter with tremendous care and generously offered corrections, caveats and extremely pertinent, additional reading (any errors or omissions are mine alone). I would like to thank the staff and students of the following universities who hosted me, talked with me or otherwise contributed to this research: Japan Women's, Nihon, Takasaki, Tokyo, Toyo and Waseda. In addition to those academics cited throughout this article, my sincere thanks to Aoki Keiko, Endo Hanako, Rosalind Fielding, Igarashi Hirohisa, Samantha Landau, Matsuda Yoshiko, Ve-Yin Tee, Alex Watson and Laurence Williams. I am profoundly grateful for the British Shakespeare Association's impetus to found, and its continued support for, the free, online magazine for cross-sector educators, *Teaching Shakespeare*.

NOTES

1. Entering the term into a Google search in the UK, while I write, yields Oprah (Winfrey—her last name was not given in the search result, further suggesting her iconic status), Nelson Mandela and Muhammed Ali as foremost results.
2. 'Westernisation,' *Oxford English Dictionary Online*, accessed April 27, 2019. http://www.oed.com. Tsuneyoshi Ryoko, ed. *Globalization and Japanese "Exceptionalism" in Education: Insiders' Views into a Changing System* (London: Routledge, 2018). 3. This effect is sometimes described as 'MacDonaldization', foregrounding its western capitalist or neoliberal aspects.
3. Tsuneyoshi, *Globalization and Japanese*, 3–4, 25.

172   S. OLIVE

4. Daniel Gallimore, 'Shakespeare in Contemporary Japan', in *Shakespeare in Hollywood, Asia and Cyberspace*, edited by Alexa Alice Joubin and Charles S. Ross, 109–120. Indiana: Purdue University Press, 2009. Dominic Shellard and David Warren, 'Shakespeare in Japan: A Great! Collaboration', *Shakespeare* 9.4 (2013): 373–382. Warren does note the stalling of British influence, including the place of Shakespeare, in Japan during the period post-World War I until the 1980s.
5. Dominic Shellard and David Warren, 'Shakespeare in Japan', 379, 375.
6. Lei Bi-qi Beatrice, Judy Celine Ick and Poonam Trivedi, eds, *Shakespeare's Asian Journeys: Critical Encounters, Cultural Geographies, and the Politics of Travel* (London: Routledge, 2016). 3.
7. Gallimore, 'Shakespeare in Contemporary Japan'. Cho *Political Shakespeare in Korea*. Kohei Uchimaru, 'Teaching Shakespeare in Japanese Secondary Schools: a study of Shakespeare's Reception in Locally Produced EFL School Readers'. MA diss. (University of Birmingham, 2016).
8. See also Kawachi Yoshiko, 'Introduction: Shakespeare in Modern Japan', *Multicultural Shakespeare: Translation, Appropriation and Performance* 14.29 (2016): 7–12 and Daniel Gallimore, 'Tsubouchi Shōyō and the Beauty of Shakespeare Translation in 1900s Japan', *Multicultural Shakespeare: Translation, Appropriation and Performance* 13.28 (2016): 69–85.
9. Uchimaru in Chapter 4 (103).
10. Roland Kelts, *Japanamerica: how Japanese popular culture has invaded the US* (London: Palgrave Macmillan, 2008). *Galapagosuzation* is used critically (including within Japan) to suggest that the country is losing touch with international developments, and should adjust to more "universal" standards'. Tsuneyoshi, *Globalization and Japanese*, 19.
11. Uchimaru in Chapter 4 (103).
12. Sonia Massai, *World-wide Shakespeares: Local Appropriations in Film andPerformance* (London: Routledge, 2006), 4. Reiterated in Susan Bennett and Christy Carson, *Shakespeare Beyond English: A Global Experiment* (Cambridge: Cambridge University Press, 2013), 4.
13. Massai, *World-wide Shakespeares*, 4.
14. James Brandon, 'Some Shakespeare(s) in Some Asia(s)', *Asian Studies Review* 20.3 (April 1997): 1–26. R.S. White, 'Introduction', in *Shakespeare's Local Habitations*, edited by Krystyna Kujawińska-Courtney and R.S. White (Łódź: Łódź University Press, 2007). Koichi Iwabuchi, Stephen Muecke and Mandy Thomas. *Rogue Flows: Trans-Asian Cultural Traffic* (Hong Kong: Hong Kong University Press, 2014). Yang Lingui, 'Modernity and Tradition in Shakespeare's Asianization', *Multicultural Shakespeare: Translation, Appropriation and Performance* 10.25 (2013): 5–10. https://doi.org/10.2478/mstap-2013-0001. See

also Alexa Alice Joubin, *Chinese Shakespeares: Two Centuries of Cultural Exchange* (New York: Columbia University Press, 2009).

15. Thea Buckley, '*In the Spicèd Indian Air by Night*': *Performing Shakespeare's Macbeth in Postmillennial Kerala.* PhD diss. (University of Birmingham, 2017), 18–19. This is something, Jacqueline Lo and Helen Gilbert have successfully done in relation to East Asian modern theatre, establishing a conceptual framework for acknowledging the multilateral, or 'cross-cultural', flows between east and west in 'Toward a Topography of Cross-Cultural Theatre Praxis'. *The Drama Review* (2002): 46.3. 31–53. Iwabuchi et al., *Rogue Flows.* Systematically overemphasising west-east flows, continually underestimating or neglecting the ways in which Asia influences or outstrips the west, is something that the work of Adele Lee in chapter two, and Kishore Mahbubani in his recent polemic, *Has the West Lost It?*, argues western scholars, educators, politicians, policy-makers, economists, commentators and their publics have done at their peril (London: Allen Lane, 2018).

16. It is more usual to be completing a PhD while holding a higher education teaching position in Japan than it is in twenty-first-century British higher education, where a PhD is more usually a pre-requisite for such posts.

17. Private universities are very common in the region as part of a twentieth-century solution to increased demand for higher education. Tan Jee-Peng and Alain Mingat, *Education in Asia: A Comparative Study of Cost and Financing* (Washington, DC: World Bank, 1992).

18. Machi, 'Beyond the Language Barrier', *Teaching Shakespeare* 7 (Spring 2015): 12–13.

19. Tsuneyoshi, *Globalization and Japanese*, 4, 8.

20. Although, anecdotally, EAL speakers during the course of this research have also reflected to me about feeling liberated when working in English from the social norms of their native culture in a way that can aid verbal interactions, particularly hierarchical ones such as student-teacher—this resonates with the findings of Alison Phipps about researching multilingually. See Phipps, 'Giving an Account of Researching Multilingually', *International Journal of Applied Linguistics* 23 (2013): 329–341.

21. Sarah Olive, 'To Research, or Not to Research? Some Dilemmas of Insider-Outsider Research on Shakespeare in South East/East Asian higher education', *Researcher Stories Blog. British Sociological Association*, accessed 5 May 2017, https://bsapgforum.com/2017/05/05/dr-sarah-olive-to-research-or-not-to-research-some-dilemmas-of-insider-out sider-research-on-shakespeare-in-south-easteast-asian-higher-education/.

22. Morinaga Koji, 'Initiating the Language of Shakespeare', *Teaching Shakespeare* 16 (Autumn 2018): 13–15.

23. Kenneth Chan, 'Teaching Shakespeare to College Students', *Teaching Shakespeare* 6 (Autumn 2014): 5–6.
24. Igarashi, 'Improving Understanding Through Shakespeare', 5–7.
25. Igarashi, 'Improving Understanding Through Shakespeare', 5-7.
26. Igarashi, 'Improving Understanding Through Shakespeare', 5–7.
27. Uchimaru adds that 'Shakespeare himself appeared in *Fate/Apocrypha*, a version of the most popular Japanese game and anime series, where his secret weapon is the "First Folio"'. 'Editorial: Teaching Shakespeare in the Japanese English as a Foreign Language (EFL) Classroom', *Teaching Shakespeare* 16 (Autumn 2018): 3–4.
28. Igarashi Hirohisa, 'Improving Understanding Through Shakespeare', *Teaching Shakespeare* 16 (Autumn 2018): 5–7. Kenneth Chan, 'Teaching Shakespeare to College Students', 5–6.
29. Anthony Martin, 'Editorial', *Teaching Shakespeare* 13 (November 2017): 3.
30. Matsuyama Kyoko, 'Teaching English Literature in Japanese Universities', *Teaching* Shakespeare 13 (November 2017): 4–6. Chan, 'Teaching Shakespeare to College Students', 5–6. Suzuki Shinichi, 'Encouraging Various Points of View', *Teaching Shakespeare* 13 (November 2017): 13–15. Marie Honda, 'Undergraduate and Lifelong Learners of Shakespeare', *Teaching Shakespeare* 6 (Autumn 2014): 19. Marie Honda, 'Shakespeare's Teenage Film Adaptations and Japanese Comics: From *10 Things I Hate About You* to *Hana Yori Dango*', *Teaching Shakespeare* 13 (November 2017): 7–9.
31. Matsuyama, 'Teaching English Literature in Japanese Universities', 4–6.
32. See also Yoshifumi Saito, 'Globalization or Anglicization? A Dilemma of English-Language Teaching in Japan', in *Globalization and Japanese "Exceptionalism" in Education*, edited by Tsuneyoshi Ryoko (London: Routledge, 2018). 178–189.
33. Phillipe Van Parijs, *Just Democracy: The Rawls-Machiavelli Programme* (ECPR Essays Series, 2011), 21.
34. Morinaga, 'Initiating the Language of Shakespeare', 13.
35. Tsuneyoshi, *Globalization and Japanese,* 10.
36. Daniel Gallimore, 'Teaching Sheikusupia', *Teaching Shakespeare* 6 (Autumn 2014): 6–8.
37. Tsuneyoshi, *Globalization and Japanese*, 4, 8–9, 34. Yonezawa Akiyoshi and Shimmi Yukiko, 'Japan's Challenge in Fostering Global Human Resources: Policy Debates and Practices', in *Globalization and Japanese "Exceptionalism" in Education*, edited by Tsuneyoshi Ryoko (London: Routledge, 2018). 43–60, 46.
38. Shudo Sachiko and Yasunari Harada, 'Designing a Syllabus for Integrated Language Activities', *Humanitas* 47 (2008): 1–12. 1. Quoted in Motoyama, Tetsuhito. 'Teaching Shakespeare to Law Students', *Teaching*

Shakespeare 6 (Autumn 2014): 10–11. 10. A superb account of government policies concerning global *jinzai* and higher education written in English is given by Yonezawa and Shimmi, 'Japan's challenge'. Also, Yoshifumi Saito, 'Globalization or Anglicization?' 183.

39. Motoyama, 'Teaching Shakespeare to Law Students', 10.
40. Motoyama, 'Teaching Shakespeare to Law Students'.
41. Their sentiment is echoed by an educator from another institution, Morinaga who—in problematising MEXT's emphasis on a communicative model of English—says 'Background knowledge of Shakespeare, along with that of the Bible, Roman and Greek mythology, is vitally significant in understanding British and American culture'. 'Initiating the language of Shakespeare', 13–15.
42. Umemiya Yu, 'Teaching Shakespeare in the Current HE Context', *Teaching Shakespeare* 6 (Autumn 2014): 16–18. 17.
43. Umemiya Yu, 'Teaching English Stress Pattern Through Shakespearean Verse', *Teaching Shakespeare* 20 (forthcoming). The potential of Shakespeare to train students' 'ears to English basic rhythm, iambic pentameter' is also advocated by Morinaga. 'Initiating the language of Shakespeare', 13–15.
44. Poonam Trivedi and Minami Ryuta, eds, *Replaying Shakespeare in Asia* (London: Routledge, 2010). 4. Kodama Keita, 'Introducing Shakespeare to Young EFL Learners', *Teaching Shakespeare* 16 (Autumn 2018): 11–13. Morinaga, 'Initiating the Language of Shakespeare': 13–15.
45. Chapter three and Suzuki, 'Encouraging Various Points of View', 13–15. Uchimaru, 'Editorial', 3–4.
46. This has been noted in chapter four of this book by Uchimaru, as well as by Minami Ryuta, '"No Literature Please, We're Japanese"': The Disappearance of Literary Texts from English Classrooms in Japan', in *English Studies in Asia*, edited by Masazumi Araki, Lim Chee Seng, Minami Ryuta and Yoshihara Yukari (Kuala Lumpur: Silverfish Books, 2007), 145–165; Morinaga, 'Initiating the Language of Shakespeare': 13–15; and Suzuki, 'Encouraging Various Points of View', 13–15.
47. Van Parijs, *Just Democracy*, 21.
48. Chan, 'Teaching Shakespeare to College Students', 4. Gallimore, 'Teaching Sheikusupia', 7. See also Yaguchi Yujin, 'The University of Tokyo PEAK Program', in *Globalization and Japanese "Exceptionalism" in Education*, edited by Tsuneyoshi Ryoko (London: Routledge, 2018), 131–143. 132.
49. James Tink, 'Teaching the History Plays in Japan', *Teaching Shakespeare* 6 (Autumn 2014): 12–13. Chan, 'Teaching Shakespeare to College Students', 4. Umemiya, 'Teaching Shakespeare in the Current HE Context', 16. Koizumi Yuto, 'First Year Shakespeare Through Film', *Teaching Shakespeare* 6 (Autumn 2014): 15.

50. Koizumi, 'First Year Shakespeare Through Film', 15.
51. Desmet, 'Import/Export', 9.
52. Desmet, 'Import/Export'.
53. Lei Bi-qi Beatrice, Judy Celine Ick and Poonam Trivedi, eds, *Shakespeare's Asian Journeys: Critical Encounters, Cultural Geographies, and the Politics of Travel* (London: Routledge, 2016), 2.
54. 'Purportedly' because western hegemony tends to forget its histories of discrimination against the LGBTQ+—Lesbian, Gay, Bisexual, Transgender, Queer and other sexual identities—community. Machi Saeko, 'The Appeal of Gender-Crossing in *Twelfth Night*', *Teaching Shakespeare* 14 (Spring 2018): 14–15. Machi, Saeko. 'Beyond the Language Barrier.'
55. R.T. Pithers and Rebecca Soden, 'Critical Thinking in Education: A Review', *Educational Research* 42.3 (2000), 237–249. 238–239. Linkon, *Literary Learning*, x. Goddard, *English, Language and Literacy 3 to 19*, 47.
56. Ellis, 'English as a Subject', 11, 13-14. Peel et al., *Questions of English*, 2. Curtis, *Teaching Secondary English*, 4, 13. Hall, N. 'Literacy as Social Experience,' in *Teaching English to Children: From Practice to Principle*, edited by Brumfit, Christopher, Jayne Moon and Ray Tongue (Cheltenham: Nelson ELT, 1991), 244–259. 245, 249. Matthewman, Sasha. *Teaching Secondary English As If the Planet Matters*. Abingdon: Routledge, 2011. 1. See also Brumfit, Christopher, Jayne Moon and Ray Tongue, eds, *Teaching English to Children: From Practice to Principle*. Cheltenham: Nelson ELT, 1991. For more on subject English as producing world citizens and fostering social justice see Angela Goddard, *English, Language and Literacy 3 to 19*, 4.
57. Machi, 'The Appeal of Gender-Crossing in *Twelfth Night*'.
58. Machi, 'The Appeal of Gender-Crossing in *Twelfth Night*', 15.
59. Machi, 'The Appeal of Gender-Crossing in *Twelfth Night*'.
60. Honda, 'Undergraduate and Lifelong Learners of Shakespeare', 19.
61. Tink, 'Teaching the History Plays in Japan', 12–13.
62. Chan, 'Teaching Shakespeare to College Students', 4–5.
63. Such as Kobayashi Akio's *Let's Read English Poems* (Tokyo: NHK Publishing, 2007) cited in Morinaga, 'Initiating the language of Shakespeare', 13–15.
64. Morinaga, 'Initiating the Language of Shakespeare', 13–15. Honda, 'Undergraduate and Lifelong Learners of Shakespeare', 19. Honda, 'Shakespeare's Teenage Film', 8–9.
65. Matsuyama does note that some are more popular with female students, because they are produced and marketed as *shojo-manga*, girl manga in a publishing industry that continues to demarcate texts along binary gender lines. 'Teaching English Literature in Japanese Universities', 4.
66. Matsuyama, 'Teaching English Literature in Japanese Universities', 5.

67. It would be possible to read this as evidence of creative heeding of Sōseki and Fukuhara's call, to students and literary critics identified in the previous chapter, to avoid regurgitating western interpretations of Shakespeare and instead to produce readings that are inflected with a strong sense of Japanese national identity—thereby, they suggested, Japan could avoid reinforcing western hegemony
68. Martin, 'Editorial', 3.
69. This is a trend observable in Shakespeare studies in relation to theatre and film, see Asian Shakespeare Intercultural Archive (A|S|I|A) (website), accessed 28 November 2018, http://a-s-i-a-web.org/en/home.php. Mark Thornton Burnett, *Filming Shakespeare in the Global Marketplace* (Houndmills: Palgrave, 2007).
70. Umemiya, 'Teaching English Stress Pattern Through Shakespearean Verse'.
71. See chapter four. Todd Andrew Borlik, *'Reading Hamlet Upside Down: The Shakespeare Criticism of Natsume Sōseki,'* Shakespeare 9.4 (2013): 383–403. Minami Ryuta, 'Shakespeare as an Icon of the Enemy Culture: Shakespeare in Wartime Japan, 1937–1945', in *Shakespeare and the Second World War: Memory, Culture, Identity*, edited by Irena Makaryk and Marissa McHugh (Toronto: University of Toronto, 2012), 163–179.
72. Sarah Olive, 'Vox Pop', *Teaching Shakespeare* 9 (Spring 2016): 2–5. 5.3. The fit between Shakespeare's rhetoric and *manga* devices is espoused by Gallimore, who favours the use of Self-Made Hero's *manga* editions in his classes, as well as Matsuyama. 'Teaching Sheikusupia', 6–8, and 'Teaching English Literature in Japanese Universities', 4–6.
73. It is worth noting that bowdlerisation is still in evidence in texts used in some American states, so the 'western norms' I invoke here do not represent a unanimous consensus on or treatment of Shakespearean bawdy.
74. It is important to note that such English-language versions continue to be published and used in the school system in the United States, and Velda Elliott and Sarah Olive found some wariness about what sexual content is appropriate for school students—though I have not encountered existing literature dealing with these considerations in higher education despite broader debates about trigger-warnings for content containing sexual, and other forms of, violence. 'Secondary Shakespeare in the UK: what gets taught and why?' *English in Education* (2019).
75. Ayami Oki-Siekierczak, 'The Treatment of Bawdy in Japanese Classrooms', *Teaching Shakespeare* 6 (Autumn 2014): 9.
76. Oki-Siekierczak, 'The Treatment of Bawdy in Japanese Classrooms', 9.
77. Machi, 'Beyond the Language Barrier', 12–13.
78. Similarly, Marie Honda reports that, when asked to write comparatively about the Luhrmann and Zeffirelli films of the play they had been shown,

some students criticise the kiss scene [in Zeffirelli Romeo kissing Juliet 'from chin to neck'] as being obscene and disgraceful'. See also Machi, 'Beyond the Language Barrier', 12–13. Honda, 'Shakespeare's Teenage Film, 7–9.

79. Machi, 'Beyond the Language Barrier', 12–13.
80. Machi, 'Beyond the Language Barrier', 12–13.
81. Motoyama, 'Teaching Shakespeare to Law Students', 10.
82. Motoyama, 'Teaching Shakespeare to Law Students', 10.
83. Yang, 'Modernity and Tradition in Shakespeare's Asianization', 7.
84. Kitamura Yuto, 'Global Citizenship education in Asia', in *Globalization and Japanese "Exceptionalism" in Education*, edited by Tsuneyoshi Ryoko (London: Routledge, 2018), 61–76, 67. Although Tsuneyoshi offers a counter argument that graduates of such universities tend to go to well-known domestic firms who do not require or assess the students on English. *Globalization and Japanese*, 4.
85. Yonezawa and Shimmi, 'Japan's Challenge', 56.
86. I use this term here to encompass active, practical and performance methods outlined by the likes of Rex Gibson, James Stredder, the Royal Shakespeare Company's and Shakespeare's Globe education departments.
87. Kevin Bergman, 'A Boys' Drama Club Performs *Romeo and Juliet*', *Teaching Shakespeare* 6 (Autumn 2014): 14.
88. Martin, 'Editorial', 3. Sarah Olive, 'Editorial: Teaching Shakespeare in Hanoi,' 3–5.
89. Kodama, 'Introducing Shakespeare to Young EFL Learners', 11.
90. Umemiya, 'Teaching Shakespeare in the Current HE Context, 15.
91. Umemiya, 'Teaching Shakespeare in the Current HE Context, 15.
92. Umemiya, 'Teaching Shakespeare in the Current HE Context, 15.
93. Umemiya, 'Teaching Shakespeare in the Current HE Context, 16.
94. Umemiya, 'Teaching Shakespeare in the Current HE Context, 16.
95. Kevin Wetmore, Siyuan Liu and Erin Mee, *Modern Asian Theatre and Performance, 1900–2000* (London: Bloomsbury, 1999).
96. Peel et al., *Questions of English*. Pithers and Soden, 'Critical Thinking in Education', 239. Tink, 'Teaching the History Plays in Japan', 12–13. Gallimore, 'Teaching Sheikusupia', 6–8. Chan, 'Teaching Shakespeare to College Students', 4.
97. Koizumi, 'First Year Shakespeare Through Film, 15.
98. Motoyama, 'Teaching Shakespeare to Law Students', 10.
99. Motoyama, 'Teaching Shakespeare to Law Students', 10.
100. Suzuki, 'Encouraging Various Points of View', 13–15.
101. Honda, 'Undergraduate and Lifelong Learners of Shakespeare', 19.
102. Honda, 'Undergraduate and Lifelong Learners of Shakespeare', 19.

103. R.S. White, 'Introduction', in *Shakespeare's Local Habitations*, ed. Krystyna Kujawińska-Courtney and R.S. White (Łódź: Łódź University Press, 2007). Lee Hyon-u, Shim Jung-soon, and Kim Dong-wook (ed). *Glocalizing Shakespeare in Korea and Beyond* (Seoul: Dongin, 2009).
104. Chan, 'Teaching Shakespeare to College Students', 4.
105. Yang, 'Modernity and Tradition in Shakespeare's Asianization', 7.
106. Hiroko Willcock, 'Western Thought, and the Sapporo Agricultural College: A Case Study of Acculturation in Early Meiji Japan', *Modern Asian Studies* 34.4 (2000): 977–1017.
107. Dominic Shellard and David Warren, 'Shakespeare in Japan: a Great! Collaboration', 373.
108. Tink, 'Teaching the History Plays in Japan', 12–13.
109. Terms such as 'medieval' and 'middle ages' have currency to describe similar historical periods in both countries. Mizoguchi Kazuhiro, 'A Study of Value Education in Teaching History: A Case Study of Teaching Materials in History for Political Literacy', *Research Journal of Educational Methods* 20 (1994): 127–136.
110. Tink, 'Teaching the History Plays in Japan', 12–13.
111. Tink, 'Teaching the History Plays in Japan', 12–13.
112. Buckley, 'In the Spiced Indian Air', 14.
113. The exclusive emphasis on heteronormative relationships here as well as the omission of any pejorative shorthand for female equivalents of the 'herbivores' reflects the original article. Honda, 'Shakespeare's Teenage Film', 8–9.
114. Honda, 'Shakespeare's Teenage Film', 8–9.
115. Honda, Shakespeare's Teenage Film', 9.
116. Dominic Shellard and David Warren, 'Shakespeare in Japan: A Great! Collaboration', 375.
117. Oki-Siekierczak, 'The Treatment of Bawdy in Japanese Classrooms', 9. Honda, 'Shakespeare's Teenage Film', 8–9. Motoyama, 'Teaching Shakespeare to Law Students', 10.
118. Elliott and Olive, 'Secondary Shakespeare in the UK: What Gets Taught and Why?' *English in Education* (2019).
119. Yang Lingui, 'Modernity and Tradition in Shakespeare's Asianization,' 5.
120. Mahbubani articulates the impact of Asians' studying abroad on their values and ideas, often further disseminated in Asia on their return. *Has the West Lost It?* 12, 26.
121. Rebellato, *Theatre & Globalization*.
122. Rebellato, *Theatre & Globalization*.
123. Brandon, 'Some Shakespeare(s) in Some Asia(s),' 19.
124. Bhandari, Rajika and Alessia Lefébure, eds, *Asia: The Next Higher Education Superpower?* (New York: Institute of International Education, 2015). ix.

125. Tsuneyoshi, *Globalization and Japanese*, 7.

References

Asian Shakespeare Intercultural Archive (A|S|I|A) (website). Accessed 28 November 2018, http://a-s-i-a-web.org/en/home.php.

Bennett, Susan and Christy Carson, *Shakespeare Beyond English: A Global Experiment*. Cambridge: Cambridge University Press, 2013.

Bergman, Kevin. 'A Boys' Drama Club Performs *Romeo and Juliet*'. *Teaching Shakespeare* 6 (Autumn 2014): 14. https://www.britishshakespeare.ws/wp-content/uploads/2014/10/TS6_AW_WEB1.pdf.

Bhandari, Rajika and Alessia Lefébure, eds, *Asia: The Next Higher Education Superpower?* New York: Institute of International Education, 2015.

Brandon, James R. 'Some Shakespeare(s) in Some Asia(s)'. *Asian Studies Review* 20.3 (April 1997): 1–26.

Brumfit, Christopher, Jayne Moon and Ray Tongue. *Teaching English to Children: From Practice to Principle*. Cheltenham: Nelson ELT, 1991.

Buckley, Thea. *'In the Spicèd Indian Air by Night': Performing Shakespeare's Macbeth in Postmillennial Kerala*. PhD diss., University of Birmingham, 2017.

Chan, Kenneth. 'Teaching Shakespeare to College Students'. *Teaching Shakespeare* 6. *Teaching Shakespeare* 6 (Autumn 2014): 5–6. https://www.britishshakespeare.ws/wp-content/uploads/2014/10/TS6_AW_WEB1.pdf.

Curtis, David. *Teaching Secondary English*. London: Open University Press, 1992.

Desmet, Christy. 'Import/Export: Trafficking in Cross-Cultural Shakespearean Spaces'. *Teaching Shakespeare* 10 (Autumn 2016): 7–9.

Dillon, Michael. *Contemporary China: An Introduction*. Abingdon: Routledge, 2009.

Elliott, Victoria and Sarah Olive. 'Secondary Shakespeare in the UK: What Gets Taught and Why?' *English in Education*. 2019.

Ellis, Viv. 'English as a Subject'. In The Routledge Companion to English Studies, edited by Constant Leung and Brian Street. London: Routledge, 2014. 3–15.

Duty, Lisa and Merry M. Merryfield. 'Globalization'. In *The SAGE Handbook of Education for Citizenship and Democracy*, edited by James Arthur, Ian Davies, and Carole Hahn. London: Sage, 2008. https://doi.org/10.4135/9781849200486.n8.

Gallimore, Daniel. 'Shakespeare in Contemporary Japan'. In *Shakespeare in Hollywood, Asia and Cyberspace*, edited by Alexa Alice Joubin and Charles S. Ross, 109–120. West Lafayette, IN: Purdue University Press, 2009.

Gallimore, Daniel. 'Teaching Sheikusupia'. *Teaching Shakespeare* 6 (Autumn 2014): 6–8. https://www.britishshakespeare.ws/wp-content/uploads/2014/10/TS6_AW_WEB1.pdf.

Gallimore, Daniel. 'Tsubouchi Shōyō and the Beauty of Shakespeare Translation in 1900s Japan'. *Multicultural Shakespeare: Translation, Appropriation and Performance* 13.28 (2016): 69–85.

Goddard, Angela. *English, Language and Literacy 3 to 19: English 16–19.* Leicester: Owen and UKLA, 2015.

Hall, N. 'Literacy as Social Experience'. In *Teaching English to Children: From Practice to Principle,* edited by Brumfit, Christopher, Jayne Moon and Ray Tongue. Cheltenham: Nelson ELT, 1991. 244–259.

Hawkes, Terence. *Meaning by Shakespeare.* London: Routledge, 1992.

Hodgdon, Barbara. *The Shakespeare Trade: Performances and Appropriations.* Philadelphia: University of Pennsylvania Press, 1998.

Honda, Marie. 'Shakespeare's Teenage Film Adaptations and Japanese Comics: From *10 Things I Hate About You* to *Hana Yori Dango*'. *Teaching Shakespeare* 13 (November 2017): 7–9. https://www.tes.com/teaching-resource/teaching-shakespeare-13-11933304.

Honda, Marie. 'Undergraduate and Lifelong Learners of Shakespeare'. *Teaching Shakespeare* 6 (Autumn 2014): 19. https://www.britishshakespeare.ws/wp-content/uploads/2014/10/TS6_AW_WEB1.pdf.

Houlahan, Mark. 'Girdles 'Round the Earth: Globe to Globe (or "There and Back Again")'. Paper presented at the 'Rethinking the Global' Seminar of the Shakespeare Association of America Annual Meeting, Los Angeles, CA, April 2018.

Joubin, Alexa Alice. *Chinese Shakespeares: Two Centuries of Cultural Exchange.* New York: Columbia University Press, 2009.

Kawachi, Yoshiko. 'Introduction: Shakespeare in Modern Japan'. *Multicultural Shakespeare: Translation, Appropriation and Performance* 14.29 (2016): 7–12.

Kobayashi, Akio, *Let's Read English Poems.* Tokyo: NHK Publishing, 2007.

Kodama, Keita, 'Introducing Shakespeare to Young EFL Learners'. *Teaching Shakespeare* 16 (Autumn 2018): 11–13.

Koizumi, Yuto. 'First Year Shakespeare Through Film'. *Teaching Shakespeare* 6 (Autumn 2014): 15. https://www.britishshakespeare.ws/wp-content/uploads/2014/10/TS6_AW_WEB1.pdf.

Igarashi, Hirohisa. 'Improving Understanding Through Shakespeare'. *Teaching Shakespeare* 16 (Autumn 2018): 5–7.

Iwabuchi, Koichi, Stephen Muecke, and Mandy Thomas. *Rogue Flows: Trans-Asian Cultural Traffic.* Hong Kong: Hong Kong University Press, 2014.

Jameson, Fredric. *Nationalism, Colonialism and Literature: Modernism and Imperialism.* Dublin: Field Day, 1998.

Kelts, Roland. *Japanamerica: How Japanese Popular Culture Has Invaded the US*. London: Palgrave Macmillan, 2008.

Lee, Hyon-u, Shim Jung-soon, and Kim Dong-wook, eds, *Glocalizing Shakespeare in Korea and Beyond*. Seoul: Dongin, 2009.

Lei, Bi-qi Beatrice, Judy Celine Ick and Poonam Trivedi, eds. *Shakespeare's Asian Journeys: Critical Encounters, Cultural Geographies, and the Politics of Travel*. London: Routledge, 2016.

Linkon, Sherry Lee. *Literary Learning: Teaching the English Major*. Bloomington: Indiana University Press, 2011.

Lo, Jacqueline and Helen Gilbert. 'Toward a Topography of Cross-Cultural Theatre Praxis'. *The Drama Review* 46.3 (2002): 31–53.

Machi, Saeko. 'The Appeal of Gender-Crossing in *Twelfth Night*'. *Teaching Shakespeare* 14 (Spring 2018): 14–15. https://www.tes.com/teaching-resource/teaching-shakespeare-issue-14-11933306.

Machi, Saeko. 'Beyond the Language Barrier'. *Teaching Shakespeare* 7 (Spring 2015): 12–13. https://www.britishshakespeare.ws/wp-content/uploads/2014/01/TS7_AW_WEB2.pdf.

Mahbubani, Kishore. *Has the West Lost It? A Provocation*. London: Allen Lane, 2018.

Martin, Anthony. 'Editorial'. *Teaching Shakespeare* 13 (November 2017): 3. https://www.tes.com/teaching-resource/teaching-shakespeare-13-119 33304.

Massai, Sonia. *World-Wide Shakespeares: Local Appropriations in Film and Performance*. London: Routledge, 2006.

Matsuyama, Kyoko. 'Teaching English Literature in Japanese Universities: Teaching Unfamiliar Materials with Familiar Resources'. *Teaching Shakespeare* 13 (November 2017): 4–6. https://www.tes.com/teaching-resource/teaching-shakespeare-13-11933304.

Matthewman, Sasha. *Teaching Secondary English as if the Planet Matters*. Abingdon: Routledge, 2011.

Minami, Ryuta. '"No Literature Please, We're Japanese"': The Disappearance of Literary Texts from English Classrooms in Japan'. In *English Studies in Asia*, edited by Masazumi Araki, Lim Chee Seng, Minami Ryuta and Yoshihara Yukari. Kuala Lumpur: Silverfish Books, 2007. 145–165.

Minami, Ryuta. 'Shakespeare as an Icon of the Enemy Culture: Shakespeare in Wartime Japan, 1937–1945'. In *Shakespeare and the Second World War: Memory, Culture, Identity*, edited by Irena Makaryk and Marissa McHugh. Toronto: University of Toronto, 2012. 163–179.

Mizoguchi, Kazuhiro. 'A Study of Value Education in Teaching History: A Case Study of Teaching Materials in History for Political Literacy'. *Research Journal of Educational Methods* 20 (1994): 127–136.

Morinaga, Koji. 'Initiating the Language of Shakespeare'. *Teaching Shakespeare* 16 (Autumn 2018): 13–15.

Motoyama, Tetsuhito. 'Teaching Shakespeare to Law Students'. *Teaching Shakespeare* 6 (Autumn 2014): 10–11. https://www.britishshakespeare.ws/wp-content/uploads/2014/10/TS6_AW_WEB1.pdf.

Oki-Siekierczak, Ayami. 'The Treatment of Bawdy in Japanese Classrooms'. *Teaching Shakespeare* 6 (Autumn 2014): 9. https://www.britishshakespeare.ws/wp-content/uploads/2014/10/TS6_AW_WEB1.pdf.

Olive, Sarah. 'Editorial: Teaching Shakespeare in Hanoi'. *Teaching Shakespeare* 12 (Summer 2017): 3–5. https://www.britishshakespeare.ws/wp-content/uploads/2017/05/TeachingShakespeare12_AW_Web1.pdf.

Olive, Sarah. *Shakespeare Valued: Education Policy and Pedagogy in England, 1989–2009.* Bristol: Intellect, 2015.

Olive, Sarah. 'TNT's Twelfth Night at Japan Women's University.' *British Shakespeare Association Education Network Blog*, 16 May 2017, https://www.britishshakespeare.ws/shakespeare-in-education/tnts-twelfth-night-at-japan-womens-university/.

Olive, Sarah. 'To Research, or Not to Research? Some Dilemmas of Insider-Outsider Research on Shakespeare in South East/East Asian Higher Education.' *Researcher Stories Blog. British Sociological Association*, 5 May 2017, https://bsapgforum.com/2017/05/05/dr-sarah-olive-to-research-or-not-to-research-some-dilemmas-of-insider-outsider-research-on-shakespeare-in-south-easteast-asian-higher-education/.

Olive, Sarah. 'Vox Pop'. *Teaching Shakespeare* 9 (Spring 2016): 2–5. https://www.britishshakespeare.ws/wp-content/uploads/2016/02/TS9_AW_Web.pdf

Oxford English Dictionary Online. 'Westernisation'. Accessed April 27, 2019. http://www.oed.com.

Peel, Robin, Annette J. Patterson and Jeanne Gerlach. *Questions of English: Ethics, Aesthetics, Rhetoric, and the Formation of the Subject in England, Australia, and the United States.* London: Routledge, 2000.

Phipps, Alison. 'Giving an Account of Researching Multilingually'. *International Journal of Applied Linguistics* 23 (2013): 329–341.

Pithers, R. T. and Rebecca Soden. 'Critical Thinking in Education: A Review'. *Educational Research* 42.3 (2000): 237–249. https://doi.org/10.1080/001318800440579.

Rebellato, Dan. *Theatre & Globalization.* Houndmills: Palgrave Macmillan, 2009.

Saito Yoshifumi. 'Globalization or Anglicization? A Dilemma of English-Language Teaching in Japan'. In *Globalization and Japanese "Exceptionalism" in Education*, edited by Tsuneyoshi Ryoko. London: Routledge, 2018: 178–189.

Shellard, Dominic and David Warren. 'Shakespeare in Japan: A Great! Collaboration'. *Shakespeare* 9.4 (2013): 373–382.

Shudo, Sachiko and Yasunari Harada. 'Designing a Syllabus for Integrated Language Activities'. *Humanitas* 47 (2008): 1–12.

Suzuki, Shinichi. 'Encouraging Various Points of View'. *Teaching Shakespeare* 13 (November 2017): 13–15.

Tan, Jee-Peng and Alain Mingat. *Education in Asia: A Comparative Study of Cost and Financing*. Washington, DC: World Bank, 1992.

Taylor, Gary. *Reinventing Shakespeare: A Cultural History from the Restoration to the Present*. New York: Oxford University Press, 1989.

Thornton Burnett, Mark. *Filming Shakespeare in the Global Marketplace*. Houndmills: Palgrave, 2007.

Tink, James. 'Teaching the History Plays in Japan'. *Teaching Shakespeare* 6 (Autumn 2014): 12–13. https://www.britishshakespeare.ws/wp-content/upl oads/2014/10/TS6_AW_WEB1.pdf.

Trivedi, Poonam and Minami Ryuta, eds, *Replaying Shakespeare in Asia*. London: Routledge, 2010.

Tsuneyoshi, Ryoko. *Globalization and Japanese "Exceptionalism" in Education: Insiders' Views into a Changing System*. London: Routledge, 2018.

Uchimaru, Kohei. 'Editorial: Teaching Shakespeare in the Japanese English as a Foreign Language (EFL) Classroom'. *Teaching Shakespeare* 16 (Autumn 2018): 3–4.

Uchimaru, Kohei. 'Teaching Shakespeare in Japanese Secondary Schools: A study of Shakespeare's Reception in Locally Produced EFL School Readers'. MA diss., Birmingham: University of Birmingham, 2016.

Umemiya, Yu. 'Teaching English Stress Pattern Through Shakespearean Verse'. *Teaching Shakespeare* 20 (forthcoming).

Umemiya, Yu. 'Teaching Shakespeare in the Current HE Context'. *Teaching Shakespeare* 6 (Autumn 2014): 16–18. https://www.britishshakespeare.ws/ wp-content/uploads/2014/10/TS6_AW_WEB1.pdf.

Van Parijs, Philippe. *Just Democracy: The Rawls-Machiavelli Programme*. ECPR Essays Series, 2011.

Wetmore, Kevin, Siyuan Liu and Erin Mee. *Modern Asian Theatre and Performance, 1900–2000*. London: Bloomsbury, 1999.

White, R.S. 'Introduction'. In *Shakespeare's Local Habitations*, edited by Krystyna Kujawińska-Courtney and R.S. White. Łódź: Łódź University Press, 2007.

Willcock, Hiroko. 'Western Thought, and the Sapporo Agricultural College: A Case Study of Acculturation in Early Meiji Japan'. *Modern Asian Studies* 34.4 (2000): 977–1017.

Yaguchi, Yujin. 'The University of Tokyo PEAK Program'. In *Globalization and Japanese "Exceptionalism" in Education*, edited by Tsuneyoshi Ryoko. London: Routledge, 2018, 131–143.

Yang, Lingui. 'Modernity and Tradition in Shakespeare's Asianization'. *Multicultural Shakespeare: Translation, Appropriation and Performance* 10.25 (2013): 5–10. https://doi.org/10.2478/mstap-2013-0001.

Yonezawa, Akiyoshi and Shimmi Yukiko, 'Japan's Challenge in Fostering Global Human Resources: Policy Debates and Practices'. In *Globalization and Japanese "Exceptionalism" in Education*, edited by Tsuneyoshi Ryoko. London: Routledge, 2018. 43–60.

CHAPTER 6

Yamasaki Seisuke and the Shakespeare for Children Series in Japan

Rosalind Fielding

Abstract This chapter examines the history, performance and reception of the Shakespeare for Children series, established in 1995 by actor and director Yamasaki Seisuke at the Tokyo Globe. This series, which creates specially adapted productions of Shakespeare for younger audiences, has staged over twenty productions and toured both nationally and internationally. Yamasaki's series is considered within the wider context of theatre for young audiences in Japan, which had reached its 100th year in 2003. The chapter addresses the techniques employed by Yamasaki to create accessible shows, and these are examined in detail through case studies of *Cymbeline* and *A Midsummer Night's Dream*. Little has been published on the Shakespeare for Children series in either Japanese or English, and so this chapter aims to address this gap, taking its inspiration from the 'Shakespeare for Children series: For children today' event held at Waseda University, Tokyo, in May 2017.

R. Fielding (✉)
University of Birmingham, UK

© The Author(s), under exclusive license to Springer Nature
Switzerland AG 2021, corrected publication 2021
S. Olive et al., *Shakespeare in East Asian Education*, Global Shakespeares,
https://doi.org/10.1007/978-3-030-64796-4_6

187

Keywords Shakespeare · Japan · Children · Theatre · Performance · Yamasaki Seisuke · Shakespeare for Children · Tokyo Globe

6.1   Overview of Theatre
for Young Audiences in Japan

This chapter focuses on the Shakespeare for Children series, taking its opening from the event 'Shakespeare for Children series: For children today', a public talk held on 29 May 2017 at Waseda University in Tokyo. Unlike many of the other chapters in this book, this section is not concerned with formal education, nor is it concerned with Shakespeare as a means of studying English, since the company perform in Japanese. Rather, it considers the Shakespeare for Children series (*Kodomo no tame no sheikusupia*, occasionally also translated as the 'Shakespeare for Children Company'), a series of specially adapted performances of Shakespeare for young audiences. The series has performed over twenty productions to audiences across Japan since it was established in 1995. The Shakespeare for Children series is well regarded by critics for its combination of theatricality and accessibility for audiences both young and old, and it is unique in Japan for its dedication to introducing children to Shakespeare through performance and workshops. The series is a valuable example of Shakespeare outside the formal classroom setting in Japan and as a demonstration of the different ways that children can encounter Shakespeare. Additionally, it illuminates Sarah Olive's suggestion in the previous chapter that Japanese-language teaching resources trouble notions of Shakespeare as a westernising force in local education.

This chapter aims to address how the company was founded, to consider its place in the wider context of Shakespearean performance and children's theatre in Japan, and how the series stages Shakespeare for its young audiences. Very little has been published on the Shakespeare for Children series in English, and surprisingly little has been published in Japanese, which is a clear discrepancy given the number of publications in both languages dealing with the contemporary performance of Shakespeare in Japan. Notable exceptions include a mention in Kawai Shoichiro's article 'More Japanized, Casual and Transgender Shakespeares' (*Shakespeare Survey*, 62), Fukahori Etsuko's 2015 review of *Hamlet* (*The Kwassui Review*, 58) in English and *Richard II* (2002) and *Measure for Measure* (2006) in Japanese (both also in *The Kwassui Review*), amongst a few others. The company's work has been made increasingly accessible internationally thanks to the Asian Shakespeare Intercultural Archive, which hosts videos of their *A Midsummer Night's Dream* (2007) and *Cymbeline* (2008) on its platform, subtitled in multiple languages.[1] With this in mind, I will discuss the history of the series in considerable depth as it is hard to find this information gathered together in English. Many of the quotations from Yamasaki come from the Waseda event and are translated by me. The event was hosted by Dr Hida Norifumi (Waseda University) at the Tsubouchi Memorial Theatre Museum, which frequently hosts exhibitions and events on both contemporary and historical theatre.

Before moving onto the series itself, I will first briefly discuss the current situation of theatre for young audiences in Japan to better ground the later case studies. Although I will not explore the history of theatre for children in Japan in extensive detail, it is worth noting that 2003 marked the 100th anniversary of theatre for young people in Japan: Kobayashi Yuriko argues that the first professional production for young audiences was *Otogi-shibai* (*The Fairy Play*) staged by *shinpa* ('New School', a theatre movement from the nineteenth century) actor Kawakami Otojirō and his wife Kawakami Sadayakko in 1903.[2] The inspiration for *The Fairy Play* came from novelist and pioneer of children's literature Iwaya Sazanami, who saw theatre for young audiences in Germany and then worked with the Kawakamis, who were also influential figures in Shakespeare's reception in Japan, to produce *The Fairy Play*. In an introduction to theatre for young people in Japan, Fujita Asaya writes that one of the characteristics of early post-war Japanese children's theatre was that since very few companies had their own theatre, artists had to collaborate with schools to create productions in ordinary spaces such as gymnasiums ('gymnasium theatre').[3] In 1986 Robin Hall wrote that in Japan 'children's theatre is considered part of the cultural heritage', meaning that 'every schoolchild has the opportunity to see one or two performances every year', adding that children's theatre 'seems less a stepchild than a legitimate offspring of theatre for adults',[4] thereby implying that not only was theatre for children easily accessible at the time but that it was also regarded as an important part of their education. This resonates with Adele Lee's discussion in Chapter 2 and Olive's in Chapter 3 of this book about the important relationship between educational settings, schools and universities, and the development of modern theatre across East Asia.

Fujita writes that, during its heyday, there were around 200 dedicated companies for children, but he suggests that the genre is currently
facing problems caused by decreasing audience numbers.[5] One of the
best sources for information about contemporary young people's theatre
in Japan is the *Theatre Yearbook: Theatre in Japan*, published annually by
the Japanese Centre of the International Theatre Institute. Each edition
of the *Yearbook* contains an article by theatre critic Yokomizo Yukiko,
charting notable productions, tours and festivals for young audiences
as well as considering funding, audiences and social issues in the arts.
Yokomizo describes the difficulties Japan's falling birthrate is causing
theatre for young audiences, writing how it has been 'heavily affected by
the reduced numbers of children in Japan', and that—due to falling population numbers—in some areas, elementary schools (attended by children
aged six to twelve) and middle schools (ages twelve to fifteen) have been
consolidated, leading to a decreasing number of institutions requesting
performances.[6] Consequently, troupes dedicated to performing work for
young audiences have found it increasingly difficult to operate and have
seen a 'drastic decrease in the number of performances' they can hold
each year.[7] Fujita concludes that the decreasing audience and performance
numbers are a result of the cost of staging this kind of work: while he
also cites the declining birthrate, he states that since many companies
recover their expenses through 'membership fees paid by the children as
well as entrance fees', few companies are able to perform at schools with
a small number of students. He states that consequently 75% of children
at elementary schools and 83% at middle schools have been 'abandoned'
by the theatre due to 'financial circumstances'.[8]

The main associations and groups for children's theatre in Japan are
Jienkyo (Japan Union of Theatrical Companies for Children and Young
People), established in 1975 and the Japanese Centre of ASSITEJ (Association Internationale du Theatre pour l'Enfance et la Jeunesse), founded in
1979. ASSITEJ has National Centres in around 100 countries and serves
to unite theatres, companies and individual artists who create theatre for
young audiences. Jienkyo is prominent in sponsoring theatrical events for
children, including the Summer Vacation Children and Youth Theatre
Festival held in two theatres in Tokyo (Space Zero and PUK Puppet
Theater). There is also the Great Theatre Exposition for Children, previously known as the Forum for Children to Encounter the Stage Arts,
which is held at the National Olympics Memorial Youth Center during

the summer. The Tokyo Metropolitan Theatre also hosts TACT/Festival, a family-oriented festival featuring international performances.

There are a number of other festivals aimed at young audiences outside of Tokyo, including the TACT/FEST Osaka International Arts Festival for Children, which brings together national and international companies, and the Kid's Circuit in Saku which has been held in Nagano prefecture since 2016. Toyama prefecture holds the World Festival of Children's Performing Arts once every four years, hosting local, national and international companies. In Okinawa, the southernmost prefecture in Japan, the ricca ricca*festa International Theater Festival OKINAWA for Young Audiences is held every summer. It was established in 1994 and was then restarted on a larger scale in 2005, and has been held every July–August since, inviting a large number of companies from across the world. There is also the Theatre for Young Audiences Inclusive Arts Festival launched in January 2019 by TYA Japan with the theme 'Inclusive Arts' which includes performances by disabled artists and performances created for disabled audiences, and which emphasises that it is open to anyone whatever 'sexuality, culture and/or race you may be'.[9]

There are a number of outreach projects aiming to bring children into contact with the arts, including the Children Launching Project, created by playwright Noda Hideki (artistic director of the Tokyo Metropolitan Theatre), dancer and actor Moriyama Mirai and playwright Iwai Hideto. This project held storytelling workshops for children aged six to twelve which were then used as the basis for the professional theatre production *Namuhamudahamu* (a word invented by the children in the workshops as a 'word to mourn the dead'), which was performed at the Metropolitan Theatre in 2017.[10] The NPO Children Meet Artists arranges the Performance Kids Tokyo series, which brings artists working in dance, music and theatre into schools and cultural facilities to conduct workshops with children, leading to a showcase performance on the final day of training. There are also some initiatives to introduce children to Japan's traditional performing arts such as *noh* and *kabuki* (art forms dating from the fourteenth and the seventeenth centuries, respectively), including performances aimed at younger audiences (e.g. at the Kabuki-za, a major venue for *kabuki* performance in Japan, which has held the '*Kabuki* Class for Children' lecture and performance event since 1952) and the Traditional Performing Arts for Kids programme, in which children train with professional artists in genres such as *noh*, *Nihon Buyo* (traditional dance) and *Sankyoku* (music played on a *koto*, a thirteen-stringed instrument) for several months before putting on a public show at the end of the programme.

Another major feature of theatre for young audiences in Japan is the Regional Tour of Children's and Youth Theatre, sponsored by the Japan Arts Council, which tours across Japan to bring theatre to audiences living outside of the major cities. It was held for the 59th year in 2018. There is another touring project sponsored by the Agency for Cultural Affairs that is part of the Strategic Project for the Encouragement of the Creation of Artistic Culture, which visits rural areas and remote islands in the spring and autumn. Shiki Theatre Company, which was founded in 1953 and is one of the largest theatrical groups in Japan (responsible for long-running productions of musicals such as *Cats* and *The Lion King*) has its own major touring programme known as Heart Theatre (*Kokoro no gekijo*). The project was launched in 2008 and gives free performances to children across Japan: Shiki's website describes it as part of its 'priority' of 'conducting social contribution activities for children across the country'.[11] In 2015, Shiki toured three shows to 166 cities from Hokkaido to Okinawa, giving a total of 483 performances to 560,000 children (although the Shiki website gives the more conservative number of 360,000 children).[12]

The Nissei Theatre (Tokyo) has two major family-oriented events, the Nissei Masterpiece Series and the Nissei Theatre Family Festival. The Masterpiece Series presents free performances to children aged eleven to twelve across Japan, and since its beginning in 1964 it claims to have been attended by over 7,770,000 students.[13] In 2015, it toured to twelve cities and presented puppet shows, classical music concerts and operas. The Family Festival has been held since 1993, the year of the theatre's thirtieth anniversary, with the intention of introducing children to attending performances in a professional theatre space.

The number of festivals and projects discussed here suggests that there is fertile ground for theatre for young audiences in Japan, despite the move away from school performances and a changing population. Indeed, the Japanese Centre of International Association of Theatre for Children and Young People (ASSITEJ) refers to over 100 active companies for young audiences with an annual audience of 'over eight million'.[14] Although much of the work for young audiences (and indeed, much theatre in general) is focused on Tokyo and its surrounding areas, the festivals and touring companies visit many regions across the country, from the northernmost prefecture of Hokkaido to the southernmost Okinawan islands. Out of the projects described here, the Shakespeare for Children series is the only such programme dedicated to performing Shakespeare for young audiences in Japan. However, there have of course been other family-oriented productions of Shakespeare outside of this series, including Gekidan Chojugiga's *The Complete Works of Shakespeare (Abridged)*, a translation of the Reduced Shakespeare Company's production, which has been running since 2002 and has appeared at events such as the Kid's Circuit in Saku festival in 2016 and at the Children's Theatre in Onomichi, Hiroshima prefecture, in 2006.

The uniqueness of the Shakespeare for Children series makes it valuable as an example of the strategies for adapting Shakespeare for young audiences in Japan. As already mentioned, this series has received little academic recognition, perhaps reflecting Janice Bland's description of the 'lack of critical discussion of plays for young adults'.[15] Peter Hollindale writes that given the 'historical depth of children's drama, the long tradition of children's creative involvement as participants, not just spectators, the diversity of educational gains which it affords, and the omnipresence of drama in contemporary adult life' it should 'no longer be acceptable for children's drama to be the impoverished curricular and theatrical Cinderella which it currently is'.[16] As it stands, theatre for young audiences has been 'implicitly devalued in academic and pedagogical discourse and practice'.[17] To counter this trend, this chapter aims to consider how children can 'encounter' Shakespeare through the work of the Shakespeare for Children series, and the adaptation techniques used that allow the series to be accessible.[18] In the following, I will discuss the history of the series and its connection to the wider trends in Shakespeare performance in Japan at the time, which is particularly important given the close connection between the series and the Tokyo Globe Theatre, a former hub of Shakespearean performance in Japan. I will also consider the performance history and style of the Shakespeare for Children series, besides discussing how Yamasaki uses language and the translated Shakespearean text to adapt the plays for a younger audience, and give case studies of two productions from the series.

6.2   Yamasaki and the History of the Shakespeare for Children Series

The Shakespeare for Children series was founded by actor and director Yamasaki Seisuke in 1995 at the Tokyo Globe Theatre. Yamasaki was born in Kitakyushu, the largest city on the southwest island of Kyushu, and alongside other companies he has worked with the Seinenza Theater Company, founded in 1975 and known for its productions of modern (*shingeki*, 'New Theatre') drama. During the Waseda event, Yamasaki mentioned that he had attended acting classes in Britain but he described the experience as 'not that much fun', with what he found to be an over-emphasis on studying the play-text. Yamasaki does however place much importance on the script in his productions, so this is not at all to suggest that he has an aversion to text. In 1991 Yamasaki joined the Tokyo Globe Company which was housed at what was then the Panasonic Tokyo Globe Theatre, located in the Shinjuku district of Tokyo.

Opened in 1988, the Tokyo Globe is a recreation of the Second Globe Theatre (built in 1614). The theatre's founders cited Sam Wana-maker's Shakespeare's Globe Theatre project in London (based on the earlier 1599 incarnation) as grounds for recreating the 1614 building,[19] although construction of the Tokyo Globe was finished long before Shakespeare's Globe (completed in 1997). The creation of this Jacobean theatre in the middle of Tokyo was more an accident of construction laws and the economic boom of the 'bubble period' (1986–1991) than anything else, but its opening had an undeniable impact on the Shake-spearean performances that came after it. Critics such as Anzai Tetsuo have argued that the opening of this space marked the beginning of a new stage in Shakespeare's history in Japan: Anzai sets the opening of the Tokyo Globe as the fifth stage in his reception theory, following on from Meiji era adaptation (nineteenth century), the *shingeki* period (early twentieth century), Fukuda Tsuneari's translations and produc-tions (1955–1970) and the *shogekijo* ('Little Theatre Movement') period (1960s).[20] The theatre itself was part of a high-rise apartment complex, built under a deal to acquire land owned by the Tokyo Government: given the requirement to include a cultural facility in their plans for a residential development on former government land, the developers (a consortium of sixty-six real estate firms) chose to construct the Tokyo Globe. Unlike the Wanamaker project in London, the designers did not use construc-tion techniques or materials from the Jacobean era. Tamura Seiya, the theatre's senior manager during its early period, stressed that the Tokyo Globe was a 'recreation, not a reproduction' of the historic Globe,[21] and as a result, and taking its location close to some disruptive train tracks and Tokyo's annual rainy season into account, the designers decided on a roof to cover the theatre in addition to seats, a lighting rig and a pink finish to the outside of the building. With its thrust stage, the theatre sat

650 people, although the stage was made moveable to fit an extra fifty people inside.

During its heyday, the Tokyo Globe was a centre for Shakespearean performance in Japan and hosted both experimental Japanese productions and famous international companies. The Tokyo Globe was the first theatre built in Japan specifically for the purpose of staging Shakespeare, but despite being described as a 'monument to Japanese Shakespeare'[22] it also operated under the motto of 'Shakespeare and before, Beckett and after'[23] since it was also open to non-Shakespeare productions. It opened with a three-month-long festival that included the English Shakespeare Company (ESC)'s *The Wars of the Roses* series, three shows from the National Theatre of Great Britain (*Cymbeline*, *The Winter's Tale* and *The Tempest*) and two by Ingmar Bergman (*Hamlet* and *Miss Julie*), alongside workshops by the Royal Shakespeare Company (RSC). Later, it hosted the National Theatre's *Richard III* (1990), Shakespeare's Globe Theatre's *As You Like It* (1998) and the RSC's *Macbeth* (2000). At the same time, it was also a central site in the diversification of Shakespearean performance in Japan, providing a space for experimentation and innovation. Notable productions included *The Braggart Samurai* by the Mansaku-no-kai Company in 1991, a *kyogen* (a traditional theatre genre from the fourteenth century) adaptation of *The Merry Wives of Windsor* by Takahashi Yasunari that sparked further experiments with traditional genres such as the *Kyogen of Errors*, an adaptation of *The Comedy of Errors* staged in 2001 at the Setagaya Public Theatre.

Despite its artistic influence, the theatre struggled with low attendance rates and with its finances, having been built on very expensive land during the economic boom. Following the economic downturn caused by the bursting of the 'bubble' in 1991, the theatre struggled financially and in 1998 it dropped 'Panasonic' from its name to attract new investors, but it eventually closed down in 2002.[24] In 2004 it was bought by idol entertainment management agency Johnny's Production Company, more widely known as Johnny's, the agency behind popular acts such as Arashi and SMAP. Johnny's reopened the venue in 2004 with a production of *Romeo and Juliet*, starring one of its idols (Higashiyama Noriyuki) as Romeo. Following this change of ownership, the Tokyo Globe—despite maintaining its pink and abstract semi-timbered outside appearance—rarely stages Shakespeare, preferring musicals or dramas starring members of Johnny's agency. However, it does still host the occasional Shakespeare (including a production of *Macbeth* in 2016, starring Johnny's idol

Maruyama Ryuhei), but Shakespeare's plays are no longer the cornerstone of the theatre as they were before.

Yamasaki joined the resident Tokyo Globe Company in 1991 (founded in 1989) as an actor after having already performed at the Globe in productions such as Uesugi Shozo's *Broken Hamlet* (1990). This meant that when the company began its work, Yamasaki—alongside many of the other collaborators—were familiar with the particular demands of the space and how to use it to their advantage: Suematsu Michiko, amongst others, has noted that in certain ways the theatre was not 'physically audience-friendly' due to restricted views,[25] and Michael Pennington, who performed there with the ESC, also noted that although the seats were 'angled towards the stage', they 'somehow faced away from its focal point'.[26] Pennington added however that 'for all its technical shortcomings', the Tokyo Globe put its actors 'in touch with a certain magic'.[27] The early history of the Shakespeare for Children series at the Tokyo Globe therefore has some similarities with the Playing Shakespeare with Deutsche Bank series at Shakespeare's Globe in London (which has staged a production every year since 2007), in introducing Shakespeare to children within a thrust-stage space that, as W.B. Worthen has written, 'is said to restore how Shakespeare's plays "worked"', creating an experience that can 'come into visibility only in this kind of space, in this kind of relationship'.[28] Worthen does note, however, that 'we don't need Tudor timbers to frame this relationship: surely reinforced concrete would work just as well',[29] perhaps an apt statement in regard to this pink indoor Globe that hosted not only a successful series for children but also a diverse range of productions for adults too.

In 1994, one of the leaders of the Tokyo Globe suggested that they create something to introduce children to Shakespeare. The Shakespeare for Children series has now been running for over twenty years, proving the success of its founding intention. During the talk event, however, Yamasaki acknowledged that he did not expect the series to continue for as long as it has. The transferability that has seen it outlive its original home and move into new venues, besides its national and international tours, are proof of its accomplishment. This longevity, taken alongside the praise it has received from artists, audiences and critics, suggests that the series has outdone its original aims and ambitions. In her study on Shakespeare for young people, Abigail Rokison writes that 'full-scale Shakespeare productions created specifically for young audiences ... are seen as having a limited appeal, insufficient to fill a theater for a run',[30] but the longevity of this series proves otherwise. The organisers involved in planning the first Shakespeare for Children project initially floated the idea of staging a digest of Shakespeare's plays, rather than a full production of a single play. Yamasaki confessed that at the time they were unsure how best to proceed, due to an uncertainty over how to make the plays, which he described as 'really difficult to understand' for adults, easily understandable and accessible for children. They planned on staging this digest during the summer holidays (July–August) and this focus on summer performances has continued throughout the series, with an average of one play per year being put on in July or August (and in 2014, September). Summer performances are an observable trend in theatre for young audiences in Japan, with the majority of the festivals and tours described above concentrated during the summer months.

The organisers decided against staging a digest along the lines of Gekidan Chojugiga and the Reduced Shakespeare Company, and so the Shakespeare for Children series began in 1995 with a production of *Romeo and Juliet*. While Yamasaki has adapted and directed every production since, he only acted in this first show. Other original members of the series include actors who went on to form their own companies or who have been influential in recent Shakespearean performances in Japan: for example, Ayanogi Takayuki, who founded the Academic Shakespeare Company in 1996, and Yoshida Kōtarō, who founded AUN in 1997 and who often acted in Ninagawa Yukio's Sai-no-kuni Shakespeare Series. His credits with Ninagawa include *Titus Andronicus* (2004), *Much Ado About Nothing* (2008) and *Henry VI* (2010). Following Ninagawa's death in May 2016 Yoshida was announced as the artistic director of the Sai-no-kuni Shakespeare Series. There has therefore been considerable cross-over between Shakespeare for children and adults in Japan, and the productions in the Shakespeare for Children series can and should stand on their own, rather than being dismissed as inferior products. Edward Hall, director of the Pocket Propeller series whose shows are adapted from the 'adult' productions made by Propeller Theatre Company (UK), has similarly stated that the aim of the series was to deliver 'a first class theatrical experience to a young audience', and Rokison has also written about productions which, 'in terms of technical support, music, set, props and costumes', might be expected to be 'in the theatre's main repertoire'.[31] Rokison's work is especially useful in considering Yamasaki's Shakespeare for Children series since it brings into focus the differences and similarities between it and comparable productions in Britain, and provides some context for the strategies adopted by Yamasaki in terms of wider trends in adapting Shakespeare for children.

Yamasaki took over direction from the series' second production, *Twelfth Night*. He subsequently staged a production at the Tokyo Globe every summer until its closure in 2002: in order, from 1997 to 2002 their productions were *King Lear*, *Henry IV*, *Othello*, *King Lear* and *Twelfth Night* (double bill), *Richard II* and *The Merchant of Venice*. In the years after the Tokyo Globe closed, the series went to a number of different theatres across Tokyo, including the Sunshine Theatre, Setagaya Public Theatre and Kinokuniya Southern Theatre, before eventually becoming a fixture at the Owlspot Theater in Ikebukuro. In 2006 and 2007, the series returned to the Tokyo Globe with *Richard III* and then *A Midsummer Night's Dream*. The series also appeared in 2006 at the Pit Theatre (a studio space seating up to 468 people) at the New National Theatre, Tokyo, one of Japan's national theatres. Since 1997 the series has toured around Japan to reach audiences outside of Tokyo: it has toured to numerous prefectures including Kansai, Shiga, Ibaraki, Iwate, Miyazaki, Shizuoka and Saitama, a system that undermines the Tokyo-centric nature of much theatre production in contemporary Japan. In 2007 and 2008, *A Midsummer Night's Dream* and *Cymbeline* were taken to Seoul and performed in Japanese with Korean subtitles, aimed at both children and adults, implying a degree of success or popularity for the series since it was able to tour internationally.

6.3   Shakespeare for Children: Text and Performance Strategies

The Shakespeare for Children website describes the company's performances as 'not difficult Shakespeare', which 'anyone can enjoy watching'.[32] In regard to his objectives for what the audience will take away from the performance, Yamasaki describes wanting them to get a feel of the story and the characters, and to know that it is fine to not understand everything happening on the stage. He has also said that he wants them to be able to cope with a degree of uncertainty during the performance so that they do not need to 'keep checking the programme to see who's who', and Ishihara Kosai and Hirokawa Osamu have argued that '"understandable and entertaining Shakespeare for everyone" suitably expresses the style of performance of this company'.[33] In this next section, then, I will consider the tactics employed by the series to create these 'understandable' and 'enjoyable' shows, and what they mean in terms of introducing young audiences to Shakespeare.

Performances in the series are all adapted into shortened versions, cut to around two hours. This has telling similarities to the Playing Shakespeare series at Shakespeare's Globe, which aims to 'deliver thrilling 90–minute fully-staged versions of Shakespeare's plays' for secondary school students.[34] Rokison notes in relation to Playing Shakespeare's average length that it is 'substantially longer than most versions for young people'.[35] Yamasaki has stated that when staging Shakespeare the most important element for him is the text, and this is also similar to Playing Shakespeare director Bill Buckhurst, who has argued that it is important to give 'young people a full-scale production' rather than telling 'the story in as few words as possible'.[36] The longer running times of both Playing Shakespeare and the Shakespeare for Children series imply that this strategy of staging longer productions for young audiences is feasible and will not necessarily lead to the audience being unable to concentrate or understand. Yamasaki does make frequent cuts to the text, but it is through these cuts that he pinpoints the vital parts of the plot to help the younger audience both understand and remain engaged with the story. In an interview with the *Japan Times*, he said that it was important not to 'underestimate children's capability', since they can 'enjoy Shakespeare's plays just as adults do',[37] and Fukahori has argued that the cuts he makes are to 'stress the actual progress of events in the play',[38] rather than cutting because he thinks the lines are beyond the children's understanding.

Yamasaki has also compared the plays to a tree and the way he prepares the texts to the art of *bonsai*, with the story as the tree's trunk and his job being to arrange the branches to reveal this story in the best way. By 'judiciously trimming leaves and small branches' of the tree, the trunk will 'appear so clearly that even young children' can easily see it.[39] Yamasaki suggested that the way he prepares the text has changed, as he previously cut significantly more of the lines but, wanting to preserve more of the text, he now thinks about 'which lines are beautiful or interesting' for the audience. He gave his 2017 production of *King Lear* as an example of his changing approach as he made no cuts to the storm scene (3.2) and chose instead to perform it 'as is'. He has also said that he is 'especially aware of children' when he is at the scriptwriting stage, and that since the 'words are often even difficult for grown-ups, I carefully select the vocabulary to vividly appeal to children'.[40] Rokison raises the point that at least part of the cutting in Playing Shakespeare is done in response to the small cast, and this practical need certainly counts for the Shakespeare for Children series too.[41]

Since the second production (*Twelfth Night*, 1996), the series has used Odashima Yushi's (b. 1930–) translations. Odashima was the second translator to finish Shakespeare's complete works in Japanese, and his translations were all performed by Deguchi Norio with his Shakespeare Company from 1975 to 1981. Yamasaki compared the length of Odashima's translated lines to those of Shakespeare's in English, and his translations are 'widely regarded as easy to understand for the general public' due to his use of colloquial language.[42] In the 2014 *Hamlet* Yamasaki played with different translations of Shakespeare to create a 'special trigger' at the start of the play to capture the audience's attention, having *Hamlet* open with the actors delivering the 'to be or not to be' soliloquy in different translations, several of which are extremely famous in Japanese.[43] Yamasaki said that even though the speech is well-known and has several different interpretations in Japanese, 'the line doesn't especially matter to children—and anyway, most of them will be hearing it for the first time. So I intentionally repeated it in various different translations to make a strong impression at the start and grab their interest'.[44]

This tactic of rearranging the text and the story is another characteristic of the company. Although Yamasaki does not change the plot itself, he sometimes alters the order of scenes to clarify the action (*Richard II*), or adds scenes to give background (e.g. in *Richard III* he added scenes from *Henry VI Part III*, including the Battle of Tewkesbury and Richard's murder of Henry), and repetition (to go back to *Hamlet*, the 'to be or not to be' soliloquy was repeatedly performed throughout the show). Adding details such as the Battle of Tewkesbury are particularly useful in performing one of Shakespeare's history plays for children, giving them crucial background information to understand Richard's opening speech, and is particularly noteworthy when working with a young Japanese audience, whose familiarity with fifteenth-century English history cannot be counted on. Elements such as these allow the children to access the stories more easily, and also underline Yamasaki's hope that the audience will not feel the need to keep checking the programme to see who the characters are. The company's website also suggests that the way the scenes are arranged allows the play's themes to be highlighted, adding that the shows are directed 'with a heart full of playfulness',[45] an idea that will become apparent later in the performance case studies.

In addition to these changes, Yamasaki also adds visual and verbal jokes, 'idioms and new episodes designed to appeal to family audiences'[46]. For example, in *Hamlet*, he added a scene where Old Hamlet duels with the King of Norway, presented as an ice hockey game. As Fukahori notes, he also added an extremely successful visual gag (bringing the audience into 'explosions of laughter') in 1.4, where the ghost appears to Hamlet and beckons him to follow: the ghost and the other actors surrounding him beckoned to Hamlet in the same way as the *manekineko*, the beckoning cat figure regarded as bringing good fortune (often displayed outside of businesses or in the home), and one of the Chorus members was also holding a *manekineko* itself.[47] Yamasaki said that he wants to create these 'moments of relief in tough situations', and the use of a familiar figure from daily life, alongside the gag, is an effective way to disrupt any tension that might have been brought on by the arrival of the ghost.[48] Yamasaki is, as Fukahori suggests, 'sure that laughter is essential to stage a play for children', and so his productions are fast and full of entertaining moments such as this.[49]

Kawai writes that the current trend in Shakespearean performance in Japan is 'choose your own Shakespeare', in which the audience can 'pick from a long list of productions' and he argues that the Shakespeare for Children series 'may be a typical new form for Shakespeare in the twenty-first century, where people have begun to enjoy Shakespeare in a more casual manner' than that of the previous century, which was largely dominated by *shingeki* style productions.[50] As Kawai notes, contemporary audiences have a wider choice of styles and genres to choose from, ranging from traditional theatre to new adaptations, and this freedom of expression aided the creation of and now supports the ongoing success of the Shakespeare for Children series. At the event, Yamasaki himself described 'enjoyment' for him as something that does not mean only having fun, but also about being excited and experiencing various emotions, including sometimes sadness or fear: he made a comparison with going to a theme park, an activity strongly associated with childhood or 'childness' (as conceived of by Hollindale), where you might 'scream because you're scared' when you go on a ride, but ultimately you are still enjoying the experience. But he also said elsewhere that children 'cannot put up with long serious scenes like adults. They cannot concentrate for a long time, so it is necessary to let them feel relieved and then let them concentrate',[51] which is where the adaptation strategies such as jokes and physicality come in. The other problem in creating these shows for children that Yamasaki spoke of was that their interest level is 'at maximum' at the start of the performance, but that it can then suddenly drop as the event goes on. Consequently, they need various elements to keep their attention because, as Yamasaki joked, their attitude is 'ok, what's next?' Rokison describes a similar concept when she argues that the 'use of live music and sound effects, direct audience address, elements of audience participation and improvisation' are 'chosen for their ability to capture and retain the attention and enthusiasm of a young audience' in this kind of performance,[52] and I will go into more detail about how Yamasaki uses these features in the performance case studies.

As with comparable projects in Britain, such as Young People's Shakespeare, Propeller's Pocket Shakespeare, and Playing Shakespeare, the Shakespeare for Children series is characterised by its small casts. The cast takes on the role of Chorus when not acting as a particular character, and through dynamic movement and quick character changes they help to maintain the speedy pace of the production. *Romeo and Juliet* in 1995 had a cast of sixteen, but since then the series has tended to have a cast of around ten people (and in comparison, Pocket Propeller uses six, Playing Shakespeare around ten). The majority of the cast therefore take on multiple roles during the play, using quick change techniques to switch between characters: this is an interesting tactic to introduce children to the effects—or as Kawai terms it, the 'magic'—of theatre and theatricality.[53] When discussing this staging choice during the event, Yamasaki stated that it seems as though most of the audience are able to understand that the 'actors are playing different characters' within the play, sometimes of the same gender, sometimes not, and that all the characters are part of a performance.

The Chorus play a central part in each production, with an established set of conventions each time they appear: they wear long black coats and hats which are used as props or taken off to signify a switch in character, and consequently they are often referred to as the Black Coats. Productions begin with all the actors gathering onstage, dressed as the Chorus. They repeat lines together throughout the play, embody crowds and at other times act as elements of a character's psychology. In *Hamlet*, for example, the Chorus were onstage with Hamlet during his soliloquies, possibly as 'voices of the heart'.[54] In traditional Japanese theatre forms such as *noh* or *bunraku* (a traditional type of puppet theatre), the seated chorus (*jiutai*) occasionally speak for other actors, and Yamasaki has arguably adapted this technique here (see Suematsu 2017 for further discussion on this). The Chorus take an active part in the events of the play, with, for example, their coats being thrown over Ophelia's body to signify her burial, echoing Kawai's comment on the way the series uses a 'high theatricality in the style of Theatre de Complicité'[55] that has garnered it much praise from both critics and audiences. Another example of this is the Chorus calling Claudius's name several times towards the start of *Hamlet* until one of the actors took off his Chorus outfit and became Claudius. In this way, the Chorus become new characters by removing their coats and revealing another costume underneath.

The use of music in Shakespeare aimed at younger audiences is commonplace (see e.g., Rokison) and Yamasaki initially wanted the actors to play instruments onstage. However, since the actors he was working with in the beginning were not trained musicians and they did not have much rehearsal time, it was too difficult to incorporate live music into the show. He therefore decided that the 'most reasonable' instrument the actors could use would be their hands, which was the beginning of one of the other characteristic features of the series: clapping. Now each production tends to begin with the actors clapping together onstage and at other times in the show, beginning in a small way in *Twelfth Night* (1995) but incorporated more heavily from the 1997 *King Lear* onwards. *King Lear* began with the actors in a circle, clapping together, and the 2007 *A Midsummer Night's Dream* opened with the Mechanicals, who, after a brief introductory scene (described in more detail later), began to clap rhythmically together and move across the stage to mark the start of the next scene. Clapping is often used to mark a change in tone or location, and Yamasaki frequently employs this rhythmic clapping just before the interval and then at the opening of the next act. Clapping is a simple way of creating rhythm and also offers coherence and familiarity between productions for repeat viewers, but above all, it works as a method to get the audience's attention and keep them focused. Once the audience becomes familiar with the technique, it is a useful way to signpost new scenes and thereby helps them follow the flow of the story. This use of clapping to mark the end of a scene is reminiscent of the use of wooden clappers (*tsuke*) in *kabuki*, which similarly mark the beginning and end of scenes, suggesting that Yamasaki may have incorporated a feature of traditional theatre familiar to some of the audience.

As is implied by the use of clapping rather than any other instrument, Yamasaki's Shakespeare productions are often stripped-back, and this is also the case with the stage design, which is largely empty. The set is always simple, made up of wooden desks and chairs resembling those found in old elementary schools, which are moved around to form whatever is needed for the scene such as a platform or a row of chairs. In *Cymbeline* (2008), boulders were also used in the background, representing both the 'rocks unscalable' (3 January 20) of the landscape and the cave which Belarius lives in. This simplicity is often found in productions of Shakespeare for children in Britain too, although this could be inspired by the need to tour to schools or other regional venues and the ability to set up quickly in an improvised space, besides the ties it has to the simplicity of early modern stage furniture. Fukahori has suggested that Yamasaki's series depends 'almost exclusively on actors' bodies and voices' for dramatic effect,[56] but it is also worth noting, as Tanaka Nobuko argues, that although the target audiences are aged 'from 10 upwards, there is nothing patronizing or simplistic' about these staging techniques.[57] Unlike the Playing Shakespeare series, which uses a combination of contemporary and period costume, the costumes in the Shakespeare for Children series are largely historical, although they are not period specific and anachronistic elements such as the black coats worn by the Chorus are always present.

Possibly one of the most crucial elements of the Shakespeare for Children series is the use of a 'Shakespeare puppet' in each show. The puppet is 'child-sized'[58] and is operated by one actor, often Yamasaki himself, its mouth moving in time with an actor who speaks its lines. In the process of planning *Romeo and Juliet* in 1995, a discussion arose about who should play Peter. It was suggested that they could use a puppet in the role since 'he's always at the Nurse's side' and could thereby be operated by the actor playing her. They decided to make the puppet resemble the Droeshout portrait of Shakespeare in the First Folio, with long white hair (bald on top) and a little moustache and goatee. This makes Shakespeare a visible and sometimes comical presence in each show, giving the audience a stable image of the playwright to hold onto. Puppetry has a significant presence in theatre for young audiences in Japan, with Yokomizo suggesting that there may be around 2,000 puppet troupes across the country, although she adds that many of these are small companies with only one or two members.[59] Some puppet troupes are very well established, including Puppet Theater PUK (founded 1929) which has its own small permanent theatre in Tokyo and which also tours to festivals and regional venues. This prevalence of puppetry may account for the reasoning behind including the puppet in the series, and it is certainly notable that in promotional material the Shakespeare puppet is often prominently included.

The puppet takes on a different role in each show, often cleverly illuminating a particular element of the story. In *Richard III*, for example, it was used to represent Richard's damaged hand. At the end of the play, Richmond cuts the puppet from Richard's hand and places it on his own, signifying the transfer of power. Not only does the puppet serve as a method of drawing the young audience in, it also sometimes takes on the role of 'commentator', to help clarify events for the children.[60] In *Cymbeline*, the puppet was cast as Jupiter and in this role the puppet often commented on and intervened in the story, explaining details of the complicated plot and helping keep up the play's fast pace. At other times the puppet has been used to highlight relevant themes within a play, including when it was cast as the 'Ghost of Young Hamlet' (a figure carried by the Ghost of Old Hamlet) as an alter ego of the main character.[61]

A final point to make about the series' performance techniques concerns the fluid cross-gender casting it frequently employs. Yamasaki emphasised that casting is often a practical decision taken because of the sparsity of roles for women. For example, in *Richard III* Richmond was played by a female actor. He also identified the practice with Elizabethan stagecraft, referencing the practice of using boy players in female roles, and also with traditional Japanese performing arts such as *noh* and *kabuki* which historically were largely performed by men. Yamasaki described an initial concern about the way the young target audience might respond to cross-gender casting, but when Yamasaki played the Nurse in 1995 he said that he was 'surprised that no children made fun of a man in that role – they naturally accepted that theatre is fundamentally fiction and just enjoyed the play'.[62] In her discussion on Pocket Propeller, a series that was performed entirely by male actors from the Propeller Theatre Company, Rokison notes that this cross-gender casting is another element that 'helps to emphasize the fictive nature of the production, encouraging, in both actor and audience, an imaginative engagement and willing suspension of disbelief'.[63] In Yamasaki's case, it seems that he has used cross-gender casting to emphasise the production's theatricality, to reference earlier theatre forms (both Japanese and British), and to address the gender imbalance of the plays.[64]

6.4   In Performance: *Cymbeline* and *A Midsummer Night's Dream*

The Shakespeare for Children series staged *Cymbeline* in 2008 at Owlspot Theatre, having staged an earlier version in 2003. In the following section, I will use this production as a brief case study of these performance techniques in action, before considering the *A Midsummer Night's Dream* staged at the Tokyo Globe (2007). Given the relative popularity of *A Midsummer Night's Dream* (performed seventeen times in the Greater Tokyo region in 2011, and fourteen times in 2012) versus *Cymbeline* (which is rarely staged), and the complicated plot and numerous characters of *Cymbeline*, these two case studies will offer revealing examples of Yamasaki's performance style. Furthermore, *A Midsummer Night's Dream* is a popular choice for productions intended for children in Britain, and was described by Peter Holland as often being 'the way children first encounter Shakespeare',[65] and so a discussion of Yamasaki's approach to directing may illuminate some of the similarities and differences between British and Japanese theatre for young audiences.

Cymbeline opened with the cast clapping together in the darkness, with the Black Coats gradually appearing from the back of the stage. The clapping helped focus the attention of the audience and clearly demarcated the start of the performance. The Chorus opened the show by chanting Iachimo's lines from 2.4 together ('if you seek for further satisfying, under her breast... lies a mole') (2.4.133–35), beginning the production with an element of the story that would become crucial later on. Posthumus emerged from among them, the only non-Black Coat character during the introduction, and the Chorus surrounded him threateningly and although there was no music, the Chorus made a repetitive hissing noise that added to the tension of the scene. Posthumus eventually curled up on the ground and individual Chorus members began asking 'how did it end up this way?' and 'is it a rumour?'.[66] The Shakespeare puppet then appeared, operated by Yamasaki, using the onomatopoeic word '*goro-goro*' ('rumble') to announce thunder. Cast as the god Jupiter, the puppet took on a highly active role that greatly expanded the original. The Black Coats divided lines from 5.4, with the rest of the Chorus repeating the final part of the line: for example, 'In Britain where was he that could stand up his parallel' was followed by 'his parallel' (5.4.42–43). The Chorus then narrated how Posthumus had married Imogen and been banished as a result. Jupiter brought the prologue to an end by stating, 'Be merry, be merry and be merry. More haste and less speed',[67] and then in English began to say 'good morning', a phrase completed by the Chorus, after which the scene brightened and Posthumus 'woke up'. The introduction therefore highlighted some of the conflicts that were going to be crucial to the rest of the play and established the character of Posthumus and his part in the following story.

The layout of the stage remained largely the same throughout the show, with a row of tables and stools laid out as a platform in front of a backdrop of boulders. The clothes were likewise fairly simple and suggestive of period costume, although not of any one period in particular. As described in the previous section, members of the Chorus changed almost instantly into other characters; during the opening scene, for example, some of the Chorus searched for Imogen before the actor playing her removed her coat and was revealed as 'Imogen'. In other scenes, the Black Coats announced a character's name as they were revealed if they had not already been named during the course of the dialogue; if they had been named, they would simply take on the role. The Black Coats also participated in the action in numerous ways, crowding around Imogen and congratulating her on her marriage, and bringing Cloten first a *kendama* (a traditional wooden toy known as a 'sword and ball') and then a dried cuttlefish instead of his sword when he challenged Posthumus to a duel. Although their fight is reported and not seen in Shakespeare's text, Yamasaki dramatised it onstage and had the Chorus verbalise some of the violence, often using onomatopoeia. For example, when Posthumus punched Cloten, the Chorus chanted in time with the fighting, 'One, two – *bang*!' The Chorus were also used to mark the end of scenes by repeating the clapping rhythm. The first half, which ran for approximately one hour, finished with clapping that led into a blackout, and then vice versa following the interval, giving the show a recognisable structure and alerting the audience to what was going to happen.

The puppet made numerous appearances throughout the performance, both as Jupiter and as the 'Grand Master', a physician working with Cornelius. As Jupiter the puppet often intervened in the action, telling Posthumus that he needed to leave and announcing the arrival of Cymbeline during the opening scene, and then later interrupting Iachimo during his scene in Imogen's bedroom (2.2). When Iachimo approached the sleeping Imogen, saying 'That I might touch!', Jupiter interrupted and told him 'No, that is not your purpose'.[68] The puppet therefore provided some relief from the tension building up in the scene and also seemed to direct the characters' behaviour. Jupiter was also both a commentator and a confidant, taking on Imogen's lines to say 'A father cruel, and a step-dame false' (1.6.1) sympathetically to her. The scene from the opening was repeated towards the end of the performance, and Jupiter, who had up until this point been wearing the same kind of black coat and hat as the Chorus, reappeared in white robes and a diadem. Based on the stage direction 'Jupiter descends in thunder and lightning, sitting upon an eagle' (5.4), one of the Black Coats pretended to be an eagle, carrying the puppet on their back and flapping their arms as though they were wings. The other Chorus members demanded that the eagle 'screech' for them to prove it was real, to which the actor responded by mimicking a bird cry (but in reality saying 'ea-gle' in English). As with the earlier 'good morning', there were several other examples of English being used, including Cymbeline telling the court to 'shut up' when he first entered. This is a common feature of the series and it is used in a variety of ways, sometimes as a reference to the original English text, at other times as a joke or a reference to something from popular culture, and at other times as a way of teaching the audience some English vocabulary, as with the above example of the eagle.

This version of *Cymbeline*, running at two hours, took on the compli-cated plot of the play but avoided condensing it too heavily. Yamasaki retained several 'adult' parts of the original play, including the scene in Imogen's bedroom, Iachimo's description of her and the beheading of Cloten. Furthermore, the multiple confusions, mistakes and revelations that take place in the final scene were delivered lucidly and humorously, with comedic reveals of different characters who each emerged from the back of the stage and stated 'I've been listening to everything'.[69] Perhaps a surprising number of characters and storylines were kept in this version, very different to some of the productions described by Rokison which, 'with a young audience in mind', prioritise 'brevity'.[70] As suggested earlier, this reflects Yamasaki's determination to not patronise or underes-timate the audience's abilities. The *A Midsummer Night's Dream* in 2007 was the last performance of the series in recent years to be produced at the Tokyo Globe. As with Yamasaki's other productions, *A Midsummer Night's Dream* opened with the Black Coats, although here they were also wearing hard hats. The Mechanicals removed their coats and thus exited the Chorus, while the rest of the Black Coats joined in as unnamed members of the group. In the opening scene, the Chorus brought on the desks and chairs that made up the set and laid them out as a platform, before beginning to rehearse their performance of *Pyramus and Thisbe*. In colloquial, everyday language they gradually revealed the background to the play and introduced the individual members of the group. Puck was brought into the introduction, interrupting the rehearsal and fore-shadowing his later role in the play. The opening scene also contained a brief moment of audience participation, with the actors asking people on the front row to point to a lost desk which was hidden at one side of the stage. This scene also introduced an element of play and theatricality by having the Chorus find and read aloud a piece of paper with part of Puck's final speech on it.

While there was little cross-gender casting in *Cymbeline*, here Yamasaki was cast as both Hippolyta and Titania. The puppet, besides being a member of the Mechanicals, was also cast as Hippolyta's son and the child fought over by Titania and Oberon. As with *Cymbeline*, the Chorus clapped to mark the transition from one scene into another, and they also played a large role in the introduction of other characters. The Chorus often chanted the name of a character several times before they were revealed from among their ranks. For example, when Egeus says 'Stand forth, Demetrius', the Chorus chanted 'Demetrius, Demetrius' until his coat was removed and the character revealed (1.1.24). They were again involved in creating humour, with one scene in particular intended for the adults in the audience: when Helena and Hermia talked about Demetrius ('I frown upon him, yet he loves me still' (1.1.194)), the Chorus added after 'The more I hate, the more he follows me' (1.1.199), 'Oh shit!' in English. This is perhaps a surprising element to find in a production intended for a young audience, especially given the aversion to Shake-speare's scatological humour of some university students demonstrated by Olive in Chapter 5—though that was in a formal educational, rather than entertainment, setting. However, it echoes language that older members of the audience might recognise from international media.

Yamasaki's Shakespeare productions are less obviously intercultural than performances that visually or thematically locate the action in Japan, but they do contain elements of localisation. In *A Midsummer Night's Dream*, a similar visual joke to the previously described *manekineko* scene was created during the Mechanicals' rehearsal (3.1) with one of the Black Coats holding up a *noren* curtain, traditionally used backstage in Japanese theatres, to cover the door to their 'dressing room'. During the play-within-a-play performance of *Pyramus and Thisbe*, 'Wall' delivered his first lines using a vocal technique reminiscent of *kabuki*. Humour was also created by having Helena smoking a cigarette, with one of the Black Coats bringing her an ashtray. However, the scene with the four lovers (3.2) was performed in a fairly muted way, with few laughs from the audience; Helena seemed quiet and sad, particularly when she accused the others of mocking her ('can you not hate me, as I know you do, but you must join in souls to mock me too?' (3.2.149–150)), suggesting she had been bullied before. Bullying is prevalent in Japanese schools and this bullied and shy Helena could be an allusion to this, as a teaching moment for would-be bullies or a sympathetic scene for the bullied. During the event Yamasaki spoke about his then upcoming production of *King Lear* (2017), describing what he saw as its links to contemporary Japanese society. He referred in particular to *King Lear*'s representation of ageing and the elderly, a theme which has resonant echoes with the rapidly ageing society and falling birthrate facing Japan. While these are only a few examples of the way Yamasaki localised the productions for the young audience and tied them into contemporary issues or concerns, they demonstrate Yamasaki's method of making the plays accessible and addressing themes the children might hear about in daily life in a safe space or new way.

6.5   Reception and Rationales

During the Waseda event, when asked what the importance of performing Shakespeare for children might be, Yamasaki acknowledged that, two decades after the series had started, he was still thinking about whether it was necessary or not. He suggested that rather than being 'necessary' to stage Shakespeare for children in Japan, it is 'desirable' so that they are given the opportunity to see the plays live and to personally experience the arts. Part of his thinking seemed to concern a perceived lack of opportunity for Japanese children to encounter Shakespeare and the desirability of redressing that. Yamasaki also holds workshops for children, allowing them to not only watch theatre but to try it for themselves. Answering a question from the audience about these acting workshops with children, Yamasaki emphasised his belief that it is fine for them to be shy, that being shy is good and it is normal to be scared, but that what is important for the children involved is how they control that and change themselves in performance to express themselves clearly.

Yamasaki was also emphatic that he wants the plays to be enjoyable to watch. The techniques discussed in the previous sections are evidence of this motivation, and it is a measure of his success that the series (alongside Yamasaki's Chekhov project) won the prestigious Kinokuniya Drama Award in 2010. His determination that the plays be enjoyable for children recalls director Kelly Hunter's take on her own practice in creating Shakespeare for young audiences, that her 'motivation was not to introduce Shakespeare to children in order that they become well-behaved theatre go-ers', but to 'invigorate their souls at the particular moment in their lives, right then and there in the room'.[71] The elements in the Shakespeare for Children series that are there to help a young audience 'encounter' Shakespeare also serve to invigorate and to welcome the children into the theatre.

Many critics have noted the popularity of Shakespeare for Children with both younger audiences and adults. As the performances draw in sizeable adult crowds, it suggests that Yamasaki's adaptations do successfully appeal to older audiences as well, a phenomenon that Olive has noted in relation to the Royal Shakespeare Company's productions for children such as *The Comedy of Errors* (2009), at least as staged in their theatres at Stratford-upon-Avon (2015).[72] Rokison also noted a similar phenomenon at performances of Pocket Propeller's *Pocket Dream* held at the Underbelly in London in 2011.[73] Yamasaki himself has stated that he wants to 'make Shakespeare plays more familiar for anyone to enjoy as great entertainment',[74] and the series website further adds that the series intends to put on 'shows that children and adults can enjoy together in the same space'.[75] The intergenerational interest in the series is indicative of the playfulness of the adaptation techniques, and of the non-patronising nature of the shows themselves.

It is worth noting, however, that while the series has many similarities to comparable projects in Britain, many of the British examples involve a degree of participation that is largely lacking in Yamasaki's work. Rokison suggests that British productions prioritise 'active involvement' alongside 'clarity' and length as elements that have the 'potential to involve and enthral young audiences'.[76] This contrast implies the different expectations from audiences in Japan and the UK in terms of participation within the theatre, and demonstrates that this kind of active involvement is not universally necessary to attract young audiences. In this way, perhaps the series offers an example of resisting the twenty-first-century globalising and anglicising influences on Shakespeare in East Asian education discussed by Lee and Olive in Chapters 2 and 5. Additionally, while it is true that the Tokyo Globe has always operated differently to Shake-speare's Globe (particularly as it lacks a standing audience in the yard), there are significant differences between the Playing Shakespeare productions at Shakespeare's Globe and the Shakespeare for Children series at the Tokyo Globe. Playing Shakespeare productions make frequent use of the yard and every level of the theatre, bringing the actors out into the audience and making the whole space part of the performance, while the Shakespeare for Children series largely keeps the action contained on the stage, although Yamasaki does sometimes engage in audience participation and brings actors onto the stage through the auditorium. This is not to criticise Yamasaki for taking a different approach, merely to note that these differences exist and that they are particularly notable given the similar spaces Playing Shakespeare and the Shakespeare for Children series take place in. Occasional Playing Shakespeare director Joanne Howarth suggested that theatre for young people needs to be 'energetic' and needs to 'look at the issues in the play that are relevant to that audience',[77] and whatever the stylistic differences between Playing Shakespeare and Shake-speare for Children it is clear that Yamasaki has successfully met these 'needs'.

The continuing popularity of the Shakespeare for Children series, as described by Yamasaki at the Waseda event and as demonstrated by its standing and longevity, is evidence that it has been able to connect with young audiences and also suggests that it has succeeded in its goal of creating productions of Shakespeare that are both understandable and enjoyable for its audiences. The accessibility of the productions, which has been much commented on by critics such as Fukahori and Kawai, proves that it has accomplished its founding intent of staging Shakespeare that 'anyone can enjoy'.[78] Not only that but if, as Fiona Banks (a member of the Globe Education team involved in creating Playing Shakespeare) suggests, being part of an audience at a theatre can 'empower students', and that if they then 'feel engaged with a performance and form feelings and opinions about their experience they are instantly theatre critics', then these productions may also be seen as offering a valuable introduction to performance to its audiences.[79] The commitment to touring to multiple venues is likewise of note, as it provides the opportunity to watch the show to a wider group of people. Furthermore, the theatricality of the productions and the confidence to stage plays which are less familiar or less popular (such as *Cymbeline* or *Measure for Measure*) has brought the company recognition and helped to establish their reputation. The Shakespeare for Children series makes a valuable contribution to theatre for children and is particularly of note as a unique example and as a potential inspiration to other artists working in this area, both in Japan and internationally. I would also suggest that the use of playfulness and irreverence, alongside references to more serious issues such as bullying or isolation, is key to Yamasaki's technique of adapting the plays for young audiences and is an essential element in how the series first invites young audiences to encounter Shakespeare and then encourages them to come again.

NOTES

1. Asian Shakespeare Intercultural Archive (A|S|I|A) (website), accessed 28 November 2018, http://a-s-i-a-web.org/en/home.php.
2. Kobayashi Yuriko, 'Drama and Theatre for Young People in Japan', *Research in Drama Education* 9 (1, 2004), 93.
3. Fujita Asaya, 'Jubilee—Introduction to TYA in Japan', *ASSITEJ*, accessed 4 February 2019, http://www.assitej-international.org/en/2015/06/jub ilee-introduction-of-tya-in-japan.
4. Robin Hall, 'Children's Theatre in Japan', *Asian Theatre Journal* 3 (1, 1986), 108.
5. Fujita.
6. Yokomizo Yukiko, 'Children's and Youth Theatre and Puppet Theatre', In *Theatre Yearbook 2017: Theatre in Japan*, edited by the International Theatre Institute (Tokyo: Japanese Centre of the International Theatre Institute, 2017), 76.
7. Ibid.
8. Fujita.
9. 'About', *TYA Inclusive Arts Festival*, accessed 19 February 2019, http://tyafes-japan.com.
10. 'Children Launching Project', *Arts Council Tokyo*, accessed 10 February 2019, https://www.artscouncil-tokyo.jp/en/events/13477.
11. 'Conveying the "Excitement of Life" and "the Joy of Living"', *Shiki*, accessed 20 January 2019, https://www.shiki.jp/en.
12. Yokomizo Yukiko, 'Children's and Youth Theatre and Puppet Theatre', in *Theatre Yearbook 2015: Theatre in Japan*, edited by the International Theatre Institute (Tokyo: Japanese Centre of the International Theatre Institute, 2015), 71. Shiki, 'Conveying'.
13. 'Performances and Programs', *Nissei Theatre*, accessed 20 January 2019, http://www.nissaytheatre.or.jp/en/outline/business.html.
14. 'TYA in Japan: Yesterday and Today', *ASSITEJ*, accessed 4 February 2019, http://assitej-japan.jp/?page_id=258.

15. Janice Bland, 'Slipping Back in Time: *King of Shadows* as Play Script', in *Shakespeare in the EFL Classroom*, edited by Maria Eisenmann and Christie Lütge (Heidelberg: Universitätsverlag Winter, 2014), 334.
16. Peter Hollindale, 'Drama for Children', in *The Cambridge Guide to Children's Books in English*, edited by Victor Watson (Cambridge: Cambridge University Press, 2001), 220.
17. Jan Wozniak, *The Politics of Performing Shakespeare for Young People: Standing up to Shakespeare* (London: Bloomsbury, Arden Shakespeare, 2016), 11.
18. Abigail Rokison, *Shakespeare for Young People: Productions, Versions and Adaptations* (London: Bloomsbury, Arden Shakespeare, 2013), 1.
19. Stuart Varnam-Atkin, 'Tokyo's "Fayrest that Ever Was"', *Japan Times*, 11 December 2013, https://www.japantimes.co.jp/culture/2013/12/11/stage/tokyos-fayrest-that-ever-was/#.WpD9UMnqZnE.
20. Anzai Tetsuo, 'A Century of Shakespeare in Japan: A Brief Historical Survey', in *Shakespeare in Japan*, edited by Anzai Tetsuo et al. (New York: Edwin Mellen, 1999), 3–12.
21. Dennis Normile, 'Globe's Sound and Fury Strut Tokyo Stage', *Japan Economic Journal*, 29 October 1988, 8.
22. J.R. Mulryne, 'Introduction', in *Shakespeare and the Japanese Stage*, edited by Sasayama Takashi, J.R. Mulryne and Margaret Shewring (Cambridge: Cambridge University Press, 1998), 6.
23. Normile, 'Tokyo Stage'.
24. Varnam-Atkin, 'Fayrest'.
25. Suematsu Michiko, 'The Tokyo Globe Years, 1988–2002', in *Shakespeare in Hollywood, Asia and Cyberspace*, edited by Alexa Alice Joubin and Charles S. Ross (West Lafayette: Purdue University Press, 2009), 127.
26. Michael Bogdanov and Michael Pennington, *The English Shakespeare Company: The Story of the Wars of the Roses, 1986–89* (London: Nick Hern Books, 1991), 137.
27. Ibid., 138.
28. W.B. Worthen, 'Reconstructing the Globe: Constructing Ourselves', *Shakespeare Survey* 52 (1999), 45.
29. Ibid.
30. Rokison, *Shakespeare for Young People*, 17.
31. Edward Hall, 'About Pocket Propeller: An Introduction from Edward Hall', *Propeller*, accessed 1 February 2019, https://www.propeller.org.uk/education. Rokison, *Shakespeare for Young People*, 6.
32. '*Engeki*', *Canon Kikaku*, accessed 10 February 2019, http://www.canonkikaku.com/engeki.
33. Ishihara Kosai and Hirokawa Osamu, 'A Survey of Shakespearean Performances in Japan from 2001–2010', *Komazawa University Foreign Language Studies* 16 (2014), 15.

34. 'Playing Shakespeare with Deutsche Bank', *Shakespeare's Globe Theatre*, accessed 15 January, https://www.shakespearesglobe.com/education/tea chers/playing-shakespeare.
35. Rokison, 19.
36. Rokison, 93.
37. Tanaka Nobuko, '*Hamlet* Marks Take #18 in Shakespeare for Children Series', *Japan Times*, 3 September 2014, https://www.japantimes.co.jp/culture/2014/09/03/stage/hamlet-marks-take-18-shakespeare-children-series.
38. Fukahori Etsuko, 'Staging Shakespeare for Children: Yamasaki Seisuke's 2001 Production of *Richard II*', *The Kwassui Review* 54 (2011), 13.
39. Fukahori Etsuko, 'Staging *Hamlet* for Japanese Children: Seisuke Yamasaki's 2014 Production of *Hamlet*', *The Kwassui Review* 58 (2015), 3.
40. Tanaka, '*Hamlet*'.
41. Rokison, 19.
42. Fukahori, 'Staging *Hamlet*', 4.
43. Tanaka.
44. Ibid.
45. Canon Kikaku, '*Engeki*'.
46. Fukahori, '*Richard II*', 13.
47. Fukahori, 'Staging *Hamlet*', 5.
48. Quoted in Fukahori, 'Staging *Hamlet*', 4.
49. Fukahori, 'Staging *Hamlet*', 4.
50. Kawai Shoichiro, 'More Japanized, Casual and Transgender Shakespeares', *Shakespeare Survey* 62 (2009), 262–263.
51. Fukahori, 'Staging *Hamlet*', 4–5.
52. Rokison, 107.
53. Kawai, 'Shakespeares', 263.
54. Quoted in Ishihara and Hirokawa, 'Survey', 18.
55. Kawai, 263.
56. Fukahori, '*Richard II*', 13.
57. Tanaka.
58. Ibid.
59. Yokomizo Yukiko, 'Children's and Youth Theatre and Puppet Theatre', in *Theatre Yearbook 2014: Theatre in Japan*, edited by the International Theatre Institute (Tokyo: Japanese Centre of the International Theatre Institute, 2014), 73.
60. Ishihara and Hirokawa, 'Survey', 15.
61. Fukahori, '*Hamlet*'.
62. Tanaka.
63. Rokison, 116.

64. See also Olive's Chapter 5 for discussion of some Japanese university students' response to cross-gender casting in a touring production of *Twelfth Night*.
65. Peter Holland, *William Shakespeare's A Midsummer Night's Dream* (Oxford: Oxford University Press, 1998), i.
66. Mika Eglinton, 'A *Midsummer Night's Dream* Translation,' *Asian Shakespeare Intercultural Archive*, accessed 15 January 2019, a-s-i-a-web.org.
67. Eglinton.
68. Ibid.
69. Ibid.
70. Rokison, 121.
71. Kelly Hunter, *Shakespeare's Heartbeat: Drama Games for Children with Autism* (London: Routledge, 2015), 2.
72. Sarah Olive, *Shakespeare Valued: Education Policy and Pedagogy 1989–2009* (Bristol: Intellect, 2015).
73. Rokison, 122.
74. Tanaka.
75. Canon Kikaku, *'Engeki'*.
76. Rokison, 121.
77. 'The Director', *Playing Shakespeare with Deutsche Bank*, accessed 15 January 2019, http://2008.playingshakespeare.org/text_in_perform ance/item/4.
78. Canon Kikaku, *'Engeki'*.
79. Fiona Banks, *Creative Shakespeare: The Globe Education Guide to Practical Shakespeare* (London: Bloomsbury, Arden Shakespeare, 2014), 197.

REFERENCES

Anzai, Tetsuo. 'A Century of Shakespeare in Japan: A Brief Historical Survey'. In *Shakespeare in Japan*, edited by Anzai Tetsuo and Others. New York: Edwin Mellen, 1999. 3–12.
Arts Council Tokyo. 'Children Launching Project'. *Arts Council Tokyo*, February 2017. https://www.artscouncil-tokyo.jp/en/events/13477.
ASSITEJ. 'TYA in Japan: Yesterday and Today'. *ASSITEJ Japan*, 2019. https://assitej-japan.jp/?page_id=258.
Banks, Fiona. *Creative Shakespeare: The Globe Education Guide to Practical Shakespeare*. London: Bloomsbury, Arden Shakespeare, 2014.
Bland, Janice. 'Slipping Back in Time: *King of Shadows* as Play Script'. In *Shakespeare in the EFL Classroom*, edited by Maria Eisenmann and Christine Lütge. Heidelberg: Universitätsverlag Winter, 2014. 331–346.
Bogdanov, Michael, and Michael Pennington. *The English Shakespeare Company: The Story of the Wars of the Roses, 1986–89*. London: Nick Hern Books, 1991.

Canon Kikaku. '*Engeki*.' *Canon Kikaku*. Accessed 10 February 2019. http://www.canonkikaku.com/engeki.

Eglinton, Mika. '*A Midsummer Night's Dream* Translation'. *Asian Shakespeare Intercultural Archive*. Accessed 15 January 2019. a-s-i-a-web.org.

Fujita, Asaya. 2015. 'Jubilee – Introduction to TYA in Japan'. *ASSITEJ—International Association of Theatre for Children and Young People*. Accessed 4 February 2019. http://www.assitej-international.org/en/2015/06/jubilee-introduction-of-tya-in-japan.

Fukahori, Etsuko. 'Staging Shakespeare for Children: Yamasaki Seisuke's 2001 Production of *Richard II*'. *The Kwassui Review* 54 (2011): 1–14.

———. 'Staging *Hamlet* for Japanese Children: Seisuke Yamasaki's 2014 Production of *Hamlet*'. *The Kwassui Review* 58 (2015): 1–7.

Hall, Edward. 'About Pocket Propeller: An Introduction from Edward Hall'. *Propeller*. Accessed 1 February 2019. https://www.propeller.org.uk/education.

Hall, Robin. 'Children's Theatre in Japan'. *Asian Theatre Journal* 3 (1, 1986): 102–109.

Holland, Peter. *William Shakespeare's A Midsummer Night's Dream*. Oxford: Oxford University Press, 1998.

Hollindale, Peter. 'Drama for Children'. In *The Cambridge Guide to Children's Books in English*, edited by Victor Watson, 216–220. Cambridge: Cambridge University Press, 2001.

Hunter, Kelly. *Shakespeare's Heartbeat: Drama Games for Children with Autism*. London: Routledge, 2015.

Ishihara, Kosai, and Osamu Hirokawa. 'A Survey of Shakespearean Performances in Japan from 2001–2010'. *Komazawa University Foreign Language Studies* 16 (2014): 1–44.

Kawai, Shoichiro. 'More Japanized, Casual and Transgender Shakespeares'. *Shakespeare Survey* 62 (2009): 261–272.

Kobayashi, Yuriko. 'Drama and Theatre for Young People in Japan'. *Research in Drama Education* 9 (1, 2004): 93–95.

Mulryne, J.R. 'Introduction'. In *Shakespeare and the Japanese Stage*, edited by Sasayama Takashi, J.R. Mulryne, and Margaret Shewring, 1–11. Cambridge: Cambridge University Press, 1998.

Nissei Theatre. 'Performances and Programs'. *Nissei Theatre*. Accessed 20 January 2019. http://www.nissaytheatre.or.jp/en/outline/business.html.

Normile, Dennis. 'Globe's Sound and Fury Strut Tokyo Stage'. *Japan Economic Journal* 29 (October) 1988.

Olive, Sarah. *Shakespeare Valued: Education Policy and Pedagogy 1989–2009*. Bristol: Intellect, 2015.

218   R. FIELDING

Playing Shakespeare with Deutsche Bank. 'The Director'. *Playing Shakespeare*. Accessed 15 January 2019, http://2008.playingshakespeare.org/text_in_perf ormance/item/4.

Rokison, Abigail. *Shakespeare for Young People: Productions, Versions and Adaptations*. London: Bloomsbury, Arden Shakespeare, 2013.

Shakespeare, William. *A Midsummer Night's Dream*, edited by Sukanta Chaudhuri. London: Bloomsbury, Arden Shakespeare, 2017.

———. *Cymbeline*, 3rd series, edited by Valerie Wayne. London: Bloomsbury, Arden Shakespeare, 2017.

Shakespeare's Globe Theatre. 'Playing Shakespeare with Deutsche Bank'. *Shakespeare's Globe Theatre*. Accessed 15 January 2019. https://www.shakespeares globe.com/education/teachers/playing-shakespeare.

Shiki. 'Conveying the "Excitement of Life" and "the Joy of Living".' *Shiki*. Accessed 20 January 2019. https://www.shiki.jp/en.

Suematsu, Michiko. 'The Tokyo Globe Years, 1988–2002'. In *Shakespeare in Hollywood, Asia and Cyberspace*, edited by Alexa Alice Joubin and Charles S. Ross, 121–128. West Lafayette: Purdue University Press, 2009.

———. 'Verbal and Visual Representations in Modern Japanese Shakespeare Productions'. In *The Oxford Handbook of Shakespeare and Performance*, edited by James C. Bullman, 585–598. Oxford: Oxford University Press, 2017.

Tanaka, Nobuko. '*Hamlet* Marks Take #18 in Shakespeare for Children Series.' *Japan Times*, 3 September 2014. https://www.japantimes.co.jp/culture/ 2014/09/03/stage/hamlet-marks-take-18-shakespeare-children-series.

TYA Inclusive Arts Festival 2019. 'About'. *TYA Inclusive Arts Festival*. Accessed 19 February 2019. https://tyafes-japan.com.

Varnam-Atkin, Stuart. 'Tokyo's "Fayrest that Ever Was"'. *Japan Times*, 11 December 2013. https://www.japantimes.co.jp/culture/2013/12/11/ stage/tokyos-fayrest-that-ever-was/#.WpD9UMnqZnE.

Worthen, W.B. 'Reconstructing the Globe: Constructing Ourselves.' *Shakespeare Survey* 52 (1999): 33–45.

Wozniak, Jan. *The Politics of Performing Shakespeare for Young People: Standing up to Shakespeare*. London: Bloomsbury, Arden Shakespeare, 2016.

Yokomizo, Yukiko. 'Children's and Youth Theatre and Puppet Theatre'. In *Theatre Yearbook 2014: Theatre in Japan*, edited by the International Theatre Institute, 67–75. Tokyo: Japanese Centre of the International Theatre Institute, 2014.

———. 'Children's and Youth Theatre and Puppet Theatre'. In *Theatre Yearbook 2015: Theatre in Japan*, edited by the International Theatre Institute, 70–79. Tokyo: Japanese Centre of the International Theatre Institute, 2015.

———. 'Children's and Youth Theatre and Puppet Theatre'. In *Theatre Yearbook 2017: Theatre in Japan*, edited by the International Theatre Institute, 76–85. Tokyo: Japanese Centre of the International Theatre Institute, 2017.

CHAPTER 7

Afterword: Technology in Teaching Shakespeare in Taiwan

Chen Yilin

Abstract Chen Yilin concludes that Shakespeare came to East Asia more than a century ago and it has been taught at school through English language education. *Shakespeare in East Asian Education* is the first book exploring the ways in which Shakespeare has been incorporated into classrooms across the region, including both subjects of English and Theatre studies. She argues that the book is important for western readers not only to understand traditional approaches to teaching Shakespeare in this region, but also to reflect on new pedagogies in terms of making Shakespeare relevant to local cultures in the global context nowadays. Foregrounding the latter, Chen offers an insight into the rationale and pedagogies of the Global/Local Shakespeare MOOC. She focuses in particular on the MOOC's incorporation into Taiwanese higher education using a flipped classroom and Bloom's Taxonomy of Educational Objectives to align objectives, teaching and assessment, from manga to mobile apps.

C. Yilin (✉)
Department of English, Providence University, Taichung City, Taiwan

S. Olive et al., *Shakespeare in East Asian Education*, Global Shakespeares,
https://doi.org/10.1007/978-3-030-64796-4_7

219

Keywords Taiwan · MOOC · Digital · Bloom's taxonomy · Flipped classroom · Visual literacy · ICT literacy · Manga

Shakespeare has been a feature of the classroom in East Asia for more than a century. In the introduction to this book, the authors pointed out that a problem with the current English-language publications on teaching Shakespeare in Asia is the lack of sustained critical analysis in the field. To counter this, their chapters have looked at regional and global influences on the ways Shakespeare has been taught in and performed for young people in East Asia, based on the existing discourse of Shakespeare in colonial and postcolonial education, including Hong Kong as a former colony of British Empire and Taiwan as a former colony of Japan.

This monograph's main chapters began with Adele Lee's investigation into how Shakespeare is taught in Hong Kong to argue the extent to which Chinese educational reform might help the future direction of teaching Shakespeare in the west. As Lee indicates, the experience of teachers and students in Hong Kong classrooms may illuminate its colonial past with the British Empire and its present ties with the Chinese education system. The well-known Chinese Universities Shakespeare Festival (CUSF), hosted by the Chinese University of Hong Kong, was launched in 2005 after educational reform was proposed to promote life-long learning for the twenty-first century. Lee's research in 2014 suggested that Shakespeare was set to become a staple of a liberal arts curriculum in Hong Kong schools. Her research reflects the situation in Hong Kong, a site of rapid and dramatic political change, in the recent past rather than the present moment, where tensions between Hong Kong and mainland China have significantly escalated. Yet, unfortunately, the CUSF was suspended in the same year without a reason—although Sarah Olive's Chapter 3 explores possible contributing factors for its discontinuation. The CUSF offered a successful example of bringing university students from greater China to develop important skills for the twenty-first century, and through their performances, participating members, including students from China, Macau, and Taiwan, could have an experience of collaboration, as well as competition, and making Shakespeare relevant to them. As a former British colony, Hong Kong has a long history of including Shakespeare in education from school to university. Shakespeare's lines were featured in high school textbooks as early as 1842. Similarly, as Kohei Uchimaru observes in Chapter 4, Shakespeare was incorporated into textbooks for English language learning in Japan during the late nineteenth century, due to its national policy of modernisation when the British Empire's model of a superpower nation state in the world appealed to its leaders. It is common in East Asia that Shakespeare is used in English language courses as literary works through which students can improve their language skills. However, since the issue of World Englishes was first mentioned in 1978, there has been a trend to claim legitimacy for localised varieties of English. As English has become a global and pluralised medium of communication, attitudes towards Shakespeare as an example of an elite language are also gradually changing.

Rosalind Fielding's chapter explores the way in which the Shakespeare for Children series in Japan is portrayed by its makers as an effective way to encounter Shakespeare at an early age. Indeed, Shakespeare's plays were written for performance. In higher education, performance is often integrated into Asian curricula, as the numerous examples given in this monograph demonstrate. Through performing Shakespeare in English, as shown by the perspectives Olive draws on in Chapters 3 and 5, students not only study the literary texts and acquire English language skills, but also develop other soft skills, such as teamwork and interpersonal communication.

Taiwan has featured in very few discussions of Shakespeare in education so far, especially with regard to new pedagogies for the digital generation. I would like to share with readers the ways in which technology has facilitated the teaching of Shakespeare in Taiwan. Online learning, a new type of distance education, has become much more important since access to the Internet was identified as a fundamental right by the World Summit on the Information Society in 2003. Furthermore, online teaching has abruptly became a staple of, rather than ancillary to, formal education in countries affected by the COVID-19 pandemic since 2020. Traditional distance education offered video lectures, readings and problem sets, and yet very limited interactions with learners. The emergence of MOOC (Massive Open Online Courses) around 2008 overcame the limitation, and provided forums, quizzes and assignment feedback for learners. Funded by the Taiwan Ministry of Education (MoE), the Global/Local Shakespeare MOOC was the first open-access resource in Taiwan dedicated to teaching Shakespeare in English online.

Launched in September 2014, the Global/Local Shakespeare MOOC is a thirteen-week online course that aims to teach Shakespeare in a global context.[1] In order to include various viewpoints and voices, this course invited participation from several globally-known scholars and *manga* artists from Canada, Japan, Taiwan and the United States. Lectures were created by several well-known Shakespearean scholars.[2] In addition to academics, educators on the course were drawn from publishing, such as Meng Chen, a Taiwanese artist and the author of the *manga* adaptation of *Hamlet*, published by Maxpower Publishing; Elie Lin, General Editor at Maxpower Publishing; and Sanazaki Harumo, a Japanese *manga* artist and the author of a collection of *manga* Shakespearean plays, including *Romeo and Juliet*, *Macbeth*, and *A Midsummer Night's Dream*.[3]

I have published previously on this course in three book chapters.[4] Here, however, I would like to emphasise how technology can change the learning objectives of Shakespeare in East Asia generally and Taiwan in particular. This MOOC contains seventy-eight instructional films to cover several themes, including critical analyses of selective readings in Shakespeare's works, an introduction to Shakespeare in graphic novels and *manga* adaptations. The films are about ten to twenty minutes in length. This course examines the British publisher SelfMadeHero's *Manga Shakespeare* series; Chen's *Hamulete: Fuwangde Youhun* (*The King Father's Ghost*); and Sanazaki's *manga*.[5] Online learners are able to pause, rewind, and replay the films based on their pace of learning. This course hopes to increase awareness of the globalisation, localisation, and glocalisation phenomena to investigate in what ways these phenomena are correlated to Shakespeare. Besides watching these videos, the online learners can share opinions of learning Shakespeare and to develop a capacity to explore the relationship between Shakespeare and their own cultures (Table 7.1).

Furthermore, based on Bloom's Taxonomy to design the various activities and assessments, this course fulfils the different levels of cognitive domains. The formative assessments include tests on the films (unit test 20%), reading Shakespeare's texts—online learners need to select a scene and read one character's lines with the emotions implied in the scene (practice-by-doing assignment 10%), and analysing Shakespearean adaptations (two case studies 10%). The summative assessments are role-playing (a midterm 30%), and staging a Shakespeare scene (a final presentation 30%). The unit test will be taken online, and learners will be tested while or after they watch a video film. As for the practice-by-doing assignment, after watching a video concerning Shakespeare's *Sonnet 20*, online learners

Table 7.1 Course assessment and Bloom's Taxonomy

Assessment Percentage	Assessment	Bloom's Taxonomy
Assessment Percentage Unit Tests 20%	Assessment Twenty multiple choice questions, automatically graded by computer to give immediate feedback to the students	Bloom's Taxonomy After watching an instructional film, students will take a multiple choice test to assess their learning. The assessment is to evaluate a learner's knowledge and comprehension of the lectures. It responds to the cognitive domain of remembering and understanding
Practice-by-Doing Assignment 10%	A film of a sonnet recitation, graded by the student's peers and the instructor In week two, students have to submit a film of reading a sonnet to ShareCourse platform. The film will be randomly assigned to and graded by their peers and then by their instructor	After studying the sonnets, online learners need to select a scene and read one character's lines with emotions implied in the scene. Students learn to apply their knowledge of Shakespeare's text to create a film. Afterwards, they will evaluate their classmates' works. The assessment hopes to achieve the cognitive domains of remembering, understanding, applying, creating and evaluating
Case Studies 10%	Two short papers, graded by the instructor In week four, students have to analyse one Taiwanese adaptation of Romeo and Juliet. They will use materials available online to explain in what ways Shakespeare's Romeo and Juliet was adapted to, appropriated within or parodied in a Taiwanese context and makes Shakespeare accessible to young people In week nine, students will analyse Act III Scene 4 in a film, a performance, or a manga version of Hamlet to explain in what ways the interpretation reveals different attitudes towards the confrontation between Gertrude and Hamlet	The two assignments aim to assess a learner's cognitive domains of applying, analysing, and evaluating

(continued)

Table 7.1 (continued)

Assessment Percentage	Assessment	Bloom's Taxonomy
Midterm Exam 30%	A written exam, taken online, asks students to analyse and explain Shakespeare's texts in the cultural and social contexts Students will be instructed to take this test and to analyse one of the five speeches taught in the MOOC lectures. Students can choose one character's speech in a specific Shakespearean scene and explore it using five questions: • Who is the speaker? • What is his/her purpose or motivation in this speech? • What is his/her action? (the method to get what he or she wants in the speech) • Has he/she met any resistance (anyone or anything (i.e. inner conflicts, circumstance or social surroundings) which stops the character from getting what they want? • Has the character overcome the resistance by the end of his/her speech?	The written exam aims to evaluate a learner's cognitive domains of remembering, understanding, applying, analysing, and evaluating
Final Presentation 30% (summative assessment)	After the midterm, students have to stage a scene. They use five questions to analyse a character, and begin to recite and memorise the lines. Once they are confident of their speech, they can rehearse the scene with movement. They should upload a film of their work	Staging a scene requires synthetic skills, including all the cognitive domains of remembering, understanding, applying, analysing, evaluating and creating

are encouraged to practice it. They are instructed to recite and record the *Sonnet*. The two case studies are to examine Shakespearean adaptations that are taught in the films. The midterm and final exams relate to performing a scene. Both the curriculum contents and the assessment design are diverse.

More importantly, this course incorporated the transnational dissemination of *manga* Shakespeare into teaching, and examples were given to explain the glocalisation of Shakespeare. I believe *manga* and comics are more suitable than films and other motion picture films to be the means for studying Shakespeare because they are still images, and students can take their time to observe the relation between the text and pictures. In popular culture, *manga* adaptations embrace local values to re-examine Shakespeare's text.[6] This course also invited both Japanese and Taiwanese *manga* artists to share their interpretations of Shakespeare's texts. Therefore, by studying these *manga* adaptations, learners had a chance not only to learn Shakespeare's texts with a global perspective, but also to understand them in the relevant cultural contexts.

Given the growing importance of visual literacy, images, charts, and graphics are frequently used in contemporary daily life.[7] For the digital generation, the ability to read and understand information given in visual content is as important as that in literary works. Flipping the Global/Local Shakespeare MOOC explores the ways in which transliteracy can be integrated into classes on Shakespeare. The term transliteracy was first developed in 2005 as part of research into online reading. It hopes to 'encompass different literacies and multiple communication channels that require active participation with and across a range of platforms, and embracing both linear and non-linear messages'.[8] In other words, transliteracy is an ability to combine all the literacies, i.e. information, ICT, communication and collaboration, creativity and critical thinking.

The Global/Local Shakespeare MOOC offered films that could be used to conduct a flipped classroom in an interactive environment, where the educator guides students to apply concepts and engages them to explore the higher-level cognitive skills of Bloom's Taxonomy (1956). The original taxonomy includes the cognitive domains of knowledge, comprehension, application, analysis, synthesis and evaluation.[9] Revised in 2002, David Krathwohl proposed that the new cognitive skills of taxonomy should be remembering, understanding, applying, analysing, evaluating, and creating.[10] To conduct a flipped classroom, an educator needs to design two parts of a curriculum. The first part is self-learning materials which students engage with before coming to the classroom. The second part is activities conducted in the actual classroom. The self-learning materials, in the flipped classroom for the Global/Local Shakespeare MOOC, were the films and online unit tests. Students needed to remember and understand the contents in these videos before coming to the classroom. In the actual classroom, the educator provided interactive instructions to complete tasks through applying, analysing, evaluating, and creating. The following two lesson plans are flipped classroom activities which educators can use to develop these higher-level cognitive skills.

Two lesson plans of flipped classroom for the Global/Local Shakespeare MOOC are provided as a reference for helping students to develop twenty-first-century skills. The first lesson plan featured here aims to cultivate visual literacy while the second emphasises ICT literacy. Before coming to the flipped classroom, students need to complete self-learning materials, i.e. the films and online tests of the Global/Local Shakespeare MOOC on the website. When they come to the actual classroom, they are asked to do activities based on the films they watched. The first lesson plan comprises films from the Global/Local Shakespeare MOOC.[11] Students acquire knowledge through watching the video, and in the flipped classroom, they participate in visualisation activities to identify and analyse visual information in Shakespeare's text. According to my previous research, the visualisation activities also enhance the student's understanding of the text and improve their reading comprehension.[12] For instance, students explore the possible meanings of a sonnet and a soliloquy through watching the films. In class, students are divided into groups to find metaphors in the text. After identifying the metaphors, each student needs to examine the text and draw appropriate images representing the metaphors. Then they try to use their own words to interpret Shakespeare's text. Below is a worksheet completed for a soliloquy in *Romeo and Juliet*. The column for metaphors/images provides space for students to draw a picture in correspondence to a keyword or a phrase in a line. By doing so, students not only can enhance their understanding of the text, but also develop their capacity for using visual resources in communication (Fig. 7.1).

The second lesson plan helps students obtain twenty-first-century skills, i.e. critical thinking and problem-solving, creativity and innovation, communication and collaboration and digital literacy (information

Metaphors/Images	Text	Interpretation (I hear, feel, I taste, I smell, I touch, I see, etc.)
	The clock struck nine when I did send the Nurse.	I feel she's uneasy and stares at the clock.
	In half an hour she promised to return.	I feel she just can't relax herself and stop watching the clock.
	Perchance she cannot meet him.	I feel she's worried.
	That's not so.	I hear she denies her own question.
	Oh, she is lame!	I think she's thinking too much.
	Love's heralds should be thoughts, Which ten times faster glide than the sun's beams, Driving back shadows over louring hills.	I feel her emotion is complex.
	Of this day's journey, and from nine till twelve Is three long hours, yet she is not come.	I feel she's hard to get through the time of waiting.
	Had she affections and warm youthful blood, She would be as swift in motion as a ball.	She hopes her nurse can swift like a youth to bring back the message, but I think she asks her nurse too much.
	My words would bandy her to my sweet love, And his to me.	She relies on her nurse a lot.
	But old folks, many feign as they were dead, Unwieldy, slow, heavy, and pale as lead.	I feel she almost gives up and her mood turns to very down to use many pessimist words.
	O God! she comes. O honey nurse! what news?	I think she's too happy for seeing her nurse.
	Hast thou met with him? Send thy man away.	I feel Julie's deep love to Romeo.

Fig. 7.1 A worksheet for Juliet's soliloquy in *Romeo and Juliet*

literacy, media literacy, and information communication technologies literacy) by designing Shakespeare educational applications for EFL (English as a Foreign Language) students in middle school. This lesson plan encourages students to develop their verbal, visual, and technology abilities in the flipped classroom. The second lesson plan also incorporates the films from the Global/Local Shakespeare MOOC into the flipped classroom, which employs different activities and technology to boost students' cultural awareness, visual comprehension, and creativity. The films offer an exploration of themes concerning Shakespeare's sonnets, soliloquies, and scenes from *Romeo and Juliet*. Students learn diverse artistic approaches to reading and interpreting Shakespeare in different *manga* adaptations. Before they can develop an application, they are also required to play one selected Shakespeare-related application each week for at least fifteen to twenty minutes, and they should complete quizzes related to the game they played afterwards. By playing these apps, students observe the mechanism of current popular games for learning Shakespeare via games. They are asked to pay attention to what learning objectives the game has set for students, such as remembering the plot of a Shakespeare play or to learn English, and so on. In the flipped classroom, they are divided into five groups and guided to create an online learning application. Through scaffolding instructions, students learn how to identify metaphors in Shakespeare's works and translate Shakespeare's text into images. Every week, students are taught to use graphic design software to create images for the themes in a sonnet, a soliloquy or a scene. By means of these activities and resources, students are inspired to write their game proposal. Once their proposals are approved, they start learning the software, called Smart Apps Creator (SAC) to develop their educational applications.

In recent decades, Shakespeare's texts, performances, and adaptations have been available online, and they are now easily accessed through applications.[13] In 2017, there were 259 Shakespeare-related apps in Google Play Store and 200 in the iTunes Apps store. Many of these Shakespeare-related applications featured Shakespeare's works and/or story guides, while very few contained both educational and entertainment purposes. Given that games can increase learning interest, motivation, retention, critical thinking, and problem-solving skills, this flipped classroom helps students to design mobile game-based learning (MGBL) applications for first-time Shakespeare learners.[14] Until February 2017, only twenty-one free games inspired by Shakespeare were available in Google Play Store, and again very few of these Shakespearean apps were educational or entertaining.[15] The attempt to create a good educational and entertaining mobile application for learning Shakespeare or learning English through Shakespeare for EFL students is innovative in higher education in Taiwan. This flipped classroom was instrumental in integrating critical thinking and problem-solving, creativity and innovation, collaboration and ICT literacy into a Shakespeare course. By the end of the course, students successfully produced five educational applications. Their games were brought to local high schools, and played by 250 high school students. According to a survey conducted and collected in one school, it showed that thirty-six high school students believe the applications motivated them to learn Shakespeare and they would continue using the apps for learning.[16]

Traditionally, Shakespeare's plays are often treated as literature in English departments in Asia. Alternatively, his plays are adapted and performed as a medium for learning English language—as several chapters in this book have demonstrated. However, the growing importance of transliteracy in the Information Age urges a revolution in education. Moreover, the online learning is becoming increasingly mainstream during the COVID-19 pandemic. The Global/Local Shakespeare MOOC helped students to learn online and enabled both native English speakers and non-native English speakers to meet and study Shakespeare through an intercultural perspective. Besides, through the face-to-face flipped classroom, Shakespeare became accessible for the local Taiwanese students. They not only examined the ways in which Shakespeare is read and interpreted in *manga* adaptations, but also developed transliteracy through learning Shakespeare's texts.

The Global/Local Shakespeare MOOC and these two examples of a flipped classroom demonstrate how the digital technology brings new approaches to teaching Shakespeare. Information spreads far and wide in the cyber world, and in the very near future, AI (Artificial Intelligence) technology will make a revolutionary change in education.[17] With the rapid growth of information, the purpose of schools and academia is not only to teach knowledge, but also to assist students in finding and using information. Learning through a game could be an effective supplement to assist students in learning subjects and important cognitive skills. As this monograph explores, Shakespeare has shifted from an Anglophone icon into a cross-cultural public property due to globalisation. Teaching Shakespeare in Asia should not be limited to the purpose of acquiring

English language skills and cultural knowledge. The learning objectives of a Shakespeare class can extend to the ways in which Shakespeare is interpreted and adapted in different social, political, cultural, and political contexts.

NOTES

1. The course was first offered in September 2014 for eighteen weeks on the Sharecourse platform: https://sharecourse.pu.edu.tw/sharecourse/course/view/courseInfo/125.
2. These include Alexa Alice Joubin (Professor of English, Theater and Dance, George Washington University, USA); Lia Wen-Ching Liang (Assistant Professor of Foreign Languages, National Tsinghua University, Taiwan), Ian MacLennan (retired Associate Professor of Theatre Arts, Thorneloe University, Canada), Minami Ryuta (Professor of English, Shirayuri Women's University, Japan), and Yoshihara Yukari (Associate Professor of Humanities and Social Science, University of Tsukuba, Japan).
3. Sanazaki Harumo. Shakespeare's Romeo and Juliet (Tokyo: Futabasha, 2003).   http://www.ebookjapan.jp/ebj/title/16382.html?volume=1. This volume also contains the other play titles listed here.
4. The previous discussions of Global/Local Shakespeare MOOC are: Chen Yilin and Tsai Yi-ren, 'The Flipped Global/Local Shakespeare MOOC Curriculum for the New Media Age Learners: Translating Verbal Metaphors into Visual Images', in *Epoch Making in English Teaching and Learning: Evolution, Innovation, and Revolution*, edited by Y. Leung (Taipei: Crane, 2016); Chen Yilin, 'MOOC "Global/Local Shakespeare"': New Approaches to Teaching Shakespeare in Taiwan and Beyond', in *Doing English in Asia: Global Literature and Culture*, edited by Patricia Haseltine and Ma Sheng-mei (Lanham, MD: Lexington Books, 2016), 133–146.; and Chen Yilin, Jou Yan-An, Chen Yi-chung, and Chen Hong-Yuan, 'Interdisciplinary Curriculum for Future Mobile Learning: An Evaluation of the Design of Shakespeare Educational Apps in the Flipped Classroom in Taiwan', in *Reconceptualizing English Language Teaching and Learning in the 21st Century: A Special Monograph in Memory of Professor Kai-Chong Cheung*, edited by Y. Leung, J. Katchen, S. Hwang, and Y. Chen (Taipei: Crane, 2018), 417–419.
5. Meng Chen, *Hamulete: Fuwangde Youhun (The King Father's Ghost)* (Quanli: Maxpower, 2006).
6. See my discussion of Meng's *Hamulete*, a *manga* adaptation of *Hamlet* in Chen, 'MOOC "Global/Local Shakespeare', In Meng's adaptation,

Gertrude accidentally falls down from a tower and dies. The artist particularly explains that she rewrote the plot because of her concern about Gertrude's 'incestuous' affair with her brother-in-law.

7. Chen, MOOC 'Global/Local Shakespeare', 145.

8. Sue Thomas, Chris Joseph, Jess Laccetti, Bruce Mason, Simon Mills, Simon Perril, and Kate Pullinger, 'Transliteracy: Crossing divides', *First Monday* 12.12 (2007). Susie Andretta, 'Transliteracy: Take a Walk on the Wild Side', World Library and Information Congress: 75th IFLA General Conference and Assembly, Milan, Italy, 23–27 August 2009 [Conference paper].

9. María Luisa Sein-Echaluce, Ángel Fidalgo-Blanco, and Francisco José García-Peñalvo, *Innovative Trends in Flipped Teaching and Adaptive Learning* (Hershey, PA: IGI Global, 2019), 113.

10. David Krathwohl, 'A Revision of Bloom's Taxonomy: An Overview', *Theory into Practice* 41.4 (2002): 213–217.

11. Instructional films for this flipped classroom include the topics regarding Shakespeare's *Sonnets*, a soliloquy or a scene analysis, selected readings of *Romeo and Juliet*, Shakespeare and Japanese *manga*, reading Japanese *manga*, and so on.

12. A questionnaire was made to collect student feedback on visualisation activities after the final task. Results showed that most students agreed discussing their visualisation increased their comprehension of the text. All students agreed that their understanding of Shakespeare's text improved after reading it with assistance of illustrations. According to the statistics, most students claimed that visualising the pictures after reading the text greatly helped them understand what they read.

13. Christie Carson and Peter Kirwan, *Shakespeare and Digital World* (Cambridge: Cambridge University Press, 2014); J. L. Ailles, 'Is There an App for That?: Mobile Shakespeare on the Phone and in the Cloud', in *OuterSpeares: Shakespeare, Intermedia, and the Limits of Adaptation*, edited by Daniel Fischlin (Toronto: University of Toronto Press, 2014), 75–110.

14. Marc Prensky, 'Digital Game-Based Learning', in *Computers in Entertainment* (CIE) 1.1 (2003), 21; Mike Sharples, Josie Taylor, and Giasemi Vavoula, 'Towards a Theory of Mobile Learning', *Proceedings of mLearn* 2005 1.1 (2005), 1–9; and Richard Van Eck, 'Digital Game-based Learning: It's Not Just the Digital Natives Who Are Restless', *EDUCAUSE Review* 41.2 (2006): 16.

15. Amy Suen and Andy Fung, 'Shakespeare in the Apps: Mobile Technology in Education Context', *International Journal of Information and Education Technology* 6.9 (2016): 731–736.

16. Chen, Jou, Chen and Chen, 'Interdisciplinary'.

17. Anthony Seldon and Oladimeji Abidoye, *The Fourth Education Revolution* (London: Legend, 2018).

References

Ailles, J. L. 'Is There an App for That? Mobile Shakespeare on the Phone and in the Cloud'. In *OuterSpeares: Shakespeare, Intermedia, and the Limits of Adaptation*, edited by Daniel Fischlin. Toronto: University of Toronto Press, 2014. 75–110.

Andretta, Susie. 'Transliteracy: Take a Walk on the Wild Side', World Library and Information Congress: 75th IFLA General Conference and Assembly, Milan, Italy, 23–27 August 2009 [Conference paper]. https://nlabnetworks.typepad.com/transliteracy/Andretta_Transliteracy.pdf.

Chen, Yilin. 'MOOC "Global/Local Shakespeare": New Approaches to Teaching Shakespeare in Taiwan and Beyond'. In *Doing English in Asia: Global Literature and Culture*, edited by Patricia Haseltine and Ma Sheng-mei. Lanham, MD: Lexington Books, 2016. 133–146.

Chen, Yilin, and Tsai Yi-ren, 'The Flipped Global/Local Shakespeare MOOC Curriculum for the New Media Age Learners: Translating Verbal Metaphors into Visual Images'. In *Epoch Making in English Teaching and Learning: Evolution, Innovation, and Revolution*, edited by Y. Leung. Taipei: Crane, 2016.

Chen, Yilin, Jou Yan-An, Chen Yi-chung, and Chen Hong-Yuan. 'Interdisciplinary Curriculum for Future Mobile Learning: An Evaluation of the Design of Shakespeare Educational Apps in the Flipped Classroom in Taiwan'. In *Reconceptualizing English Language Teaching and Learning in the 21st Century: A Special Monograph in Memory of Professor Kai-Chong Cheung*, edited by Y. Leung, J. Katchen, S. Hwang, and Y. Chen. Taipei: Crane, 2018. 410–427. 417–419.

Krathwohl, David. 'A Revision of Bloom's Taxonomy: An Overview'. *Theory into Practice*. 41.4 (2002): 213–217.

Meng, Chen. *Hamulete: Fuwangde Youhun (The King Father's Ghost)*. Quanli: Maxpower, 2006.

Prensky, Marc. 'Digital Game-based Learning'. *Computers in Entertainment* (CIE) 1.1 (2003): 21–26.

Sanazaki, Harumo. Shakespeare's Romeo and Juliet. Tokyo: Futabasha, 2003. http://www.ebookjapan.jp/ebj/title/16382.html?volume=1.

Sein-Echaluce, María Luisa, Ángel Fidalgo-Blanco, and Francisco José García-Peñalvo. *Innovative Trends in Flipped Teaching and Adaptive Learning*. Hershey, PA: IGI Global, 2019. 113.

Seldon, Anthony, and Oladimeji Abidoye. *The Fourth Education Revolution*. London: Legend, 2018.

Shamoon, Deborah Michelle. *Passionate Friendship: The Aesthetics of Girls' Culture in Japan*. Honolulu: University of Hawaii Press, 2012. 104–105.

Sharples, Mike, Josie Taylor, and Giasemi Vavoula. 'Towards a Theory of Mobile Learning'. *Proceedings of mLearn* 2005. 1.1 (2005): 1–9.

Suen, Amy, and Andy Fung. 'Shakespeare in the Apps: Mobile Technology in Education Context'. *International Journal of Information and Education Technology*. 6.9 (2016): 731–736.

Thomas, Sue, Chris Joseph, Jess Laccetti, Bruce Mason, Simon Mills, Simon Perril, and Kate Pullinger. 'Transliteracy: Crossing Divides'. *First Monday*. 12.12 (2007).

Van Eck, Richard. 'Digital Game-Based Learning: It's Not Just the Digital Natives Who Are Restless'. *EDUCAUSE Review*. 41.2 (2006): 16.

Correction to: Shakespeare in East Asian Education

Sarah Olive, Kohei Uchimaru, Adele Lee,
and Rosalind Fielding

Correction to:
S. Olive et al., *Shakespeare in East Asian Education,* **Global**
Shakespeares, https://doi.org/10.1007/978-3-030-64796-4

In the original version on this book the given name and family name of
the author Kohei Uchimaru were mixed up. This has now been corrected
to Kohei (given name) and Uchimaru (family name).

The updated version of the book can be found at https://doi.org/10.1007/
978-3-030-64796-4

© The Author(s), under exclusive license to Springer Nature   C1
Switzerland AG 2021
S. Olive et al., *Shakespeare in East Asian Education,* Global Shakespeares,
https://doi.org/10.1007/978-3-030-64796-4_8

INDEX

CPSIA information can be obtained
at www.ICGtesting.com
Printed in the USA
LVHW100356270522
719857LV00004B/38